Praise for Anna Loan-Wilsey
A Lack of Temperance

"Ms. Loan-Wilsey writes with vivid imagery that immediately brings to life the late nineteenth century in this engrossing and thoroughly enjoyable tale. Miss Hattie Davish is a force to be reckoned with, and I'm eagerly awaiting more of her adventures."
  —Kate Kingsbury

"Fans of historical mysteries should be delighted with this debut."
  —*Mystery Scene*

"A wonderful read from a welcome addition to the genre. This one shouldn't be missed—it has it all!"
  —Emily Brightwell

"*A Lack of Temperance* shows no lack of a fresh setting, spunky amateur detective, fascinating characters, and intriguing mystery. Anna Loan-Wilsey has a real talent for pulling the reader into a past world of both charm and chaos. Heroine Hattie and her typewriter certainly travel well! I can't wait to read her next adventure."
  —Karen Harper, *New York Times* bestselling author of *Finding Mercy*

"Eureka Springs is usually a peaceful spa resort, but when Hattie Davish arrives with her typewriter she finds the town in an uproar. Temperance ladies are attacking saloons and her new employer is missing. This is a fast-paced and fascinating read, peopled with feisty females, giving us a glimpse of how far women were actually prepared to go for the cause."
  —Rhys Bowen, Agatha and Anthony award–winning author of the Molly Murphy Mysteries and the bestselling Royal Spyness series

Books by Anna Loan-Wilsey

A LACK OF TEMPERANCE

ANYTHING BUT CIVIL

Published by Kensington Publishing Corporation

ANYTHING BUT CIVIL

ANNA LOAN-WILSEY

𝒦

KENSINGTON BOOKS
www.kensingtonbooks.com

KENSINGTON BOOKS are published by

Kensington Publishing Corp.
119 West 40th Street
New York, NY 10018

All Kensington titles, imprints, and distributed lines are available at special quantity discounts for bulk purchases for sales promotion, premiums, fund-raising, educational, or institutional use.

Special book excerpts or customized printings can also be created to fit specific needs. For details, write or phone the office of the Kensington Special Sales Manager: Kensington Publishing Corp., 119 West 40th Street, New York, NY 10018. Attn. Special Sales Department. Phone: 1-800-221-2647.

Kensington and the K logo Reg. U.S. Pat. & TM Off.

ISBN-13: 978-0-7582-7636-0
ISBN-10: 0-7582-7636-2
First Kensington Trade Paperback Printing: October 2013

eISBN-13: 978-0-7582-7637-7
eISBN-10: 0-7582-7637-0
First Kensington Electronic Edition: October 2013

10 9 8 7 6 5 4 3 2 1

Printed in the United States of America

To my mother,
Joan Suzanne Loan

Acknowledgments

I'd like to thank Rachel O'Neill at the Galena History Museum for her quick and gracious responses to questions about some very minute details of Galena's storied past. Steve Repp, historical librarian at the Galena Public Library, helped me navigate the invaluable resources in the Alfred Mueller Historical Collections.

I'm grateful for the support of the team at Kensington, including my editor, John Scognamiglio; Barbara Wild, copy editor (who's as much of a stickler for historical detail as I am); Vida Engstrand, my publicist; and the art duo of Kristine Mills and Judy York for such wonderful covers—I couldn't be happier.

And most of all, I'd like to thank my family, especially my husband Brian, for their votes of confidence, editorial comments, genuine interest, and love.

Deep-seated are the wounds dealt in civil brawls.

—Marcus Annaeus Lucanus, A.D. 39–65

CHAPTER 1

"Is he dead?"

"Yes," I said, knowing he wouldn't like the answer.

"Damn!"

Sir Arthur paused for a moment from his pacing, lifted his cigar again, and after a long inhale blew several rings of smoke, that floated toward me like dissipating halos. I sat poised with my finger on the brittle, yellow paper waiting for his word.

"Read me the details, Hattie."

I glanced down to the paragraph detailing the officer's demise and read, " 'The rebels have lately been playing a sharp game in front of a part of our line, near Appomattox. At this point there is a small creek in front of our works, across which they have built a dam, which has threatened to force back our picket line to a dangerous extent. To counteract this, Lieutenant Colonel Regan had devised works which he superintended personally. On visiting a part of the line, a rebel sharpshooter succeeded, after several attempts, in fatally wounding him, the ball entering the right side of the neck.' "

"What's the date on that newspaper?"

"The fifteenth of November 1864," I said. I made a few notes in my book, checked Lieutenant Colonel Regan from the list, and then returned the newspaper scrapbook to the shelf, lining it carefully up with the others.

"Bloody hell!" Sir Arthur plopped down into the leather sofa and slapped his knee sharply. "I would've bet a pint Regan was at Appomattox. No wonder we haven't been able to track him down. The man's dead. Well, check him off the list, Hattie. Ah, General Starrett." The last remark Sir Arthur directed to the elderly gentleman who appeared in the doorway. I rose from my chair as Sir Arthur jumped up to meet the man, shaking his hand vigorously. The old man winced in pain. "Good to finally meet you, General."

"Is it? Well, I'm glad to be of service."

Despite the roaring fire and the almost-stifling heat of the room, General Cornelius Starrett was dressed in layers, evident from the bulk beneath the charcoal gray velvet smoking jacket he wore. His eyes, slightly sunken, were bright blue and his skin taut and pale. The only hair on his head was a wreath of dark gray wisps. He stood slightly bent at the waist, leaning on a cane. The general closed the door behind him and motioned for Sir Arthur to return to the comfort of the sofa, which he did, puffing again from his cigar.

Tap, tap, tap. His cane marked the old man's slow, methodical shuffle as it connected with the bare wooden floor at the edge of the Persian area rug, centered in the middle of the room. I unconsciously leaned toward him, ready to assist him if he faltered.

"Oh, do sit down, young lady." His voice, husky and deep, boomed, its vibrant command at odds with the feeble body that housed it. I immediately complied with the general's order, dropping quickly onto the chair.

"My secretary and I were availing ourselves of your newspaper clippings while we waited," Sir Arthur said without a hint of apology in his voice.

Both us had been at our wit's end waiting. Sir Arthur had paced the floor and smoked two cigars. I'd straightened every book on the shelf, read a chapter from three separate intriguing books on gardening I'd come across, and counted to one hundred in French. If this interview, our third attempt, wasn't pivotal to Sir Arthur's work, we wouldn't have waited. And then Sir Arthur had found the scrapbooks of newspaper clippings.

"You don't mind, do you, old boy?" I winced at Sir Arthur's familiarity, but the general, either slightly deaf or being diplomatic, appeared not to notice.

"Of course not, of course not, Sir Arthur. That's what you're here for, isn't it? To pick my brain? Why not my library as well? My wife, Lavinia, put those scrapbooks together. Hope they were useful."

"I guess you could say so," Sir Arthur said, reminded of his disappointment in finding Regan had died five months too early.

"You have quite a diverse collection," I said. "I noticed a number of botanical books. Are you interested in botany, General?"

Sir Arthur frowned at me. I'd done it again. My job was to record the conversation and not divert it with my own questions. Yet I was forgetting this more and more lately.

What's gotten into me?

"That's Fred's department. So you've had time to look around. Am I late for our appointment then?" the general asked, settling himself into an overstuffed leather chair across from Sir Arthur and setting his cane across his lap. "We did say two o'clock, didn't we? What time is it now?" Instead of looking at the clock on the large marble fireplace mantel, General Starrett looked at me.

"Half past three, sir," I said.

"Oh, well, nothing could be done." He kneaded his bony thigh. The skin on his hand was almost transparent. "These legs aren't worth a damn these days. Pardon my language, young lady." I fought the urge to smile. Sir Arthur had sworn a dozen times while waiting without giving it a thought.

"Nothing is, the legs, the eyesight, the hearing (*so it was deafness and not diplomacy after all*), nothing. But don't you worry, Sir Arthur," the general said, tapping his head with his index finger. "Everything's all right in here. Now, what is it you want to know?"

He reached into the breast pocket of his jacket and retrieved a sterling silver engraved pocket cigar case. He opened the case, chose a cigar, ran the length of the cigar under his nose, and rolled it between his thumb and index finger before closing the case with a snap. He snipped the tip off the cigar.

"Don't mind, do you, young lady?"

"Of course she doesn't," Sir Arthur replied, brandishing his own cigar. "Miss Davish is far too professional to object to a man's guilty pleasures." He tipped his head in my direction. "Working for me, she probably doesn't even smell the smoke anymore. Do you, Hattie?"

"No, of course I don't mind," I said, avoiding the question of smoke. I could've enlightened them on the nights spent laundering my suits and dresses since starting again in Sir Arthur's employ. But I enjoyed working for Sir Arthur, and wanting to stay in his employ, I instead glanced at the bison head mounted on the wall above the built-in bookcases across from me. Then, repressing the urge to inquire about the procurement of the bison and distract the old man further, I studied a pair of silver table lighters, both in the shape of a ship's lantern, one with green-colored glass, the other with red, sitting on the table. The general reached for the one with the red glass.

The general chuckled, lit the cigar, and took a series of quick inhales, then coughed.

"My, my. A woman who doesn't object to smoking. You've found a gem in this one, Sir Arthur. Now if only Adella would agree. My library or not, the girl won't even enter the room if I've been smoking. And the irony is . . ." A laugh gurgled up from his chest and exploded through his nose, followed by a series of deep, dry hacking coughs. He pulled the handkerchief from his breast pocket, one silver star stitched into the corner, and held it tightly to his lips. "Damn, old age! Pardon my language, young lady, but I can't even have a good laugh anymore without having a fit. Should've died on the battlefield."

"What's so ironic?" Sir Arthur said.

"That Adella, my granddaughter, objects to my smoking cigars, but has no objection to Frederick making them." He dabbed the handkerchief at the corners of his lips and frowned, looking at the puzzled expression on our faces. "Oh, never mind," he said gruffly. "What do you want to know?"

As Sir Arthur explained our presence and need, as he had countless times before, I pushed aside the brown velvet curtain and glanced out at the lengthening shadows, stretching across the leaf-strewn yard, the dusting of snow that had fallen this morning all but a memory.

We may not have a white Christmas after all, I thought.

The narrow Galena River, once twice as wide and thronging with Mississippi River steamboats, was still and silent, filmed over with a thin sheen of ice, bits of which reflected brightly in the afternoon sun. Somewhere out of sight a horse snorted.

"Now if you're ready, General," Sir Arthur said. "We'll get started." I let the curtain fall and turned back to the task at hand.

I dipped my pen in ink and marked in longhand at the top of the page: *December 17, 1892, 3:38 p.m., Brigadier General*

Cornelius Starrett, Union Army of the Cumberland. I propped my notebook in my lap and prepared to take dictation.

"Eeee!" someone squealed. The chandelier bounced up and down, the glass prisms jingling, as something thumped on the floorboards above us.

"What the devil was that?" Sir Arthur exclaimed as we both stared up at the ceiling.

"Oh, never mind that." General Starrett chuckled. "It's just Adella's children romping around upstairs. Now what were you saying?"

"As I said in my letter," Sir Arthur began, glancing at the swaying chandelier, "I'm writing a book about the men at Appomattox Court House the day of April ninth, 1865, you, of course, being one. I've spent the better part of a month researching those men, only to find by chance that one of the officers on my list wasn't even there. Before you begin your personal account, General Starrett, would you be able to recall those present?"

"Of course! Does a skunk stink? Seventeen soldiers were in the room," the general said without hesitation, "us boys from Galena, some of Grant's men, and of course Lee and his aide. I remember because it was my lucky number. I started out with the Seventeenth Illinois Infantry and married Lavinia on the seventeenth of June." As General Starrett counted off the names on his fingers, I wrote them down to compare to our list later.

1. Ulysses S. Grant★
2. John Rawlins★
3. Ely Parker★
4. Cornelius Starrett★
5. Robert E. Lee

★Galena resident when mustered in

6. Orville Babcock
7. Horace Porter
8. Robert Lincoln
9. Theodore Bowers
10. Phillip Sheridan
11. Rufus Ingalls
12. Adam Badeau
13. George Sharpe
14. Michael Morgan
15. Seth Williams
16. Charles Marshall
17. Edward Ord

"Of course, men milled about in other parts of the house and in the yard then and over the next day or two; Lee's man Longstreet was one of them. Chamberlain was in charge for the formal surrender. I don't remember the others."

"Very good, thank you, General," Sir Arthur said when I indicated with a nod that I had all the names. He beamed at the old man. We were finally getting the information Sir Arthur needed. "Now in your own words, please describe everything you can from that day."

The general sat back a little more in his chair, his cigar dangling from his mouth. "Reveille was at 0500 hours," the general began. "Grant was already up and complaining of a terrible headache—"

And that's when the brawl erupted.

CHAPTER 2

"Traitor!"

"You're a swine, Henry!" another man bellowed.

The general, startled by the shouting, stopped mid-sentence, almost dropping his cigar.

"Copperhead! Traitor!" Henry answered.

Sir Arthur rushed over to the window as I drew back the curtain. A one-horse buggy, its wheels sliding sideways in the mud, stopped abruptly in the middle of the street. Its owner, a tall, lean man with white bushy eyebrows and a salt-and-pepper beard wearing a brown derby, stood up and shook a clenched fist at a man standing with his back to us on the edge of General Starrett's lawn.

A single train engine, with one bar of the cowcatcher bent in, rumbled past less than twenty yards beyond the house. Its wheels clanking and its motor hissing made the men's shouts inaudible until it chugged down the tracks that ran along the riverbank toward the depot and the railroad yard down the hill.

"—should've seen you and your rebel friends hang!" Henry, the tall, rotund man on the lawn, was shouting.

"You're a relic, Henry!" the man in the buggy shouted. "The war ended over twenty-five years ago. You should've gone down with one your ships."

"Y-y-you . . . I'll," Henry stammered with rage. "You're gonna regret that, Jamison."

"Ambrose, Ambrose!" the housekeeper cried from somewhere inside the house. "Get the mistress. Go get Mrs. Reynard. Now!"

The general, looking slightly disoriented, frowned and inched to the edge of his chair.

"What's all the shouting?" he said. "What's going on out there?" He pointed his cane toward the window and shook it as hard as his weak hands would allow. His face was red with anger. "Go see what all the fuss is about." I knew the order wasn't for Sir Arthur and so I rose to investigate.

"Spineless traitor!" Henry yelled.

"Bloody hell," Sir Arthur said before I took more than two steps toward the door.

Someone screeched in pain. A neighborhood dog barked, another followed, and soon a cacophony of yelping and howling arose. I rushed back to the window in time to see the large man, Henry, punch the driver of the buggy, wrench him from his seat with both hands, and drag him onto the dirt. Fists and gravel flew as the two men grappled on the ground. The horse, spooked by the commotion, reared slightly and then bolted down the street, the bells strapped around his neck jingling a frantic tune. A red and blue plaid heavy wool lap blanket, twisted into one of the buggy's wheels, flapped with every turn. The horse barely missed running over the men struggling in the street. Henry, having the upper hand, landed several calculated jabs to the other's head before standing up, leaving the man lying groaning on the ground. He delivered one last kick to his victim's side before brushing the dirt from the road off his coat, turning his back on his victim, and walking toward the house. I gasped.

Henry was Santa Claus, albeit slightly younger; his girth, his white beard and mustache, and the plump rosy cheeks matched the image of the rotund, jolly Saint Nick on the displays I'd seen lately in shop windows and in advertisements printed in the newspaper. He was dressed in a brown sealskin overcoat trimmed at the collar and the cuffs in black fur, a shaggy brown fur cap, and tall brown boots. And I'd watched him force a man from his carriage and pummel him senseless in the street.

I hope there aren't children about, I thought.

"Is he okay?" I wondered aloud while watching people from neighboring homes converge and stare down on the prostrate figure in the street.

"I don't know," Sir Arthur said. Three men lifted the unconscious figure, his head flopping, and carried him away.

"At least the dogs have quieted down," I said.

We turned away when the door to the library burst open and the culprit of the grisly scene stood in the doorway. Instead of the traditional sack over his back, this Saint Nick carried his gloves and a large valise in one hand and with the other pulled his hat off his head. A bleeding scratch above his left eye and a purple bruise on his left cheek marked where his victim had struck a blow. The housekeeper, Mrs. Becker, hovering behind him, the keys at her waist jingling inharmoniously, was unable to enter the room as long as he was blocking the door. He laughed heartily at her distress and again upon seeing the startled expressions on our faces. He dropped his valise down with a thud.

"Well, Merry Christmas, General!" Henry, the Santa Claus look-alike, declared. "Surprised to see me?"

"Come with me, you rabble-rouser," Mrs. Becker said from the hallway. "How dare you burst in here uninvited." She grabbed the man's arm, attempting to pull him back toward the hall. She was a large, tall woman but no match for the stranger, and sensing her efforts were in vain, she appealed to the general.

"I'm so sorry, sir. He pushed right past me. I've sent Ambrose for the mistress. Should I send for the police?" Her comment elicited another hearty laugh from the intruder.

"The police? Now that's a good one. I know it's been a while but—"

Mrs. Becker reached beyond him and confiscated the man's valise. "I don't know who you think you are, but either you leave right now or I am calling the police."

He ignored the housekeeper's threats, and to my discomfort, the strange man took a few steps into the room toward me. He glanced at Sir Arthur, dismissing him with a turn of his head, and then grasped my hand and kissed it.

"My, my, my. You definitely keep better company than the last time I was here, General."

I fought the desire to slap him, to shout at him, "Who do you think you are?" but instead tried pulling my hand away. He wouldn't let go.

"It's all right, Becker. No need to call the police," General Starrett said, then turned to face the stranger. "Fighting Jamison in the street, Henry? What did you think you were doing, training for a prize fight with John L. Sullivan?" The general pushed himself up with the aid of his cane, his body shaking. The cost of restraining his anger was clearly written on his face. "You didn't kill the man, did you?"

Saint Nick let go of my hand, shrugged out of his coat, and tossed it over the back of the sofa, a sleeve brushing against me. I immediately moved as far away from him as possible and rubbed my hand on my skirt. I looked up to see Sir Arthur scowling. Before I could apologize for my coarse behavior, he handed me his handkerchief, without taking his eyes off the new arrival.

"He deserved a beating," Henry said in answer to the general. "You heard what he said to me." Henry looked at the general and noticed, as I did, that the old man's strength was leaving him, that he began to sway on his feet. Again I was concerned the old man might fall. "Well, maybe you didn't hear it, but they did." The stranger pointed in Sir Arthur and my direction. "Trust me, General. He deserved it."

"I've heard it before, Henry. And Jamison's right, you know. It was a long time ago. It's not important anymore. Forget it, forget him."

"Never," Henry said.

"Well, my boy," the general said as he eased back into his chair. "Life's never boring when you're around, I'll give you that." He chuckled under his breath, shaking his head as he did. His anger was gone. "No, never a dull moment. Though you could've come at a more opportune moment."

I couldn't agree more, I thought. We were finally getting some work done.

"General," Sir Arthur said, "I'm afraid I am at a loss. Would you be so kind as to introduce me to your guest?" I could tell from Sir Arthur's formal tone that he was more than at a loss; he was livid. His interview had been interrupted, his secretary had been imposed upon, he was being rudely ignored, and he felt the sting of the offense.

"Guest?" Henry said, pointing his finger at Sir Arthur. "You, sir, are the guest here and don't forget it." Sir Arthur struggled to maintain a calm countenance, but the hands he held behind his back were clenched. It took all my experience with impertinent-behaving employers not to allow my jaw to drop. No one spoke to Sir Arthur as this man had. No one.

"Pardon me?" Sir Arthur said. "I think you've forgotten yourself, sir."

"I think it's you who have forgotten your place, whatever your name is," the man said, taking a step toward Sir Arthur. Henry was a good half foot taller. Images of him pounding on the head of the man outside flashed into my mind. Sir Arthur was a brilliant man, but he was no physical match for this perverse Santa Claus.

"I'm Sir Arthur Windom-Greene, sir. And you are?"

"Oh, so sorry, Sir Arthur, I've forgotten my manners," General Starrett said. "Sir Arthur, this is Captain—"

Before he could finish, the sound of footsteps tripping rapidly down the staircase reached us. The captain turned as a woman in her thirties burst into the room. Dressed in a pale gray walking dress, a few tendrils of blond hair loose about her face, she breathed in effort after her flight down the stairs. She stood a moment in the doorway, a book, *Journeys in Persia and Kurdistan,* clutched to her chest. She looked at the stranger as if he were a ghost.

"Adella," Henry said. He opened his arms and she, bursting into a radiant smile, tossed the book and flew into them.

"Daddy," she squeaked like a child, "you've come home!"

". . . Henry Starrett," the general said, finishing his introduction, "my son."

CHAPTER 3

"Blast! What a damn nuisance," Sir Arthur said, almost spitting the words. "We were finally making progress with the old boy. But bloody hell, what cheek that son of his had."

We faced each other in Sir Arthur's glass-front Landau carriage as it rumbled across the Spring Street Bridge toward the west side of the Galena River. Sir Arthur fiddled with his hat, a faded Civil War officer's slouch hat that could've been blue once or could've always been a nondescript gray. In winter weather, I'd hoped he'd wear a fur cap. At his age (was he over sixty now?) and with little hair left to warm his head, he could easily succumb to the cold. I should've known he wouldn't wear anything else.

"Bloody hell." Sir Arthur yanked the hat over his eyes.

Since abruptly leaving the general's house, Sir Arthur had fumed in silence. It was unsettling, seeing his anger stifled, but I knew Sir Arthur. He couldn't hold it in for long. I was relieved when he finally spoke.

"And what did he call himself, Captain Starrett?" Sir

Arthur said sarcastically. "I've never even heard of him. Have you?"

"No, I was as surprised as you were, sir," I said. "I haven't come across any mention of General Starrett having an officer for a son." I pulled my hands out of my new fox fur muff and flipped the pages of my notebook until I came to my notes on General Starrett. "We knew he had a son and at least the one granddaughter, Adella. But I don't see any references to his son being a Union officer."

"He's obviously an ass, but to be thorough we must find out more about him." I'd worked with Sir Arthur enough to recognize when it was time to poise my pen for dictation. I also knew when he said "we" he meant me. I made a list of the questions Sir Arthur ticked off on his fingers.

1. In what battles did Captain Henry Starrett fight?
2. How did he earn his commission?
3. What unit did he lead?
4. Had he suffered any battle injuries?
5. Where was he mustered in and out?
6. Where has he been since the war?
7. Why is there little record of him?

"I want any official records you can find, Hattie," Sir Arthur said. "I need to know if Captain Starrett should be included in the general's biography."

Sir Arthur, a millionaire several times over, was a self-taught scholar on the Civil War who had moved from London to Virginia almost ten years ago to "shake the hands of heroes, both dead and alive." Although Sir Arthur's preoccupation with our civil war changed my life, it also confounded me. Why would someone be obsessed with someone else's history? I knew better than to ask.

"Yes, sir."

"It may also require some below-stairs work on your part," he said, his way of saying he wanted me to glean what I could about Captain Henry Starrett from the housekeeper, cook, and maids at the general's home.

"Yes, sir."

"And I want to know what you can learn by the time we meet with the general again, whenever that will be. Tomorrow, I hope."

"Yes, sir."

"Good." Sir Arthur stared out the window. "Did you notice he didn't mention Custer?"

"Yes, I did. You were right; Custer wasn't in the room."

"Yes, it never added up. But we'll ask the general specifically about him before we cross Custer off our list. Good, we're here."

We were on "Quality Hill," an area of opulent mansions dotting the high bluffs overlooking the wide, flat river valley below. The entire town was laid out before us, the bustling Main Street that ran parallel with the curving river at the base of the hill, Grant Park and the rows of houses on Park Avenue across the river on the eastern ridge, the train depots, the winding tracks that ran along both sides of the river and the river itself. The view was spectacular, one of the best in town.

Leave it to Sir Arthur to rent a house visible from any point in town, I thought as we entered his fully furnished, fully staffed three-story redbrick Federal-style home.

William Finch, a blond-haired man in his thirties, dressed in an evening tail coat, long, black tie, and formal striped pants, yawned as he held the door open for us, the mingled scent of coal, furniture polish, and gingerbread greeting us as we entered. William took Sir Arthur's coat and hat. I usually came in through the back door, so I stood in the foyer with my coat and boa draped over my arm and my hat and muff in my hand, not sure what to do.

"Finch, take Hattie's things," Sir Arthur said. "We'll be in my library until tea."

"Sir," Finch said, awkwardly taking my things, "the mail came a few minutes ago. Do you want me to bring it to you at tea?"

"No, bring it now," Sir Arthur said.

"B-b-but," the butler stammered, nearly throwing my things on a chair, "tea's in a few minutes. I don't think I'll have time to bring the mail and then the tea." I flinched at William's ill-timed complaint. He obviously hadn't worked long for Sir Arthur.

Sir Arthur pulled out a pocket watch. "It's 3:54. You have six minutes until tea. Plenty of time." He looked up directly at William. "If you want to still be here for dinner, that is." He turned and didn't see the distraught fellow dash away.

I followed Sir Arthur into the library and shivered slightly from the cold. The overstuffed leather chairs and sofa sat in shadow as the last rays of the setting sun streamed in through the bay window, reflecting in the glass doors of the wall-length mahogany bookcase. Only the outlines of the numerous books, manuscripts, and bric-a-brac inside were distinguishable. An ivory elephant, left behind by a previous occupant, cast an eerie shadow across the leather surface of the large walnut desk. The last of the fire's embers glowed in the fireplace. Sir Arthur turned up the gas lamp, flooding the room with light. It was again my favorite room in the house.

Sir Arthur went to his desk and retrieved several pages of handwritten paper from a drawer. He handed them to me. "I need these for tomorrow." I took them and turned to leave. "Jolly good show today, Hattie, uncovering Lieutenant Colonel Regan's death. I can see now why you were invaluable to the Eureka Springs police."

"Thank you, sir." I beamed with pride. Sir Arthur was generous with his money but never with his compliments, especially when he was feeling ill-humored. I only wish he hadn't linked my research skills with my helping the Eureka Springs police discover who killed my previous employer.

"Maybe you'll uncover something new at Grant's home. I've arranged for you to accompany me on the G.A.R. tour tomorrow. By the way, I'd like you to look into this Jamison man too."

Finally, I thought. I'd been hoping to discuss Mr. Jamison and his violent altercation with Captain Starrett from the moment we saw them in the street, but to my chagrin and surprise Sir Arthur never brought the matter up. Until now. Captain Starrett had called Mr. Jamison a traitor. Serious talk, especially in a town built on its Civil War pride. But why?

A knock on the door prevented me from commenting and Finch entered the room, carrying a salver covered with several envelopes. Sir Arthur took them and shuffled through them quickly. From the decorative envelopes, many were Christmas cards. He pulled one out of the pile.

"Here's one for you, Hattie," he said, handing me a card. I was thrilled. Having no family and few acquaintances, I rarely received Christmas cards. "Miss Shaw has kindly remembered both of us this year." He chuckled and then pulled out his pocket watch again. "Four o'clock, Finch. Time for tea."

CHAPTER 4

Dismissed without further discussion, I retired to my own room to work, a simple, whitewashed room on the third floor with a sloping ceiling, a fireplace that Ida always kept burning, and a small window that looked out on the back of the houses on High Street. Modestly furnished, it contained only a small brass bed with a white crocheted bedspread, a darkly stained pine washstand with a chipped washbasin with pink lilies painted on one side, a wooden ladder-back chair, a small dresser, and, unlike the rest of the staff's rooms, an oak rolltop desk. My plant press lay on top of the stack of wooden hatboxes piled next to the dresser, and several botany books and the most recent issues of *La Mode Illustrée,* my preferred source for the newest fashion in hats, lined the one bookshelf in the room. It was adequate for my needs but a long way from the luxury of the Arcadia Hotel. Before typing up the pages of Sir Arthur's manuscript that he'd handwritten in his illegible scrawl, I sat at the desk and deciphered them. As always, it confounded me how a man like Sir Arthur, so meticulous in his research, could be so slovenly in his handwriting. But then again, I was grateful for it; it's one of the reasons why he'd hired me.

When I was done, I picked up the Christmas card that had arrived earlier. The envelope was postmarked Eureka Springs, Arkansas. I sliced it open with my pearl-handled letter opener. Fringed in blue silk, one side of the card showed a richly colored bouquet of red roses, wheat, and blue forget-me-nots and it read: "Happy may your Christmas be." On the other side, it read: "May Christmas Peace keep Winter from thy heart." I read the brief note Miss Lizzie, the dear elderly woman I'd met during my time in Eureka Springs, had included, written on Arcadia Hotel stationery.

They weren't coming! She and her sister, Miss Lucy, friends of Sir Arthur's, had planned to visit for the holidays, but Miss Lucy had come down with a coryza and Dr. Grice didn't recommend that she expose herself to the cold winter weather.

How disappointing, was my first thought. *Ah, Dr. Grice,* was my second.

Dr. Walter Grice, a physician I'd also met in Eureka Springs who, only after a brief acquaintance, had become dear to me and, I think, me to him. But the reality of our lives intervened and separated us. The situation was impossible, but it hadn't stopped me from anticipating and relishing every letter I'd received from him.

I was replying to Miss Lizzie's letter when someone tapped on my door.

"Come in," I said. Ida Hollenbeck, maid-of-all-work for Sir Arthur, opened the door tentatively. Ida was at least ten years younger than me, with big bones and big hands that were strong, calloused, and stained with something she'd been helping Mrs. Monday, the cook, with in the kitchen. She had a wide face and small eyes and often mixed her German and English without realizing it. She wore a dark apron over a blue working dress and two unmatched boots, which she alternated every other day, so "to wear them down evenly." Brown frizzy hair stuck out from under her white cap.

"*Verzeihung*—Excuse me, Hattie, but *he* wants to see you, in the library, *ja?*" Ida, in awe of her employer, could never bring herself to call him by name. She seemed to be slightly frightened of even me. At least I convinced her to call me Hattie.

"Thank you, Ida." I didn't have to ask her when Sir Arthur wanted to see me, the answer was always "now." I brushed my dress off, picked up my notebook and pencil, and followed Ida down the stairs.

"*Gute Nacht*—Good night, Hattie, *ja?*" Ida said as we separated at the bottom of the stairs, Ida toward the kitchen and me toward the library.

I knocked and then opened the door. "You wanted to see me, Sir Arthur?" I said.

"Sit down, Hattie. There's a matter I'd like to discuss," he said. He was settled in his favorite leather chair, smoking a cigar and reading the local newspaper, the *Galena Gazette*. A stack of newspapers were folded up on the table beside him.

I found a seat opposite him and flipped over to a blank page on my tablet. As he folded the paper and set it on top of the stack, he pointed to a headline, SHOPLIFTER STRIKES ST. LOUIS STORE, MAKES OFF WITH HUNDREDS OF DOLLARS' WORTH OF GOODS. "Not my idea of getting into the Christmas spirit, eh, Hattie?"

"No, sir."

"Anyway, I received news this afternoon. Philippa has decided not to join me here in Galena for Christmas. She wants to stay in Richmond with the grandchildren." I was crushed, first Miss Lucy gets sick and Miss Lizzie cancels, and now this.

When Sir Arthur had hired me directly from my disastrous assignment in Eureka Springs, I was elated to accept in part because I hated spending Christmas alone. I was looking forward to a jolly holiday with Sir Arthur's large and boisterous family. Lady Philippa was a wonderful hostess, but with only a few days before Christmas I'd begun to wonder when his family would arrive. Finch and Ida had prepared all the rooms, but they'd remained empty. I'd wanted to ask Sir Arthur when we should expect Lady Philippa, but it was not my place to ask. Now I had my answer. Christmas wasn't going to be festive after all.

"I had suspected as much when she wrote of her ambivalence in her previous letter. So I decided to invite some old friends of mine for the holidays," Sir Arthur said, holding up two letters, "and they have both accepted." Suddenly things didn't look so bleak after all. "But that will mean more work for the staff, preparing for the holidays, decorating, trimming the tree, that sort of thing. Philippa usually takes care of all that. I want you to do it, Hattie."

"Sir?" I wasn't a hostess. I'd spent the last eleven years of my life alone on Christmas and the seven years before that it was only my father and me. I didn't know the first thing about preparing for a proper holiday. "I've never done anything like this."

"I want you to oversee everything, Hattie. Coordinate the menus with Mrs. Monday and work with Finch in arranging for the guests. And I want you to supervise all of the holiday preparations, the tree, the greenery, the ribbons and bows, whatever you want. All of my decorations are in Richmond with Philippa, so you'll have to either buy or make what you need. And since Philippa usually buys the staff's presents for Boxing Day, I'll need you to do that too."

"Yes, sir," I said. "Though I'm concerned I won't have time to do everything properly." My subtle hint was as far as I could question Sir Arthur.

"You'll have Finch, Harvey, Mrs. Monday, and the maid to help you. Besides, I have proofreading I need to do in the next few days, which should free you up to attend to these extra responsibilities. I can count on you, can't I, Hattie?"

I was elated about enjoying such an elaborate Christmas but overwhelmed by the fact that I had to plan it all. *Just another challenge,* I told myself.

"Of course, sir," I said.

"Good," Sir Arthur said. I poised my pencil to paper again. "Lieutenant Triggs and his wife, Priscilla, are due to arrive any minute now. You remember the lieutenant, don't you, Hattie? He acted as our guide and liaison in Kansas City."

I did remember Lieutenant Morgan Triggs. I'd only been working for Sir Arthur for four days when he insisted I accompany him to the Westport battlefield site he was researching. Lieutenant Morgan Triggs was the man who volunteered to escort us and answer any questions Sir Arthur might have. For three days, the two men trampled every inch of what remained of the battlefield discussing every nuance of strategy while I, straggling along behind them, diligently recorded every word they said. Once, while taking notes, I tripped over a fieldstone and fell sprawling on the ground at Lieutenant Triggs's feet. He helped me to rise. I thanked him, brushed myself off, and continued taking Sir Arthur's dictation without comment.

"Now that's loyalty," the lieutenant said to Sir Arthur, pointing over his shoulder at me with his thumb. "I've seen a pack of bloodhounds during a hunt less diligent and steadfast than your Miss Davish." Sir Arthur stopped in his tracks and gestured to the field around them.

"You were in the infantry, Twenty-Ninth Missouri Volunteers, if I recall right," Sir Arthur said. The lieutenant nodded. "Isn't that what you soldiers did every day of the war?"

"I'd never thought of it like that," Morgan Triggs said.

"Loyalty," Sir Arthur had said. "That's what this war was all about, loyalty to your country, to your principles, to your commanding officer, to your God." He had turned to face me then, as I'd finished recording his last words. "That's what I expect from you, Miss Davish. Nothing less than complete loyalty. Give me that, girl, and I can open doors you never knew existed."

I'd been too dumbfounded at the time to capture the words on paper, but I've never forgotten them.

"We kept up a correspondence and I've enjoyed a hunt with the lieutenant several times since," Sir Arthur said. "John Baines and his wife will be arriving Monday morning, from Chicago. I don't know the exact time." I oddly knew nothing about the acquaintance between John Baines and Sir Arthur. But with Sir Arthur, one learns to stifle one's curiosity. It was a lesson I'd learned from him long ago that has served me well in my profession. Except in Eureka Springs, of course. I'd allowed my curiosity free rein there. Even now I marveled at the thought.

What was I thinking?

"I'll look it up, sir," I said.

"Good, now as to the menu, I had Mrs. Monday start a proper pudding several days ago, but I also want a goose, not a turkey, a goose. And I want wassail punch for Christmas Eve and Christmas cake, with extra walnuts, for Christmas Day tea."

"Would you also like mince pies, sir?" I said.

"Yes, I would." He sent a ring of smoke into the air. "I knew I could count on you, Hattie."

The clock struck half past five and the doorbell rang almost simultaneously.

"He's right on time," Sir Arthur said. "I knew I liked that fellow."

"Welcome to my home away from home," Sir Arthur said as William Finch helped Lieutenant Morgan Triggs off with his coat. Lieutenant Triggs was a small man, only a few inches taller than me, but muscular under his well-fitted suit. He was in his mid-fifties, with salt-and-pepper hair. He had a round, clean-shaven face that made the scar that crossed his right eyebrow and stretched to the corner of his ear all the more prominent. Although soft-spoken, he had a friendly openness to his demeanor that made him excellent company for Sir Arthur. Lieutenant Triggs had treated me with respect and I'd liked him for it.

Sir Arthur took Mrs. Triggs's hand, then shook the lieutenant's. "Glad you could make it, Triggs. How was the train ride? You remember Hattie, don't you?"

"Ah, Miss Davish," the lieutenant said. "Sir Arthur's penwielding Galahad! I'm glad to know Sir Arthur had the brains to hire you back again." He turned to the woman beside him and put his hand against her back. "May I introduce my wife, Priscilla? You know Sir Arthur, but I don't think you've ever met Miss Davish, have you, darling?"

"No," Priscilla Triggs said softly. "Pleased to make your acquaintance, Miss Davish."

Priscilla Triggs was a short, slightly built woman, who seemed dwarfed by everyone around her. She wore a dark purple dress of plain material, embellished with only a trim of beads, and an older purple and black full crown lace bonnet, which she seemed reluctant to take off. Her hair was still dark red and she had pale, freckled skin. Yet Mrs. Triggs seemed older than she was, which was probably late forties. She stood with a slight stoop to her shoulder and had sad eyes that she raised with visible effort. She stood in stark contrast next to her vibrant husband.

"Please to meet you, ma'am," I said.

"When Sir Arthur was in Missouri, Miss Davish here was his right hand," Lieutenant Triggs explained. "And his left!"

"She probably knows as much about the battles of West-port as you or I do now, Morgan," Sir Arthur added.

"I wouldn't doubt it. Priscilla, you should see her fingers fly over that typewriter of hers, like the rapid fire of the enemy line."

"You're Sir Arthur's secretary then, Miss Davish?" Mrs. Triggs said.

"Yes, ma'am. I assisted when he was writing an article on the battles of Westport. That's when I met your husband."

As the men exchanged pleasantries, I watched Mrs. Triggs. Her eyes were cast down during the entire conversation.

"Shall I show them to their rooms so they may freshen up before dinner, sir?" William Finch suggested after several minutes of us standing in the hall. Sir Arthur was already discussing his newest project with Lieutenant Triggs and, as usual, had forgotten all about his guests' comfort.

"Of course, of course. I'll meet you in the library when you're ready."

"If it's all the same to you, Sir Arthur, I'm in no need of a break. After hours on the train, I'm like a private who's been flicking weevils into the fire just for something to do. I'm intrigued by your new book and would relish some stimulating conversation." Sir Arthur's eyes lit up. I could see why they had continued their friendship. "If that's all right with you, darling?" Lieutenant Triggs said to his wife.

"Yes, but I think I will lie down."

"Hattie, see to anything Mrs. Triggs may need," Sir Arthur said as the lieutenant kissed his wife on the cheek. The two men began their conversation where they'd left off and walked toward the library, us women completely forgotten. William picked up Mrs. Triggs's suitcases and bag.

"If you'd follow me, ma'am."

"I'd like a glass of water before I go up, if you don't mind," Mrs. Triggs said. William dropped the bags with a thud.

"One moment, please." William disappeared down the hall. Mrs. Triggs gave me a pained smile, then walked over to the Albert Bierstadt painting *Forest Stream* hanging on the wall. She studied the large, tumbled moss-covered boulders beside the still pool in silence for several moments.

"Oh, how I envy you, Miss Davish," she said, without turning around.

I was taken by surprise and didn't know what to say. I waited for her to say more, but she didn't. William returned with the glass of water. She turned, drank the entire contents of the glass without taking a breath, and then handed it back to the butler.

"Thank you," she said, grabbing my arm and pulling me toward her. I stiffened at her familiarity. She leaned into me and said, "I know we'll get along just fine, Miss Davish. Morgan has nothing but praise for you."

"Thank you, ma'am," I said. William and I exchanged puzzled glances.

"Oh, do call me Priscilla," she said. "And I'll call you Hattie." She squeezed my arm to punctuate our new acquaintance.

"If you'd follow me now, ma'am," William said. We started up the staircase. Priscilla walked beside me, with her hand on my arm, almost as if climbing the stairs took too much effort and she needed my support. We approached her room in silence. William opened the door, showed her in, and set up her suitcases.

"The maid can assist you in unpacking if you'd like," the butler said. "Dinner will be served at seven. If that will be all, ma'am?"

"Yes, thank you," Mrs. Triggs said.

"Is there anything you need, Mrs. Triggs, I mean Priscilla?" I said. I resented Sir Arthur offering my services first as hostess, now as a housekeeper or maid, but both my loyalty to him and the familiarity this woman imposed upon me compelled me to inquire.

"No, it's too late for me, Hattie," she said, pulling the drape back from the window. A delivery wagon laden down with pine trees piled several feet high rumbled past in the street below. "It's just too late." I glanced at the clock on the mantel. It was only half past five.

What does she mean by that? I wondered as I slipped out the door and hastily closed it behind me.

CHAPTER 5

"It was the greatest adventure of our lives," a man with only one leg and a long, flowing white beard said. Every head in the room, with the exception of mine and Sir Arthur's, nodded in solemn agreement.

"I'll never forget the time I got up to water the trees in the middle of a moonless night," the one-legged man said. "Just as I finished up and turned around, I bumped right into a rebel, I did. Must of been a scout or something. Well, I be damned if I didn't pull up my britches and run as fast as I could go. I looked back once, trying not to get shot, and wouldn't you know, the damn reb was running the other way!" He slapped his one knee and let out a loud guffaw, spreading laughter through the room.

What was Sir Arthur thinking, bringing me here? I wondered.

When Sir Arthur, Lieutenant Morgan Triggs, and I had arrived at the monthly meeting of the #502 Edward D. Kittoe Post of the Grand Army of the Republic, otherwise known as the G.A.R., heads weren't nodding, but beards were wagging and eyes were raised. Women were not allowed at the meetings and my presence set the men, mostly feeble old men, into passionate complaints. But Sir Arthur had been asked to attend as a special guest, and with General Starrett's assurances, for he was the Senior Vice Commander of the post, I was allowed to stay and take notes as long as I sat in the shadowed corner and didn't speak. As the one-legged man's tale attested, the men quickly forgot I was in the room at all. At least most of the men. In an attempt to shield myself from the coarse men, I vainly buried myself in my shorthand. It didn't work.

"Who can forget the 'horizontal entertainment'? " another man added, chuckling.

Horizontal entertainment? I wondered as several men shouted, "Hear, hear!"

One of the men, with a scruffy gray mustache and several moles on his cheek, looked directly at me and winked. I dropped my gaze, tugged my hat down as far as it would go, and pressed my back against the wall. A moth landed on my tablet, methodically searching the paper for food. When I shooed it away, the man with the moles was still staring at me. I didn't look up again.

After taking roll call, which I had dutifully captured in my notebook, the Post Commander, Lieutenant Colonel Issac Holbrook, a tall, elderly man with thick white hair that protruded from his head and ran in various directions, read the minutes of the last meeting, including a description of the "sham battle" the men put on for the town. He then reminded everybody of the "Great Men of Galena" house tour scheduled for tomorrow that was organized by the G.A.R. specifically for Sir Arthur, though everyone was invited to attend. Then General Starrett officially introduced Sir Arthur, who in turn introduced his guest, Lieutenant Triggs. The general had allowed Sir Arthur a few minutes to speak to the group. Sir Arthur described his purpose for moving to Galena and then asked if anyone was willing to tell their impression of the war.

Contrary to his normal dominating personality, Sir Arthur never passed on the chance to live vicariously through men who had actually fought in the war.

"We had to walk fifteen to twenty miles a day, share our short rations of rancid bacon and hardtack with the worms, use our rifle butts to crush coffee beans, sleep out in the rain with only our coats to cover us, and yet we enjoyed ourselves capitally," the old one-legged, bearded soldier said.

"Damn near got myself killed three times over," another said, "but I'd have to agree with Rufus here. I had one hell of a time!" Unlike the other veterans, Lieutenant Triggs did not smile nor did he nod his head in response.

"But you were at war," Sir Arthur said. "How could you describe your experiences with such joy?"

"I didn't say it weren't hell, Mr. Englishman," the old soldier named Rufus replied. "A man's not supposed to see his own leg tossed onto a pile of severed limbs like so much refuse or whittle away his hours between battles betting on how long a tick can crawl on a man before it bites him. No, it was war all right but if you've never lived through it, you have no idea what we here are talking about." Sir Arthur flinched. The old soldier didn't realize it, but he cut right to Sir Arthur's one known vulnerability. He would've given his title and lands for a chance to experience the war as these men had.

"There's a pride in it, sir," a small, round-faced, spectacled man said in response to Sir Arthur's open expression of bewilderment, suspicion, and hurt pride. "I know you are interested mostly in the big men that came from here, like General Grant or Dr. Kittoe, but for us ordinary folk, who never traveled more than twenty miles from home before the war, there's a pride and a sense of importance in being a part of beating the rebs and keeping this country together." A preponderance of head wagging followed.

"Yeah, we Union men stuck together, fought together, and

lots of us died together. But those of us who lived, we can hold our heads up higher than before because we did what was right."

"Unlike those Southern-loving rich folk!" one man cried.

"Or those lousy Southern-loving copperheads," someone else added.

"I'd heard a certain segment of Galena society had ties to the South, especially those relying on the Mississippi River trade," Sir Arthur said. "But I didn't know there were copperheads."

I'd learned about the Copperhead Movement while helping Sir Arthur with his first book. A Northern faction of the Democratic Party, they were called by President Lincoln "the fire in the rear" and by their enemies who hoped to stigmatize them like venomous snakes "copperheads." Among other things, they believed the Union could never be restored by war and demanded peace at any cost. To undermine the war effort they were known to fight the draft, encourage desertion, talk of helping rebel prisoners of war escape, and take money from the Confederacy. Even unsuccessful efforts to organize violent resistance occurred. When the Union suffered losses, the movement had strong support. After Sherman's victory in Atlanta, support for the movement waned and some movement leaders were tried for treason. Copperheads in Galena could've split the town apart.

"It sounds like living in Galena during the war was . . . complicated," Sir Arthur said, in what I took to be a vast understatement.

"Oh, no, sir," the round-faced man said. "Like General Grant once said, 'There are but two parties now, traitors and patriots.' "

"Hear, hear, Charlie!" Rowdy applause erupted and several men slapped the round-faced man named Charlie on the back.

Before the clamor settled down and Sir Arthur could ask another question, the door swung open.

"Who's a traitor and who's a patriot?"

"Henry!" a simultaneous cry went up as Henry Starrett was welcomed heartily into the room. Sir Arthur scowled. Lieutenant Triggs stared at the newcomer with an unreadable expression.

"You old rascal!" someone said.

"We heard that you were back."

"Break any hearts lately?"

"Sink any ships lately?"

Men clambered over to shake Henry Starrett's hand. I couldn't shake the impression of ancient boys vying for Santa Claus's attention.

"Now what's this about a copperhead I'm hearing?" Henry Starrett said.

"The men were graciously answering questions for my book, Captain Starrett," Sir Arthur said. "We weren't talking about 'a copperhead.' "

"No, actually, he's right, mister," Charlie said. "That's one of the reasons your questions got us so fired up. There's talk that Enoch Jamison is back in town, visiting his ailing mother for the holidays."

"And who is Enoch Jamison?" Sir Arthur said, knowing full well he was the same man we witnessed being beaten.

"One of the most vile creatures to walk the earth, Sir Arthur," Henry Starrett said. "Am I right?" The men began grumbling among themselves. "Am I right?" he said again.

"Oh, Henry," General Starrett said. "Don't be ridiculous. It was over twenty-five years ago."

"Again, I ask," Sir Arthur said, getting annoyed at his time being wasted. "Who is Enoch Jamison?"

"One of Galena's most notorious copperheads," the man

with the moles on his cheek said. "He spent time at Fort Delaware for treason."

"I believe he was honorably discharged, Mr. Groat," General Starrett said.

"That was a mistake, sir," Mr. Groat, the man with the moles, said.

"Yeah, some say he should've hanged," Charlie added.

"Which is why he has some nerve showing his face around here again," Henry Starrett said.

"Yeah," a few men said in vague agreement as a middle-aged man with brown hair, a large, floppy mustache, broad shoulders, and big, muscular arms stood and made for the door. He shook a fist at Henry Starrett. In India ink, O.C.K. was marked on the back of his left hand. He was clearly angry. *But why?*

"Speaking of copperheads," Henry said, glancing at the man in the doorway.

"Damn you, Starrett!" the man shouted before slamming the door behind him. More grumbling came from the group. Henry either didn't notice or pretended not to.

"I think something should be done about it," he said.

"Like pull the man from his buggy and give him a lashing in the street, Captain Starrett?" Sir Arthur said calmly. The room fell silent and all eyes were on Captain Starrett.

"That's right, by God!" he said, slapping the back of the man nearest him. Chaos erupted. Several men jumped up and shook Henry's hand while everyone spoke at once.

"Pulled him from his buggy?"

"Doesn't he have a sick mother to tend?"

"Did you kill him?"

"Henry, you are a madman," one man yelled, "but I'm sure Jamison deserved it!"

"Damn right he did," Henry said, "and more if I have anything to do with it. I'll have him regretting he ever came back to town."

"Hear, hear!" several men shouted in approval.

"If I may," Sir Arthur said, ignoring the growing tension in the room, "I have a few more questions for you gentlemen."

No one seemed to hear Sir Arthur as the men all talked, almost shouting, among themselves, gesturing with their hands and canes.

"Order, order!" Lieutenant Colonel Holbrook shouted about the din. "We still have the newly purposed charity works to discuss."

I quickly gathered my things and, being careful to stay out of arm's reach of Mr. Groat, followed as Sir Arthur stomped toward the door. Lieutenant Triggs scrambled through the crowd to catch up with us.

"Order, order!" Lieutenant Colonel Holbrook shouted again. "Please, gentlemen."

"Oh, where's your fighting spirit, Holbrook? Let the old codgers have some fun." Henry Starrett pointed to two men who were red faced and arguing over something I couldn't hear. One minute the room had been filled with reminiscing old men and now it was filled with angry ex-soldiers who were eager for one last battle. How had Henry Starrett's surprise appearance turned a routine meeting into a mob scene?

"Sir Arthur, please don't leave!" Lieutenant Colonel Holbrook shouted. Sir Arthur, knowing he wouldn't be heard without shouting back, and Sir Arthur never stoops to shouting, shook his head and waved. Lieutenant Triggs hesitated slightly and looked back once before leaving.

"Don't forget. The tour starts at eleven," was the last coherent statement I heard as I gladly followed Sir Arthur and the lieutenant out the door.

★ ★ ★

BOOM!

The house shook and I heard Mrs. Monday downstairs scream. The explosion was still ringing in my ears as I raced down the stairs and found the entire household congregating in the foyer. Sir Arthur was still dressed, but the Triggses, William Finch, and Mrs. Monday, a reed of a woman in her mid-sixties, were still in their robes, having been startled awake.

"What the devil was that?" Sir Arthur said. Sweat ran down Lieutenant Triggs's face and he was shaking. He shook his head as his wife clung to his arm.

We followed Sir Arthur out the front door and looked toward a plume of smoke rising above Grant Park across the river. The street was filling with people as they poured out of their homes, most still in their dressing gowns and robes. I was happy that I'd been working late and like Sir Arthur was still modestly attired.

When Sir Arthur dismissed me after the G.A.R. meeting, I'd headed straight to my room to type up the meeting notes; I was too distressed to sleep. With that done, I had further tried to distract myself from the unpleasantries of the evening by starting a list of everything I could think of that needed doing before Christmas. I sat at my typewriter for an hour trying to recall everything I'd ever seen in magazines or read about in books, because that was the only place I'd seen the Christmas finery that Sir Arthur expected.

1. Arrange menus with Mrs. Monday for Christmas Eve and Christmas Day
2. Shop for presents for staff from Sir Arthur
3. Shop for presents from me
4. Cut down tree with Harvey
5. Buy greenery, hothouse flowers, bows, and ribbons
6. Buy ornaments, confections, walnuts, Brazil nuts

7. Make cornucopias, garlands
8. Decorate halls, mantels, tables with Ida and William
9. Organize games: snapdragon, charades, button, button, who's got the button

The exercise had worked. I'd finally started to feel excited again about the upcoming festivities when the explosion had occurred.

"That was cannon fire," a neighbor explained when Sir Arthur inquired.

"Well, bloody hell," Sir Arthur said. We all strained to see movement in the dim gaslight that glowed over Grant Park. A crowd was gathering there too. "Finch, go get Harvey."

"You wanted me, sir?" Harvey, the middle-aged grounds-keeper and coachman, said. He stood only a few feet away. He was fully dressed but still rubbing his eyes. The cannon blast had aroused him from his room in the carriage house.

"Yes, Harvey. Bring the gig around. I want to see what all the commotion is about." Harvey went back toward the carriage house. "Lieutenant? Care to join me? I'll wait for you to dress."

Triggs looked down at his wife and kissed her brow. "Sorry, Sir Arthur," he said without his usual jovial tone, his wife still clutching his arm. "Too reminiscent of Vicksburg for my tastes."

Sir Arthur turned to me. "Since you're prepared as always, Hattie, fancy a midnight drive?"

Why not? I thought.

Within minutes, Sir Arthur and I were rumbling over the Green Street Bridge toward Grant Park. Since coming to Galena a few weeks ago, I made a stop at Grant Park a regular part of my morning hikes. Spanning almost two blocks of Park Avenue, it was a place of meandering walkways and strategi-cally located benches, all with a superb view of the river, the bluffs, and downtown, on the river's eastern bank. It was flanked on one end by a monument honoring the Civil War soldiers from Galena and a bronze "Napoleon" cannon marked with a deep impression of some past battle, and by a statue of Ulysses S. Grant on the other. Between the two was a lovely fountain installed last year by the Ladies' Auxiliary of a female figure, on bended knee, elevated on a pedestal. Four nude cherubs, sitting on rocks, held shells aloft from which, had the fountain been turned on, water would spray. Its pool was empty but for last autumn's fallen leaves. I could only imagine how pleasant a spot it was in summer. Even stark and cold, the park was a peaceful place that I often had to myself. Not tonight. We'd been right about a crowd. Dozens of people had gathered in the northwest corner of the park, near the soldier's monument. And they sounded angry.

"Stomp on the copperhead! Stomp on the copperhead!"

Sir Arthur and I pushed our way through the shouting crowd for a better view. Sir Arthur stopped short.

"Astonishing. Isn't that . . . ?" Sir Arthur said, speechless.

"Santa Claus," I said, finishing Sir Arthur's thought. He looked at me perplexed.

"Santa Claus?"

"I'm sorry. I mean Henry Starrett," I said. Sir Arthur looked at the man in the fur-trimmed overcoat and fur cap standing next to the cannon.

"I didn't see it before, but you're right, Hattie. Captain Starrett does bear an uncanny resemblance to Father Christmas. But what is he doing?" The captain had climbed onto the cannon, which had been turned around to face Park Avenue, and was now straddling it as if it were a horse. He waved his cap in the air as the crowd clapped and cheered him.

"Do you think that got his attention?" Henry yelled.

"Again!" several in the crowd cried.

"It didn't hit his house!" someone else yelled.

"Enough of this," Sir Arthur said as he pushed his way to the front of the crowd and confronted the man on the cannon. "What is the idea, Captain, disturbing the peace like this?"

"Disturbing the peace?" Captain Starrett said as he deftly leaped down from the cannon. "We're just getting started!" He stooped over and retrieved a sack that had been lying on the ground. He waved his arm above his head. "To the copperheads!"

Captain Starrett purposely cut across the park and crossed the street. The crowd followed. As I walked among them, I recognized many of the men who had been at the G.A.R. meeting earlier this evening. They held shovels or horse whips or carried sacks or pails filled with I knew not what. I was surprised to see that I was not the only woman, but the proximity of others of my sex did not make me feel more secure. Two separate women, bent upon staying with the mob, had heedlessly trampled a brown derby hat that lay abandoned on the ground. I stayed as close to Sir Arthur as was appropriate.

We didn't walk far. The crowd stopped suddenly in front of a small, two-story redbrick house, with green shutters and a white, pillared portico, a block from the park. Henry Starrett reached into his bag and retrieved a large, rancid cabbage.

"Now!" shouted Captain Starrett, smashing the wilted, slimy cabbage into the front door. The cabbage slid down the length of the door, leaving an oily, putrid-smelling streak. Already at the edge of the throng, I instinctively took several steps back.

With that order, men and women shouted, laughed, and gloated as they bashed windows, trampled hedges, and volleyed eggs, rotten vegetables, and animal feces at the house. Even a man with one arm missing below the elbow lobbed tomatoes at the house, creating what looked like splatters of blood. It was horrible to watch and the stench was almost unbearable.

So why am I still here?

"My God!" Sir Arthur cursed from behind the handkerchief he held to his nose. "This is barbaric."

Mere minutes had passed when, with the damage done, Captain Starrett held up his hand and bellowed, "Come out and face us, Jamison, you traitor, you coward!"

Jamison? Was Captain Starrett going to attack the man again? Hadn't he suffered enough?

The mob miraculously fell silent and all eyes stared at the front door. Would he come out? The door slowly opened and a man took a firm step onto his porch. A rocking chair beside him was still swaying from the impact of a brick. With gaslight from the street and a few lanterns that swayed in the midst of the crowd, it was difficult to see the man's face clearly. Then he raised a lantern above his head, casting light on both himself and his immediate foe. I gasped. The man's face was swollen. One eye was circled by black and purplish bruises and his nose looked slightly off center. With the evidence of Captain Starrett's savage beating written on the man's face, I knew Enoch Jamison at once.

"What do you want?" Enoch Jamison said. He suddenly dodged his head to the side as a rotten potato missed him by inches. "Don't have anything better to do than attack the home of a feeble, old woman? Cowards!" he yelled.

"Traitor!" someone shouted in reply.

"Go home," Jamison said. "Go home and frighten your own wives and mothers with your savagery." The man whom they had called a coward then turned his back on his attackers. "And Merry Christmas!" he shouted over his shoulder before slamming the door behind him.

"Astonishing," Sir Arthur said as the crowd slowly dispersed. Some shaking their heads, others mumbling. Most seemed ashamed of what they'd done. Not Captain Starrett. He shook hands with anyone who would take his hand and congratulated them on a job well done.

"We showed him," I heard Captain Starrett say over and over. What was he trying to prove? He had attacked the man physically and now had succeeded in terrorizing him in his mother's home. But why? Because of a political stance Enoch Jamison had held over a quarter of a century ago? I didn't think I would ever understand.

As the crowd dispersed, Sir Arthur approached Captain Starrett, who now stood alone in Enoch Jamison's front yard.

"Why?" Sir Arthur asked, wondering as I had.

"Why what?" Captain Starrett said.

"Why would you do such a thing?"

"I can't abide copperheads." Captain Starrett shrugged. "Plus," Captain Starrett said, slapping Sir Arthur on the back, sending my employer forward a few inches. "It sure beats the usual evening's entertainment," he said, laughing as he gathered up his belongings and headed toward General Starrett's home a few blocks away. He whistled a strain of the "Battle Hymn of the Republic" as he went.

Sir Arthur stood still, his face flush with anger, watching until Captain Starrett was out of sight. I'd never seen anyone treat Sir Arthur with disrespect. And with the exception of his wife, Lady Philippa, I'd never even seen anyone touch Sir Arthur. Captain Starrett had done both in one day. I didn't know how Sir Arthur would respond, but I knew better than to say anything.

"The impudence! The . . ." Sir Arthur was speechless with fury.

He stormed toward the horse and gig he had left tied up at the edge of the park, with me struggling to keep up. We rode back across the river and up the hill to Prospect Street in silence. Harvey was asleep on the step when we arrived. I envied his repose. I knew I wasn't going to get any sleep tonight. Sir Arthur, after nudging Harvey awake with his foot, handed him the horse's reins. A deep imprint of the porch banister Harvey had been leaning on marked his cheek. He rubbed it absent-mindedly. As I stepped down from the gig, Sir Arthur turned on me with a pointed finger inches from my face. Startled, I took a step back, hitting my elbow against the rim of the wheel.

"I don't care if he served as Grant's aide-de-camp," Sir Arthur said, turning then and stomping toward the door. "That man will not be mentioned in my book!"

CHAPTER 6

The next morning, I took an early walk before Mass down the entire length of Main Street. My boots clicked on the dry boardwalk and, like a pioneer, I made a new discovery with every bend in the road. This downtown thoroughfare, just wide enough for two carriages to pass, was level but, unlike the straight main streets of most Middle West towns, snaked around for almost a mile, parallel to the original path of the river. With the sun not yet above the three- and four-story buildings that lined the road like a continuous wall of red brick, I was walking through a tunnel punctuated with color-ful wooden awnings. At each crosswalk, I'd emerge where I could see the river or the bluffs above. But gazing at natural wonders would have to come later, I was here to peek at the shops: Henning's bakery, Geo. Young's books & stationery, Grumme's confections, the Fair Store, the St. Louis Depart-ment Store, Barry Bros. Dry Goods, Siniger & Siniger's Drugs, LeBron and Son, Jewelers, Killian's fine groceries, Kuhn's Meat Market, and my favorite, Mrs. Edwards' Millinery. Fortunately for me with my extra Christmas duties, Main Street still re-

flected the wealth and prosperity of the town's heyday of pro-
ductive lead mines and steamboat traffic. I'd be able to find
anything I needed.

So what? Christmas is already spoiled.

The thought popped into my head as I stood in the same
spot I had occupied the night before. After my walk down
Main Street, I'd crossed the footbridge and strolled through
Grant Park. The park was vacant, of people and of evidence
that anything extraordinary had occurred. Another dusting of
snow had fallen in the early morning hours, enough to cover
any traces of last night's mob. I brushed away the snow from a
bench and sat down, setting my plant press on my lap to keep
it dry. In the few weeks I'd been in Galena, I had only found
two new specimens for my plant collection, red-osier dog-
wood, with its bright red branches, and blue ash twigs with
winter buds. I'd gotten spoiled in Eureka Springs, where I had
collected something new almost every day. But it was too cold
here to find almost anything that wasn't dead, brown, and
shriveled up. So I had given up bringing my plant press along
on my hikes. But today I'd brought it along as a case of false
optimism. For despite the exciting day I had planned ahead of
me, a melancholy had taken hold of me during the night. I'd
barely slept. I looked out across the river valley to the town of
redbrick buildings on the bluffs built from where the water's
edge used to be. Without the slightest breeze, smoke from
chimneys and smokestacks rose unwavering straight up into
the sky.

What's wrong with me? I wondered.

Images of Captain Henry Starrett came to mind, his
mocking of Sir Arthur, his brutal attack on Mr. Jamison in the
street and then on the man's house, all in the name of a
"night's entertainment." Men had been injured and insulted
and yet all I could think of was that Santa Claus wasn't who
we thought he was. The Santa Claus of my childhood had

given me the book I'll treasure forever. With her inscription inside it, he had given me back my mother, for an instant. He was the Santa Claus who with every glimpse of him on a card or in a newspaper or in a church hall filled me with the hope of recapturing the magic, peace, and love of that Christmas-time almost twenty years ago. I'd been excited about planning the Christmas festivities, but seeing a version of Santa Claus be so cruel had put a damper on my exuberance and had made me wonder if I'd ever enjoy Christmas again.

How absurd, I thought, having felt sorry for myself when Mr. Jamison was the one who deserved my pity. Captain Starrett wasn't Santa Claus. So why should he ruin my Christmas?

I felt immensely better. I stood, shook the snow off the hem of my dress, straightened my hat, and headed back across the bridge toward Sir Arthur's house to change for Mass at St. Michael's.

"You're going back to the general's house, Hattie." Sir Arthur waved a simple gold-bordered white card in one hand and his cigar in the other. "Starrett sent word that he's ready to talk again, now. So you'll have to go without me."

"Yes, sir," I said, trying to hide my disappointment.

I'd planned to attend the G.A.R.-sponsored home tour. I'd raced back from St. Michael's, changed into a less formal day dress, and fetched a pencil and tablet of paper from my room before meeting Sir Arthur and Lieutenant Triggs in the foyer. I'd been especially looking forward to seeing the late Dr. Kittoe's greenhouse.

"Take down everything Starrett feels up to talking about," Sir Arthur said. "You know the topics I'd like him to cover, including the Custer question. I look forward to reading the material tonight."

"Starrett?" Lieutenant Triggs asked, surprised.

"Not to worry old chap, I'm not talking about the brute

but his father, General Cornelius Starrett of the Army of the Cumberland, Fourth Corps. I'm interviewing him for my book. You saw him at the G.A.R. meeting, I believe."

"Well, I'll be. So that was him? My brother served with the general at Missionary Ridge, though he was Major Starrett then. Had nothing but praise for the great soldier. Amazing he's the sire of . . ." Morgan Triggs didn't finish his thought. He didn't have to. "I didn't know the general was living here."

"Well, come along after the tour then if you'd like. Bring Mrs. Triggs too if she's up to it. I've been invited for tea." Only Sir Arthur would invite two additional guests to someone else's tea. Sir Arthur looked at his watch.

"Right!" he said. "It's time to go."

The tour, arranged by the G.A.R. weeks ago for Sir Arthur during his visit to Galena, began and ended with U. S. Grant's homes, with several of Galena's other famous men in between, including the former homes of General John Rawlins on Hill Street, Dr. Edward Kittoe's on S. High Street, the statesman Elihu Washburne's former home on Third Street, an impressive Greek Revival house that had appeared in *Harper's New Monthly Magazine,* and General William Rowley's on Park. At each home, the Union Army veterans' group had arranged someone to show the tour group around and answer any questions Sir Arthur might have.

While he was still a clerk in his father's leather-goods store in 1860, Grant and his family lived at 121 S. High Street, a modest brick house, only a block from Sir Arthur's rented home. After his triumphal return in 1865, the people of Galena presented Grant with a beautiful Italianate brick house high on the hill overlooking Galena from the east side of the river. Although Grant had died seven years ago, the home was still owned by his children, who on this occasion allowed the caretaker to show the G.A.R. members and Sir Arthur around the house. So the tour was to begin with Grant's more humble beginnings on one side of the river and finish in the grand home on the other side.

I followed Sir Arthur and Lieutenant Triggs out the door as Sir Arthur questioned the lieutenant about his brother's experience with General Starrett. The two men carried on a lively conversation as they waited, while I unobtrusively took notes. The only exception was when Sir Arthur asked Lieutenant Triggs if he knew anything about Captain Starrett, the general's son.

And I thought Sir Arthur didn't want anything more to do with the man?

Lieutenant Triggs spit on the ground.

"That's what I think too," Sir Arthur said, laughing at his friend's reaction as two Rockaway carriages arrived with Lieutenant Colonel Holbrook, his hair as tousled as last night, as if he hadn't combed it in days, and two other men I remembered seeing at the G.A.R. meeting but was never introduced to. Lieutenant Triggs smiled and waved to me as they pulled away. I tentatively waved back, before heading down the Washington Street stairs.

The lieutenant's reaction puzzled me. Why would Morgan Triggs spit at the mentioning of Captain Starrett's name? I didn't think Triggs even knew the man.

After crossing the river at the Green Street Bridge and traversing the park, I approached the scene of last night's pandemonium, the home of Enoch Jamison, the so-called "copperhead," on my way to General Starrett's home. Hoping to go unnoticed, I stood behind a delivery cart, piled high with crates labeled: *Martin Dairy,* stopped in the road across the street. Except for the trampled, muddy lawn and two rhododendron bushes that looked as if someone had bedded down for the night in them, the home showed little evidence that anything had occurred to disturb its peace last night. The walls and windows, last night streaked with egg and rotten vegeta-

bles and other filth, had already been cleaned. The broken
window was boarded up and the glass cleared away. As the
milkman returned carrying two empty milk bottles, Enoch
Jamison's door opened. But instead of Mr. Jamison, the man
who stepped out was young, only a few years older than me,
bespectacled, short, and pudgy. I wouldn't have given him a
second glance except that the man wore a black suit that had
gone out of fashion ten years ago. It was so faded it appeared
perpetually covered in dust. And on his head was a dented
foot-tall black stovepipe hat. In an unladylike manner, I stood
staring, even after the milk cart pulled away and the man
walked down the street in the opposite direction. I hadn't seen
a stovepipe hat like that in years.

"Come in," someone said. "Ah, here she is," the general
said when I opened the door. "Sir Arthur said you'd be on
time."

The old general was seated in a rocking chair near the fire.
He indicated a chair across from him. "Ready?" he said enthusiastically, smiling and rubbing his hands together. He lit his
pipe as I retrieved my notebook from my bag, flipped to the
last entry, and sat poised to take down his every word.

"As I was saying when my son interrupted us yesterday,
reveille was at 0500 hours. Grant was already up and complaining of a headache. The general had received a message
from Lee the night before requesting a meeting at 1000 hours
the next day, but at 1150 that morning we were only about
four miles west of Walker's Church. . . ."

It was as if he were recounting the events of the day before. Every detail, every thought, every emotion from that day
almost thirty years ago had been stamped on his memory like
a photograph. Twice I had to scramble to catch up with the
dictation, having been mesmerized by the general's story.

". . . Lee, with his man Marshall, and Babcock had arrived

first and were waiting for the general in the home of Wilmer McLean. Funny one that McLean. Claimed that the war began in his front yard and ended in his front parlor!" The general burst into a fit of laughter that turned into coughing. He waved me away when I rose to help. "Doggone it! I hate getting old. Now where was I?"

He stared up at the ceiling for a moment. I followed his gaze to the wallpaper border of brown deer leaping through a swirl of olive and blue–colored leaves, flowers, and birds. A cobweb stretched across the corner above the general's head.

"Oh, yes, I remember," he said. "We arrived in Appomattox Court House around 1300 hours. Grant had us wait outside on the front lawn while he went in to meet Lee. I whittled two sticks to straws I was so anxious waiting until he summoned us. Hats in hand, we entered quietly and arranged ourselves on either side of the large parlor room. I'll never forget what a contrast those two made. Grant, short, in his rough traveling suit, without a sword, and with barely any insignia, was sitting in the middle of the room, at a small oval table. Lee, a tall, commanding man, was wearing a new uniform and bejeweled long sword and sat beside a marble-topped table in the corner facing him. The silence was heavy, as if we entered a dying patient's sick chamber. But then Grant said, 'I met you once before, General Lee, while we were serving in—' "

A knock on the door interrupted the general mid-sentence.

"Oh, what is it now?" the general said peevishly. Adella Reynard opened the door.

"Oh, Papa, must you smoke that thing?" she said, waving her hand about to dispel the smoke from the air.

"What do you want, Adella? I'm about to dictate my story to Sir Arthur's secretary," the general said.

"I know that, Papa," Adella said, kissing her grandfather's almost bald head. "I wanted to give her something." She handed me an envelope with gold foil trim. "Give this to Sir Arthur, won't you?"

"Yes, of course," I said.

"What is it?" General Starrett asked.

"It's an invitation for tomorrow night."

"Oh," General Starrett said, raising his pipe to his lips.

"Now don't let him talk too long, Miss Davish. He tires easily," Adella said as she plucked a book from the shelf, *A Woman's Trip to Alaska,* and then made for the door. She waved her hand in the air again. "And do put that pipe away, Papa." As the door closed behind the young woman the general shook his head, then smiled.

"Means well, that one," he said. He lifted his pipe slightly away from his lips.

"Do you really not mind the smoke, dear girl?" he asked.

"Actually, the smell of a pipe is sweet and pleasant. My father smoked a pipe." I knew better than to completely contradict Sir Arthur and mention my abhorrence for cigars.

"Sir Arthur's right. You are a treasure," the general said, and then took a long puff. "Now where was I?"

CHAPTER 7

"I have to have the rest no later than Tuesday." As I stepped into the hall from the library, I heard the insipid man's voice insist. "No later than Tuesday!"

"I'm not a child, Mott. I heard you the first time." I recognized the second man's voice. It was Captain Henry Starrett. The two men were speaking in hushed tones, but I could hear them arguing. They were in the back parlor, a few steps down the hall.

The general had been in a talkative mood and spent the remainder of the morning and some of the afternoon dictating his life story. He had his midday meal brought to him on a tray. He only stopped when Sir Arthur and Lieutenant Triggs arrived and Adella came to escort him to tea, admonishing me for keeping him from his afternoon nap. It was then that I'd realized that I was famished, not having been offered lunch when the general had his. I hoped Mrs. Cassidy might have something I could eat.

"If I may be so bold to say so, you act like one sometimes, Mr. Starrett," the man called Mott said.

"I beg your pardon?" Captain Starrett said. "How dare you speak to me like that!" Was this conversation too going to come to blows?

"But I ask, what man comes all this way and then puts everything we've worked for in jeopardy?" Mott asked. "Maybe you fail to see the significance of what I've told you. Maybe you don't care."

"Of course I care," Captain Starrett growled. "But I may have . . . miscalculated."

"Miscalculated?" Mott said. "You're not telling me you've wasted my time, everyone's time, are you, Captain Starrett?"

"No."

"Do I need to remind you that—"

"Enough!" Henry Starrett shouted, then lowered his voice once again. "You'll have it by Tuesday. All of it."

"Good. But let me remind you, just in case, that if I don't, I won't be held responsible for the consequences," the man named Mott said condescendingly. "They won't wait forever, Captain." I wished I could see who Henry Starrett was talking to, but I didn't dare move a muscle or they might know I was in the hall, eavesdropping. "By the way, may I ask how you intend to hold up your end of the bargain?"

"None of your business."

"It is my business; everything's my business. Who do you think will have to answer for your . . . miscalculation?"

"You're scum, Mott. If I thought I could do this without you, I'd . . ."

"You'd what?" Mott said. "Have it by Tuesday, Captain, and you won't have to deal with me again."

"You'll have it, damn it! Now get out of my house."

"Oh, that reminds me, I spoke with Jamison."

"Well? What did the snake have to say?"

"Forgive me, Mr. Starrett but I quote, he said, 'Go to Hell.'" The captain growled. "Good day to you, sir," Mott said.

Before I could hide myself, Mott was in the hallway. To my astonishment, it was the man I'd seen coming out of Enoch Jamison's house, this morning. What could this man have possibly said to Enoch Jamison that interested Henry Starrett? And why? With my curiosity piqued, all thought of retreat was gone.

As he approached me, Mr. Mott lowered his face so as to see above his spectacles but down his nose. His neck was in an awkward position as he tried to look me up and down. It was comical, for as I was taller than he was, he ended up looking at my chin. He carried a small leather Gladstone traveling bag. What was inside? I wondered.

"Charming," he said, grinning without showing his teeth. He tipped his old-fashioned hat to me and left by the front door without another word.

Did anyone else see him? He obviously wasn't concerned that I had or that I'd overheard the conversation. Did anyone else hear Mr. Mott and Captain Starrett arguing? What was it that the captain had to give to Mott by Tuesday? Why was it so important? Before Captain Starrett caught me eavesdropping in the hall, I strode toward the kitchen. But I was too late. I walked right into him as he stormed out of the back parlor door.

"Pardon me," I said, backing away as quickly as possible. His face was flush and his mouth was twisted into a scowl. He was obviously furious. And as before, it was all the more disturbing due to his resemblance to Santa Claus.

Would I ever be able to think of jolly Saint Nick the same again?

"You?" Captain Starrett grunted, and swung his arm toward me. I closed my eyes and braced for the impact of the blow. Instead Captain Starrett knocked into a side table, sending an Oriental flower vase smashing to the floor. The mosaic of colored pieces of porcelain crunched under his footsteps as he pushed past me down the hall. I didn't give him a chance to turn back and ran to the kitchen.

"Thank you for your hospitality, Mrs. Reynard," Sir Arthur said, taking that lady's hand. "Come now, Triggs, we must be going."

"Again, my wife sends her regrets," Lieutenant Triggs said. The sound of small feet pounded on the floorboards above us. The lieutenant pointed to the ceiling. "She'll especially regret not meeting your lovely children." Then he saluted the general and warmly shook his hand. "It was an honor to meet you, sir. A real honor."

"Good to meet you too, old boy," the general said. "Send my regards to your brother."

They were all in the foyer as I left the kitchen after tea. Mrs. Cassidy had been kind enough to offer me a cup of coffee and several each of her toffee bars and pumpkin bread, which had done wonders to calm my nerves. The front door opened and a man entered.

"Darling," Mrs. Reynard said, greeting her husband at the door.

"Adella, my sweet," the man said, kissing his wife on the cheek. He handed her a parcel. "That book you wanted came in." Except for the odd way he spoke, slightly out of the side of his mouth, and the red and white variegated amaryllis on his lapel, Frederick Reynard was unremarkable in every way, average build, average height, sandy hair and mustache, brown and gray single-breasted sack suit. I wouldn't be able to pick him out of a crowd. Yet his countenance and manners were charming, as it was evident that he adored his wife. His eyes followed her every movement, even as he handed his coat, hat, and gloves to the butler, a tall, thin black man. Frederick hung on her every word and seemed unabashed at showing her affection in front of complete strangers.

"Oh, Frederick," Adella said, ripping the paper from the book, *Girl's Winter in India*. "Thank you, darling. Oh, forgive me. Frederick, this is Lieutenant Triggs and Sir Arthur Windom-Greene. Sir Arthur is writing a book about Papa. Lieutenant Triggs is a guest of Sir Arthur." Frederick looked up questioningly at my approach. "And this is his secretary, Miss Davish."

"Should've had you along, Hattie," Sir Arthur said as way of introduction. "Mrs. Mahoud, the Grant home caretaker, gave us a most illuminating tour. Needed your pen. I won't remember half of what she told us," Sir Arthur said, half laughing, to the general.

"Yes, she is most kind," Adella said. "When we toured the house, she went out of her way to show us the president's personal belongings, including a satin *mouchoir* handkerchief case, a wooden tea caddy, and a mother-of-pearl cigar case, that were still in the house."

"Yes, I think Sir Arthur's favorite item was the .41-caliber Colt derringer on which Grant himself had carved 'U.S. Grant 1863,' " Lieutenant Triggs said, smiling, as Sir Arthur nodded enthusiastically.

"It was brilliant," Sir Arthur said. "It would be the crown jewel of my collection. If only the Grants would sell it."

"Glad it was worthwhile," General Starrett said. "Lieutenant Colonel Holbrook and I thought it might—" He stopped mid-sentence as Henry Starrett stomped down the stairs. His scowl hadn't softened. "Well, hello, Henry. Haven't seen you all day. Late night?"

Henry, ignoring his father, looked about the foyer, then focused his attention on Sir Arthur. "You get around, don't you, Englishman? Well, you should keep a better leash on your girl. I'm sick of finding her underfoot in my own house."

Sir Arthur's face reddened as he took a step forward.

"Father," Adella said, trying to ease the tension, "you haven't met Lieutenant Triggs."

"That's all right, ma'am," Lieutenant Triggs said, stepping next to Sir Arthur and laying a hand on his shoulder. It was the second time in less than twelve hours that a man had laid a hand on Sir Arthur and I anticipated that poor Lieutenant Triggs was about to have Sir Arthur's fury flung at him. I was wrong.

"Thank you for tea, Mrs. Reynard," Sir Arthur said calmly, removing Morgan Triggs's hold on him. "And the tour, General. As I said, it was most illuminating." Without another word to acknowledge Henry Starrett, Sir Arthur turned his back on us and left.

"Does he always leave a room like this?" Lieutenant Triggs asked me as we scrambled out the door to catch up with Sir Arthur.

"No," I said, pondering the question I'd been asking myself. "Only when Henry Starrett enters it."

CHAPTER 8

I'd spent the entire evening and part of the night transcribing my notes from General Starrett's interview. Sir Arthur's disappointment for not having them in hand earlier in the evening had been assuaged by their sheer volume. He had graciously given me until morning to finish.

Well before sunrise, with the notes on Sir Arthur's desk, I stood at the top of the Washington Street stairs, wearing my rubber boots, recently purchased from Strohmeyer's, for the first time. Although I'd have little time to actually hike this morning, I was excited; it had snowed several inches during the night. Even in the faint light of the quarter moon, everything glistened. Snow crystals clung to the tree branches and the muddy street was sparkling white, a single wagon track running down the middle. The view from the top of the stairs revealed that throughout the entire town every awning, lamppost, bench, boardwalk, parked wagon, and rooftop was blanketed in snow. And the stillness was absolute.

Not a single footprint marked the newly fallen snow on the stairs. I gingerly stepped on the top stair, holding the railing, then decided that I didn't want to be the first to test the slipperiness of the untrodden stairs. Instead I walked down Prospect to the Green Street, or as the pupils who have to climb them for class every day call them, the High School stairs. Here many footprints marked the passage of other early morning risers, mostly merchants and clerks who worked on Main Street below. I followed in their path and descended the hill to Bench Street without incident. My goal this morning was Mrs. Brendel's first, to order holly, greens, and several bouquets of cut flowers for the Christmas decorations, and then to the river path that followed the train tracks toward the Mississippi River.

I arrived at Mrs. Brendel's a few minutes before she opened. I'd planned it that way. Mrs. Brendel had the best selection of cut flowers and Christmas greenery in town, but she was first and foremost a milliner. I'd spent hours since arriving in Galena pursuing the wares of Mrs. Edwards' Millinery and especially Miss Burke's, which I passed on Main Street every time I walked to the Green Street Bridge, but I'd never been to Mrs. Brendel's. I now took the opportunity to admire her latest creations in her shop front window until a young girl with bows in her hair, obviously not Mrs. Brendel, unlocked the door. It took all of my restraint to order only the holly, evergreen rope, and flowers I'd come for. As I left, I pledged to myself I'd be back at a more convenient time for the fancy lace braid hat in the window. The wide satin trim and large spray of velvet forget-me-nots would match my navy brilliantine suit perfectly.

I crossed the river on the footbridge and walked up Park Avenue. When I passed the Starrett house, most of the curtains were still drawn. From previous early morning hikes, I'd presumed that Mrs. Reynard and her grandfather, General Starrett, were both late risers. It seemed Captain Henry Starrett was as well. Mr. Reynard, on the other hand, was always gone to work before even I passed by. This morning seemed to be an exception, as evidenced by the three sets of footprints on the steps leading down from the lawn to the road. As I followed the train tracks south, I noticed that two of those sets of footprints had followed the same path. Who else had been hiking this way this morning from the Starrett house? I got my answer in the form of a distinct giggle a few yards away. Suddenly a snowball whizzed by my head and smacked against an elm behind me. Shouts of glee from the two children filled the still air.

"Can't a body pass in the early morning without being assailed by a missile of snow?" I mockingly declared. A little girl shrieked.

"It's not Mrs. Becker," a boy of ten said. "It's some lady in funny clothes." I looked at the short hemline of my hiking skirt and my boots. What was so funny about them? "You can come out now, Sis." A girl about eight came out of hiding from behind a tree.

"You're not going to Mama, are you?" his sister said.

"I don't know, who might your mother be?" I asked.

The boy stood tall and puffed out his chest. "Mrs. Frederick Reynard. I'm Master Edward Reynard and this is my sister, Gertrude." I knew the Reynards had children, having heard their squeals and the pounding of running feet above General Starrett's library, but I'd not yet met them.

"Well, Master Reynard, Miss Reynard, I'm pleased to make your acquaintance. And I am not some lady in funny clothes; my name is Miss Davish and I'm wearing my very practical hiking costume. And no, Miss Reynard, I'm not going to tell your mother. But I do think an apology is in order," I said, trying not to laugh.

"Sorry, Miss Davish," the children said in unison. Edward brushed the snow on the ground with his boot and stared down.

"Apology accepted," I said, offering my hand. Edward smiled and shook it heartily. Gertrude giggled and smiled at me before running back toward the trees. Her brother immediately followed his sister.

Chuckling under my breath, I continued on my hike. Yet before I'd gone a hundred yards, a high-pitched screech came from the direction of the children I'd left behind. I ran back the way I'd come.

"Help, help!" Edward was flying over the snow toward me screaming. "It's Gertie!" He grabbed my hands and began pulling me down toward the river. "Come on, we have to help Gertie."

I let him lead me to the edge of the river, all the while hearing screams and cries from Gertie. But when we got there she was nowhere in sight.

"Where's your sister, Edward?" I asked. He pointed to a black hole in the river about ten feet from the edge, where the ice had broken completely. The snow around the hole had been scraped away on the side closest to the riverbank.

"Oh my God. She's fallen through the ice?" I asked.

"We were playing and . . . the ice broke and . . . ," Edward replied. "You have to get her out!"

Suddenly the little girl resurfaced, gasping for air and wildly thrashing about in the freezing water. She obviously couldn't touch the bottom of the river.

"Ned! Ned! He-e-e-el-l-lp-p-p!" Gertie screamed, madly clutching for a hold on the slippery edge of ice. She burst into convulsive sobbing; her breathing sounded sporadic. Without thinking, I threw off my coat, dropped to my knees, and then crawled on my belly toward the break in the ice, pulling my coat behind me.

"I'm coming, Gertrude. Keep swimming. I'm almost there."

I inched toward the struggling girl praying that the ice

would hold my weight. Not wanting to get too close, I stopped about three feet from the hole and I threw the end of my coat toward it.

"Grab my coat, Gertrude!" I cried. "Grab my coat!"

As the little girl snatched the end of my coat, the weight of her pulled me toward the hole. The ice creaked and then stopped. I pulled my coat toward me and held my breath. The ice creaked again, but I could see that Gertrude had her elbows on the ice. A bald eagle circled silently above us.

"Hang on, Gertrude, and I'll pull you out."

"It's hard!" the little girl cried. "My hands hurt and I can't feel my legs!"

"Just hold on and everything will be all right." I tried to sound convincing and keep the worry from my voice.

"Hold on, Gertie!" her brother shouted encouragement from the river's edge. "She'll get you out."

It seemed to help. I could feel the coat draw taut as I slowly drew the little girl toward me. I inched backward painfully slow, trying to keep my weight evenly distributed, while pulling Gertrude from the water. When her legs and feet finally surfaced, I dragged her as quickly as I could to me. Her lips were blue and she was shivering uncontrollably. I wrapped her in my coat and pulled her tightly to my chest. I crawled back to the edge of the river and safety, on my knees.

"I want my mama!" Gertrude whimpered, her breathing shallow. I stood up with Edward's helping hand.

"We're going to get your mother right now, Gertie," I said, starting to walk up the hill toward the path. I glanced over my shoulder at the sound of wings flapping behind us. The bald eagle had landed next to the break in the ice.

"Don't worry, Gertie," Edward said, patting his sister's back. "You're going to be all right now."

"Edward's right," I said. "He's going to see that you have warm clothes, a fire, and warm milk waiting for you." I nodded to Edward, who immediately dashed back toward the house. I followed him as fast as I could.

"C-c-c-cold," the child whispered, becoming lethargic and heavy in my arms.

"We'll be home soon," I said. I too was starting to feel the effects of the cold. I wasn't wearing a coat and while I was crawling across the ice my gloves and clothes had gotten wet. My back ached, my ears and cheeks burned, and I too was losing feeling in my hands and feet. I'd only gone up the hill and a few yards along the path when I heard adult voices approaching. I kept moving.

A woman cried, "Gertie! My baby!"

"Mama," Gertie barely whispered.

"See," Edward said. "I told you Miss Davish rescued Gertie."

"What on earth were you doing?" a man's voice yelled.

"Father," Mrs. Reynard said as Henry Starrett came into view. I'd thought his comment was directed at the children until I heard the tone Adella used. Henry Starrett was speaking to me.

"Silly woman," Henry said sharply, "we might've had to rescue both of you." I didn't have the strength to remind him that that had been unnecessary.

Less than a minute later, Gertie was wrapped in dry blankets and lifted from me into her mother's outstretched arms, while someone put a blanket around my shoulders. I took a step forward and stumbled. Captain Starrett and the butler, each lifting me by an arm, supported me as we walked back to the house. A small crowd had gathered with several well-wishers patting me on the back or shaking my hand. I flinched at the pain each encounter shot through my body.

"You're a fool," Captain Starrett said under his breath as Adella wept over her shivering child. "You could've gotten my granddaughter killed."

"I'm sorry you feel that way, Captain," I said, my teeth chattering. "She was drowning and I couldn't think of what better to do."

"You should've called for help and let one of us get her."

"There wasn't time. Besides, you would've been too heavy for the ice," I said. "As it was, it barely supported me." I said this last sentence nonchalantly but inside quaked at the thought of the ice breaking beneath me. The captain was right; I'd been impulsive. But I wasn't going to admit that to him.

"Thank you, Miss Davish," Adella said, approaching us, after Mrs. Becker whisked Gertrude into the house. "You've saved my daughter's life. We will be forever grateful."

"You're welcome, Mrs. Reynard," I said, not wanting to voice the doubts and fears I still had for the child's recovery. "I'm only glad I was at hand and could help."

The crowd slowly dispersed as we approached the house. Captain Starrett and the butler released their hold on me. In her shock, I heard Adella admonishing her son.

"Ned, I told you never to go near the river alone. Wait until your father hears about this."

"Gertie's okay," Ned said, pleading. "Do you have to tell Father? I promise never to go near it again."

"Come with me, Hattie," Mrs. Cassidy said, walking toward the kitchen in the back of the house as the family went to the front door. Instead of following her, I hung back. I was shivering, filthy, and exhausted and had to get back to work.

"Thank you, Mrs. Cassidy, but I'm already late getting back," I said. "They're delivering the greenery today and Sir Arthur has more guests arriving this morning."

"Come on, girl," the older woman said as she physically led me into her warm kitchen. "You'll catch your death if you don't come in and warm up. I'll make us a fresh pot of coffee." She sat me down in front of the fire and left the room for a moment. When she returned, she had a man's cloak and gloves.

"This is all I have, but you can wear them while we launder your own," Mrs. Cassidy said, helping me put the cloak on. "You saved that girl, you know." My whole body shook. My fingers and toes tingled and burned as I began to warm up. "You're a hero, Miss Davish."

"I'm no hero, Mrs. Cassidy. I did what anyone would have." The cook shook her head as she handed me a cup of coffee.

"No, not everyone would've done what you did. It took real bravery to do what you did."

"But I didn't even think about it. I was acting on instinct."

"Should've known you'd be so brave," she said as if she hadn't heard me. "People said you faced down a murderer after all." I flinched at her reference to the murder of my previous employer.

"I'm not brave, Mrs. Cassidy. And I'm certainly no hero." I looked down at myself. I was a mess. I was wearing a man's coat, several sizes too big for me; my dress was filthy, wrinkled, and torn in several places. Even my new rubber boots were covered with ice, mud, and grime. I touched my head and could only imagine the state of my hair. And my hat, where had I left my hat? "I'm simply cold, filthy, and slightly embarrassed."

Granted I couldn't think of what else I should've done. The child was drowning. But what would Sir Arthur think of my escapade? Would he approve of my rescuing the girl or merely think me impulsive? I glanced at the kitchen clock.

It won't matter if I don't get back right now, I thought. The Baineses' train was about to arrive any minute and I'd be out of my job.

Chapter 9

When I returned to Sir Arthur's house, all I wanted to do was run up the back stairs, get to my room without being seen, and change my clothes. None of that happened. Instead, as I came out of the kitchen, before I could even get to the stairs, Ida was in the doorway, blocking my way.

"Oh, *mein Gott!*" she declared. "What happened to you, *ja?*"

"It's a long story and I need to change quickly. The Baineses will be here any minute."

"Too late, *meine Freundin*. They're already here, *ja. He* wasn't pleased you weren't here to greet them. I was sent to find you."

"Oh, I better be quick."

"*Nein, nein.* You have to come with me now." She took my arm, as if she expected me to dash out the door and escape Sir Arthur's reprimand, and pulled me toward the parlor door. "If you don't come, it will be my trouble, *ja?*"

"All right, all right." I tossed the borrowed gloves and cloak over Ida's outstretched arm but didn't know what to do

with my boots. "This is ridiculous, Ida. I can't go in there with
boots on and looking like this." I attempted to repin my hair
in place without the aid of a mirror.

"But you must," Ida said, helping me with my hair. "You
go in and I'll get your shoes. You can change later, *ja?*"

Ida escorted me to the parlor and knocked. "I found Hattie, *Herr,*" she announced. As I entered the room, my worst
fears were confirmed. Sir Arthur was not alone. Lieutenant
Triggs and his wife turned at my approach. A tall, handsome,
impeccably dressed man in his fifties with a full head of silvery-
blond hair and a short, tidy mustache stood leaning against the
wall next to the fire. He winked at me. I blushed, confused
until he did the same thing a moment later when he was looking elsewhere. I'd come to recognize it as a nervous twitch in
his eye. But what did he have to be nervous about?

Also in the room, seated on the settee closest to the fire,
chatting about the barely palatable breakfast she had been
served on the train, was a woman in her early fifties, who,
though still attractive, must have been striking in her youth.
Her light brown hair showed not a single streak of gray; her
complexion was creamy and flawless except the few wrinkles
etched into the corners of her eyes and mouth. Her day dress
of cream and pink printed silk was exquisite, expensive, and
probably mail-ordered from Paris or New York. She didn't
smile when she saw me. Nor did she stop talking.

"Don't you agree, Mrs. Triggs?" Before Mrs. Triggs had a
chance to reply, the woman continued. "And the food they
served was simply atrocious. The omelet was cold, the salmon
was slimy—" She glanced at me again. She screamed. "Oh my
God, Sir Arthur! The filthiest vagrant creature I've ever seen is
standing in your doorway!" She turned her head away. Sir
Arthur started when he saw me. "John, Sir Arthur, somebody,
please make it go away."

"My, my, Miss Davish, you look like Saint George battling

the dragon. Did the dragon win this time?" Lieutenant Triggs laughed at his own joke.

"Gentlemen, ladies, if you will excuse me for a moment." With a scowl Sir Arthur indicated that he wanted me to pre-cede him out of the room. The moment he closed the door behind him, he turned on me.

"Hattie, what the devil have you been doing this morn-ing?" he scolded, scrutinizing my torn and filthy dress and wet rubber boots. "As you could see, our guests have arrived. And yet you were nowhere to be found, only to appear in my par-lor as an unkempt vagabond. I don't need to tell you how dis-appointed I am. I've come to expect more from you than this. I demand an explanation."

"I'm sorry, sir, my appearance is unacceptable, even to me, but with good cause, I assure you."

"And what would that be?"

"Gertie Reynard fell through the ice on the river this morning and I was the only one about to help. I was running late and didn't have time to change."

Sir Arthur stared at me for a moment and then roared with laughter. "My God, Hattie Davish, is there nothing you can't do?" Then he sent me upstairs to change. Once presentable again, I returned to the parlor.

". . . And I'd be more than happy to help with the—" The woman by the fire was cut off mid-sentence by Sir Arthur.

"Ah, there's the secretary I know. Hattie, I'd like to intro-duce you to our new guests," Sir Arthur said, indicating the man by the fire and the woman who had been talking when I came in. "Mr. and Mrs. John Baines, my secretary and personal assistant, Miss Hattie Davish. Despite her awkward appearance earlier, she is extremely capable and will aid you in anything you need here during your stay."

"Charmed," John Baines said, tipping his head. His eye twitched again.

His wife, with a blank expression on her face, said, "Good. As I didn't bring my maid and yours did clean up well, I'll need help unpacking. And I'd like a bath drawn before ten."

"Rachel," her husband hissed, "I don't think that's what Sir Arthur meant."

"But I'm simply exhausted from my journey, darling," she said.

Relieved that Mr. Baines had come to my rescue, I said, "Ida will be more than happy to help you, Mrs. Baines."

"Yes, Hattie's probably been too busy this morning typing up manuscript notes and rescuing little girls to see to anything else," Sir Arthur said.

"Rescuing little girls?" Mrs. Triggs said, swinging her head around to look at me.

"That's why Hattie appeared before us in tatters," Sir Arthur said. "She's been out on the river near General Starrett's house. Tell them the story, Hattie." I related the story of this morning's adventure. Everyone seemed riveted by my tale, everyone except Mrs. Baines, who stood up and yawned.

"Excuse me, I'm going to my room now," she said. "I'm simply exhausted by the journey. John, are you coming?" Her husband didn't appear to hear her. "John? John? Jack!"

"Yes?" John Baines said.

"I said, are you coming?"

"I'll be up in a moment," he said. "Please, Miss Davish, you had me on the edge of my chair." His wife stared at him, and then she glanced over at Lieutenant and Mrs. Triggs, who also seemed eager for the conclusion of my story.

"Mrs. Triggs," Mrs. Baines said, "you look as exhausted as I feel. Wouldn't you like to retire to your room?"

Mrs. Triggs's shoulders drooped and all the color, except two rosy spots on her cheeks, left her face. She dropped her eyes to her lap.

"I didn't notice it before," Lieutenant Triggs said, "but you look unwell, Priscilla. Maybe you should lie down." Mrs. Triggs visibly wilted before my eyes.

"But what about Hattie's story and the little girl?" Priscilla Triggs said, almost in a whisper.

"You don't need to hear the whole thing. We know the girl's okay, right, Miss Davish?" Priscilla's husband said. I nodded slowly, saddened by the sudden turn of events. Mrs. Triggs looked miserable as Rachel Baines took her arm.

"That story's nothing," Rachel Baines said. Priscilla Triggs looked over her shoulder at me, her eyes wide and filling with tears.

"But . . . ," Priscilla said as Rachel Baines escorted her from the room.

"Did you know I was a nurse in the war?" Mrs. Baines said. "Well, let me tell you about the time I saved three boys from . . ."

Soon afterward, I excused myself to tend to the delivery that had arrived from Mrs. Brendel's shop. With Ida's and Harvey's help, I spent the remainder of the morning decorating Sir Arthur's house. We put bouquets of red and white roses in every room, except the Triggses' bedroom, for flowers made the lieutenant sneeze. We laid boughs of holly across every windowsill and mantel throughout the house. We wrapped evergreen roping on the porch balustrade and pillars and draped it over every doorway, filling the house with the scent of fir and pine. As Harvey hung a branch of mistletoe from the entranceway chandelier, I couldn't help but wish Walter were here.

All that was left was the red velvet ribbon to be draped from the dining room chandelier, and, most important, the Christmas tree. Although a vendor at Market House Square sold trees, I'd arranged for Harvey and me to take the horse and sleigh into the countryside to cut one down. I'd discovered a nice stand of white pines on one of my hikes. I was dressed to go and ready to leave when Ida came running out of the kitchen.

"*He* wants to see you, *ja?*" she said. Sir Arthur knew we were going to get the Christmas tree; what could it be now?

"*Un, deux, trois. . . ,*" I began to count under my breath.

I'd been looking forward to getting the tree. I'd made an effort all morning to enjoy the decorating and not dwell on the incident with Gertie and the consequences that followed. We hadn't heard how the little girl fared and it took all of my discipline not to let it occupy my thoughts. But no Christmas was complete without a tree. I used to cut down our Christmas tree with my father when I was a little girl and had eagerly awaited doing it again for the first time as an adult, even if my only company was a gruff carriage driver. I was frustrated and let out a big sigh.

"Can you wait a few minutes, Harvey?" I asked.

"Yeah," he said, "but I won't wait too long. Got too much shoveling to do."

Sir Arthur was in the library.

"Come in," he called after I knocked. "Ah, Hattie. This stuff is brilliant." He had the notes General Starrett had dictated to me spread out on his desk before him. "I have a few points of clarification, but we'll go over those later. First, this arrived for you." He handed me an envelope of what looked like another Christmas card. It was postmarked St. Louis. I couldn't recall knowing anyone from St. Louis. Then he picked up a simple, gold-bordered white card and waved it at me. I recognized it as General Starrett's stationery. "Second, I have some interesting news for you."

Tap. Tap. Tap. Someone knocked on the door. "Come in."

"Sir Arthur, I was looking at what the servants have done in the front parlor and I thought"—Rachel Baines stopped

when she saw me, but only momentarily—"that the front parlor mantel was too plain for the prominence of the room. I
think it needs more embellishments, like red ribbon and gold-
painted pinecones. Several different-sized candles would do
nicely as well. When we decorate our home in Chicago, we always have—"

"Certainly, Rachel. I want you to feel at home. If you want
more candles and ribbon, I'm sure that can be easily arranged."

"And gold-painted pinecones?" she asked.

"Of course." Sir Arthur looked at me. I nodded my assent
to take care of it. "Anything else?"

"Well, I would also like to discuss the menu for Christmas
dinner."

"Of course, if you don't mind waiting. I was about to relay
some news to Hattie, here. We won't be long, as she's off to cut
down our Christmas tree." I was pleased that he remembered
but growing impatient to hear about Gertrude Reynard's recovery. I was careful not to allow my countenance to reveal either emotion.

"Of course. For you Sir Arthur," Rachel Baines said, "I'll
wait." But instead of excusing herself from the room, she deliberately sat down. Sir Arthur didn't seem to notice, but I did.

"Hattie, this is an invitation from the Reynards for their
dinner party tonight," Sir Arthur said, waving the card at me
again.

"Yes, sir," I said. What was his point? I'd been the one who
had delivered the invitation myself. What more did that have
to do with me? And what about the little girl? What about
Gertrude Reynard?

"I'm looking forward to meeting Mrs. Reynard and this
infamous General Starrett," Mrs. Baines said. "Unfortunately,
someone didn't warn me that we would be invited out." She
playfully wagged her finger at Sir Arthur. "I packed all wrong.
Now I'll have to go shopping."

"Um, yes. Main Street has every shop you could need," Sir Arthur said, not knowing how to handle this interruption.

"And who is this Captain Starrett? I can't seem to get any-one to tell me about this mysterious man," Mrs. Baines said, laughing nervously. Now what did she have to be nervous about?

"Like I was saying, Hattie," Sir Arthur said, not deigning to reply to this second interruption, "this invitation is for you."

"Excuse me?" Rachel Baines and I said simultaneously. She scowled at me.

"Excuse me, Sir Arthur, but why would a servant be in-vited to a dinner party? I don't understand. Are rules of society different here than everywhere else I've been?" She sounded sincerely confused.

"Sir, I don't understand either." I had to admit I actually agreed with Mrs. Baines. When Adella Reynard had men-tioned the dinner party to her grandfather, I had not been mentioned as a possible guest. What had changed?

"You saved Gertrude Reynard," Sir Arthur said, in re-sponse to my unvoiced question.

"So the little girl will recover?" I asked.

"Fully," Sir Arthur said. I was relieved.

"What little girl?" Mrs. Baines said. "Who is Gertrude Reynard?"

"She is the daughter of Frederick and Adella Reynard. The one from Hattie's story this morning," Sir Arthur said. "General Starrett's great-granddaughter."

"But what does that have to do with your secretary being invited to our dinner party?"

"Because, Mrs. Baines," Sir Arthur said, handing me the envelope, "Adella Reynard is expressing her gratitude by invit-ing Hattie to be her guest."

"Do you think I should accept?" I didn't want to do any-thing that Sir Arthur would disapprove of.

"Of course you shouldn't accept," Mrs. Baines said, coming to her feet. "It's inappropriate. I know it and you know it. You'll feel uncomfortable at a table with your betters. What a way to express gratitude! You'd think Mrs. Reynard would be more sensitive."

"Actually," Sir Arthur said, smirking, "I think it's a fine idea. You deserve it, Hattie, and I heard, through the grapevine, that Mrs. Monday has even helped out with some of the desserts."

"But, Sir Arthur, the girl will be woefully unprepared. What about the rules for everything from which fork to use to which topics of conversations are appropriate? She couldn't possibly know how to conduct herself at a dinner table. Not to mention her lack of wardrobe. She'll embarrass you, Sir Arthur." Mrs. Baines turned on me suddenly and took my hand. "You wouldn't want to embarrass Sir Arthur, would you, girl?"

I was mortified. Of course I didn't want to embarrass Sir Arthur, but I also knew that I wouldn't. I took great strides, and a good portion of my salary, to see that my wardrobe was fashionable, and Mrs. Chaplin's School for Women didn't only teach me shorthand and typewriting. I've been properly trained in all types of etiquette—just don't ask me to paint or play the piano.

"No, Mrs. Baines, you do our Hattie an injustice. I can't think of another woman I'd rather carry on a conversation with at the dinner table." Mrs. Baines flinched, but Sir Arthur seemed oblivious to the affront he'd made. "Hattie, accept the invitation. It may mean working late afterward, but I think you'll enjoy yourself."

"Thank you, sir," I said. I removed myself from the library. I had to find Harvey to postpone cutting the Christmas tree down. I had a little shopping of my own to do.

I had mixed emotions about going to the party. The dinner

promised to be elegant, with exquisite food and interesting conversation, but Mrs. Baines was right about me not being the typical dinner party guest. And what if, like Mrs. Baines, Captain Starrett objected to my presence? He wasn't approving of my actions when I rescued his granddaughter. What would he do when I arrived at his house as a dinner guest? And how would Sir Arthur react?

It doesn't matter, I thought. *I may as well try to enjoy myself.* Sir Arthur told me to accept the invitation and I would be attending the dinner whether my presence was disruptive or not. For despite the fact that Mrs. Baines was still arguing with Sir Arthur "on my behalf" as she put it when I left, I knew Sir Arthur enough to know that once he's made up his mind not even the wiles of a lovely woman could change it. Which proved to be right, for when I returned to my room after talking to Harvey a note from Mrs. Baines was on my bed. It read:

Despite my best efforts, I'm afraid Sir Arthur won't change his mind. You'll have to go to the dinner party. It will be tedious, but don't worry; I will be there to assist you. If you follow my instructions, it'll be possible to avoid the faux pas and pitfalls that await you. We can only hope our hosts are as gracious at overlooking your shortcomings as they were in extending this ill-conceived invitation.

Mrs. R. Baines

P.S. Be sure to show me your dress and hair before dinner.

She probably meant well, I thought. *But then why did she always make me feel bad?*

It was with this thought that I opened the Christmas card postmarked St. Louis, the glitter and gold foil sparkling under the light of the gas lamp I'd had to light on this gloomy day. I cringed and dropped the card right side down when I saw the Santa Claus, dressed in a brown robe and hat with flowing white beard and piercing blue eyes. I'd had enough of Captain Henry Starrett resembling Santa Claus. Then I saw the inscription on the back. My heart skipped a beat. It was from Walter: *Spending Christmas with Mother in St. Louis, but wishing I was in Galena with you. Ever your friend, Walter Grice.*

I wish you were here too, Walter, I thought.

And the thought was triggered an hour later on Main Street when I espied Enoch Jamison exiting a store. I'd been shopping at the St. Louis Department Store to buy red velvet ribbon for the dining room, a few German glass ornaments for the Christmas tree, and lace for my dress, at Siniger & Siniger's Drug Store for gold paint, and at Owens Confectionery for ribbon candy. I'd been among a crowd enthralled with an elaborate puppet display in the show window of Barry Bros. Dry Goods when I spotted him. A full papier-mâché moon had shone down on children sleeping in a humble thatch-roof cottage when clouds had parted. Santa Claus, driving his sleigh, laden with gifts and drawn by two reindeer, had appeared from around a mountaintop, blowing his horn.

Toot-toot! Toot-toot! "Merry Christmas!" Puppet Santa Claus declared.

Everyone clapped and cheered, everyone except Enoch Jamison. He stood, purplish-black bruises circling his eyes, his arm in a sling, glancing about him furtively, as if waiting impatiently for someone. *He's the antithesis of Walter,* I thought, watching Enoch Jamison, beaten and cheerless, flinch when a man thumped him on the back.

"Merry Christmas, Enoch," the man said. "We're on your side. Hope you heal up quick!" Mr. Jamison bobbed his head slightly and mumbled an inaudible reply. The urge to see the strength in Walter's eyes and the reassurance in his smile overwhelmed me.

Pull yourself together, I thought, and the moment passed. I brushed my sleeve of snowflakes that had drifted down from the store awning above me and readjusted my hat. Mr. Jamison caught a glimpse of me and frowned; I'd been staring at him.

Why did I feel compelled to spy on this poor man, anyway? I wondered.

Ashamed of myself, I abandoned the puppet show but stopped when Mr. Jamison grew agitated and approached another coming toward him. It was the man with *O.C.K.* in India ink on his hand. The two put their heads together and spoke furtively but indistinctly. I couldn't understand a word. Who was this other man? He had left the G.A.R. meeting disgusted by Henry Starrett's arguments. Was he too a "copperhead" from days gone by? But then why attend a Grand Army of the Republic meeting? Still in conference, they navigated through the now-dispersing crowd of window-shoppers and disappeared around the bend. What were they talking about? All I could do was wonder as I made my way back to Prospect Street and an afternoon of finding the perfect Christmas tree with Harvey and making cornucopias, garland, and a mess in the kitchen with Mrs. Monday and Ida. I vowed to write Walter tonight.

CHAPTER 10

"*Mein Gott!*" When I descended the back stairs, Ida almost dropped the bucket she was carrying. "*Sehr schön,* very beautiful. Mrs. Monday come see Hattie, *ja?*"

Mrs. Monday, in her usual highly starched, spotless white apron, strolled into the hallway, wiping her hands on a towel. Despite the heat and demands of the kitchen, not even a single strand of gray hair was displaced from her bun. She grinned. "My, my, don't you look handsome."

I looked down to admire my emerald green brocade evening gown. I'd bought it two years ago and only had a chance to wear it once. The lace I'd bought and sewn on the scooped neckline and sleeves this morning was the added touch it needed to make it feel new.

"Thank you," I said, beaming.

"It matches the color of your eyes, *ja?*" Ida said.

"What on earth are you doing in the servants' hall?" Rachel Baines, dressed in what must have been the latest fashion from Paris, a royal blue velvet gown, with a belt of satin and a bertha collar of antique lace veiling the sleeves and draped in front with an exquisite rose gold, amethyst, and pearl brooch, was stalking down the hallway. She shooed Ida and Mrs. Monday with her hand. "Stay away. Do you want to soil the girl's gown?"

Mrs. Monday bowed her head and sulked back to the kitchen with Ida, lugging a pail of soapy water, on her heels. "If you're going to be treated like a lady, even for one night, you'd better act like one," Rachel Baines said.

This wasn't the way it should've been. It hurt to see Ida and Mrs. Monday treated so. If the entire evening was going to be like this, Mrs. Baines was right; I never should've been invited in the first place.

"I was concerned that you'd dress above your station or show too much skin," she said, appraising my dress, shoes, and hair, "but you managed to look tasteful. Thank goodness you won't stand out," she said, escorting me into the front foyer where the men were waiting.

Sir Arthur was looking at his watch. When he saw us arrive, he nodded. "Good, we'll leave in precisely three minutes."

Lieutenant Triggs whistled. "Ladies! I had no idea we would be graced by such beauty tonight!" he exclaimed, taking Rachel Baines's hand and kissing it. "Which one are you, dear lady, Aphrodite or Helen of Troy?"

"Aphrodite," John Baines answered. His wife giggled with delight.

Lieutenant Triggs turned to me. "Then you must be Helen of Troy." I blushed from the scrutiny I was getting from every pair of eyes in the hall. "I heard you were joining us, Hattie. I'm thrilled, absolutely thrilled."

"You do look smashing, Hattie," Sir Arthur said. "New dress?" He looked at his watch again. "Where's your wife, Lieutenant?"

"I must apologize, Sir Arthur," he said, glancing at the hall clock. "She'll be down soon, I'm sure."

"Is she unwell?" Sir Arthur couldn't imagine any other excuse for tardy behavior.

"More of a malaise, I'd say," Lieutenant Triggs said. "Difficult time of year for her, you know, but she'll be fine. Dinner should cheer her up."

"Good, glad to hear it," Sir Arthur said, checking his watch again.

"How do you like my new dress, Sir Arthur?" Rachel Baines said.

"It's lovely, Mrs. Baines."

"Why did you need a new dress?" John Baines asked, his eye twitching.

"Aren't I worth a new dress?" she said, taking his arm. "Don't I look nice in it?" Her husband wrapped his arm around her tightly.

"You're the prettiest woman I've ever seen." Rachel Baines beamed while her husband blushed, realizing he had forgotten himself in front of an audience.

"Priscilla," Lieutenant Triggs said, in obvious relief. Priscilla Triggs descended the staircase and joined us. She was dressed in a brown heavy brocade gown accented with a white ribbon sash about her waist, black lace and white bows about the neckline and shoulders. She looked very elegant, except her eyes were puffy and red, as if she'd been crying. She smiled weakly when her husband offered her his arm. "Shall we, darling lady?"

"I must have a glass of water before I go," Priscilla said. Sir Arthur looked at his watch.

"Yes, I know. Right here, my darling," Lieutenant Triggs said, pointing to a hall table with a pitcher of water and a single glass set on a silver tray.

"Well, I never," Rachel Baines said, watching as Priscilla drained the glass and set the glass on the tray, averting her eyes from the questioning stares.

"I'm ready now," Priscilla Triggs said.

All six of us arrived together at the Reynard/Starrett house exactly fifteen minutes before the hour named on the invitation, partially from Sir Arthur's fanatical revulsion of tardiness and Frederick Reynard's kind offer to complement Sir Arthur's sleigh with his own horse and sleigh. Ned and Gertie, dressed in their finery, threw open the door and ran out to greet us.

"Mother, they're here. They're here!" Ned yelled as Gertie threw her arms around my legs. She seemed to have made a speedy and full recovery. Priscilla Triggs reached out and touched Gertie on the head. I picked Gertie up in my arms.

"Are you all better now, Gertie?" I asked. She nodded shyly. "And you're not going to go near that river again, are you?" She shook her head. "Good girl." Gertie beamed.

"Hattie!" Rachel Baines exclaimed. "Put that child down. She has wet feet. You do want to be presentable to our hostess, don't you?" She shook her head in disbelief as I set Gertie down. "I'll have to watch you closer than I thought."

"Come on, everybody," Ned called, waving his arm and running back toward the house.

"Charming lad," Lieutenant Triggs said, chuckling. "He'll make a fine officer."

"The boy does have spirit," John Baines said.

Gertie grabbed my hand and then Priscilla Triggs's, whose face lit up and who, for the first time since I'd met her, smiled broadly. Gertie led us into the warmth and light of the house, where the sweet aroma of pine announced the arrival of Christmas here as well. The chandelier, the banister, the doorways were all draped in ropes of evergreen. The household staff had been industrious since I'd been here. Gertie dropped our hands, then disappeared with her brother into one of the parlors. Adella Reynard, dressed in a rich silk gown of burgundy with collar and cuffs of fine lace, was in the hall welcoming everyone while the butler, the black man who had helped me down by the river, was taking everyone's cloaks.

"Miss?" he said, extending his arm. As I let him help me off with my cloak, I said, "Ambrose, is it?" He nodded. "I never got to thank you for helping me yesterday, Ambrose. I'm Hattie, by the way."

"You're sure welcome, Miss Hattie. I was glad to hear the missus invited you. That was a brave thing you did."

"Not so brave," I said. "You would've done the same if you'd been near."

"Nice of you to say so, miss. Well, enjoy yourself." He looked around and, seeing the other guests following Adella into the front parlor, said conspiratorially, "And don't forget to stop by the kitchen before you leave. I hear Mrs. Cassidy set some of the truffle desserts aside for you, for later." I laughed, already looking forward to the sweet confections, and joined the rest of the party. Rachel Baines was speaking when I entered.

". . . lovely home. I know I speak for everyone when I say I'm delighted to be here." She continued on for some time before Adella had a chance to introduce the guests whom we hadn't met yet.

"I'd like you all to meet our dear friends Mrs. Powers and Mrs. Kaplan."

Mrs. Powers was a small woman in her late fifties with a disproportionately large nose. She wore all black, which matched the color of her hair, and seemed in a somber mood, given the festive occasion.

"Mrs. Powers's late husband," Adella explained, "was one of Frederick's partners at the factory." Priscilla Triggs gravitated toward her almost immediately and the two struck up a conversation.

"Mrs. Kaplan is the widow of an old friend of Papa's," Adella said. Mrs. Kaplan was an elderly woman with a humped back and a shock of white, frizzy hair. She held a sturdy wooden cane, with a sterling silver cap, in her hands. She and General Starrett sat next to each other, exchanging observations that inevitably made the other laugh. She too wore black.

"Mrs. Powers, Mrs. Kaplan, and oh, Mrs. Holbrook," Adella said to Lieutenant Colonel Holbrook's wife, a plump, stately elderly lady in a charcoal gray evening gown who had arrived with her husband moments earlier. "I'd like to introduce Sir Arthur Windom-Greene, who is visiting Galena from England via Richmond. He's writing a book about Papa."

Sir Arthur nodded his head, mumbling, "Charmed, ladies," before quickly returning to his conversation with Lieutenant Colonel Holbrook, who had joined the cluster of men by the fireplace the moment he stepped into the room.

"And I wouldn't want to forget Sir Arthur's guests for the holidays," Adella Reynard said, "Lieutenant Triggs and his wife and Mr. Baines and his wife."

Suddenly the children reappeared, racing into the room.

"Children, you're supposed to be in the nursery," Adella said.

"Do you want to see what my granddaddy gave me?" Gertie said, running up to me. I looked to Adella for instruction. She nodded her approval.

"Yes, please," I said. The little girl pulled a small lacquered wooden box from behind her back and opened it. It contained an exquisite violet hand-painted fan with mother-of-pearl ribs and white lace. Gertie waved the fan around in the air a few times and then folded it up again. Just as I thought she would put it away, she used it to whack her brother on the head.

"Now, Gertrude, nice young ladies don't hit their brothers," Adella said as Ned stuck his tongue out at his sister.

"May I see?" Priscilla Triggs, who hadn't said a word to us since we'd arrived, reached for the fan. Gertie moved closer so that the woman could get a closer look. Mrs. Powers leaned closer too.

"Granddaddy said it's special, like me," Gertie said proudly.

"My daughter had something similar when she was your age," Mrs. Powers said. "Hers was blue."

"It is special. Thank you for showing us," Priscilla Triggs said. Gertie then stuck her tongue out at her brother.

"Yeah, well, my present's better." Ned, who had climbed up and was standing on a chair, jumped down and ran over to a corner table. He ran back with his prize in his hand, pointing it at me. Someone screamed. I fell out of my chair scrambling to get out of its line of fire as the other women all ducked their heads. It wasn't a toy; it was a gun.

"Ned!" his mother cried. "I told you to put that away." She snatched it from her unwilling son's hands and set it on top of a bookcase, out of the boy's reach. Still trembling, I slowly retook my seat. The men roared with laughter, finding sport in my distress.

"What quick reflexes on your girl, Sir Arthur," Lieutenant Colonel Holbrook guffawed. "Could've used her at Gideon's Bluff!"

"I knew your boy would make a good soldier," Lieutenant Triggs said, slapping Frederick Reynard on the back, "but who would've known about Miss Davish!"

I could ignore the old colonel, but Lieutenant Triggs's comment stung. *"Un, deux, trois . . . ,"* I counted under my breath. I avoided eye contact with any of the men, especially Sir Arthur. He wouldn't have approved of the expression on my face.

The elderly Mrs. Kaplan leaned over and gave my leg a pat. Her countenance was less comforting than amused. I flashed a feeble smile at her, took a deep breath, trying to calm my nerves, all the while wondering what type of man gives a ten-year-old boy a pistol?

"But Mother, Granddaddy gave it to me."

"Yes, I know, but it isn't a toy. You can have it back when your father has time to teach you how to use it. Not until then."

"But it doesn't have any bullets in it. Granddaddy kept those."

"Don't argue, Edward. It's still dangerous." Gertie triumphantly stuck out her tongue at her brother again. "Now to bed with you both," their mother said.

"Ah," Ned said, kicking the leg of a table while Gertie entertained herself by winking and making funny faces at me and the other women.

"Now," Frederick Reynard said, crossing the room toward us. Without another word, the children tore out of the room, scrambling and pushing each other for the chance to get through the door first.

"And who's this lovely girl in green?" Mrs. Kaplan said when Adella had seemed to forget to introduce me.

"Oh, I'm so sorry, Mrs. Kaplan," Adella said, blushing. "This is Miss Hattie Davish, Sir Arthur's secretary. She's taking Papa's dictation for Sir Arthur's book."

"A secretary?" Mrs. Holbrook said.

"I know it's unusual," Mrs. Baines said, feeling the need to apologize for my presence, "but I think Mrs. Reynard invited Hattie to have an equal number of men and women. It's obvious she's a thoughtful hostess."

"Actually," Frederick Reynard said, wearing another variegated amaryllis on his lapel. He stood close to his wife, their shoulders almost touching. "Miss Davish was invited in honor of the debt of gratitude this family owes her. She's quite remarkable, really."

"Indeed?" Mrs. Kaplan said. "And tell me, Frederick, what has this young lady done to deserve such high praise?"

"Be foolhardy," Captain Starrett said loudly, cutting off the buzz of conversation as he entered the parlor for the first time. He had seemed out of sorts ever since I overheard his conversation with the man he called Mott. Was it a coincidence he was directing his anger at me? "Girl shouldn't have gone out on that ice. I'm not calling your judgment into question, Sir Arthur, but that secretary of yours is a silly, thoughtless girl."

"Father!" Adella exclaimed, seeing her dinner party unravel before her eyes.

Priscilla Triggs too seemed shocked. She came to stand beside me and put a protective hand on my shoulder.

"And who was foolhardy, young man, aiming a cannon in the direction of the peaceful folk on Park Avenue?" Mrs. Kaplan said.

Several snickers followed Mrs. Kaplan's declaration. I wasn't shocked by her outspokenness; in my experience elderly ladies often spoke their minds, and this one in particular seemed to be enjoying herself immensely. But I was surprised how quickly Captain Starrett's politics had infiltrated a Christmas dinner party. I had envisioned a lively but joyous occasion. Politics had always seemed malapropos for mixed company, especially at this time of the year. I should've known better when Captain Starrett was involved.

"And before you start spouting words like *copperhead* and *traitor*—," the old woman said.

"He *is* a copperhead and a traitor," Henry said. "And he deserved more than he got. Should've burned the house down."

"What about Mrs. Jamison?" Sir Arthur said. Henry glared at him.

"Yes, what about Mary?" Mrs. Kaplan said. "Did she deserve to suffer from the ruckus you brutes made? Would you burn the house down with her in it?"

"Now, now, Ettie," General Starrett said, patting the old woman's hand. "No one's burning anyone's house down." She bobbed her head once and folded her arms across her sagging bosom, allowing herself to be mollified.

"Father," Adella said quickly, trying to avoid any further discord, "may I introduce our guests, Mrs. Triggs and Mrs. Baines?" Still glaring at Sir Arthur, Henry Starrett disregarded the nods the women gave.

"What a pleasure to meet you," Rachel Baines said, almost giggling. The admiring tone in her voice caused the object of her pleasure to regard her for the first time. He hesitated for a moment, then smiled and deliberately took the lady's hand.

"The pleasure is all mine, beautiful lady," he said. Rachel Baines blushed with pleasure while her husband stood brooding by the fireplace, his eye twitching.

Sir Arthur, during this interlude, had clenched his teeth, trying to maintain his dignity. He could restrain his tongue no longer. "You owe me and Miss Davish an apology, sir."

"Excuse me? I don't owe you anything," Captain Starrett said, smiling down at Mrs. Baines.

"I'll have you know, Captain, that the girl you described as foolhardy is the antithesis of my Miss Davish. And despite your claim, you have insulted me, sir."

"Take it as you like. But you're in my house and I'll say what I'm so inclined to say," Captain Starrett said, retaining Rachel Baines's hand but spitting the words at Sir Arthur. "Sir!"

"So you are disinclined to answer this lady's question?" Sir Arthur said, indicating Mrs. Kaplan, who gripped her cane and stuck out her chin as if expecting an answer.

"What question? Whether I thought Jamison's mother deserved to have her peace disrupted or whether I'd burn down the house with the traitors inside?"

Gasps followed, then silence. Henry's callousness was stunning.

"Father!" Adella chided.

The dinner party was on the brink of disaster, before we had even sat down at the table, when, by sheer providence, Ambrose came in.

"Dinner is served," he announced.

"Let's eat then!" Captain Starrett said with mock bravado, clapping and rubbing his hands together.

Adella quickly took her father's arm and had him escort her in. It was a breach in protocol but an obvious attempt to speak to her father and salvage her party. Sir Arthur, who should've gone in on our hostess's arm, gallantly offered his arm to the elderly Mrs. Kaplan as Frederick escorted a delighted Rachel Baines. Mrs. Holbrook with General Starrett, Lieutenant Colonel Holbrook and Mrs. Powers, and Priscilla Triggs with John Baines followed. Lieutenant Triggs offered me his arm. I took it reluctantly, the sting of his jest still smarting.

"Don't listen to that man, Miss Davish," he said with unexpected vehemence. "We all know how invaluable you are to Sir Arthur."

"Thank you," I said, rattled by the entire exchange. How had I become the catalyst of such discord? "Maybe Mrs. Baines was right, though. Maybe I shouldn't have come."

CHAPTER 11

The dining room was festive and welcoming. The roaring fire accentuated the gold rosettes stenciled on the crimson walls, and the frosted windows were decorated with wreaths of holly. The table set under the chandelier's glow sparkled off the small bands of gold encircling the plates, the painting of a cardinal perched on a sprig of holly painted on the flat rims of the plates and dishes, the etched glasses, and of course the plethora of silverware. Each place setting had a row of spoons for the fruit, soup, dessert, and coffee, a dinner knife and a salad knife, and forks, to be used in order, for oysters, fish, roast, salad, game, and dessert.

I'm glad I paid attention in "dinner table etiquette" class, I thought.

An elaborate display of white gardenias and Christmas tulips in a three-tiered, two-foot vase made of spun sugar, surrounded at the base by red amaryllis flowers, was the centerpiece. I'd seen Mrs. Brendel's inventory and wondered where Mrs. Reynard had obtained the tulips. They were fresh, beautiful, and would have been extremely difficult to find in any shop.

As we entered, Adella was setting down a place card, as if she had changed her seating arrangements. When her father helped Adella into her chair and then sat down next to her, I knew my hunch had been right. But who did she displace at her side? Lieutenant Triggs escorted me to the table and we discovered that we were sitting beside each other. I was especially grateful that Captain Starrett was at the far end of the table and that Rachel Baines sat on Lieutenant Triggs's right. She could not speak to me without impolitely leaning over the table or speaking behind the lieutenant's back. When General Starrett sat down to my left, I knew it was his place that had been swapped with that of his son. I was infinitely grateful to our hostess for sparing me the embarrassment of sitting next to the man who had called my judgment into question.

Despite the strain of earlier, everyone was quickly engaged in polite banter, and the first course was served.

"Your favorite, Father," Adella cooed when the bluepoint oysters appeared.

"Issac loves them too, don't you, dear," Mrs. Holbrook said to her husband, who was rubbing his hands together in anticipation. Henry Starrett took several from the platter, then directed Ambrose to go against protocol and serve Lieutenant Colonel Holbrook next.

"Help yourself, Holbrook. Enjoy!" Henry Starrett said as he popped the first oyster in his mouth. Lieutenant Colonel Holbrook was more than happy to oblige.

Lieutenant Triggs was an attentive dining companion, cajoling me into trying the slimy creatures when they made their way to our plates, but was often distracted by Mrs. Baines, who, not satisfied with monopolizing our host, would ask the lieutenant's opinion on this or that. At these times, I would either engage the general, if he wasn't engaged with Mrs. Holbrook, or, most often, listen to the conversation of the others. The men were reminiscing about the war.

It was one of these times when I heard Captain Starrett say, ". . . the sausage had fur growing on it, but we were so desperate for meat, Private Blair shaved it off, and we ate it anyway!" He laughed and pounded his fist on the table.

"I don't think that's appropriate dinner talk, Father," Adella said.

"That reminds me of an amusing story," Lieutenant Colonel Holbrook said. "One time we got a ration wagon of salt horse and rice. Having eaten nothing but hardtack and weevils for two days, we were excited until we slit open the bags. The beef has gone rancid and the worms had eaten half of the meat before we could!"

"Issac!" his wife remonstrated. "We're eating dinner!" The veterans all laughed.

"That's the point, dear," Lieutenant Colonel Holbrook said. "Henry's furry sausage would've been wonderful. That night we dined on rice, hardtack, and worms." Henry Starrett burst with laughter, spittle forming on his lips. He wrapped his arms around his middle as his whole body convulsed.

"Good one, Holbrook. Good one," Henry said as he brought himself under control.

"But not very appetizing, I'm afraid," Rachel Baines said, pushing her plate away.

"Oh, Father," Adella said, desperate to change the dinner topic of conversation. "Tell us the Farris' Camp story." She turned to Mrs. Powers to her right. "Father told such wonderful stories when I was a little girl."

"My heart was in my throat, but I kept on," Captain Starrett said, launching into a tale of terrifying anticipation at approaching an enemy camp. It quickly became apparent to Sir Arthur and me, both of whom had read Grant's autobiography, that the tale Captain Starrett told was an embellishment of one of Grant's own recollections. Did any of the others know Henry Starrett was misrepresenting himself? Would they think less of him if they did?

"We approached the hilltop and looked down. The enemy's camp was visible, but Farris and his men were gone. They'd been more afraid of me than I of them!" Captain Starrett said. "From that moment on, I never felt alarm at facing an enemy again."

I knew without looking at him, Sir Arthur was livid. What Henry Starrett had done was kin to blasphemy to Sir Arthur. But he held his tongue and when Henry finished, Sir Arthur refrained from joining in the applause that followed. Mrs. Baines, who seemed slightly out of sorts, also kept her hands on her lap.

"Did you know that I served in the war too, *Captain* Starrett?" Rachel Baines said, stressing Henry Starrett's rank. All eyes shifted to her and she beamed.

"Astonishing, Mrs. Baines," Frederick Reynard said. "How extraordinary!"

"Yes, I was a nurse." She batted her eyelashes and looked away, feigning false modesty. "I was not yet twenty when I served on my first hospital ship." The questions for Mrs. Baines spilled across the table to the delight of the woman.

"Where did you serve?"

"Did you see any of the fighting?"

"Were you ever in danger?"

"Did you ever faint from seeing so much blood?"

"I thought Dorothea Dix only allowed old and plain nurses? How did such a beautiful, young lady get by Miss Dix?" Rachel Baines especially relished this last one.

"My father piloted a hospital ship for a while, didn't you, Father?" Adella said. The comment made Rachel Baines frown. She looked at Henry Starrett, who was staring intensely at her.

"Mostly served as a transport out of St. Louis, but yes, I did pilot a hospital ship, for a short while," he said. "Maybe our paths even crossed once, Mrs. Baines. I do remember a pretty little nurse in Cairo." He smiled and winked at Mrs. Baines, whose face reddened, but a slight smile tugged at her lips.

"Oh, you'd remember, Captain Starrett," John Baines said. "My wife is unforgettable, especially on a battlefield!" He smiled broadly at her and raised his glass slightly in a personal toast. Her eyes sparkled as she nodded to her husband's compliment. She quickly engaged Frederick in conversation.

A few minutes elapsed and I was chatting with General Starrett about Sir Arthur's book when I heard Mrs. Kaplan say, "Mr. Reynard, you never did tell me the story of that young girl." Out of the corner of my eye, I saw her indicate me with a nod. I held my breath until Captain Starrett was distracted and regaling his daughter and Priscilla Triggs with a story about one of his steamboat adventures.

"Miss Davish saved our daughter, Gertrude," Frederick Reynard said, "who had fallen through the ice on the river."

"How did a slip of a girl like that," Mrs. Kaplan said, pointing to me with a shaking hand, "save your daughter?"

"She crawled across the ice and used her cloak to pull Gertie to safety."

"Remarkable," the old woman said.

"Captain Starrett does have a point, though," Mrs. Baines interjected. "It was foolish of her not to wait for the men."

"Actually, the men wouldn't have been able to do it," Sir Arthur said, stabbing his fillet of beef with a fork. "Too heavy."

"So it was the very fact that she's made like a twig made her your daughter's perfect rescuer!" Mrs. Holbrook declared.

"Yes," Frederick said, "you could say that."

I looked down at myself. *I'm not that thin,* I thought.

"Then she should've waited and let Mrs. Reynard do it," Mrs. Baines said before she realized how inane she sounded.

"Certainly not," Frederick said. "I wouldn't have my wife endangering herself like that."

"But it's okay that Sir Arthur's secretary did?" Mrs. Kaplan said. Sir Arthur glared at Frederick Reynard, anticipating his answer.

"Well, um." I was too far down the table to deflect the conversation away from me but was grateful for once that Mrs. Baines was determined to do so.

"It's not important who saved Mr. Reynard's sweet little girl, is it? But the fact that she's safe now. I'm sure any one of us would've done all we could to see her well."

"You're absolutely right," Frederick said, relieved to see Sir Arthur's ire mollified by Mrs. Baines's comment. "Though we'll all feel better when—"

Crash! The sound of a tray dropping stopped all conversation. Ambrose, who had been serving at the table, appeared with a salver in his hand.

"Is everything all right, Ambrose?" Frederick asked.

"Yes, sir, nothing for you to worry about, sir. But a gentleman is here to see Captain Starrett."

"Well, tell him I'm having dinner with guests, man," the captain said, his face flush.

"Yes, sir, but he refuses to leave, at least until I deliver his card, sir."

"Give it to me then." Ambrose offered him the salver, and Henry snatched up the card. The captain's face blanched.

"Is everything all right, Father?" Adella said, placing a hand on his arm. "Do you need to see this man?"

Henry Starrett stood up and tossed his napkin on his chair. "If you'll excuse me for a moment." He staggered slightly. When he opened the door, I could see the reflection of Mott in a mirror that hung in the hall. He smiled when he saw Captain Starrett. Then the door closed behind them.

"That boy never did abide proper manners. Does everything his own way," General Starrett said, shaking his head but chuckling. "But never a dull moment, I grant you." He seemed to be the only one who found the interruption amusing.

"Papa, our guests," Adella said under her breath. "I'm sure Father will be back momentarily. Ambrose, will you please bring in the next course?"

CHAPTER 12

B ut Captain Starrett didn't return momentarily. In fact, he hadn't returned by the time the first dessert course, Mrs. Monday's chocolate truffle cookies, was served.

Where is he? I wondered. Why hadn't he returned, even to excuse himself to his guests? And what role did Mr. Mott play in Captain Starrett's absence? By the look on Adella's face, I wasn't the only one wondering where her father had gone. It'd been hours and the conversation had begun to lull. Several guests, who were animated and full of conversation at the beginning of the night, seemed to grow weary. I didn't know if it was due to the late hour or the heaviness of the food or both, but I too was feeling the effects. In fact, the confection I'd looked forward to seemed to turn my stomach. I refused the fruit and cheese courses and longed only for my bed. But when Adella signaled that we would all retire to the parlor, I knew it would be considered rude if I didn't stay at least a while longer. My feelings were reflected in the countenance of Priscilla Triggs, and Mrs. Kaplan snored quietly in the corner armchair, but to my surprise most of the gentleman too seemed to let somnolence overtake them. Sir Arthur, on the other hand, who was used to long dinner parties and rarely went to bed before two in the morning, was in high spirits and entertained some of the ladies with his story of meeting the Queen.

At one point I heard Adella Reynard exclaim, "I'd love to see England, Sir Arthur!"

"Why, with all your travel books, I'm surprised to hear you've never been there, Mrs. Reynard."

"I've never been anywhere but Chicago," Adella confessed, eliciting a round of laughter. I don't think she was joking.

The general too seemed himself, but I wasn't surprised when he announced he was retiring early.

"Good night, Papa," Adella said, kissing the old man on his forehead. "Sleep well."

After the old man's departure, Adella left momentarily to check on her children. As soon as she'd left the room I heard John Baines say, "What do you suppose happened to Henry Starrett? He had a visitor and then never did come back. And what was all that talk of burning down the copperhead's house?"

"I know," Mrs. Baines said, putting her hand to her throat. "I've never been so insulted by a host in my life. He barely addressed me and then disappeared. His behavior was inexcusable."

"He addressed you with compliments and flattery, my dear," her husband said. "What more do you want, his undivided attention?" He laughed halfheartedly and his eye twitched again.

"Oh, John," Mrs. Baines said, dismissing her husband's comment with a flip of her head and a wave of her hand. John Baines furrowed his brow. His retort was stifled by Adella's cheerful return.

I engaged Frederick Reynard in conversation on the topic of exotic plants. He became animated, his breath fast and shallow.

"Where is your greenhouse, Mr. Reynard?"

Although I hadn't gone on the G.A.R. home tour, I had made a point of walking by the late Dr. Kittoe's home before my hike this morning. I'd learned from Sir Arthur's research that Dr. Kittoe had been an avid gardener and greenhouse plant grower, so I suffered a twinge of sadness and disappointment that Mrs. Kittoe, the Civil War surgeon's widow, now left the structure empty. Remembering this emboldened me to ask Frederick Reynard about his obviously prospering greenhouse in hopes of getting a tour.

"It's attached to the carriage house. Adella didn't want me tracking dirt through the house." He tilted his head slightly. "How did you know I had a greenhouse, Miss Davish?"

"I enjoy collecting plants myself and was admiring both the amaryllis on your lapel and the cut flowers in the centerpiece. I've been to the shops in town and only someone with a private greenhouse would have freshly cut tulips this time of the year."

"You do have a sharp eye," he said, wiping his forehead with a handkerchief. His face was growing flush. "Yes, growing plants is my passion, Miss Davish. Right now, I'm growing tulips, gardenia, citrus, amaryllis, narcissus, carnations, azalea, hibiscus, and of course several varieties of rose. My Christmas cacti are in full bloom. Are you interested in seeing my greenhouse, Miss Davish?"

"Yes, very much so."

"It's settled then. I'll speak to Sir Arthur tomorrow. I'm sure he can spare you—"

"Help! Help!" The old general's cries of distress came from down the hall. "For pity's sake, will somebody help!"

We all leaped from our seats and ran to see what had befallen the general. But to my surprise this small exertion caused me distress. I felt light-headed when I rose from my chair and my head was pounding by the time I reached the library. I looked to Mrs. Triggs standing next to me. Her face was flush and damp. So was that of her husband.

If I hadn't already felt ill, the disarray before me would've made me swoon. I grabbed the back of the nearest chair. The library where I'd spent many hours with Sir Arthur and the general had been completely ransacked. The desk drawers were open, books were overturned, and papers were strewn about the room. Fragments of red glass, sparkling in the gaslight, lay scattered across the floor. One of the lantern-shaped cigar lighters had been smashed to pieces. It would take hours to bring the room back to order. And then I saw it: the safe, a small, steel box with a brass plate that read: *Fire and Thief Resist*; the door was open and it was empty.

"Papa!" Adella cried, running to her grandfather as everyone else slowly filtered into the room. "Are you all right?"

"What happened?" Frederick Reynard asked.

"We've been robbed!" the general declared. "And whoever did it attacked Henry." He pointed behind the settee. We hadn't noticed Henry lying there before. Of the large man all I could see was a hint of his black dress jacket and his feet sticking out beyond the sofa.

Adella screamed and fainted into her husband's arms. Under her unexpected weight Frederick lost his balance, and they both collapsed onto the settee.

"My God!" John Baines said, his eye twitching incessantly, as his wife bolted to the prone figure's side.

"Is he dead?" Morgan Triggs asked.

"Luckily, no," Rachel Baines said as a matter of fact, her nurse's training evident. "He's unconscious and his pulse is racing, but he's alive."

"Call a doctor," Sir Arthur said to Mrs. Becker, the house-keeper, hovering outside the library door. She lifted her skirts and ran.

"This is outrageous," John Baines said, his words slightly slurred. "Who could've done this?"

"That copperhead Henry's been antagonizing, Enoch Jamison, comes to mind," Mrs. Holbrook said. Several heads nodded.

Sir Arthur walked over and inspected the safe. "What was in here, General?"

"Money, stock, bonds." The general held an unlit cigar. His hand was shaking.

"Can you tell if anything else is missing?" Sir Arthur said.

"No, I'll have to go through it all to know," General Starrett said.

"When could this have happened?" Mrs. Powers said.

"It must've been while we were all at dinner," Lieutenant Colonel Holbrook said, he too growing red in the face.

"Now we know why Captain Starrett didn't return to the dining room," Mrs. Baines said.

"Yes, while we dined and laughed, Henry was lying here fighting for his life," Mrs. Kaplan said, seeming to approve of the gasps her comment elicited.

"I read in the *Gazette* about a string of burglaries of late," Lieutenant Colonel Holbrook said, wiping a handkerchief across his brow.

"Yes, I have too," Sir Arthur said. "But those were all businesses and no one had been hurt."

"Maybe the culprit is branching out," Mrs. Kaplan said, "and burglarizing people in their homes. Henry must've surprised the thief, who then attacked him."

"Then none of us is safe," Mrs. Baines said.

"Oh, dear, what about the children?" Mrs. Triggs asked.

"They're fine. They've been in the nursery since eight o'clock," Adella said, waking from her stupor. "But what about Father?"

"The doctor is coming," Frederick said. "Then we'll know if he'll live."

"Freddie!" Adella admonished.

"Sorry, darling, but we don't know what happened to him. I'm being realistic."

"You're the nurse, Mrs. Baines. Do think Henry is in mortal danger?" Mrs. Holbrook said. Then noticing the pallor of her husband's face, she added, "Are you feeling ill, Issac, dear?"

"I'm fine," he said, wiping his sweating brow with his handkerchief again. He didn't look fine and his breathing was becoming labored. "But I think it prudent that we—" He swayed on his feet and grabbed hold of his wife's shoulder for balance.

"Yes, yes," Adella said, "maybe you should retire for the evening, Colonel Holbrook."

Sir Arthur glanced around the room. I counted no fewer than four other people, Frederick Reynard, Lieutenant and Mrs. Triggs, and Mr. Baines, who had the same clammy complexions as Lieutenant Colonel Holbrook. Why was Sir Arthur looking like that at me?

"Considering the circumstances," he said, "I think that it would be wise for us all to retire, Mrs. Reynard."

"But what about the burglar?" Mrs. Baines said, her hand going straight to the brooch at her neckline. "He could still be lurking around outside waiting to steal my jewels or accost my person."

"I'm sure the culprit is long gone, Mrs. Baines, and you and your jewels are safe," Sir Arthur said without a hint of sarcasm. "Maybe you could stay until the doctor arrives?"

"Yes, of course." Mrs. Baines squared her shoulders and

nodded and without hesitation began issuing instructions to the maid.

"Thank you for a memorable evening." Sir Arthur bowed to Mrs. Reynard. "Sir," he said, shaking Frederick Reynard's hand.

"But shouldn't the police be called in?" Mrs. Powers said. "Valuables have been stolen and a man has been assaulted."

"No, no," General Starrett said. "No need for the police just yet."

"I agree with Mrs. Powers, Cornelius," Lieutenant Colonel Holbrook said, his words coming out in spurts. He was relying on his wife completely now. "For goodness' sake, man, your son was attacked." General Starrett stared down at his son, shaking his head.

"No, not yet."

"Leave everything as you found it, General," Sir Arthur said, "and I will come over first thing tomorrow morning and assist you in evaluating your loss. Hopefully Henry will be up by then and able to tell us what happened."

"That's most kind of you," the general said. It was kind of Sir Arthur and uncharacteristic. This was definitely the type of job he would normally assign to me. Why hadn't he mentioned my name?

"We'll see ourselves out," Sir Arthur said.

"Of course. Thank you, Sir Arthur," Adella said. Only Sir Arthur could dismiss the host and hostess in their own home without repercussions.

As Ambrose helped us on with our cloaks, I heard Priscilla Triggs say, "You don't suppose the visitor robbed the general, do you?"

"He was the only stranger that we know of who was in the house," Sir Arthur said.

"You don't think someone at the dinner party did it, do

you, sir?" I asked quietly. "Several guests excused themselves during dinner."

"You're too astute for your own good, Hattie," Sir Arthur said under his breath. "Let's keep quiet for now, shall we?" I looked around to see if anyone had heard me, but the others were distracted.

"Well, at least we know why Henry didn't come back. I thought he'd vanished to the North Pole," John Baines was saying, chuckling pathetically. His face was beet red.

"I thought I was the only one to notice how much he looked like Santa Claus," Lieutenant Triggs said.

"It's uncanny," Mrs. Holbrook said, helping her husband on with his coat.

"I noticed that too," I said.

"That's enough, Hattie," Mrs. Baines said as she directed a maid carrying a stack of towels toward the library. "Captain Starrett is a distinguished gentleman and doesn't look anything like Santa Claus." I didn't understand Mrs. Baines. A few minutes ago she complained about Captain Starrett's rude behavior. Now she was defending him. She turned back to her husband. "What's wrong with you, John? You're slouching. Here, let me put your coat on. John? John?" Then she shrieked, "Jack!" as that gentleman crumbled to the floor.

"Oh my, another one," Mrs. Kaplan said, licking her lips and craning her neck for a better view. "Is he dead?"

"Where is that doctor?" Rachel Baines yelled, unbuttoning her husband's vest and loosening his bow tie. From the rise and fall of his chest, he was still breathing.

"What going on?" Frederick Reynard, who had retired, stumbled down the stairs.

"Now what's wrong?" General Starrett hobbled out of the library, into the hallway.

"I'm afraid some of your guests may have taken ill," Sir Arthur said with his usual calm.

"But how?" General Starrett asked as a sudden violent wave of nausea swept over me. I slipped to my knees. Someone called my name, but I ignored them. I desired nothing more than to put my inflamed cheek against the cool parquet floor. "My God, what's wrong with them?" General Starrett demanded.

"Can't you see?" Rachel Baines said. "We've been poisoned!"

I studied the intricate medallion pattern of oak, cherry, and maple on the floor as beads of perspiration dripped down my temple.

"Oh my darling, Issac! Issac!" Mrs. Holbrook cried as her husband clutched his chest, struggled to catch his breath, and fell to the floor like a toppled tree. "Help him! Help him! Somebody help him!" the poor woman shrieked as she grabbed Sir Arthur's arm.

I flinched as the lieutenant colonel's head landed inches from my face, his wild white hair plastered to his forehead, his eyes and mouth frozen open in shock, staring at me. I wanted to look away, desperately wishing I were anywhere else, but I couldn't. Being this close, I could see that Lieutenant Colonel Holbrook's eyes were two different colors; one was blue and the other hazel. I had to stare. Rachel Baines bent over Holbrook and caught my eye. She shook her head slightly. Sweat stung my eyes and I was forced to blink. The man next to me did not.

"I'm so sorry, Mrs. Holbrook," Rachel said. "Your husband's beyond anyone's help now."

Chapter 13

"How are they, Doctor?" Sir Arthur whispered. He and another man were standing outside the open doorway, their shadows, from the dim light of the gas lamp in Sir Arthur's hand, cast against the wall.

"Well, as you know, I could do nothing for old Mr. Holbrook," the doctor said, "so I've been most concerned with the general's son, Henry. Thank goodness you found him when you did. If he'd lain there any longer without proper hydration, he might have died as well. He's still quite ill and will need to be watched closely. The others should be fine once the illness runs its course."

"But Henry wasn't attacked as we first supposed?" Sir Arthur said. "You found no injury, no evidence of a struggle?"

"No, no, he collapsed from the sickness like everyone else."

That's a relief, I thought. But what did he mean, "like everyone else"?

"Then he must've discovered the theft but collapsed before he could raise the alarm," Sir Arthur said. The doctor shrugged.

"And Hattie?" Sir Arthur looked through the doorway at me. It was too dark for him to tell I was awake.

"I can only assume, since she refused to let me examine her, that she suffers from the same sickness as everyone else. But if she has an attending physician, you may want to consult him. Otherwise, I recommend the same treatment, rest and plenty of liquids."

"I've already arranged for a regimen of liquids for each patient, Doctor," Rachel Baines said. I couldn't see her and hadn't known she was there.

"You've been a great help, Mrs. Baines. I hear you nursed in the war."

"Yes, Doctor."

"Well, it's a great comfort to know they will be under your care, madam." I didn't have to see Rachel Baines to know that the comment brought a smile to her face. "Now, it may be an inconvenience for your hosts, but I would recommend all those afflicted be allowed to recover with as little disturbance as possible. Even a short carriage ride may jar their nerves."

That's why I didn't recognize where I was. It was dark and I was still in the Reynards' home.

"I will speak to the general and Mrs. Reynard about the arrangements," Sir Arthur said.

"Good. Then if that will be all, Sir Arthur?" the doctor said.

"One more thing, Dr. Gunderson. What's wrong with them?"

"From the apparent symptoms: fever, flux, profuse sweating, dizziness, vomiting, delirium, I'd have thought milk sickness, but I haven't heard of any cases of that in Galena. It could be gastritis, intestinal colic, or cholera morbus. But since several people exhibited the same symptoms in a matter of hours during a dinner party, I would say it's most likely ptomaine poisoning."

"I recognized the signs of poison right away, Doctor," Mrs. Baines said.

"Yes, I'm sure you did, Mrs. Baines. Probably saw your share of it during the war, what with all the worms and weevils our boys ate." The doctor and nurse shared a chuckle. I closed my eyes and focused on keeping the nausea down.

"So it wasn't deliberate?" Sir Arthur asked.

"I don't know. That's for the police and the coroner's office to decide. All I know is that, intentional or not, a man is dead and several others are extremely sick."

"But I'm not sick, and neither is the general nor Mrs. Baines and most of the other ladies. Can you explain that?" Sir Arthur asked.

"The poison could've been in the food that only some of us ate," I said feebly from my bed. Sir Arthur and the doctor turned their heads suddenly toward me. Rachel Baines, carrying a candle that cast a glow across her face, stepped into view.

"Hattie, you're supposed to be resting," she said as she entered the room, setting the candle down. She put her hand on my forehead and then poured a mixture of brandy and water. "Here, drink this." The thought of anything going down into my stomach was enough to make me nauseous.

"No, thank you," I said, waving her away. I felt terrible and wanted to be left alone. I should've stayed quiet and they would've left.

"Why must you be so obstinate, girl? The doctor and I are only trying to help," Mrs. Baines said. "By the way, who's Walter?"

Walter? I wondered. What did Walter have to do with anything? And how did Rachel Baines know about Walter? Was I talking in my sleep? Had I been delirious? Did Sir Arthur hear me ranting? What else did I say?

"Hattie has a point," Sir Arthur was saying when I focused on the conversation that was going on in front of me. "Could the poison have been administered to a dish that we didn't all partake of?"

"Administered?" the doctor said. "I think I gave you the wrong impression. These people were food poisoned."

"Food poisoned?" Sir Arthur said tersely. "Blast it, Gunderson, a man died!"

"The sick and elderly are known to succumb to it," Dr. Gunderson said. "Lieutenant Colonel Holbrook was both. But of course, we'll know more after the autopsy."

"So it was an accident after all," Rachel Baines said.

"It still could've been deliberate," I said. Rachel Baines frowned down at me. She picked up a hand towel, dipped it in the washbasin, and draped it over my forehead.

"You're supposed to be resting," she said again. "So stop talking and close your eyes."

"How so, Hattie?" Sir Arthur said, ignoring my nurse's advice.

My head felt heavy and my thoughts muddled. I concentrated for several moments on nothing but keeping my nausea at bay and the cool water on my face. But I'd spent too many hours in Eureka Springs puzzling over a woman's murder not to have the thought occur to me. But it was my illness impairing my judgment that made me speak my thought out loud.

"If someone knew the food was tainted but—" I stopped, suddenly realizing that I was implicating Mrs. Cassidy, the Reynards' cook, in a possible crime. I needed to stop doing this. I needed to stop looking at the sinister side of things and focus on the more probable explanation. "You're right, Mrs. Baines. I need to rest." A look of triumph flashed across her face. She patted my arm and smiled. A wave of nausea swept over me. I closed my eyes and turned my face away.

"No, Hattie, I think you might be right," Sir Arthur said.

"We can't forget that General Starrett's library was ransacked and burglarized while we were all in the dining room. It may be no coincidence that the two events happened at the same time. Someone might've tampered with tonight's food in order to distract us from the burglary." I thought of Mr. Mott, but before I could mention him I grabbed for the bedpan and gagged.

"Either way, this is not how I expected to spend Christmas," Rachel Baines said, holding back my disheveled hair. "It was sheer bad luck to be in this house." She dabbed the corners of my mouth as she helped me lie back down.

"No more so than for Lieutenant Colonel Holbrook," I added, wondering even as the words left my mouth whether it was bad luck or something else altogether.

"Well," the doctor said, lifting his watch from his pocket, "it's quite late. I'll be on my way. I'll check in tomorrow morning on the patients' progress. Don't forget, Mrs. Baines, Mr. Starrett needs to be watched at all times."

"Yes, Doctor," Rachel Baines said. The doctor turned to leave.

"Please come by early, Dr. Gunderson," Sir Arthur said. "I'm sure the police will want to speak to you."

The police? I thought. *Oh, no, not again.*

I spent the most miserable night of my life, clammy, feverish, with abdominal pain and almost constant nausea. At one point, I woke up lying on the floor with my head in the cool porcelain washbowl, my cheek bathed only in moonlight, with no memory of putting the washbowl on the floor or getting out of bed. But luckily, by the time the sun rose I felt infinitely better. I was weak and my stomach was still queasy, but my fever, stomach cramps, and headaches were gone. I was able to get out of bed without fighting nausea. I'd conceded that a hike was out of the question, but I wasn't going to lie around in bed all day. I dressed and went down to the kitchen in search of some tea.

"Hattie!" Mrs. Cassidy said, her hands busy kneading bread. "Shouldn't you be in bed?"

"I feel much better and was hoping for a cup of tea, Mrs. Cassidy," I said.

"Still, Mrs. Baines told me that all of you were supposed to stay in bed."

"I can't stay in bed all day. I have too much to do." Mrs. Cassidy shook her head, wiped her hands, and took down a cup and saucer.

"I can relate to that," she said, pouring the tea. "I'm exhausted from preparing last night's dinner and with all the excitement . . ." Her voice trailed off. "Is it true?"

I wrapped my fingers around the warm teacup, savoring the aroma, and then took a tiny sip. "Ah," I sighed, and took another sip. "Not to be more of a bother, but you wouldn't have a hard biscuit or a slice of toast I could nibble on?" I asked. The tea tasted so good, I poured myself another cup. "Is *what* true?"

"That old Holbrook collapsed and died on the hallway floor?" Mrs. Cassidy said, slicing a piece of bread and throwing it in a hot pan on the stove. "And that a burglar snuck in the house while everyone was having dinner? Of course, I didn't see anyone suspicious, but then again . . . and that the captain himself . . ." She dropped her voice and looked about for eavesdroppers. "I heard he was lucky not to have followed in the way of old Holbrook." She pulled her finger across her throat in a grotesque gesture. "The police are due any moment." She put the toast on a plate and set it in front of me. I pulled a napkin to my lips; I was suddenly in no mood for toast.

"Did you hear anyone mention poison?" I said, pushing the plate away.

"Is that why everyone got sick?" she asked. I nodded, fighting a new wave of nausea.

"Food poisoning," I managed to say through my napkin. It took a few moments for the implication to set in, but suddenly Mrs. Cassidy's eyes flew wide open in alarm.

"B-b-but, b-b-but," she stammered, "I cooked all of that food myself!"

"I thought I should warn you ahead of time that the police are going to question you. And from previous experience, it won't be pleasant."

"They're accusing me of a dirty kitchen? I can't believe it. You can ask anyone. I'm a clean, conscientious cook. And I would never have served old or tainted food." Her eyes widened as a new thought flitted across her face. "Oh my God, do they think I killed Mr. Holbrook? And tried to kill the captain? Oh my God, oh my God!" She waved her arms about as she paced the floor in sheer panic.

"What's going on in here?" Adella Reynard said from the kitchen doorway, a policeman at her side. The man, in a spotless tailored blue uniform, had a round, open face with shaggy dark blond hair and mustache. He was only slightly taller than Adella and possible not much older. He clutched a notebook tightly in his hands, his fingers turning white. He studied the linoleum floor, a simple pattern of garnet and drab tiles. The tip of a nickel-covered harmonica poked out of his breast pocket. Adella didn't introduce him.

"Oh, Mrs. Reynard, I didn't mean it," Mrs. Cassidy said, wringing her hands in her apron. "I thought I . . . oh, I mean, oh, you've got to believe me, Mrs. Reynard. I've never done anything like this in my life."

"Calm yourself, Mrs. Cassidy," Adella said. "Whatever are you talking about?" Mrs. Reynard's ignorance seemed to calm the cook, who recognized that it was more prudent now to hold her tongue. She shook her head instead of answering.

Adella pursed her lips in annoyance. "As you know, we've had some unfortunate events occur. This policeman would like a word with you. I have his full assurance he will not take any more of your time than necessary." As the policeman took a seat without one being offered and opened his notebook in front of him on the table, Adella Reynard turned to me.

"Up from your bed so soon, Miss Davish?"

"Yes, I'm feeling much better. How are Mr. Reynard and the others?"

"Freddie and most of the others are better, though not nearly as recovered as you. Father is still quite ill, I'm afraid. I think the sickness hit him the hardest."

"That remains to be seen," the policeman said, without looking up from his notes. "Lieutenant Colonel Holbrook may have died from the same poisoning that incapacitates your father." Adella's cheeks flushed. She was a woman not used to being contradicted.

"Do you suspect another cause?" I asked. The policeman looked at me sideways and a slight smile lit his face.

"And you are?" he asked in an almost-teasing tone.

"This is Miss Davish, Sir Arthur Windom-Greene's secretary, Officer Corbett," Adella said. "And Sir Arthur would find me remiss if I didn't insist she return to her bed until Dr. Gunderson arrives."

"Is Sir Arthur here?" I asked, ignoring her order back to bed. I didn't know Sir Arthur to rise before nine o'clock.

"Yes, he's in the library with Papa," Adella Reynard said. "I'll be in the nursery if you need me, Mr. Corbett." She left the room without waiting for his response.

I turned back to the policeman. "Do you think Lieutenant Colonel Holbrook died of something other than food poisoning?"

The policeman hesitated, looked down at his notes, and smiled out of the side of his mouth again. I think he found my questions amusing, but I ignored him. I wanted to know the answer.

"We won't know until the autopsy of course, but it's possible. We have to consider both, that it may have been food poisoning or poison in the food. The medical examiner will run tests to determine which."

"You suspect foul play?" I asked. "Lieutenant Colonel Holbrook was an elderly gentleman. The timing of his death could be a mere coincidence." The policeman looked up and gave me the smile again.

"That is true, Miss Davish, but considering that the house was burglarized at the same time, we are investigating Mr. Holbrook's death as intentional."

"Murder," Mrs. Cassidy whispered.

"Yes, Mrs. Cassidy, murder," Officer Corbett said, a cold, stern tone replacing his more casual one. It reminded me of Walter, capable of both playfulness and professionalism but never mixing the two. "Now, if you will, tell me how poisoned food was served from your kitchen."

Chapter 14

"Come in!" someone shouted when I knocked on General Starrett's library door. Unlike the last time I was here, when the general was ensconced in a warm, cozy room smoking a pipe, the room I entered was in chaos.

"Hattie!" Sir Arthur exclaimed with more enthusiasm than surprise. "You're feeling better, I take it?"

"Yes, sir, much better, thank you."

"No need for a doctor's advice after all," he said.

"No, sir. I definitely don't require the services of a doctor," I said.

"I'm amazed, my girl," General Starrett said. "Frederick, Henry, and Sir Arthur's guests are all still bedridden. Though maybe it's a woman thing. Mrs. Triggs is also feeling much better, I hear."

"It probably has more to do with moderation than constitution," Sir Arthur said. It struck me as an important insight, but I didn't have the time to figure out how before Sir Arthur said, "This is a job for you, Hattie."

He explained that he was assisting General Starrett in cataloging the contents of the room. "I had planned to help him myself, with you incapacitated, but since you are fit for duty . . ." He handed me the tablet he'd been using.

"Shouldn't the girl be recuperating, Sir Arthur, and not sitting in this stuffy room?"

"Oh, no, General. You don't know Hattie. She'd prefer to be here helping you than lying in bed all day. Right, Hattie?" He did know me well.

"Yes, sir."

"Good," Sir Arthur said. "If the police need me, Hattie, you know where to find me. And let me know when my guests are fit to travel and I'll send Harvey over with the sleigh. Good day, General." And with that he turned to take his leave.

"Sir," I said.

"Yes?"

"Before I came here, I was in the kitchen while a policeman interviewed Mrs. Cassidy, the cook. They think someone might have deliberately poisoned the food." I now had Sir Arthur's and General Starrett's undivided attention.

"What else did he say?" General Starrett said, inching up to the edge of his seat. Sir Arthur sat down again.

"Tell us everything that was said," Sir Arthur said.

Although I hadn't been taking physical notes, I had made mental notes in anticipation of this moment. I knew Sir Arthur would want to know everything.

"Officer Corbett asked Mrs. Cassidy to explain how the food came to be poisoned," I said. I told them how Mrs. Cassidy had denied any wrongdoing, insisting that anyone had access to the kitchen and that several people (which was highly unusual) had visited the kitchen last night: Adella checking up on the cook's progress, Frederick Reynard looking for Adella, Oscar Killian, the grocer, personally delivering the "fancy food," the children running in and out. Mrs. Cassidy also had caught a strange man in an old black suit rummaging around in her pantry. He said that he hadn't eaten dinner and was looking for something to take with him on his long journey home. She had assumed, since he was in the house, he was a guest of the house and packed him a basket.

"I think Mrs. Cassidy might've met Mr. Mott," I said. Sir Arthur shook his head.

"I don't know of a Mr. Mott," he said.

"Mott, Mott," the general said. "I don't know that name either."

"I met Mr. Mott in the hallway after he'd been speaking to your son in the back parlor. He was a strange little man."

"When was that?" Sir Arthur asked.

"It was Sunday afternoon when I took the general's dictation," I said. "But before that, I saw him coming out of Enoch Jamison's house and then again last night during dinner when Captain Starrett was called away. I was seated where I could see the visitor in the hall mirror."

"I could see the mirror from my chair as well," the general said. "Why didn't I see him?"

"He was only visible for a moment, and at the time you had your head turned, speaking to me."

"We'll have to ask Henry about him then," the general said.

"Yes, we will," Sir Arthur said. "Go on, Hattie."

"Mrs. Cassidy also admitted to leaving the kitchen twice before dinner, once to fetch a serving tray in the dining room cupboard—the one she had planned to use was chipped—and once to 'get a bit of fresh air.' It was upon her return the second time that she found Mr. Mott in her pantry, where the household poisons are kept on a high shelf in the back."

"Well, there you go," General Starrett said. "This Mott is the culprit."

"Maybe, maybe not," Sir Arthur said. "We still don't know if it was poison added to the food or it was simply spoiled food as Dr. Gunderson said."

"Not to mention that the strychnine she keeps in the pantry to kill rats isn't the only poison available about this house," I said.

"What on earth do you mean?" General Starrett said.

"Mr. Reynard grows a variety of poisonous plants in his greenhouse," I said, "Narcissus, azalea, mistletoe, even the tulips and the holly in the floral centerpiece on the dining room table are poisonous if eaten."

"Hattie is an amateur botanist," Sir Arthur said to answer the quizzical expression on the general's face. Then Sir Arthur pulled out his watch. "Well, I must take leave of you now, General," he said, standing. "Keep me informed, Hattie."

"And don't go nibbling on any mistletoe either," General Starrett said, laughing under his breath. "Who would've known Christmas could be so dangerous."

The general and I worked for a couple of hours before the policeman found us in the library. We'd been interrupted moments earlier by Adella, followed by Priscilla Triggs, her face pinched and pale.

"Papa, are you smoking that pipe again?" Adella said, taking the pipe from where the general had hastily tried to hide it in his lap. "Do remember we have sick people in this house. Speaking of whom, Mrs. Triggs is feeling slightly better and didn't want to be alone in her room. I have my hands full tending to the children and helping Mrs. Baines nurse Father. Would you mind if she sat quietly here with you?"

"Shouldn't she be with her husband?" General Starrett asked peevishly, eyeing the pipe now out of his reach.

"He was the one that suggested I find company, sir,"

Priscilla Triggs said, taking the seat beside me. She looked at me and managed a weak smile. "I promise not to disturb yours and Hattie's work."

"Thank you, Papa," Adella said, kissing his forehead. "I'll have Mrs. Becker announce luncheon." Priscilla's face blanched. I knew what she was feeling. The thought of even the toast I had attempted to eat earlier was unsettling.

"May I just have a glass of water?" Priscilla asked.

"Of course, Mrs. Triggs," Adella said. "I'll have Mrs. Becker bring it right away."

A polite rap on the door preceded the policeman sticking his head into the room. "Can I have a moment, sir?"

"I was wondering when you were going to join us, young man," the general said.

"Had to take everyone's statement, sir," the policeman said, bowing his head to the ladies in the room without making eye contact. "May I take your statement now, sir?"

"Of course," the general said. "I didn't get your name."

"It's Corbett, Papa," Adella said. She pulled another travel book from the shelf, then quickly excused herself.

"My name's Archibald Corbett, sir, and I've been assigned to this investigation. Now would you mind excusing us, ladies?"

"That won't be necessary, Corbett. Miss Davish is here doing a job and Mrs. Triggs, well, she's all settled in. No, I've nothing to hide." Priscilla Triggs shot me a look I couldn't quite interpret. Was that a smile?

"Oh, a-l-ll right, th-then," the policeman stammered, opening his notebook. "Very well, sir. If you could tell me in your own words the events that took place here last night."

"Do you want Miss Davish to take dictation?" the general said. "Sir Arthur says she's very good." Officer Corbett glanced at me and blushed. It was not the reaction I expected.

"No, no, no, thank you," he said, burying his nose in his notebook again. "I'm used to taking my own notes. Now, if you don't mind?"

As I continued to catalog the contents of General Starrett's desk, the general detailed his account of the dinner party and subsequent illness, the ransacking of the library, and the theft of the contents of his safe. I recognized the cadence to his narrative; the disastrous night took on the same overtone as one of his war experiences.

"And did the thief take anything else beside the bank notes?"

"Can't you see that's what Miss Davish and I are trying to determine? So far, everything else is accounted for except for my great-grandson's gun."

"Gun? What gun?" The policeman's head jerked up. The old man dismissed the concern in the policeman's voice with a wave of his hand.

"It was a present to the boy from his grandfather. But what does that have to do with anything? Holbrook, poor chap, was poisoned, not shot."

"That may be, sir, but now we know that the burglar may be armed and more dangerous. What type of gun was it, General?" Corbett asked. "In case it does turn up."

"A LeMat revolver."

"Thank you, sir," the policeman said, standing. "If anything else turns up missing, or if you'd like to add to your statement, please let me know."

"Did you get Mrs. Triggs's statement, Mr. Corbett?" I asked. Priscilla Triggs put her hands to her mouth. Officer Corbett dropped his notebook. I didn't know who looked more startled, Mrs. Triggs or the policeman.

"Oh, right. I'm sorry, ma'am. The general said you'd been ill. I didn't realize you were at the dinner party last night."

"How else did you think she'd gotten ill?" the general said.

"I apologize, Mrs. Triggs. I was under the impression that none of the ladies at the dinner had taken ill."

"Oh, that's all right, Mr. Corbett," Priscilla Triggs said. "I had but a mild case compared to the others, especially poor Lieutenant Colonel Holbrook, of course."

"Dr. Gunderson said Holbrook, my son, and the others were all poisoned last night," General Starrett snapped. "Did you get that in your statements?" The policeman disregarded the old man's discourtesy and continued.

"Most mentioned the illness, but I've yet to take the doctor's statement, sir. Mr. Greene said the doctor would be coming by the house this morning. I thought that I wouldn't jump to any medical conclusions until I spoke with him."

"Yes, all right, I guess. But it's not Mr. Greene. It's Sir Arthur Windom-Greene. He's a distinguished gentleman from England." General Starrett seemed more out sorts than I'd ever seen him. I wondered if he too was getting ill.

The policeman turned to Mrs. Triggs, careful to look over her shoulder and not at her face. "If you don't mind giving a statement then, ma'am?"

"If it will be helpful, Officer," Priscilla said, a lilt in her voice I'd never heard before. She shot a glance at me and smiled before turning back to the policeman. "Though I'm sure I have nothing more to add that my husband or the others haven't already said."

I think she's enjoying this, I thought. *At least one of us is.*

"That's fine, ma'am. Now tell me, in your own words, what happened last night."

Priscilla spoke softly but assuredly, relaying the details of our arrival, the pre-dinner chatter, dinner itself, and then the discovery of the theft. I envied her memory. I would've had to refer to my notes to give such a precise account.

"So you saw the boy playing with the gun before dinner?" Officer Corbett asked.

"What? More about the gun?" General Starrett said. "I'm sure it will turn up."

The policeman ignored the general's outburst and turned back to Mrs. Triggs, patiently awaiting her response.

"Yes, the Reynards have such delightful children." She smiled slightly at the memory, but then again, she hadn't had the gun pointed at her. "Edward is a wonderful, playful boy and Gertrude is simply divine."

"Playful? Divine? Ha! They're little whirling dervishes," the general blurted out. "You obviously have never had children of your own." Priscilla Triggs's eyes went wide, her mouth slack. Her secret was out and General Starrett was oblivious to the pain he had caused. Her body was taut as she sat on the edge of her chair. I didn't know if she would lunge at him or bolt from the room. She did neither. She dropped her eyes to her lap, twisting her wedding band around and around her finger.

So that's what she meant about it being too late, too late for her to have children.

"And you yourself fell victim to the sickness, ma'am?" Officer Corbett asked. "Ma'am?" Priscilla's response was barely audible.

"Yes, though my husband suffered far more than I did." I wasn't sure if she was talking about the food poisoning or being childless. "Hattie was ill as well."

The policeman looked up from his notes at me, surprised. "But I thought . . . You're the secretary, right? You weren't even at the dinner party and you still got sick?"

"She most certainly was at the dinner party, Corbett. She was the family's special guest," the general growled. He looked at me sympathetically and then shook his head. "Sorry, my girl. Didn't mean to repay our gratitude by getting you poisoned and having old Holbrook die practically on top of you."

"Ahem," Corbett said, putting his fist to his mouth. "I'll,

uh . . . I'll have to take a statement from you as well, Miss Davish." General Starrett started fidgeting in his chair and wringing his hands.

"Then get on with it, man," he said curtly. "And by God, will you please sit down." Officer Corbett obliged. Again I wondered what was wrong with the general, why he was becoming short-tempered, until he looked over at his pipe, where Adella had placed it out of his reach.

I pushed away from the desk and stood up. The policeman jumped to his feet.

"I can make my statement brief, Mr. Corbett, by saying that I agree with everything Mrs. Triggs said. Her memory was flawless and her impressions were similar to my own. We are lucky that both of us escaped the ravage of the sickness. But I do need to ask," I said, "did anyone else mention Captain Henry Starrett's visitor?"

"Yes, yes, they have, Miss Davish. Several have mentioned that Captain Starrett was called away from the table. But no one knew who the visitor was."

"His name is Horace Mott." General Starrett sat up straight in his chair while Mrs. Triggs stifled a sound that resembled a squeak. The policeman looked me in the eye for the first time.

"That's right! I'd forgotten about him!" the general exclaimed, slapping his knee. "He's your man."

The policeman ignored the general's outburst and continued staring at me. "How do you come to know this, Miss Davish?" The policeman's tone was curious, not accusatory as I'd expected. I told him what I'd told General Starrett and Sir Arthur. He settled into his chair again.

"Can you describe him?"

"Short, pudgy, a few years older than me, wears spectacles and an old-fashioned foot-tall stovepipe hat," I said. "Ambrose and Captain Starrett will be able to describe him as well."

"I've already interviewed Ambrose, but I'll speak to him again. He didn't mention Mr. Mott. Unfortunately, Captain Starrett has been too ill to be of any help."

"What are you waiting for, Corbett?" the general said, badly hiding his annoyance. "You don't need to talk to my son. Can't you see the girl here has done your work for you? Go arrest this Mott character. He stole my money and killed poor Issac Holbrook."

"But who is this Mott? And where can we find him? What business did he have here? Without speaking to your son, I can only guess. What if—" The policeman stopped. The general's face had turned red and he was clenching his fists in his lap.

"What gives you the right to come into my home and make insinuations?"

"Oh, no, pardon me, sir. No, you misunderstood me. I never meant to imply your son had anything to do with this. I simply need to know more about Mr. Mott before I can arrest him."

"Are you done then, man?" the general said, momentarily placated.

"One more question, General," Mr. Corbett said, turning to me. "Why didn't you mention this earlier, Miss Davish?"

"Because before it was no one but my son's business who he met here," the general said. "And unlike some, Miss Davish, here knows that." The policeman continued to stare at me.

"Because I now have General Starrett's permission to tell you," I said. "Now I think we would all appreciate a rest."

"Yes, of course," Mr. Corbett said. "I'll be in touch if I have any more questions." He stood to leave, notebook in hand. "Thank you all for your cooperation."

Once the door closed behind the policeman, I picked up the pipe and handed it to the general, who sighed, then smiled broadly at me. He patted my hand paternally.

"I think we need a bit of fresh air, if you don't mind, General," I said as I took Priscilla under the arm and gently guided her out of the chair. She clung to me, almost in tears.

"Excellent idea," the general said, the pipe clenched between his teeth. He reached for the remaining of the two ship's lantern-shaped lighters, the green-colored glass one. "Yes, fresh air will do you both good. And take your time. Take all the time you need." A puff of smoke circled the old man's head before the door closed behind us.

CHAPTER 15

"I heard you identified the thief," Mrs. Monday said.
Every morning after my hike, I looked forward to sitting at Mrs. Monday's table in the warm kitchen and sharing a pot of hot, black coffee. She had trained as a pastry chef in her youth and baked some of the best pastries and cakes I'd ever had. She always had a piece saved for me. But as I'd spent this morning in bed, I had missed our time together. After the police had questioned us and I'd finished my tasks of cataloging and reorganizing General Starrett's library, Priscilla Triggs and I returned to Sir Arthur's. Mrs. Baines remained behind to nurse Henry Starrett as well as her husband and Lieutenant Triggs, who were not quite up to the carriage ride yet. So although I couldn't eat the shortbread Mrs. Monday had baked especially for me, I enjoyed a few leisure moments in her company sipping ginger tea before getting back to work.

"Who told you that?" I said.

"Word gets around, Hattie," she said. "Word gets around."

"You overheard Mrs. Triggs telling Sir Arthur, didn't you?"

She nodded and we both laughed. "Well, all I did was tell the police about the man that met with Henry Starrett during dinner. Since Captain Starrett is still too ill to talk to the police, I told them what I knew."

"Speaking of dinner," Mrs. Monday said, wiping her hands on her apron and putting the kettle on, "what courses were served? Tell me everything." I did so, but reluctantly; remembering the sight and smell of the food from last night made my stomach churn, and unfortunately Mrs. Monday insisted on the details.

"Was the fillet of beef served with mushroom sauce or horseradish? What type of wine did they have with the boiled salmon? Did the soup *à la reine* have a creamy texture or was it more like a broth?"

When she seemed satisfied she said, "Did you have the oyster course, Hattie?" I was surprised. Of all of the dishes I had described, I wondered why she'd asked me about that.

"Yes," I said. "I'd never had them raw on ice before and had originally passed, but Lieutenant Triggs was persuasive in getting me to try one. He did the same to his wife."

"Did you like it?" Mrs. Monday wondered.

"No, to tell you the truth the texture was a bit slimy."

"Yes, oysters, raw or on the half shell, are an acquired taste in my opinion. I would've served oyster pudding, dressing, or soup for a party of strangers. I think they serve them to impress. Did everyone eat them?" Again, I wondered why she was so curious about the oysters, but I thought back and tried to recall if everyone did eat the oysters.

"No. Sir Arthur didn't have any nor did Mrs. Reynard. I heard Adella say they were her father's favorite, though. Maybe that's why—Oh my goodness," I said, finally figuring out the truth. "That was the poisoned dish! It was the only course that so many people passed on. And those that passed didn't get sick." Mrs. Monday nodded as if she knew all along.

"I think you're right," she said. "I've seen a man die from eating bad shellfish."

"Like Lieutenant Colonel Holbrook," I said. The cook nodded solemnly. "It would explain why Mrs. Triggs and I recovered quickly; we only had a sample of the dish. The men, with the exception of Sir Arthur and General Starrett, consumed a great deal more than we did, with Henry Starrett and Lieutenant Colonel Holbrook each having several helpings. If that's what killed Lieutenant Colonel Holbrook then Henry Starrett is lucky to be alive."

"Yes, he is," Mrs. Monday said.

"Would Mrs. Cassidy have known if the oysters were bad?" I asked.

"Maybe, but only if she knew what to look for. Mrs. Cassidy is a plain cook. I doubt she's served oysters on ice before." I was relieved to hear that. "But the grocer might. Where did she buy them, Killian's?"

"Yes, he hand-delivered the order."

"Thought so. He's known for the best canned goods in town. But I know Oscar; he wouldn't knowingly sell bad oysters. . . ." Mrs. Monday hesitated.

"What is it, Mrs. Monday?"

"Well, I have to be careful what I say, Hattie, but as you know, there's no love lost between Captain Starrett and Enoch Jamison."

"Yes, I've unfortunately been witness to several of their altercations. Why is that?"

"Because Enoch was a copperhead, Hattie. Many, including Henry Starrett, thought he was a traitor to his own country."

"And there were many Peace Democrats who believed as Mr. Jamison did," I said.

"Yes, that's true."

"Regardless of whether copperheads were considered traitors or not," I said, "that was over a quarter of a century ago."

"Not that long in many a mind's eye," she said. "Some wounds from that war are still healing, Hattie Davish, and don't you forget it. War is a terrible thing and for some it never ends."

I knew in part she spoke from personal experience. Her husband, Mr. Clement Monday, who had been in Washburne's Lead Mine Regiment, was killed at Shiloh, leaving her with five children to raise. I'd heard her many times boast that "my Clem didn't even know General Grant here in Galena, but he proudly died for the great man that day." She never remarried.

"Does that apply to Captain Starrett as well?" I asked.

"Oh, didn't you know?" Mrs. Monday said, wiping her hands on her apron. "Those two were the best of friends before the war." Suddenly everything became clear. Like many, the war had irreparably divided them. "Since neither is often in town, this may be the first time their paths have crossed in years. And we all know what happened then."

"No, Mrs. Monday, I have no idea what happened then."

"Well, it was right after the war. As you probably know, this town loves its heroes and we've had more than our share of them, Rawlins, Rowley, Chetlain, to name a few, and of course President Grant. Well, as I said, we love our heroes, so when the men came back we threw them a parade; only the president's second homecoming in '79 was bigger. But not all our boys who came back came back heroes. Enoch Jamison and a few other copperheads returned to their own welcome. Some showered them with praise and held a bonfire in their honor. Others, who felt they should've been tried for treason, harassed them, refused to trade with them, and vilified them. Let's just say that Henry was the most enthusiastic of these and didn't rest until Enoch Jamison and the others were run out of town."

"What would bring them back to Galena now?" I wondered out loud.

"I know Enoch Jamison came to nurse his ailing mother. As to Henry Starrett"—she threw up her hands and laughed—"who knows."

"But I don't understand, Mrs. Monday. What does all of this have to do with Oscar Killian and the oysters?"

"Oscar Killian is friendly with the Jamisons. He married Enoch's cousin, Elizabeth. There's even been rumors that he was once a copperhead himself." The implications swirled in my mind.

"So you think that Mr. Killian sold Mrs. Cassidy bad oysters to spite Captain Starrett, knowing he favored them?"

Mrs. Monday carefully arranged Parker House rolls, shortbread, and cranberry tarts on a plate. "It's possible," she said.

My stomach felt queasy. I wasn't sure if it was due to the close proximity of the food or the idea that the poisoning may've been intentional and possibly unrelated to the burglary after all. I'd never considered the possibility. Could it have been a coincidence? Or was there something more sinister going on?

"I knew a cook once that poisoned a cake as revenge for losing her best assistant because the mistress of the house thought the girl too pretty," Mrs. Monday said. "She only meant to make the family sick. Maybe that's what Oscar did. To get revenge for the captain's treatment of Enoch Jamison."

"Tea ready, Mrs. Monday?" William Finch, the butler, said, poking his head into the kitchen. "He's such a stickler about punctuality."

"Yes, William, all ready." She set the plate of pastries and sandwiches on the platter next to the tea service and handed it to him.

"You said 'only meant to make the family sick,' Mrs. Monday," I said. "What happened with the cook and the jealous mistress?"

"Let's hope I'm wrong and that Oscar Killian has nothing to do with this dreadful business."

"Why?" I asked.

"Because in that case, like poor Mr. Holbrook, the master of the house ate too much and died. Cook was hanged for it!"

"May I help you?" A man in his mid-twenties with a trim little mustache and spectacles sat at a desk.

After Mrs. Monday's revelation, I'd been grateful to be expected elsewhere and excused myself quickly. I'd always found work the best remedy for a restless body or mind. Right now I had a pandemonium of thoughts swirling through the latter. Was Lieutenant Colonel Holbrook's death intentional? Were the burglary and poisoning related or coincidence? Why was I even considering these questions? Ten minutes later, I had descended the Washington Street stairs, which had been cleared of snow, and, resisting the lure of the new hat and cloaks window display at the St. Louis Department Store, crossed Main Street to the Merchants National Bank Building on the opposite corner. I walked up three flights of stairs to W. F. Scheerer's photography studio.

"Yes," I said. "I have an appointment with the photographer."

"For a sitting?" The man looked puzzled. "We don't do sittings this time of day." He pointed to the window. "Bad lighting."

"No, I'm Hattie Davish, Sir Arthur Windom-Greene's secretary. I'm here to look at your photograph collection." Sir Arthur had felt his current collection woefully lacking and had sent me here to add to it.

"Ah, yes, the British gentleman's secretary. Yes, he said you would be here." He looked at the timepiece on the wall. "My, you're prompt."

"Punctuality is one of Sir Arthur's expectations, Mr. Scheerer, is it?" I said.

"No, Mr. Scheerer is visiting relatives for the holidays. I'm his assistant, Willis Myers." The man put down the glass plate he'd been studying, stood up, and retrieved a leather-bound book from the shelf.

"If you'll have a seat," he said, indicating the table near the window. "This is the catalog to the collection." He placed the book on a table in front of me. "I don't know if it'll help you find what your employer is looking for. When you're done, I'll retrieve any specific photos you'd like to see."

I opened the book and was impressed by the meticulous care that had gone into the catalog. Each photograph had a unique number, consisting of a photograph number and the location box number, a subject heading, a date, and a description, all typed up neatly without other marks or errors. The photos were arranged by subject heading. I looked at the list I'd made of Sir Arthur's preferences.

1. All photographs of Appomattox Court House; McLean's house, the village, etc.
2. A photograph of Grant in field clothes
3. A war era photograph of Grant speaking to his men or at a table
4. A photograph of Grant on or near his horse, Cincinnati
5. A photograph of General Ely S. Parker
6. A photograph of General John Rawlins
7. A war era photograph of General Starrett

I flipped the pages to where Appomattox was listed as a subject. Only one photograph was listed: "Front view of McLean's house in Appomattox Court House." The date was June 1865. I wrote down the photograph's number, starting the list I would give to Mr. Myers, and then turned to *GRANT, Ulysses S.* Due to the sheer number of photographs on this subject, they were further classified. I glanced through *Camp Life, Headquarters.* I came across a tintype labeled: *City Point, Virginia. Lieutenant Colonel Ely S. Parker, Gen. John A. Rawlins, Chief of Staff and others at Grant's Headquarters* that I knew Sir Arthur would want, wrote down the photograph's number, and continued to *Pets and Animals.*

I had worked my way through my list and most of the catalog when I turned to *STARRETT, Cornelius A.* I was surprised to see right below it *STARRETT, Henry R.* They were all entries for photographs of Captain Starrett on board or near steamboats: "Capt. Henry Starrett, in pilothouse of the *Harold Orson,*" "View from CB&N Depot, Galena, Steamer *Adella* foreground," "Captain, pilot, and wheelman posed on deck of *K. G. Homer* river steamer." The last entry had "Captain H. R. Starrett, in uniform, *Lavinia,* 1861–1865?" No location was listed. I was intrigued. A picture of young Henry Starrett in his military uniform, on a steamship named for his mother, would be a nice change from the image I had of him as Santa Claus. I added this last photo's number to my list. Curious, I flipped back through the catalog for any entries for Enoch Jamison. There were none.

After returning to the entries for General Starrett and picking out a portrait done three years into the war, I gave my list to Mr. Myers.

"This will take me a few minutes. You aren't missing your dinner, are you?"

I assured him I wasn't missing anything. When he finally returned, I scanned the photos I'd selected and knew Sir Arthur would be pleased. Mr. Myers and I arranged to have the copies made, which I would return for when ready. He charged it to Sir Arthur. While Mr. Myers wrote out a receipt, I gave the photo of Henry Starrett on his steamboat a closer examination, even borrowing Mr. Myers's hand lens. Henry Starrett was standing on a small dock, stacked with cargo crates marked: *U.S. Army Medical Department*. He appeared to be directing the loading or unloading of the cargo. Only part of the steamship could be seen behind him. Although an innocuous scene lay before me, I couldn't shake the nagging sense that I was missing something.

"Good likeness, don't you think?" Willis Myers said. It was. The identity of the young soldier was obvious. "And I like the subject matter. So much of the photographs from the war were about the battle sites, the camps, and the dead. I find it heroic for a man to use his brains and brawn instead of his guns to win the war. Don't you?"

"I definitely appreciate the unusual pose. And delivering medical supplies must've been a vital task."

Mr. Myers nodded.

"I'll say. Hope your boss didn't want a copy of this one, though; there's no negative."

"Oh, no. It piqued my curiosity, that's all. I noticed that the book held little information about it. Do you know anything more?"

"No, what's in the catalog is all I know. It's always bothered me, but I have no idea where this was taken or by whom. It's my job to ensure the catalog is complete and accurate, but that isn't always possible."

A man after my own heart, I thought.

"A portion of the collection came from John Pooley," the photographer said, "when Mr. Scheerer bought the business, with some valuable tintypes taken by Edward Peirce during the war. And after the war, no one wanted these images, so the glass plates were sold and used to build greenhouses. So that means I don't have all the information about them, or the negative plates."

For some reason the photo drew me in. Maybe it was the

mystery surrounding it, where was it taken, when was it taken, who was the photographer, what was Henry Starrett doing at that exact moment? Or was it the inexplicable expression on Henry Starrett's face? Surprise, annoyance, fear?

"Captain Starrett piloted a hospital ship at some point during the war," I said, pointing to the label on the crates. "Maybe that's what this is?"

"Maybe." The photographer sounded skeptical. "But if so, the *Lavinia* isn't marked as one in any way. That's pretty unusual."

"Did you know that Henry Starrett is in town visiting his daughter and grandchildren?" I said.

"No, I didn't know."

"Yes. You could show him this and solve the mystery behind it."

Mr. Myers's eyes lit up. "That would be great!" Then he frowned and looked about the studio. "It would be, but without some help from Santa's elves I'll be up to my ears in work all day straight through New Year's. And it's too late to call at night."

"What if *I* asked him?" The photographer's assistant looked dubious. "I was at a dinner party at the Starrett/Reynard house last night. I'm certain to see Captain Starrett again in the next few days."

"Would you?" The spark reappeared in his eyes. I shared his enthusiasm. "The catalog would be one step closer to perfection." He rummaged through a desk drawer and pulled out an envelope. "Here." He put the picture carefully into the envelope and handed to me. "I'll loan you the tintype until you get a chance to show it to him." I was thrilled. I'd be able to look at it more closely at my leisure as well as use it to trigger Captain Starrett's memory.

"I'll take great care of it," I said.

What was I thinking?

The moment I left Mr. Myers's I began to regret taking the photograph. What had made me so careless? I had committed myself to an inquiry into Captain Starrett's past, against the expressed wishes of my employer. Had indulging my curiosity become a dangerous habit? What would Sir Arthur say if he knew? Would my position be in jeopardy?

"Excuse me, sir!" I said. With the envelope tucked under my arm, I had stepped out onto Main Street. I had hesitated before turning back, having moments ago resolved to return the photograph, when a man, not minding where he was going, crashed into me. The photograph slipped from my grip, but Frederick Reynard caught it before it touched the snow piled up next to the sidewalk. "Mr. Reynard!"

"Oh, no! Miss Davish, what are you doing here?" On the bustling street, it seemed an odd question to ask.

"Visiting Scheerer's photography studio at Sir Arthur's request." I pointed to the envelope in his hand.

"Oh." He handed me back the envelope. He seemed distracted, shoving his hands in his pockets and looking about him furtively. The ever present amaryllis was missing from his lapel and an irregularly shaped bulge protruded from inside his coat. What was he hiding?

"Mrs. Baines told me you were still recuperating, sir," I said, slipping the envelope into my handbag for safekeeping. "I'm glad to see you are up and about."

"No, no, Miss Davish, I'm not up and about." He rubbed his forehead in distress. Suddenly he grabbed my arm and pulled me out of the street into a doorway. The sign above the door said: BURRICHTER BROS, WHISKIES. He leaned in close, his breath smelling of mint. "Can I trust you?"

"Sir? I don't understand."

"Sir Arthur told the general that he prizes your discretion. Can I too rely on your discretion?"

"Regarding what?" I said. "I don't know anything."

"Good, that's right, you never saw me, and you don't know anything."

"But Mr. Reynard—"

"Please, I implore you. Tell no one." He squeezed my arm and then let go.

He looked about him one more time and before I could say another word darted south down the street, weaving his way through the shoppers. A woman in a plain black lace bonnet, laden with bags on her arms, led a throng of children, all under the age of eight, down the middle of the sidewalk. Frederick nearly tripped as he collided with two of the smaller children, who refused to release each other's hands. He stumbled through the crowd until the bend in the road hid him and the children from view. *What was that all about?* I wondered. And what did I seemingly agree not to tell?

What is going on?

A gust of cold wind rushed between the buildings and I held on to my hat. I began shivering, despite my warm cloak. Abruptly my curiosity waned. Did I really want to know? Forgetting about returning the photograph, I clutched my handbag tightly and headed in the opposite direction.

CHAPTER 16

Except for the STAPLE AND FANCY GROCERIES painted on the window in bold white letters, the building looked like any other redbrick storefront. But the sign gave me pause and I glanced above the door for the proprietor's name: KILLIAN & SONS. In attempting to distance myself from Frederick Reynard, I had inadvertently walked by Oscar Killian's grocery store. The temptation to get a glimpse of the man was too great. I pushed the door and entered.

"Good evening, miss," the man behind the counter called. I froze in the doorway, the shopkeeper's bell still ringing in my ears. It was the same man who had left the G.A.R. meeting in anger and who met Enoch Jamison on the street during the Christmas puppet display. Could this be Lieutenant Colonel Holbrook's killer? My nerves left me and I started to retreat back through the door.

"Can I help you?" the man said, walking around the counter and approaching me.

"Are you Mr. Killian?" I said hesitantly, needing to confirm my suspicion.

"Yeah, what can I do for you?" Oscar Killian wore a spotless white apron around his middle. He rested his coarse, leathered hands on his hips, the *O.C.K.* tattooed on his hand appearing upside.

"I wondered if you carried Brazil nuts?" I said. Which was true but not the reason I'd come.

Oscar Killian smiled as he retrieved a burlap bag, stamped in red block letters: PRODUCTO DEL PERÚ, from the shelf behind the counter. "You're making cornucopias for the Christmas tree, huh?"

"Yes, how did you know?" He laughed, and if I hadn't seen him angry I would've thought him incapable of killing anyone, intentionally or not.

"Ah, a good grocer can read minds," he said, tapping his forehead. "It's good business to know what my customers are going to want and when. How much do you want?" I told him, and he scooped the nuts into a brown paper bag and wrapped it up in string. Biding my time, I asked for walnuts as well.

"Now if there's nothing else I can do for you, miss? . . . ," he said, handing me the bags of nuts. I hesitated, summoning the courage to answer.

"Actually, yes, there is."

"Yeah?"

"Are you aware of the death of Lieutenant Colonel Issac Holbrook?" The grocer's smile disappeared.

"Yeah."

"Were you also aware that many others at the same dinner party, including Captain Henry Starrett, were made violently ill by some type of poison?" I paused to see his reaction. Mr. Killian immediately dropped his attention to the glass case between us, straightening and restraightening jars of mincemeat and cranberry sauce. "The police suspect food poisoning as the cause of Lieutenant Colonel Holbrook's death."

"That's terrible. I didn't know."

"You knew Lieutenant Colonel Holbrook. Can you imagine why anyone would deliberately do such a thing?"

The grocer hesitated, wiped his bulging forearm across his head, and looked slightly over my head. "Deliberately? Why do you say that? I was with him at Stones River. You get to know the nature of a man in battle. The lieutenant colonel was a good man. Who would want to harm him?"

"So you think it could've been an accident?"

"Yeah, of course. What else could it be? Something was left out to spoil or wasn't cooked properly."

"In your opinion as a grocer, could the cook have bought something already spoiled?" Oscar Killian picked up a feather duster and, turning his back to me, began dusting spotless cans on the shelf against the wall: Borden's condensed milk, Anna Case's first-quality butter beans, Shakers' string beans, Preston's sugar of lemons, Cooke's favorite tomato, Getz Bros. & Co.'s celebrated crystal wave cove oysters.

"It's possible. But not likely."

"Why?" I asked. He turned around as the bell over the door chimed and another customer came in. He forced a smile and nodded to the woman, but his jaw was clenched and eyes were wide with fear.

"Selling spoiled food is bad for business, miss," he whispered. "Very bad for business."

"Pardon me," the man said brusquely as he pushed his way past me into Oscar Killian's store. He knocked into my shoulder, sending me stumbling against the glass storefront.

For goodness' sake, I thought. Was it me or had everyone else forgotten their manners? This was the second time in less than an hour a man nearly knocked me over as I stepped out of a building on Main Street. What happened to peace and goodwill toward others? Wasn't that what Christmas was supposed to be? I was about to voice my objection when the door closed behind him. I pressed my face to the glass to see who the rude man was. It was Enoch Jamison. I was stunned. He was haggard, with dark circles under his eyes, unkempt hair, and stubble growing from his chin. His tie was loose about his neck. He looked like he hadn't slept since I'd seen him yesterday. And he looked desperate. He approached Oscar Killian, gesticulating with a violent swing of his arms. I couldn't catch every word that they were saying, but Enoch Jamison's shouts could be heard in the street. Abruptly they turned their heads and both men's eyes were upon me.

Oh, no, I thought, blanching, less from being caught staring than from the look in Enoch Jamison's eyes. I took a step back. Oscar Killian pointed at me and said something I couldn't hear. Enoch Jamison nodded and started walking toward the door, never taking his eyes from my face. I didn't wait this time to confront him.

"Hey, you! Come back! I want to talk to you!" Enoch Jamison yelled at my back as I ran as fast as I could down the crowded sidewalk.

It was dinnertime at the DeSoto House, the landmark hotel, built in 1855, that occupied half of the block at the corner of Main and Green Streets. Once five stories tall, it was as famous for its upper two stories' having been removed as it was for attracting the political notable: Abraham Lincoln gave a speech from the second-story veranda, Stephen Douglas stayed here prior to the Freeport debate with Lincoln in 1858, and Ulysses S. Grant used the hotel as his presidential campaign headquarters. Slipping in the ladies entrance, I'd hoped to find a quiet spot to catch my breath and compose myself before returning to Sir Arthur's, but the second-floor ladies parlor, and the dining rooms and bar were full of people eating, smoking, drinking, laughing. Someone down the hall was playing the harmonica. The best I could do was an unoccupied settee under the winding staircase in the lobby. I jumped the first time someone stomped on the steps above me.

How foolish, I thought, willing my heart to slow down and my hands to stop shaking when everywhere around me was gaiety and music. Why had I run away? Did I think Mr. Jamison was going to hurt me? Was I overreacting? He probably wanted to ask me some questions, to clarify what I'd told Oscar Killian. Then why did I feel safer hiding here under the shadow of the staircase when I should have gone straight back to Sir Arthur's? Was I becoming irrational and jumpy? This wouldn't do. Sir Arthur would never approve of such skittish behavior if he knew. I straightened my hat and my back and pulled my small notebook out of my handbag. I made a list.

FACTS:

1. Oscar Killian sold the Reynards oysters, among other fancy foods.
2. Only those guests who ate the oyster dish got ill.
3. Lieutenant Colonel Holbrook and Captain Starrett partook of the dish more than anyone else.
4. Captain Starrett became extremely ill, Lieutenant Colonel Holbrook died.
5. Oysters were served specifically because they were one of Captain Starrett's favorite dishes.
6. Oscar Killian denies selling any spoiled food.
7. Oscar Killian professes his fondness for Lieutenant Colonel Holbrook.
8. Enoch Jamison and Oscar Killian know each other on friendly, familiar terms.
9. Enoch Jamison and Captain Starrett are on the worst of terms.
10. Enoch Jamison looked haggard and desperate.

I studied the list, reading it twice without much success. My breathing had slowed, but my thoughts were still a jumble, my concentration almost nonexistent. I closed my eyes for a moment, focusing my mind by listening to the mingling of voices, clinking silverware, and harmonica, but couldn't pause for long. I read the list again. A pattern emerged from the facts, giving rise to more questions. I flipped to a blank page and dashed them off.

1. Were the oysters spoiled or was poison administered to them?
2. If they were spoiled, did Oscar Killian know?
3. If Oscar Killian knew, did he mean Lieutenant Colonel Holbrook harm? Or was that, like in Mrs. Monday's tale, an unintended consequence?
4. What role did Enoch Jamison play?
5. Was Lieutenant Colonel Holbrook the intended victim or was it Captain Starrett?
6. Could either Oscar Killian or Enoch Jamison have administered poison to the oysters beforehand?
7. How does the poisoning relate to the burglary? Was Oscar Killian the burglar too?
8. What was Horace Mott doing in Mrs. Cassidy's kitchen?
9. Why am I not simply letting the police figure all this out?

There! I thought, my mind at ease. *I'm done with this.*

With that I tossed pencil and notebook into my bag. I had no business thinking about or meddling in this sordid affair. If Oscar Killian or anyone, for that matter, purposely poisoned the oysters, that was a concern for the police. I had a job to do. Besides, the scents filling the lobby: the perfume, the wood smoke, the tobacco smoke, and the aromas from the dining room, were starting to churn my stomach.

"Miss Davish?" It was Officer Corbett. He was grinning. "Hello. Imagine meeting you here."

He dropped the harmonica he was holding into his breast pocket and thrust out his hand to me. It was awkward. I held my handbag and the packets of Brazil nuts and walnuts I'd bought at Killian's store in my lap. Before I could rearrange my things and take Officer Corbett's offered hand, he shuffled his feet and shoved both hands into the pockets of his jacket. His smile disappeared.

"What a coincidence, Mr. Corbett," I said, rising on my own accord. "I was thinking about you a moment ago." Streaks of crimson materialized on the man's cheeks. "Or should I say about the police's investigation into the death of Lieutenant Colonel Holbrook," I said quickly, hoping to dispel any misconception.

"Oh. What about it?"

"Could it be possible that Captain Starrett and not Lieutenant Colonel Holbrook was the intended victim?" *Didn't I just tell myself this was none of my affair?* I thought. But it was too late now; I couldn't retract my question. What would it hurt to learn the answer?

"Huh, you really were considering the case," he said, sounding surprised. He motioned to the settee and I sat down again. Without his usual hesitation, he joined me. "That's a particularly thoughtful question, Miss Davish. I too have wondered if Lieutenant Colonel Holbrook's death was unintended. Regardless of the reason behind the poisoning, a distraction to the burglary, an intentional poisoning, or an accident due to spoiled food, Lieutenant Colonel Holbrook was an unfortunate victim. But Captain Starrett is a different story. That man has enemies. I could list several possible suspects who would be happy to see Henry Starrett dead."

"Are Oscar Killian and Enoch Jamison on your list?"

The policeman chuckled. "Are you a secretary or a police detective, Miss Davish? I think we need to compare notes." I blushed. I was equally embarrassed by being caught stepping beyond my obvious duties to Sir Arthur and relieved that this policeman was congenial to the idea. It was a sharp contrast to my previous experience with police.

I pulled my notebook from my handbag and told him everything I knew or suspected.

"I'm impressed, Miss Davish. Truly," Mr. Corbett said when I'd finished. "This is definitely worth pursuing. Would you care to accompany me to Mr. Killian's store? I think he has a few questions to answer."

I hesitated only a moment, long enough to consider the work I was expected to complete for Sir Arthur by the end of the day. I'd ordered his photographs but still had manuscript pages from yesterday to type. If I skipped supper, as I had already fully intended to do on account of my still-churning stomach, and I went straight to my typewriter the moment I returned from Oscar Killian's store, I could be done by the time Sir Arthur retired for the evening.

"Yes, I would," I said, hoping I wouldn't regret it later.

When Officer Corbett and I arrived a few minutes later at Oscar Killian's grocery, it was closed and dark. Someone had posted a scribbled, handwritten sign on the door: *Gone for the holidays.* Mr. Corbett had inquired after Oscar Killian in the adjacent businesses, but no one knew anything more.

"Does this mean he's guilty?" I asked, astonished at the turn of events.

"Looks awfully suspicious to me," the policeman said. "Christmas is still days away. He must've had a compelling reason to close his store at this time of the year. I'll inquire at his home, but I'm guessing he'll have left town as soon as possible."

"I'm afraid it's my fault," I said. "Maybe I should stick to dictation and typing."

"Miss Davish, why do you say that?"

"I spoke to Mr. Killian not even an hour ago and implied he might be culpable if he knowingly sold spoiled oysters."

"It's not your fault, Miss Davish." The policeman gently touched my shoulder, then pulled his hand away quickly. "Forgive me," he muttered, then looked back at the darkened storefront of Killian & Sons. I was taken aback by his gesture. I looked about me to see if anyone was watching us.

What am I doing? I wondered.

I should be at my typewriter and not standing on the street, alone with a strange man, even a policeman, at this time of night. What would Sir Arthur think if he or someone he knew drove by at this instant? And because of me, a possible killer had fled town and justice. Had my curiosity led me to trouble again? I couldn't wait a moment longer to find out.

". . . rest assured, we'll track him down and—" Officer Corbett was speaking. I had missed some of what he said.

"I'm sorry," I said, interrupting the policeman and abruptly walking away. "I must get back."

"Of c-c-ourse," he stammered. "Let me accompany you."

"No, thank you. I'll be fine." A pang of guilt shot through me when I saw the hurt on the policeman's face my rudeness had caused. I softened my tone and smiled. "Besides, you still have Enoch Jamison to question." He chuckled.

"You are determined," he said, shaking his head and chuckling. "An inspiration, really. I'll say good night then." He tipped his hat and retrieved his harmonica from his pocket.

"Good night," I said as we went our separate ways. The soft strains of his playing echoed between the buildings, fading slowly with the growing distance between us.

CHAPTER 17

Due to my foray into police business last night, I had barely finished typing the manuscript pages when Sir Arthur retired. My mind was a whirl when I'd found that Oscar Killian had inexplicably closed his store less than an hour after I'd spoken to him. Was I right? Was he involved in the poisoning and death of Lieutenant Colonel Holbrook? Killian's behavior certainly led me to believe so. But a few hours of typing up passages about the role of General Ely S. Parker at Appomattox was just what I'd needed to calm my mind. This was my purpose. This was why I was here. With a renewed focus on my work, I almost slept through the night.

But last night's peace vanished as I walked along Main Street this morning. As I peered into storefronts, I could see shopkeeper after shopkeeper restocking shelves, sweeping floors, washing windows, lighting stoves, all in preparation for the start of the business day. But Killian & Sons was dark and empty. I peered through the window when I passed, hoping to see movement inside. All was still. This was one store that wouldn't open today despite Christmas being only a few days away. What if I'd been wrong? Could a false accusation cause as much trouble as a true one? My heart sank. Was I to blame for the fear that drove this man away? I dragged my feet slowly away. I walked block after block without noticing where I was going. When I finally looked up, I was near the Spring Street Bridge, its steel trusses covered with ice, sparkling. I waited while a road wagon struggled to cross from the other side of the river. The two horses pulling snorted in the cold. The wooden planks of the bridge were snow covered and slippery for the wagon's metal wheels. It didn't fare much better as it turned onto the slushy, muddy surface of Main Street.

Why didn't they use a sleigh? I wondered as I cautiously stepped onto the bridge.

Although it was early, two sleighs, both heading toward Main Street, had passed me before I was halfway across the bridge. To cross the river, I usually used the Green Street Bridge, but I should've realized that this one would be busy, even at this hour of the morning; Spring Street Bridge was the main bridge in and out of town. But the width of the bridge easily accommodated both pedestrians and sleighs, so I had no reason to be concerned when a sleigh approached the bridge from Main Street and started to cross. But this one was different. The horses were galloping. I turned to see the sleigh slide back and forth as the horses slipped and temporarily lost their footing. I immediately tried to get out of the way, but instead of driving on the side opposite to me, the driver headed straight for me. I ran, slipping on the icy boards and finally falling. As I struggled to gain my footing, ripping my hem, I could see the breath of the horses as they ran toward me. I scrambled to the iron railing and flung myself against it, doubled over at the waist. My hat flew off my head. The horses barely missed me as they galloped past.

My hat! I clutched the air in vain and then cried out as a sharp pain shot through my middle. I gasped for breath and watched helplessly as my felt hat, the navy blue velvet ribbon flapping in the wind, floated down onto the icy river. Tears streamed down my face. I'd purchased the hat only days before as an early Christmas present to myself. As I clung to the railing, looking down at the river below, anger welled inside me. *Who did this? I want to know. And why?* They owed me more than a new hat. I turned to see the driver as he passed, only a few feet away.

It was Enoch Jamison! His head was bare and his face was flush from the wind. His eyes were wide as he stared at me. He pulled the reins hard to the right, pulling his horses away from me. An instant later he was gone, careening off the bridge and disappearing up the hill. *What just happened?* I wondered. Had he meant to scare me? Had he meant to knock me off the bridge? He certainly seemed angry yesterday at Killian's store when he thought I knew something. Or had he lost control of his horses at the moment I'd happened to be on the bridge? I was starting to believe that a coincidence like that didn't exist.

I stood up slowly. I glanced down once more at my hat, lying on the thin ice below the bridge, only to see it picked up by the wind and blown farther downstream. I wrapped my arms around my ribs, the pain making it difficult to breathe. My gloves and dress were dirty and covered in slush and my hat was gone. Yet again I was going to have to make my way back to Sir Arthur's disheveled, dirty, and bruised. At least this time it was Enoch Jamison who was the one with some explaining to do.

"I said it was nothing," Mrs. Baines was saying to her husband and Lieutenant Triggs, both of whom were feeling much better, in tow. The two men had spent last night at the Reynards' home and were finally returning to Sir Arthur's. They both looked slightly pale but much better. Then she noticed me.

"What did you do now?" Mrs. Baines said, grimacing. She

gestured toward my soiled dress with a flip of her hand. I'd returned from my near fall off the bridge, and instead of making
it up the stairs before anyone saw me like this I'd been met in
the hall by the returning guests.

Mrs. Baines shook her head and sighed. "Why Sir Arthur
keeps you in his employ is beyond me. Here, and don't get it
wet." Instead of handing William her cloak, Mrs. Baines
handed it to me. She turned her attention back to her husband. "John, the man was delirious. He didn't know what he
was doing."

I handed the cloak to William, who shook his head slightly
in disapproval. He didn't like Mrs. Baines confusing our per-
spective roles in Sir Arthur's employ any more than I did.

"But the man was astonishingly crude to you, darling,"
John Baines said. "Considering you nursed him back to
health."

"I told you, John. It means nothing, so there's nothing
more to talk about," Rachel Baines said.

"Nothing? Nothing? At one point in time, I could demand
satisfaction over something like this!" her husband exclaimed
as his eye began to twitch.

"They're talking about Henry Starrett," Lieutenant Triggs
whispered to me behind his hand. "Thanks, but I've got this,
Finch," he said to William as the butler tried to take the over-
night bag Mrs. Triggs had sent over to her husband last night.

The exchange between the arguing couple became more
heated.

"That's enough, John! I'm the wronged party here and I
say leave it alone." Mrs. Baines stomped into the parlor.

"I will not!" her husband shouted, following after her.

"Seems Henry Starrett has recovered enough to make
lewd advances toward Mrs. Baines," Morgan Triggs explained.
"Scoundrel touched her inappropriately, though as a gentle-

man I won't say where, and he tried to kiss her . . . twice. Lucky John arrived when he did."

"My," I said, chuckling weakly, trying to hide my astonishment and my pain, "Captain Starrett must be recovering."

"And as you can see," Morgan Triggs said, "John Baines is none too happy about it."

"I'm glad to see you're feeling better, Lieutenant," I said.

"Me too," he said, smiling. "I have to admit I felt so miserable I thought it was the war and I was back in Cahaba again. Is my wife around?" he said, looking through the parlor's open door.

"I wouldn't know. I arrived only a moment ago myself." He nodded, his eyes taking in my soiled attire, and then leaned in to conspire again.

"By the way, why do you look like you've been dragged behind a sleigh through the slush and the snow?" I knew I looked unpresentable, but did I look that bad? No wonder Mrs. Baines had treated me with such disdain. "Who needed rescuing today?" He chuckled.

"It's a long story," I said, not appreciating his jest. "Now if you'll excuse me, I must change."

After changing my clothes, gratefully being able to loosen my corset, and having a quick cup of coffee with Mrs. Monday, I spent the remainder of the morning doing what I'd intended to do before the incident at the bridge, go Christmas shopping. Sir Arthur had handed me a list yesterday that his wife, Philippa, had sent detailing Christmas presents he was to give on her behalf to the staff and Sir Arthur's houseguests. Tactfully, my name wasn't on the list.

1. Gentlemen: monographed silver tobacco box
2. Ladies: a silver, embossed photograph frame

3. Cook: a set of "ornamental but useful" ready-made
   aprons
4. Maid: a bolt of new fabric
5. Butler: Money
6. Coachman: Money

Upon my return from shopping, loaded with packages and
barely able to stand up straight from the pain in my ribs, I had
trouble opening the back door. I fumbled with the knob for
the second time and the top package, an assortment of hair
ribbons I'd purchased to give to Ida for all the early morning
fires she had lit for me, had slipped from my arms into the
snow when the door opened from the inside.

"Walter!"

In my surprise, I nearly dropped everything else. Dr. Walter
Grice, his eyes sparkling in the glow of the kitchen fire, stood
on the kitchen threshold, holding the door open. In a finely
pressed tailored wool suit and silk four-in-hand tie, he was the
perfect gentleman.

What is he doing here?

My first impulse was to assume the worst. "What's happened?" I said. "What's wrong?"

"From the look of you, absolutely nothing," he said, grinning from ear to ear. He stooped over, retrieved the present
from the snow, and took several other packages from my arms.
I was instantly flooded with emotions: astonishment, joy, relief?
He held the door open and we both came into the welcoming
warmth of the kitchen.

"Then why?" I said, not needing the answer. He was here.
What else mattered?

"Because you were dangerously ill. Or so I was made to
believe." It wasn't the answer I expected or wanted to hear. I
wished I hadn't asked. "Sir Arthur telegraphed Miss Lizzie,

who in turn telegraphed me. I took the first train out of St. Louis."

"You've been on a train for almost two days? You must be exhausted. And as you can see, I'm fine." I didn't mention my ribs.

"I'm relieved to find you well."

"But your long journey was all for nothing," I said.

Walter took my hand and kissed it. "No, not for nothing."

"Well, who's this in my kitchen?" Mrs. Monday said, kindly announcing her arrival. I instinctually pulled my hand away and took a step back. She carried a tray of colorful flower corsages.

"Hello," Walter said, a grin still on his face.

"Mrs. Monday, this is Dr. Walter Grice, my . . ." I hesitated, not knowing what to call him.

"I'm Miss Davish's friend from Arkansas," Walter said. "Please to meet you, Mrs. Monday."

"Pleased to meet you, Dr. Grice. Any friend of Hattie's is certainly welcome anytime in my kitchen."

"Thank you," Walter said.

"In town for the entertainment?" Mrs. Monday asked. Walter looked at me inquiringly. I shrugged. I had no idea what she was talking about.

"What entertainment?" I asked.

"Why, the annual Christmas entertainment at Turner Hall, of course," Mrs. Monday said. "It's one of the biggest events of the year. Granted Reverend Hart insists on giving his annual dramatic reading, but if you plan it right you can skip that and arrive in time for the children's play. Then the high school choir performs their annual concert of Christmas hymns and carols. And supper will be good this year since Bertha Williams and I planned the menu. You'll love the currant and cinnamon tea cakes, Hattie." Walter smirked at me. He knew of my penchant for cake. "And don't forget the dancing." Mrs. Monday closed her eyes and swayed back and forth for a moment. "Everyone's welcome."

"Sounds very . . . entertaining," Walter said with a smirk.

"That's why it's called an 'entertainment,' " Mrs. Monday said, not realizing Walter was trying to jest.

"When is it?" I asked.

"It's tonight."

Tonight? I thought. I wasn't up to another social engagement. I touched my aching ribs. And I'd never be able to dance. How would I explain it? Walter eyed me suspiciously.

"Tonight? I'd be delighted," Walter said, "provided Miss Davish will be there."

"Of course, she'll be there," Mrs. Monday said. "The whole town will be there." I unconsciously touched my ribs again.

"You are all right, aren't you, Miss Davish?" Walter said. I smiled, trying to deflect his professional attention from me. Mrs. Monday instead did it for me.

"By the way, Mr. Reynard sent these over," Mrs. Monday said as she placed the corsages in a bowl of water. "He provided these fancy ones for you, Mrs. Baines, and Mrs. Triggs to wear tonight. The simple white rose boutonnieres are for the gentlemen." It was obvious by the arrangement and fragrance that the flowers had come fresh from Frederick Reynard's greenhouse.

"For me too?" I said, surprised to be included due not only to my social status but also for the strange way he'd behaved toward me yesterday. "They're beautiful." Accented by ivy, rosebuds, and tiny yellow celandine flowers, each had a different flower as its centerpiece: a white lily for Mrs. Triggs, magenta orchids for Mrs. Baines, and a pink camellia for me.

"Like I said, it's quite the event," Mrs. Monday said.

"But isn't Lieutenant Triggs allergic to flowers?" I asked.

We had strict instructions to not put any Christmas bouquets in the Triggses' room.

"That's right. I guess you're in luck, Dr. Grice," Mrs. Monday said, handing Walter the extra boutonniere.

"Why, thank you. Who's Mr. Reynard?" Walter asked, pinning it to his jacket.

"The grandson-in-law of one of Sir Arthur's research subjects," I explained.

"More like the father of the little girl whose life Hattie saved," Mrs. Monday said. Walter looked at me and raised his eyebrows in question.

"It's a long story," I said.

"Well, I hope to hear it soon," Walter said, then excused himself to Mrs. Monday, as he hadn't unpacked before coming to see me. He was staying at the DeSoto House Hotel.

"Hattie," Walter said, in earnest as we reached the front door, "may I ask a favor?"

"Of course," I said, mindful that he had left his mother for the holidays and ridden eighteen hours on the train to see after my well-being. I trembled at his voice, imagining what he would say, what he would ask of me. I trembled too knowing I would grant him almost anything. "What is it? What can I do?"

"It's obvious your dance card will fill up quickly," Walter said. "Will you promise to save a dance for me tonight?"

"Walter Grice, you may have every dance you'd like," I said, beaming and forgetting all about my bruised ribs.

CHAPTER 18

It was like a dream. I was dressed in my evening gown (twice in one week!) and in Walter's arms, dancing, surrounded by hundreds of tiny points of light. The scent of cinnamon and pine wafted through the air. I couldn't have imagined it being more perfect. When Lieutenant Triggs asked for a dance, I was delighted but cautious. When Sir Arthur asked for a dance, I was both flustered and flattered. But in Walter's arms, I floated and hadn't a care in the world. Even the pain was bearable. Knowing I was in no shape to dance, I'd broken down and sought the doctor's medical advice, admitting to Walter that my ribs hurt. With few questions and surprisingly little teasing, Walter listened to my explanation, then gave me something from his bag. It had been worth it. I'd never been happier.

Then I saw him, Horace Mott. He glanced around looking for someone and was grinning from ear to ear. He caught my eye and bowed slightly. A shiver went down my back. What was he doing here? Why did he seem to appear at every social event? Of course he was probably here for the same reason we all were. It was Christmastime and this was an event for all of Galena.

But not everyone in Galena was in attendance.

I wish he'd stayed away like Oscar Killian and Enoch Jamison had, I thought, and immediately felt a pang of guilt wishing strangers ill at Christmas. *But bad things seem to occur in his wake.*

I missed a step and without Walter's strong arms would have tripped myself.

"What is it, Hattie?" Walter said, following my gaze across the room.

"Do you see that man in the old dusty black suit?"

"The one with the awkward smile, looking down over his spectacles?"

"That's him. He's the one that I overheard arguing with Captain Starrett."

"The one the police suspect to have stolen the general's stocks and bonds?" Walter said. "If so, he has some nerve coming here." I nodded.

"A gun was taken too," I said. The music ended and Walter immediately led me to the other side of the room.

"Wait here, I'll get some punch."

As I waited for Walter, Mott approached Captain Starrett. Henry scowled and pulled the man away from his family, into the cloakroom. They were gone only a few minutes. When they reemerged, Mott immediately headed toward the door and disappeared outside. I breathed a sigh of relief. Captain Starrett swaggered back into the main hall, slapping several men on the back as he passed. He was beaming. When he reached his family, he surprised Adella by lifting her off her feet and swinging her around in the air. Adella laughed like a little girl. What could Mott have possibly done or said that would produce such an extreme turnaround in Henry Starrett's behavior? He had been brooding since the moment he'd arrived. I heard him have a sharp word with John Baines over his advances toward Mrs. Baines, and I'd heard him bark at Ned when the boy wanted to join the children's play. I'd assumed that Henry was still not feeling well. But when I had inquired after his health, Adella Reynard had assured me her father was feeling much better. She was right; he was swinging his grandchildren around like whirligigs in the air and laughing so boisterously I could hear him across the room, despite the band playing "Sellenger's Round."

"What's going on over there?" Walter asked as he handed me a glass of punch.

"Captain Henry Starrett's mood has improved. Good news, maybe?" I said. I told Walter what he had missed. "If you'd like to meet him, this may be a good time." We approached Sir Arthur, talking to Lieutenant Triggs and his wife, and asked him if he'd mind introducing Walter to the Starretts and Reynards. Sir Arthur was kind enough to oblige.

"Dr. Grice, eh?" Henry Starrett said, the smell of whiskey on his breath. "Where were you when someone tried to poison me?" He waved his pointed finger at Walter, laughing. No one else was amused.

"Father!" Adella said. "We still don't know if it was intentional."

"Then why was I the sickest of everyone? I noticed this harebrained secretary didn't get sick. Unlike you and me, eh, Fred." Captain Starrett laughed and slapped Frederick Reynard on the back.

Both Sir Arthur and Walter took a step forward while Frederick Reynard brushed the shoulder of his jacket where his father-in-law had touched it.

"Henry, a man died," Frederick said, trying to keep the contempt out of his voice.

"Yeah, but Holbrook was an old man. It was probably his

time anyway." A collective gasp rose from all those around Starrett.

"Have some respect, sir," Sir Arthur said.

"So what about it?" Henry said, lightly punching Walter in the shoulder. "What do you have to say for yourself?"

"I wasn't here, sir," Walter said, trying to be gracious but looking like he was about to take a swing at the man, "because I was in St. Louis at the time. And as to Miss Davish, I am her personal physician and dear friend and I am insulted, sir. I can assure you that she is neither harebrained nor immune to toxins. Like half of your dinner party, she too suffered from the poison, sir." Sir Arthur was nodding seriously.

"Father didn't mean to insult you or Miss Davish, Doctor. And we all truly regret Lieutenant Colonel Holbrook's passing. Father's merely being playful on this festive occasion. Aren't you, Father?"

"Yes, yes, of course. I'll be nice. It's Christmas after all. If we're naughty, Santa Claus won't bring us any presents." He winked at Ned and Gertie, who giggled and clapped their hands in anticipation. He laughed again and it eerily sounded again like "ho, ho, ho." This was one Santa Claus I didn't want coming down my chimney.

"Didn't you have something you wanted to ask Captain Starrett, Miss Davish?" Walter said, trying to change the subject. I had shown Walter the photograph of Henry Starrett on the steamboat *Lavinia*. Walter had suggested I bring it in case the opportunity arose to ask Henry about it.

"What is it? Something about my father for that book of yours? The stories I could tell you about the old man." The captain laughed. "They could straighten your short hairs!"

"Father!" Henry Starrett laughed again and patted Adella's cheek. She grinned, pleased to be the focus of his affection, but I saw it as a condescension.

"No, I was hoping you could tell me more about this." I retrieved the tintype from my handbag and handed it to Henry Starrett. His grin disappeared as he studied the picture.

"Where did you get this?" he asked, his brow knitted in concentration.

"From Mr. Myers, one of the photographer's assistants in town. He didn't know much about it, as it was part of a collection his employer bought from a former photographer. He wondered if you could tell him more about it."

"I have no idea."

"That is you, isn't it, Captain?" I asked.

"Ah, yes, that Adonis is me, but I couldn't tell you the first thing about it." He looked at it again. "Nope, never seen this before and I have no idea who took it or why."

"But it was during the war?" I asked.

"Well, that's obvious but . . . oh, well." He shrugged. "Now if you'll excuse me. I need another drink." He tossed the tintype in my direction and walked away. Several people, including me, scrambled to pick up the picture before it was trampled. Lieutenant Triggs was the first to reach it.

"I wonder what he was doing?" the lieutenant said, studying it for a moment. He handed the photo back to me. "Where do you think it was taken?"

"I don't know. That's what I was hoping to find out," I said.

Sir Arthur finally took it and studied it with the eye of an experienced historian. "If it was during the war, we should be able to find out easily enough, assuming we know what regiment he was in." He handed the tintype back to me, frowning. He fiddled with his sagging boutonniere, trying to unpin it. "Damn thing!" Sir Arthur said under his breath when the pin pricked his finger. He pulled the boutonniere off and tossed it in the wastebasket.

"Sorry, Fred," he said, "nice thought, but the thing keeps

354555

flopping over." Frederick shrugged. "But as I said before, Hattie, Captain Starrett is not of interest to me." It was the closest Sir Arthur came to reprimanding me for disregarding his wishes.

"Nor to anyone, I suspect," Frederick, looking at the photo over my shoulder, said so softly I could barely hear him.

"You should be more careful, Henry," the woman's voice was full of concern. The man laughed heartily and I knew immediately it was Captain Henry Starrett. He was obviously still in a jolly mood.

Turner Hall was packed with townspeople of every sort, and the mingling of overheated bodies, heavily applied perfume, and aromas from the ten-foot buffet table of food had gotten to be too much. I'd left Walter in the company of Sir Arthur and John Baines and stepped outside for a moment of fresh air. Priscilla Triggs, who had been smiling from the moment the children started their play, joined me. With the cause for her melancholy revealed, the tension I usually felt in her presence had evaporated. For the first time, I was pleased to have her company. The air was crisp but cold. I hadn't planned to linger long. As I turned to go back inside, I heard a woman's voice in the dark. I didn't see anyone in front of the building and assumed she must be in the recess around the corner.

"Don't laugh. We're lucky John thinks you were delirious and doesn't suspect anything."

"I was delirious, Rachel." Rachel? Rachel Baines? "Your beauty always did drive me mad. My lips could melt into these hands."

What would John Baines think of this secret rendezvous? Was there something to his suspicions? I didn't want to know more and reached for the door. Priscilla grabbed ahold of my arm and raised her finger to silence my objection. She pointed toward the voices and pulled me along as she moved closer.

What should I do? Offend one of Sir Arthur's guests by neglecting her by leaving or offend the other by staying and eavesdropping on her? I chose to appease Priscilla Triggs and stayed where I was, hugging my arms around myself to keep warm.

"These hands have liver spots and wrinkles now," Rachel said.

"But they still belong to an angel," Henry said, his voice soft and tender. I thought I heard the distinct sound of a kiss.

"Oh, Henry, you always were a charmer and a good liar." But Mrs. Baines had said that she and Captain Starrett had never met before. Had she been lying? All was quiet for a moment or two and then I heard Mrs. Baines sigh softly. "You were always a good lover too," she said.

I blushed, mortified that I was still eavesdropping on a pair of illicit lovers. Yet I could no longer blame Priscilla for my inexcusable behavior. My ears and nose burned from the cold and my feet were getting numb. But I didn't move away. I had to hear the whole conversation.

"I mean it, Rachel. You're as beautiful as the day I met you almost thirty years ago."

"Then why did you leave me?"

"It's complicated."

"No, Henry. It's not. You either loved me or you didn't."

"I've always loved you."

"But you forgot me."

"Never. We lost touch, but I never forgot you. How could I?" Rachel giggled. I didn't want to imagine what Henry had done to elicit that response.

"I thought you were dead," Rachel Baines said.

"Me? No, you should've known I was tougher than that."

"I couldn't believe it when I heard your name."

"I couldn't believe it when you walked in my door."

"But then why not acknowledge me?" Rachel's tone was suddenly sharp.

"What would your husband think? Would I now be able to do this?" A slight moan escaped Rachel Baines's lips. Priscilla put her hand to her mouth to stifle a giggle.

"I think you don't want your precious daughter knowing her father is a liar and a cheat."

"Why do you say it like that?" Henry said. "Adella's a good girl."

I glanced toward the door as the aforementioned woman stepped outside. She saw me and Mrs. Triggs, smiled, and took a few steps toward us. She was opening her mouth to say hello when Rachel Baines spoke.

"Because I figured it out, Henry. Adella was a baby when we met, wasn't she? You were married, weren't you? Why didn't you tell me that you were married?" Her voice rose in anger.

"Because I never loved Sarah. I loved you." Adella looked at me with wide eyes, her mouth still open in a frozen gasp, and then fled back into the building. I hesitated, not knowing whether to follow Adella or not. I wish I had sooner. The next moment was filled with the sound of Henry distinctly kissing Rachel passionately.

"You're a rake, Henry Starrett," I heard Rachel Baines say playfully as I reached toward the doors. "And you're going to pay for it someday."

Adella was running across the room to her husband and children when I followed her back inside. I wanted to apologize for what Adella overheard, irrationally feeling responsible. But when I approached her, she quickly turned her back to me, kneeling down to say something to her daughter, Gertrude. The two of them walked toward the dance floor, hand in hand. As Adella passed, my attempt to say something was thwarted by the shame and embarrassment that flooded across the woman's face as she looked me in the eye. She quickly looked away, her cheeks flush. I wouldn't want to talk about it either, if I were her, so respecting her privacy I started to walk away.

"Miss Davish," someone yelled, "wait!" It was Frederick Reynard. He whispered something to his son, Ned, who raced away to join his mother and sister on the dance floor.

"You won't say anything, will you?" Frederick said.

"Of course not, Mr. Reynard. What Captain Starrett said is between him and his daughter. It's not my place to be involved in it anyway." He knitted his brow and looked at me with confusion in his eyes.

"What are you talking about?"

"The exchange outside," I said. "What Adella overheard her father say to Mrs. Baines." The startled look on Frederick's face made me realize I'd already said more than I should. "I'm sorry. I need to get back to my friends." I turned to go but felt a restraining hand on my arm.

"You have to promise again you won't say anything. . . ." Frederick looked around the room before his eyes settled on his children, in the process of climbing up on their newly returned grandfather's back; Adella stood silently nearby. "Not a word about seeing me the other day." His grip tightened.

"Mr. Reynard, you're hurting me." He looked abashed and immediately let go. I was relieved to see Walter approach. I couldn't tell whether he had seen the exchange.

"Please, Miss Davish, don't give me up," Frederick pleaded under his breath. "I'm relying on your discretion."

"Ah, Miss Davish, I found you," Walter said. "Mr. Reynard." He bowed his head slightly and spoke congenially, but I knew Walter; he was eyeing Frederick with suspicion. Walter had seen the exchange. "They're going to light the town Christmas tree."

When we arrived we had admired the tree and I'd anticipated seeing it lit up but no longer. Between seeing Mr. Mott
again, the intimate exchange between Henry Starrett and
Rachel Baines revealing secrets I hadn't wanted to know, and
Frederick Reynard's alarming insistence that I keep his secret,
the magic and holiday spirit of the night had all but vanished,
leaving me feeling empty, confused, and exhausted. And my
ribs were starting to ache again. I wanted to go.

"Or maybe I should take you home," Walter said, reading
the emotions on my face. I nodded and gratefully took Walter's
arm. We said our quick good-byes, collected our coats, and
stepped outside.

It had begun to snow. We stood at the top of the stairs as a
family clambered into their sleigh on the street below us. The
sleigh's departure was almost silent except for the quiet jingle
of the bells and the snorting of the horses, their breath visible
in the air. Music played mutely inside, but the night was calm
and quiet.

"The morphia is wearing off, isn't it?" Walter asked. I nodded and leaned on him a little more. "Can you walk?"

"Of course," I said, ruing the day I wouldn't be able to
walk, even in pain. Arm in arm, Walter and I slowly made our
way up the Washington Street stairs to Prospect Street. We
strolled in companionable silence until we had almost reached
Sir Arthur's house.

"Is something wrong, Hattie?" Walter said. "Besides the
pain in your ribs, that is."

"No," I said, knowing he wouldn't believe me. We walked
a few more steps and then I stopped. "Oh, Walter, it was so
wonderful, all the candles and the music and dancing with you
and then . . ." His face lit up when I mentioned dancing with
him but quickly clouded over at my retraction.

"Something happened, didn't it? I can tell." I told him

about the exchange I'd overheard between Henry Starrett and Rachel Baines.

"Until that moment, they had pretended not to know one another. And they denied that anything untoward occurred while she was nursing Henry back to health. It's a conversation I wish I'd never heard."

"Strange," Walter said. "Unless of course if they're conducting a love affair right under John's nose."

"It certainly sounded that way. And then Adella came out. . . ." I told him about what Henry Starrett said and how Adella reacted. "She may never want to talk to me again. I think she was ashamed to have me witness it all. I've known secrets before; it's inevitable in my position, but this one . . ." I struggled to put words to the way I felt. "The last few days, what with the food poisoning and the burglary and Enoch Jamison running me down on the bridge . . . and Frederick Reynard's strange behavior. At first he seemed so congenial and friendly. He's been quite generous and kind to me." I pointed to the beautiful corsage on my dress. "But then, everything changed."

"How?"

"He's threatening."

Walter clenched his teeth. "He's threatening you? How dare he." Walter was seething.

"He's not dangerous, Walter, but I wish he'd leave me alone."

"But why? Why would he threaten you? And about what?" he said quizzically, his anger abating. "Isn't this the man whose daughter you saved?"

"Yes, but I think he has a secret and he somehow thinks I know what it is."

"Do you? Do you know his secret?"

"No." Unless he didn't want anyone to know he was on Main Street at the time I saw him. I didn't even know where he'd been or where he was going. "I don't think so. Oh, Walter," I sighed, suddenly on the verge of tears.

Images flashed through my head: of Lieutenant Holbrook's two different-colored eyes, unblinking, as he lay dead beside me, Frederick Reynard's look of desperation as he squeezed my arm too tight, my brand-new hat blowing away down the icy river, the retreating sleigh of Enoch Jamison as I struggled for breath, Henry Starrett, as Santa Claus, laying a hand on Sir Arthur in anger, the blush on Adella Reynard's cheeks as she caught my eye tonight, Gertrude as she emerged gasping from the frozen water. I hugged Walter's arm, putting my cheek on his shoulder, hiding the tears streaming down my face.

"It's Christmastime, Walter. Is there no joy, no peace, no goodwill toward men? Am I naive to want these things?"

"No, Hattie, you're not naive," Walter said sadly. He pulled me closer. "It's what we all want."

CHAPTER 19

Even before Walter bid me good night I was regretting the self-pity I'd momentarily given in to. What was wrong with me? I'd weathered much worse. So what if this wasn't the routine assignment I'd expected from Sir Arthur? I had steady, interesting work to do and I was grateful for it. What if this Christmas wasn't the joyous, festive holiday I'd anticipated? Walter was here, wasn't he? I wouldn't spend Christmas alone. What more could a girl ask for? When I closed my bedroom door behind me and saw my typewriter, I knew. Peace of mind. I sat down and started to type.

1. Who is Mr. Mott? And what does he have to do with Captain Starrett?
2. Did Mott steal the money and gun from the general's library? If not, who did?
3. Was the poisoning deliberate? If so, by whom and why?
4. Were Oscar Killian and Enoch Jamison involved in the poisoning?

5. If not, why did Oscar Killian close his store and leave town?
6. If not, why did Enoch Jamison try to run me down on the bridge?
7. Was Lieutenant Colonel Holbrook's death intentional or accidental?
8. Could Captain Starrett have been the target?
9. Why had Mrs. Baines and Captain Starrett pretended not to know one another?
10. Were they having an affair right under John Baines's nose?
11. What was the real reason Captain Starrett returned to Galena after so much time?
12. Where was the picture of Captain Starrett taken?

A pattern had developed to my questions. Everything seemed to revolve around Captain Henry Starrett. But it was of no consequence what my questions were. I was merely performing an exercise in order to find mental peace. Lieutenant Colonel Holbrook's death, the burglary, the poisoning, these were all matters for the police.

None of this has anything to do with me, I reminded myself as I prepared for bed. My job was to type Sir Arthur's manuscripts, organize his research material, take any dictation, and get his household prepared for Christmas. I pulled the sheet of paper from the typewriter and climbed into bed. I looked at my questions again; the type was blurry as I tried to stay awake. I had organized my thoughts, but the peace I'd sought didn't come.

Maybe I should show this to Officer Corbett, was my last thought before falling asleep.

"Stepping out with your *Verehrer* again, Hattie?"

I jumped at the sound of her voice. Ida had startled me as I tried to quietly open the kitchen door. She was setting more coals on the fire and I hadn't seen her there in the dark.

"My *Verehrer?*" I asked. I didn't know what *Verehrer* meant, but I could guess. "If you mean Dr. Grice, yes. He agreed to meet me in Grant Park."

"But it's still dark, *ja?*"

"It'll be light soon. I don't normally go out when it's this dark, but Walter wants to go up to the top of the hill behind Grant's home and watch the sunrise."

"Ah, *sehr romantische,* how romantic." She batted her eyes at me teasingly. "But cold, *ja?* You will have to hold him close for warmth, *ja?*"

"Oh, Ida," I said, dismissing her teasing with a wave of my hand and heading out into the cold. Despite my heavy wool cloak and fur-lined gloves, I shivered after leaving the warmth of the kitchen.

If I still had my felt hat . . . , I thought, adjusting the inadequate straw one I was wearing. *I'll have to buy a new one, I guess.*

With that happy thought, I rubbed my hands quickly up and down my arms and then set off at a rapid pace; a brisk walk would warm me up quicker than standing in the doorway. I headed to Grant Park but took the long way. I took High Street over to Franklin and down the hill, which was tricky. Patches of ice hid beneath the snow. I had to take small, carefully placed footsteps to avoid slipping. With my tender ribs, if I fell I might not be able to easily get back up. And then what would Walter think? At Main, the sidewalks had been cleared, with the snow piled in the middle of the road. Mrs. Monday recalled winters when the snow piles were so high, it was difficult to cross the street and impossible to travel by sleigh at all. Imagining how amusing that would be, I turned onto Meeker at the end of Main, passed the smelters, and took the wagon bridge.

On the northwest side of the river, I was passed by several

sleighs and an occasional person on foot heading to work. Now the sidewalk I decided to take along this edge of the river was deserted. It was so still and silent I could hear myself breathe. The only other sound was the crunching of snow beneath my boots. I took a wooden staircase up to Park Avenue. The houses I passed as I made my way to Grant Park were mostly dark, with the occasional faint glow of a candle or lamp in an upstairs room. General Starrett's house was still dark too, though several tracks in the snow suggested that Frederick Reynard, as usual, had already left for work. But whose were these other tracks? Had the dairyman already delivered the morning's milk? Were Gertie and Ned disobeying their parents and sneaking off to the river again? I hoped not. I knew many a maid and cook were already working by the dim light from kitchen fires not visible from the street. Maybe Mrs. Cassidy or Mrs. Becker had already been out on an errand this morning. How many other souls were up and about on this peaceful morning? I wondered. I was never one to lounge in bed but was grateful that many preferred to. It gave me the chance to enjoy the illusion that for a few minutes I had the town to myself.

Like the street, the park was empty. On the northern end of the park was the soldier's monument, a limestone obelisk with the sites of Civil War battles inscribed on all four sides. The names of the dead, inscribed on the pedestal and steps, were only readable when I stepped up close. Next to the monument was the cannon that only a few days ago was aimed at Enoch Jamison's house. I reflected on the contrast between the chaos and noise of that evening and the silence and solitude that surrounded me now. I preferred the present, the anticipation of seeing Walter only adding to the moment. I leaned on the cannon and gazed across the river, unable to distinguish Sir Arthur's house from the other buildings on the hill in the dark. I lingered as lights appeared, the town preparing to wake. First, high on the hill like a beacon, light streamed from St. Matthew's church, then the Methodist church, where President Grant had attended services when he lived here and where Sir Arthur, despite being Anglican, insisted on going and sitting in Grant's pew. Then other churches lit up, Grace Episcopal, St. Michael's where I attended Mass, and South Presbyterian. And then light blazed from the riverside warehouses and shops on Main Street. Windows in the DeSoto House Hotel flickered on, first one, then another. Was one of those lit rooms Walter's? I hoped so. I left the cannon and monument and followed the curving path that transected the park toward the bridge where Walter would cross. I passed the fountain, gaslight reflecting off its cherubs and female statuette encrusted with ice. I crested the small hill where Grant's statue was prominently installed, his back to me. As I rounded the statue to look at the front, I suddenly realized I wasn't alone. Someone was sitting at the base of the statue.

"Good morning," I said. The man didn't reply. He was wearing a fur coat but no hat and leaned with his head resting back against the pedestal steps. He looked exhausted or ill.

The ground all around him had been trampled so much that blades of grass stuck up through the snow.

"Are you all right, sir?" I said, taking several steps toward him and laying my hand on his shoulder. Oddly, he had a slight scent of lily of the valley about him.

I looked down at his face. It was one of a monster. He'd been beaten brutally. His nose was crushed unnaturally toward one side of his face and his lips, cut in several places, were swollen. His cheeks were red with bruises, and trickles of blood from his nose and swollen lips had seeped into his mustache and beard. But his eyes were the worst. One eye was swollen shut and ringed with red bruises; the other looked directly at me, unblinking. I jerked my hand back and screamed!

It was Captain Henry Starrett and he was dead.

★   ★   ★

"Hattie!" I could hear him running across the bridge.

"Over here, Walter, over here!" I shouted. When Walter reached the statue, all I could do was point.

"What happened?" Walter immediately picked up the man's hand and felt for a pulse at his wrist.

"I don't know. I found him this way. Did someone beat him to death?" I pointed to the trampled snow. "You can tell a struggle went on here."

Walter did a cursory examination of the man's head and found nothing. "No blunt-force trauma to the head that I can tell, despite how badly his face appears." Then he began examining other parts of the dead man's body. He bent the man's arm at the elbow and then his fingers. "No rigor mortis," Walter said, almost to himself. He next pulled off the man's boots and wool hose. Captain Starrett's feet looked normal. "No visible liver mortis either."

Then, after replacing the dead man's boots, Walter pulled back Captain Starrett's coat.

Oh my God!

Blood drenched the dead man's entire chest: vest, shirt, and skin. Two tiny white pearl buttons dangling from a thread, all that remained from when Walter ripped open the shirt, glowed in stark contrast to the red stain. Walter peeled back the sticky, bloody clothes, revealing a wound in the man's chest, a roundish gaping hole straight through his heart. The earth moved beneath my feet and I turned my back on the gory scene. Nausea threatened to overwhelm me. I bent over, resting my hands on my knees and ignoring the pain in my ribs, and took a few deep breaths of the crisp morning air. I thought I was going to get sick or faint but did neither. My experience in Eureka Springs had obviously steeled me for discovering dead bodies.

"Are you all right?" I looked over at Walter, who was mercifully closing the man's eye. I nodded. "How long had you been in the park before you found Captain Starrett, Hattie?"

"Ten, fifteen minutes. Why?" The tone of Walter's voice unnerved me. What did my being in the park have to do with Captain Starrett's death?

"Did you see anyone or hear anything usual?"

"No, why?" Walter still hadn't answered my question.

"Good thing," Walter said, draping the flaps of Captain Starrett's shirt and vest back over the wound. "This man's been shot within the past hour." I shuddered at the thought that Henry Starrett could've been murdered as I strolled along the river or about the park.

"Shot? Who would've done this?" I asked out loud.

"I have no idea," Walter said, scooping up some snow and rubbing away blood from his fingers. It'd been a rhetorical question, but Walter had no way of knowing that I was already compiling a list of suspects in my head. After trying to run me down on the bridge, Enoch Jamison was first on my list.

"It's barbaric, beating up a dead man," I said, slowly standing upright. I was shaking but tried not to let Walter see how upset I was.

"The size, shape, and color of the bruises indicate they occurred before the man died. Someone beat him up first and then shot him. With so little blood in the snow, he was probably already in this prostrate position."

"It's so horrible," I said, wrapping my arms around my shoulders to stop myself from shaking.

"Yes, it is," Walter said. "We have to notify the police."

"And Sir Arthur."

"Sir Arthur?"

"Trust me. I've worked for dozens of wealthy, influential people and one common thread that ties them together is their desire to control: control their own money, their own families, and definitely their own fates. They hate scandal and rarely involve the police. And since General Starrett is in no shape to be here, Sir Arthur's going to want to be here in his stead when the police arrive."

"You're joking?" Walter said.

"No, I'm not. If Lieutenant Colonel Holbrook hadn't died suspiciously, General Starrett would never have involved the police when his home was burgled." I could tell by the expression on Walter's face that he was seeing me in a new light, one that I was afraid wasn't flattering. "Why do you think I'm successful? Granted I'm good at what I'm hired to do, but I'm also discreet. I once told you I keep my employer's secrets to myself the same way you keep your patients'. I was in earnest. You'd be shocked what I could tell you about some of this country's most prominent citizens."

"But a man's been murdered, Hattie."

"Believe me I know," I said, trying desperately to keep the nausea down. "And I'm agreeing with you, Walter. We have to telephone the police immediately. I'm merely suggesting that we call Sir Arthur first. In fact, I may lose my job if I don't."

"I had no idea, Hattie. You once tried to tell me, but I didn't fully understand until now. You do work at the whim of these people."

Does he truly understand? I wondered. *Does he think less of me because of it?*

"Sir Arthur is generous and fair, but he doesn't abide disloyalty of any kind."

"All right. I'll stay with the body. You go to the DeSoto House and telephone Sir Arthur and the police."

I ran toward the bridge, relieved to put some distance between me and the dead man. I stopped to look back at Walter, who had covered Henry back up in his coat. If I hadn't seen the wound, I would've thought Henry Starrett had simply fallen ill and Walter was tending him. But I knew different. It was a tableau out of a nightmare, by gaslight. Walter, the man who I was becoming more than fond of, stood in blood-splattered, trampled snow at the base of the statue of a war hero next to the body of a dead Santa Claus. I didn't look back again.

CHAPTER 20

"You did right, Hattie." Sir Arthur was at the reins as the sleigh flew across the Green Street Bridge. I'd telephoned him first. Sir Arthur had departed immediately, instructing William Finch, the butler, to telephone the police after he'd left, ensuring he would have a few minutes before they arrived. Sir Arthur saw me returning from the hotel and drove me the rest of the way. "I knew I could trust you to think of my interests first."

"Dr. Grice," Sir Arthur said with a nod as we alighted from the sleigh. He looked down as the sunrise Walter and I had planned to watch together caused our shadows to cross Henry Starrett's beaten body. "Hattie says the man's been shot."

"Yes, though I've looked around a bit and haven't found the gun," Walter said.

"No, I wouldn't expect that you would. How long has he been dead?"

"I'd guess less than an hour, but the medical examiner will be able to give us a better idea after the autopsy."

"And you think that the man was beaten before he died?"

"Yes," Walter said. "Again the medical examiner will know more, but my guess is that he was beaten but still alive when he was shot, and that's what killed him."

Sir Arthur looked up from studying the prone figure on the ground. "Hattie, what are you doing?" I was on my knees at the base of the statue.

"Looking for anything that might help," I said, "like this!" I held up several small green leaves in the palm of my hand. I'd found them in a footprint a few feet away.

"Leaves?" Sir Arthur said. "How are they going to help?"

"No disrespect, Sir Arthur," Walter said, "but Hattie used cedar needles in part to solve the Eureka Springs murder." Sir Arthur looked at me expectantly. I hoped he didn't expect me to solve this murder as well.

"So what are they?" Sir Arthur asked impatiently.

"I don't know," I conceded. "They look like oak willow or black willow tree leaves, but the former doesn't grow anywhere near Galena and the latter is deciduous; the leaves wouldn't still be green. Beside, these leaves don't have closely toothed margins. See?" I pointed to the edges of the leaves. Sir Arthur frowned. "Maybe they're from a houseplant or a tropical tree, like those that Frederick Reynard grows in his greenhouse."

"Then how did they get to be in the snow next to a murdered man?" Walter said.

I shrugged. "I have no idea."

"Maybe Frederick Reynard can answer that," Sir Arthur said. I nodded. The same thought had occurred to me. "Find anything else, Hattie?"

Before I could answer, Officer Corbett and two other policemen arrived on a sleigh. Their horse snorted, his breath steaming out in a cloud in the cold air. They stopped on Park Avenue and, leaving one man holding the bridle of the horse, ran up the hill.

"Don't anybody move!" Corbett shouted. He held his fellow officer back with an outstretched arm as he gingerly walked toward us. "We don't want to disturb the footprints."

At his admonition, I looked about me again at the myriad of footprints I'd noticed before, some coming from the direction of the bridge, others from various points in the park, but all converging on Grant's monument. Since it only stopped snowing early this morning, they must've all been made since then. Who were all these people? Besides mine, Walter's, and Sir Arthur's, at least three, maybe four other sets of footprints were distinguishable, one or two large enough to be that of Henry Starrett and one that was definitely made by the boot of a woman. *Could a woman have done this?* I wondered, looking down at the dead man. I immediately dismissed the idea. No woman I knew was capable of beating a large, strong man like Henry Starrett almost to death, even with a cane or a pan in her hand. Then why? Why was the woman here that early in the morning?

Officer Corbett stopped and knelt down next to the body, repeating Walter's action of trying to find a pulse. The harmonica was not in its usual place in Corbett's breast pocket.

"Is he dead, Archie?" the policeman minding the sleigh shouted.

"Yes!" Corbett shouted as he lifted up one side of Henry Starrett's coat and revealed the blood-splattered vest. Corbett stood up and regarded us all for the first time. "Thank you for notifying us, Sir Arthur." He tipped his hat slightly. "Miss Davish?" he said, surprised. "I didn't expect to see you here." He smiled. It was an odd reaction as we stood next to a murdered man.

"She discovered Starrett's body," Walter said, putting his arm around me. I was still shaking. Corbett flinched. "Oh, Miss Davish, I'm sorry to hear that. And you are?" he said to Walter.

"Dr. Walter Grice."

"Oh," Corbett said, nodding but anticipating further explanation. When he didn't get it he looked me in the eye for a moment, then dropped his gaze to the man lying in the snow. "I'll get detailed information later, but if you could tell me briefly, Miss Davish, how you came to find Henry Starrett?"

"I walked to the park for my usual morning hike and found him as you see him," I said.

"Why are you here, Dr. Grice?" Corbett asked.

"Miss Davish and I had arranged to meet this morning in the park. I arrived moments after she discovered the body." Corbett's gaze shot up to meet mine.

"Oh," he said, biting his lip, his face slightly flush. He quickly averted his eyes back to Henry Starrett's body. "And you, Sir Arthur? What brings you here?" Sir Arthur bristled at having to explain his presence. He wasn't used to having to explain anything.

"Damn it, man! Why do you think I'm here? Having a picnic? My secretary had just found a dead body. Of course I accompanied Hattie back after telephoning you."

"Well, thank you," the policeman said. "I will need to question you all thoroughly once we are done examining the grounds and transporting the body to the medical examiner's office. Where can I find you?"

"General Starrett's house isn't far from here," Sir Arthur said. "If you will allow me to tell him of his son's death, we will all be there."

"Yes, of course," Corbett said. "And thank you, Sir Arthur." Sir Arthur hesitated. "I didn't relish the idea of telling the general."

"Yes, well, it'll be best coming from me. I'll be off then. Hattie? Dr. Grice?" Sir Arthur said as he walked toward his sleigh.

Walter took one look at me and read my mind. "I think we'll walk and meet you there," he said.

"Of course," Sir Arthur said, and climbed into the sleigh. He yanked on the reins and drove across the park.

"I'm truly sorry you're involved in this," Mr. Corbett said. I nodded blindly, the shock of the morning settling in.

I took a step forward and stumbled. Corbett and Walter both reached out to help. I took Walter's hand, steadied myself, and then wrapped my arm around his.

"Looks like you're in good hands, Miss Davish," the policeman said, his nonchalance sounding forced. "Take care of her, Doctor."

Walter studied Corbett for a moment and then nodded. "I will. Let's go, Hattie." I clung to him as he guided me slowly down the hill.

"Are you all right?" Walter asked after a few minutes of companionable silence.

I thought about it for a moment. When I had discovered Henry Starrett, I'd been panicked, repulsed, and mystified. Now that I no longer had to look at the dead man's body, I simply felt exhausted. I was shaking again, but I knew it would pass.

"Yes, I think so."

I didn't mention the questions whirling in my head. If I could sit at my typewriter, I could still my mind as well.

"Good. Come here." Walter took me in his arms, cradling my head against his shoulder, and unexpectedly chuckled under his breath. "Remember how I once accused you of inviting danger?" I nodded, remembering. "And how I offered to chaperone you more?"

"Yes," I said.

"I think you'd better take me up on my offer." He squeezed me gently, mindful of my aching ribs, and kissed my forehead. "Agreed?"

"Agreed." *But exactly what have I agreed to?* I wondered. At this moment, wrapped in Walter's arms, I didn't care.

★ ★ ★

Ambrose was waiting for us on the porch when we arrived. "Come now, quickly, Dr. Grice, Miss Davish. Sir Arthur's been waiting for you." The butler escorted us directly into the general's library.

"Please sit down," General Starrett said, his expression somber but not what I'd expect of a grieving father. I looked at Sir Arthur for approval and he nodded.

"I've already told him," Sir Arthur said.

"I'm so sorry for your loss, General." I indicated Walter with a glance. "We both are." Walter nodded. "May I ask after Mrs. Reynard?"

"Adella is devastated, Miss Davish," General Starrett said, with pity in his voice. He took a puff of his pipe. "Poor girl adored that brute. We all did."

"Dr. Grice," Sir Arthur said matter-of-factly, "the general has a request for you."

"Yes," Walter said. "What can I do for you, General?"

"I want you to be present at my son's autopsy." By Walter's reaction, he was surprised as I was.

"General, I don't think—"

"Please, Dr. Grice," the general said, holding up his hand, cutting Walter off in mid-sentence. "I don't know the medical examiner, personally, but the coroner is a business rival of Frederick's. It would be a great comfort to us all if we had someone we could trust, someone who will be sensitive to our family's wishes, involved in this necessary but ugly event."

"Yes, of course," Walter said. "If it'll bring you and your family comfort." Walter immediately stood and took his leave.

The three of us remained sitting for a few moments in awkward silence.

"Ironic, isn't it?" General Starrett said finally.

"What is, General?" Sir Arthur asked.

"Less than an hour ago, I'd discovered someone had returned the money that was stolen from my safe."

"Really? That's excellent news, General," Sir Arthur said. The old man nodded slowly.

"I suspect one of the servants must've felt remorse and returned it before the police uncovered the truth. I was relieved. 'All's well,' I'd thought. 'All's well.' "

I couldn't disagree more that the untimely death of Lieutenant Colonel Holbrook and the unresolved case of the poisoning at his own dinner party constituted everything being all well. But the man had lost his son today, and not in battle, but to senseless violence days before Christmas. I pitied him.

"Since it's Christmastime, I'd been prepared to tell the police to drop the matter and we'd be done with it." The general hesitated, and when he spoke again a slight break in his voice betrayed his sorrow. "And now this."

CHAPTER 21

"We'll be discreet," Sir Arthur said. He had proposed that we search Henry's rooms.

"But is it necessary?" General Starrett said.

"The police will turn this whole house on end. I think we should have a look first, don't you?" Sir Arthur had a way of phrasing that made one feel that he was doing you a favor by getting his own way. The general pointed his pipe at me.

"No offense to either of you, but why must Miss Davish be involved? It's highly irregular."

"But General, you yourself admitted that Miss Davish is the soul of discretion."

"Yes, yes, but it's not that. I'm not sure a woman should be poking around a gentleman's room." Sir Arthur seemed taken aback, as if the idea never occurred to him. I wasn't a woman to him. I was his secretary.

"Woman or not, Miss Davish is the most methodical, observant person I know. She must be allowed to assist me." High praise indeed. It took all of my discipline not to blush when both men turned and stared at me.

"All right," the general said. "You're a good sort, Miss Davish. I can't imagine you'd do anything lewd. Promise me, though, that you'll never tell Adella, and please, for goodness' sake, do be discreet!"

Not wanting to involve the house staff, the general insisted that Sir Arthur and I find our own way to Henry's room on the second floor. We were more than happy to oblige and stood in front of Captain Starrett's room minutes later. I'd stopped shaking and was glad to be doing something constructive. Instinctually I glanced down the hall to my right and then my left. The hall was empty. Sir Arthur opened the door and we both slipped in quickly, shutting the door behind us. With the drapes closed and no fire, we couldn't see a thing. I groped along the wall until I found a gas lamp. Even after I turned it up, the room, adorned with mahogany wood paneling and bottle green wallpaper, was dark.

No wonder Captain Starrett slept in most mornings, I thought, opening the drapes to let the sunlight in. *So what got him out of bed early this morning?*

"I'll take the dressers and closets," Sir Arthur said. "You search his desk." I shook my head in dismay at the chaos covering the desk. The top had been rolled back and a half a dozen drawers left open. Blotting paper, letters, blank stationery, empty envelopes, books placed open upside down, and two empty crystal ashtrays, being used as paperweights instead of for their intended use, cluttered the desk. My compulsion was to organize everything immediately, but Sir Arthur expected me to find something that would illuminate why someone would want Captain Starrett dead. I forced myself to focus on the task at hand. I picked up the first piece of paper, a correspondence from a Wallace McKinney, scanned the contents, and set it down. As I scanned each letter or scrap of paper, I couldn't resist at least piling them in stacks, letters here, bills there, a large stack of them, I noted, miscellaneous, such as

a train ticket from Chicago dated December 14, in a third pile.
I pulled out my pocket notebook to write down any questions
that arose. When I'd perused every scrap of paper on the desk,
I moved on to the books, glancing at their titles as I shelved
them, *Appleton's Illustrated Railway and Steam Navigation Guide,*
Loper's Steamboat Chartering, Frank on the Lower Mississippi, Prac-
tical Miner's Own Book and Guide, and, confirming a suspicion I
had at the dinner party, a copy of *Personal Memoirs of U.S.*
Grant. I flipped through them for notes or letters that may have
been tucked inside. I found nothing. I moved on to the desk
drawers, starting on the upper left side, opening them one by
one, if they weren't already, and mentally cataloging their contents. All were empty except for three: one contained a pen, an
empty inkwell, and a journal book, another contained a simple
gold watch fob but no watch, and the main bottom drawer
contained an oval gold brooch dominated by a large amethyst
encircled by pearls. Mrs. Baines had been wearing one exactly
like it the night of the dinner party.

I flipped through the journal, which was blank except for a
smattering of meeting notes and dates corresponding to the last
few weeks. *Mott* and *SMLM* were repeated several times. Despite reading Henry's correspondence and his journal, I still had
no idea who Mott was or what business he had with Captain
Starrett. Everything involving Mr. Mott was written cryptically.

How frustrating, I thought. Instead of illuminating a possible
motive for murder, Starrett's papers merely added more questions to my list.

1. What did SMLM stand for?
2. When did Captain Starrett actually arrive in Galena?
   A train ticket in his belongings was dated several days
   earlier than he supposedly arrived. Why would he lie?
3. Where was Captain Starrett's watch?
4. Why did Captain Starrett have Mrs. Baines's brooch?

I turned to speak to Sir Arthur, having finished searching the desk, but he'd disappeared into Henry's closet. I walked over toward the closet so Sir Arthur could hear me and stepped on something, a woman's hairpin. *Who lost this?* I wondered. I immediately put my hand to my hair. It wasn't mine. Despite the wisps of curl about my face, all of my pins were in place. It could've belonged to anyone, the maid, Adella, even Rachel Baines from when she was nursing Henry back to health. I set it on the nightstand next to me. "Sir Arthur, I've finished with the—"

I stopped mid-sentence having glanced toward the fireplace. The fire had gone cold hours ago. Why hadn't the fire been lit this morning? Though that was unusual in itself, I was more intrigued by what I found after sifting through the ashes with the poker. Careful not to get the ashes on the carpet or my dress, I retrieved several fragments of unburnt paper.

"Hello, what's this?" Sir Arthur said, coming out of the closet and seeing the paper in my hands.

"These were in the fireplace."

"Brilliant, Hattie," he said, leaning over my shoulder as I laid the burnt fragment out on the desk. "I don't have my spectacles. What do they say?"

One word leaped off the page. " 'Traitor,' " I said. Sir Arthur looked at me and I at him. What could this mean?

"Quickly, Hattie," Sir Arthur said, motioning to the fragments on the table. I set to organizing the fragments and had to rearrange them several times before it became clear that they were all written in the same hand and most likely all pieces of the same letter. When I was as certain as I could be, I read the parts of the letter left to us, occasionally making a guess what a partial word might be.

" '. . . I tried to avoid you but . . . ,' " I read. "Several intact single words follow before it's coherent again," I said. I took a

deep breath before reading on. " '. . . unforgivable . . . hypocrite . . . traitor . . . you may not remember me but you ru-
ined . . . must meet . . . park. . . ."

I took a step back, overwhelmed with the insinuations
spelled out on the yellowed and blackened paper before me.
"That's it."

"No signature? No proof it was addressed to Henry and
not written by him?"

"No," I said, part of me wondering who wrote the letter
and who was being called a traitor, part of me wishing the letter had burned to ashes.

"Well, until we know . . . ," Sir Arthur said, scooping up
the fragments and stuffing them into his breast pocket. "No
need to worry the general or mislead the police. I can rely on
your discretion as always, I hope, Hattie."

"Of course, sir," I said, aghast that he was going to keep
this a secret, even for a short while. I started to feel queasy and
wondered if I'd fully recovered from the shock of this morning
after all. Or was it my experience in Eureka Springs warning
me that I'd been holding another letter from a murderer? *Letters are my stock-in-trade*, I thought. *Am I going to have to find another occupation?*

"What should we do with this?" I said, showing Sir Arthur
the brooch.

"Bloody hell," Sir Arthur swore under his breath. "How
the devil did Henry get that?" I knew it was rhetorical and
kept my opinions to myself. Sir Arthur didn't want to know I
thought Henry was either a lecher or a thief. "Same instructions. No one needs to know. You keep it and make sure it gets
back to its proper owner." He purposely avoided using Mrs.
Baines's name.

"Sir, did you happen to find any toiletries with the scent of
lily of the valley in the dressers or closet?" I asked.

"No. I found an old shaving brush, which the man obviously hadn't used of late, but not much else. Why?"

"Because Henry Starrett had that scent about him," I said.

"Blast, that's odd," Sir Arthur said. I had to agree.

So where did the scent come from?

"And that's all you found?" General Starrett said when Sir Arthur and I returned to the library. Sir Arthur had told him about only the journal and the merchants' bills, never mentioning the brooch and the burnt letter.

"I'm afraid so, yes," Sir Arthur said, with a calm voice I could never match when lying.

"So nothing too helpful. Too bad," General Starrett said. "Though now I know it's safe to let the police search the room. That is, if you can confirm you were thorough."

"Yes, General, you can count on Hattie to have been exhaustive in her search."

"Good, that's that then," he said, sitting back in his chair and taking a puff from his pipe.

"I do have a question though, if I may," I said. Sir Arthur nodded his approval.

"Yes," General Starrett said.

"Your son's journal mentions Horace Mott several times but is cryptic as to their association. Do you recall anything about Horace Mott, sir?" I asked.

"No, I don't. Had never heard of the man until you mentioned him the other day."

"What about SMLM?" I asked.

"Don't know what that is either. Is that all, missy?" General Starrett said, sounding tired and altogether weary of the day that wasn't half-over.

"I'm sorry, sir," I said. "But actually, I have a favor to ask."

"Hattie?" Sir Arthur said, looking at me dubiously. "I think General Starrett's had enough for today."

"Yes," General Starrett said, "and those lousy police are due any minute."

"Could I have your permission to visit Mr. Reynard's greenhouse?" I said.

"Hattie!" Sir Arthur said, scowling. "I'm surprised by you. You're not normally this frivolous."

The color rose in my cheeks as I tried not to let the sting of Sir Arthur's accusation weaken my will to do what I needed to do. I gently pulled a handkerchief from my pocket and un-wrapped the leaves I'd found next to Henry Starrett's body.

"It's necessary if we are to discover if these leaves, that were in the snow next to Captain Starrett, could've come from Mr. Reynard's greenhouse, sir."

"Oh, I see," Sir Arthur said.

"It might also help to know what species they belong to," I said.

I held them up for the general's inspection. The old man leaned over to within inches of my hand and, using a magnify-ing glass, looked at them suspiciously. "You say these were near where Henry died?" I nodded.

"What do you say, General? Hattie is an excellent amateur botanist. She might be able to clear up the question of these leaves with the police none the wiser." It was Sir Arthur's way of apologizing for misunderstanding my intentions.

"Yes, if you must," General Starrett said. "Ask Ambrose for the key."

It was breathtaking. With the sky overcast and the world full of gray outside, I walked slowly down the aisle engulfed in color: red amaryllis, purple dahlia, and orange hibiscus. Even the white gardenias seemed to pop from their pots and join the swirl of glorious color surrounding me. Baskets of fuchsia, geranium, and ivy hung from the metal pipe that was used in the summertime to vent the glass roof. I closed my eyes for a moment and breathed deeply of the perfume of flowers mingling with the rich scent of soil. For an instant I forgot my mission and simply marveled at the beauty and the miracle of a thriving garden of exotic plants, all growing in late December. What mastery Frederick Reynard must have to cultivate such a thriving community. And with all the palmettos! What a joy it must be to escape to this paradise even for a few moments a day!

The palmettos! Suddenly it hit me what was odd about the photograph of Henry Starrett's steamboat. The foliage in the picture had contained switch cane and palmettos, subtropical foliage. For some reason I'd only envisioned Henry piloting in northern waters. *What had put that into my head?* It didn't matter now. *At least that's one mystery solved,* I thought. I took a deep breath, reveling in the bouquet of scents, earthy and floral at the same time. A sense of renewal and peace welled up inside me.

"Do you know what you're looking for?" Ambrose said behind me, breaking the spell. It was a cold December day again and I had work to do.

"Actually, I think I do."

The moment I'd seen the leaves, I had a suspicion that I'd seen them somewhere else, recently. I methodically looked for all of the species that had been used to decorate the hall or table at dinner the night we all fell ill. But nothing matched. Then I looked at all the flowers I'd seen in a corsage or boutonniere worn by anyone in the past few days, including Frederick Reynard and his dinner guests, attendants of the Christmas entertainment, and men from the G.A.R. Even Enoch Jamison wore a carnation in his lapel at one time. But none of the leaves matched. With those possibilities exhausted, I began looking for plants with similar characteristics in leaf color, shape, and size. Minutes passed as I tried not to become discouraged.

"Eureka!" I said. "I found it." Ambrose, who had been waiting for me at the greenhouse door, was suddenly by my side. "See how the leaves on this plant and in the handkerchief are both narrowly lanceolate, approximately three inches long with margins entire?" Ambrose shook his head and shrugged. In my excitement, I'd forgotten myself and used technical terms.

"You mean they look the same?"

"Yes, exactly. I'm quite confident these leaves came from this species of plant."

"What's its name?" Ambrose asked, softly stroking one of its branches.

"It's an olive tree," I said. "And here I'd been looking for a flower."

Ambrose scowled. "Should've known, having seen it so much."

"You've seen this before, Ambrose?" I asked.

"Oh, yes, miss. Mr. Reynard often uses these leaves in his boutonnieres." I knew I'd seen these leaves recently. Now I could recall where I'd seen them, in almost every corsage or boutonniere made by Frederick Reynard. Even my corsage from last night had a small olive branch tucked in among the camellia, rosebuds, and ivy. How could I have missed it? I should've recognized the leaves immediately.

You're getting careless, I told myself.

"Well, Hattie?" Sir Arthur said upon my return to the library, preempting the general, who was opening his mouth to speak. "Did you find what you were looking for?"

"Yes, sir."

"I'll send for Fred then, shall I?" the general said.

"I think it would be for the best," Sir Arthur said.

Within moments of sending Ambrose to find him, Frederick lumbered into the room, dropping into the nearest chair.

"You wanted to see me, General? Is there news?"

"In a way, Fred. It's a terrible business, but I wanted to ask you before the police get here."

"Whatever do you mean by that?" Frederick said, with no malice in his voice, only shock and dismay. The general nodded in my direction and I took that as my cue.

I pulled the handkerchief from my pocket and unwrapped the olive tree leaves. "I found these near the body of your father-in-law."

"What are they, Fred?" General Starrett said as Frederick stood and examined the leaves in my hand.

"They're from an olive tree."

"You have an olive tree in the greenhouse, don't you? You wore a sprig of it in your boutonniere last night too, didn't you, Fred?" Fred looked at the general like a man in shock. "Don't deny it, Fred. Miss Davish, here, found the tree growing in the greenhouse." Fred shot a glance at me before facing the general again.

"Of course, I don't deny it, but—"

"How did olive leaves come to be near my son's dead body, Fred?"

"I don't know what you're talking about."

The general had stood up and was shaking his finger at Frederick Reynard. "Where's your boutonniere now, Fred?"

"Are you accusing me of killing Henry, General?" Frederick Reynard said, aghast.

"Nobody is accusing you of anything, Reynard," Sir Arthur said, indicating with a nod toward the general for me to help the old man back into his chair. Sir Arthur did the same with Frederick, who then slumped over, his head in his hands.

"But we need to know if there were olive leaves in your boutonniere yesterday," Sir Arthur said. I'd remembered seeing Frederick wearing a boutonniere to the Christmas entertainment last night. He had two rosebuds, one red and one white, but I couldn't remember the accompanying greenery. Had he worn a boutonniere to work this morning as well? He was hardly ever without one.

"I can't believe this is happening," Frederick Reynard said.

"Answer the question, Fred," General Starrett said, between tight lips.

"Yes," Fred said, looking up straight into the general's eyes. "But I didn't kill anyone!"

"Mr. Reynard, did you give your father-in-law a boutonniere with olive leaves? Maybe what we found was all that was left of his own boutonniere?"

"No, no," Frederick said, shaking his head. "I gave him a simple yellow carnation, with no greenery."

"He's telling the truth," I said. "I saw it when Walter unbuttoned his coat. It was crushed but still relatively intact."

"I have to ask you this, Mr. Reynard," Sir Arthur said, "for everyone's peace of mind."

"Yes?" Frederick said, with dread in his voice.

"Where were you when your father-in-law was killed, between six and seven this morning?"

"At work," he said. "Where else would I be? I only came home when we got the news about the captain."

General Starrett abruptly looked away as Sir Arthur nodded. I wondered if they were thinking the same thing I was; Frederick Reynard could've beaten and killed Henry Starrett and then simply continued to work as usual. Only someone at the cigar factory arriving before Frederick would know if he arrived later than usual or not.

"Do you own a gun, Mr. Reynard?" Sir Arthur asked.

"No, I don't own a gun. I'm going to check on Adella," Frederick said, leaping to his feet. His shock over Henry's death had transformed into disgust at the accusations against him. "That is, if you don't mind?" He didn't wait for a response and stormed out of the room.

The silence he left behind was awkward. General Starrett was taking short nervous puffs of his pipe. Sir Arthur lit a cigar. The two men sat smoking and stewing in their own thoughts. Finally, with the cigar smoke irritating my eyes, I couldn't keep quiet any longer.

"Do you believe him?" I said to the room at large.

The general took a long draw and then sighed. "I never would've believed it of him. I still don't want to believe it. Frederick has always been a good provider and loving husband to my Adella. I know he wasn't fond of Henry," he said, then snorted, "but—"

"But do you think he could've killed Henry?" Sir Arthur said.

"I don't know," the general said, shaking his head.

"Do you think Frederick purposely gave your son the yellow carnation boutonniere?" All three men looked at me with knitted brows. "In the language of flowers," I explained, "which, as a gardener, Mr. Reynard would be fluent in, the yellow carnation means disdain. Ironically, the olive leaves I found next to Captain Starrett's body mean peace."

"I see what Dr. Grice meant," Sir Arthur said. "Your botanical prowess may prove valuable after all, Hattie."

"All I know," General Starrett said, "is that Frederick is lying. He didn't go to work when he said he did."

"How do you know?" Sir Arthur asked.

"I had slept all night here in the library as I sometimes do. Frederick came in to retrieve something. He tiptoed into the room and thought he hadn't woken me. But he had. I looked at the clock after he left. It was six thirty."

CHAPTER 22

"Dr. Grice!" General Starrett said. "You're back already?" Walter was standing in the doorway to General Starrett's library, Ambrose helping him off with his coat. He wore no jacket or vest, and the sleeves of his shirt were rolled up to his elbows. His hands and forearms were red as if he had scoured them with a steel brush. Little flecks of blood stained his cuffs.

"Excuse my appearance, sir," Walter said, rolling his sleeves down, "but I've come straight from the autopsy. They were shorthanded and allowed me to assist. I thought you'd want to know immediately what the medical examiner said."

"Yes, of course," General Starrett said. "Please come in and close the door."

"Let me convey my deepest sympathies again, General," Walter said. "They will bring your son home tonight, sir, so you can plan the funeral."

"Thank you, Doctor," General Starrett said, with some difficulty.

"Doctor," Sir Arthur said, cutting off anything else General Starrett might've said. "What did you find?"

"I was right. The cause of death was a single shot to the heart. They found the bullet in the body. The medical examiner said it was from a .44-caliber revolver."

"What did the bullet look like?" Sir Arthur asked.

"Like the shape of the wound, round, like a ball," Walter said. "From an older gun, I'd think."

"We'll want to see the bullet," Sir Arthur said, "to verify that is was from a .44-caliber pistol."

"I'm sure the police will accommodate you, sir," Walter said.

"Are these types of guns common, Sir Arthur?" I asked, knowing nothing of firearms. "Can we track down the gun knowing the type of bullet it used?"

"Yes and no," Sir Arthur said. "We know the caliber of the bullet, which helps, and since it's round it's from a cap and ball percussion revolver, as the doctor said, an older-model gun. But both Colt and Remington Army models were ball and cap .44s and standard issue for Civil War officers. Galena is rich in Civil War officers. Anyone could've got ahold of one these."

"We may not have far to look," I said. Both men looked at me. "Ned Reynard received a pistol as a present from his grandfather. I heard him say it was an officer's gun. It's been missing since the burglary. The police suspect the burglar took it."

"Oh, God," General Starrett said. "I forgot about that."

"Did Henry give the boy ammunition to go with the gun?" Sir Arthur asked.

"I don't know," I said, "but it could be that Ned's gun killed his grandfather."

"Quite! . . . ," Sir Arthur said, uncharacteristically hesitating. "There's another possibility, I'm afraid." All eyes were on Sir Arthur. "As you know, I too had a .44 in my possession."

"Had?" General Starrett said.

"It too has gone missing. I noticed it after last night's entertainment. With the servants also at the soiree, someone must've taken it while the house was empty. I wasn't going to mention it unless it was a .44 that killed the captain."

"No possibility it was simply mislaid?" Walter asked.

"No," Sir Arthur said.

I pictured someone breaking into Sir Arthur's rental house and wandering around until they discovered the gun cabinet. It wasn't a reassuring thought.

"So Henry Starrett's murderer could've used either gun," I said. "Or another gun altogether?" *Did Enoch Jamison ever carry a gun?* I wondered. *What about Oscar Killian?*

"Yes," Sir Arthur said. "It'll make difficult work for the police and some unpleasantness ahead for us all. Now," he said, lighting a second cigar as if to dismiss the recent discovery as trivial, "is that all they found in the examination, Dr. Grice?"

"Actually, no. The man had been beaten, as you know, quite savagely. As I suspected, the bruises were made before he died but not long."

"So his killer beat him first and then shot him," Sir Arthur said.

"Most likely."

"Did they confirm when it happened?" I asked.

"As I'd thought, between six and seven in the morning," Walter said, glancing at me. "I also have news about Lieutenant Colonel Holbrook's death."

"What is it?" General Starrett said.

Walter continued to look at me. "Only the police know at this point, but the medical examiner was quite talkative during the autopsy."

"Well," Sir Arthur said, growing impatient. "What did the man say?"

"The tests revealed Lieutenant Colonel Holbrook died of heart failure. The medical examiner uncovered no traces of arsenic in his body. Further tests did confirm, from the sample the police took, that the oysters were toxic and Lieutenant Colonel Holbrook consumed a large amount. The medical examiner doesn't know if the toxic oysters caused his heart failure or whether it was a coincidence. Either way the coroner's going to rule it death by natural causes."

"So it was simply food poisoning," Sir Arthur said.

"Yes," Walter said.

"And it wasn't murder," I said. "Even if Oscar Killian knowingly sold the Reynards bad oysters?"

"Murder? No," Walter said. "But he'd be culpable in some way."

"So unless Oscar Killian stole from General Starrett's safe, the food poisoning and the burglary were unrelated," I said.

"It would seem so," Walter said.

"And since the burglar could've killed Captain Starrett with Ned's gun when he was lying incapacitated on the floor but didn't, it means that the burglar probably isn't our killer."

"Oh, Hattie," Sir Arthur said, "you are developing a mind for the criminal. I hadn't even thought of that."

"Could it be that neither the poisoning nor the burglary has any connection to Henry's murder?" the general asked.

"That's what it looks like," Walter said, shrugging. "An extraordinary coincidence."

"But what's the likelihood they could be three separate, unrelated acts?" I said.

I pictured Enoch Jamison trying to run me off the bridge and considered the conversations I'd overheard between Oscar Killian and Enoch Jamison. I shook my head. No, I couldn't believe in that big of a coincidence. The two men could've conspired to send Henry Starrett a message with the toxic oysters only to have the captain ignore them. Could their argument with the man have escalated, resulting in his murder? Before I could voice my concerns a knock came on the door.

"Come," the general said. The housekeeper, Mrs. Becker,

cracked open the door. She was already dressed in black. Her eyes were swollen and red.

"I'm sorry to disturb you, sir, but the police are here."

"Yes, yes, a necessary evil, I'm afraid, Mrs. Becker. Give me a few minutes and then send them in," General Starrett said.

"As you say, sir," the housekeeper said with a quick nod.

Sir Arthur rose suddenly. Walter and I rose from our seats as well.

"If you don't mind, General, I will take leave of you now. Please accept my deepest sympathies for your loss," Sir Arthur said as Officer Corbett arrived in the doorway.

"Sirs, Miss Davish," the policeman said. "Thank you for waiting. May we—"

"Right," Sir Arthur said, cutting the man off mid-sentence. Sir Arthur pushed his way past the startled policeman and indicated with a wave of his hand that I was to follow.

"Excuse me a moment," I said. Sir Arthur was waiting for me by the door. Ambrose, a black band of crape trimming wrapped around his right arm, was helping Sir Arthur into his coat. The evergreen garland had been stripped from the banister and the mirror on the hallstand had already been covered. Before long all Christmas decorations would be gone and the whole house would be draped in black.

How sad, I thought, tears welling in my eyes as they hadn't for Henry Starrett. For this family there'd be no lighting of the Christmas tree candles, no games of snapdragon, no caroling, no pudding or cake. Christmas was to be the second victim of this horrible crime.

"How long do you expect it will take for that man to invade my home, Hattie?"

"Sir?" I was taken aback by the question.

"You've dealt with the likes of him before. Will he follow me or be content to interview you and the doctor first?"

"I don't know. You gave him quite a start. It may've made him suspicious."

Sir Arthur opened the door before Ambrose had the chance.

"Then I must make quick work of it then, mustn't I?" With that he slammed the door behind him.

Quick work of what?

Now he was making me suspicious. Was Sir Arthur more involved in this business than I knew of? Did he have something to hide? Could it have to do with his missing gun? Or Rachel Baines's brooch, which he had charged me to hide in my purse? Or the burnt letter fragments he hid in his breast pocket? I'd always assumed my employment with Sir Arthur would be professional, straightforward, and uneventful. Had I misjudged him? Was this Eureka Springs all over again?

No, I thought. *This is Sir Arthur and I must trust in his judgment as I always have. If only he would confide in me . . .* Then again, maybe Sir Arthur knew best.

"Your cooperation saves me from running directly to the medical examiner's office, Dr. Grice," Officer Corbett said, his face bent mere inches over his notebook. I returned to General Starrett's library as Officer Corbett was interviewing Walter about the autopsy. "Your account confirms many of my suspicions after studying the body and the area around him myself. Ah, Miss Davish," he said, finally looking up. "Everything all right?" It was an odd thing to ask, but it allowed me the opportunity to cover for Sir Arthur's abrupt behavior.

"Yes, thank you. Sir Arthur had an urgent matter to attend to. He will be available at your convenience for questioning at his home anytime." Corbett nodded, his expression unreadable. Could he tell I was dissembling for Sir Arthur's sake? I glanced over at Walter, whose expression was plain: *What's going on?*

"Thank you again, Doctor," Officer Corbett said abruptly. "I will let you know if I have any more questions. Now, Miss Davish, if you would oblige me?"

"Of course." I quickly took the chair next to Walter. The policeman bent over his notebook.

"Young man, if you can't see the pages in front of your face, hand the notebook to Miss Davish," General Starrett said. "I'm sure she wouldn't mind." It was impertinent but true. I would gladly take notes, even for my own questioning. It would keep my hands occupied and my focus on the task instead of the questions I was being asked. The policeman looked up, his face flush.

"I can take my own notes, thank you," Officer Corbett said bluntly. He lowered his head again. He was angry, but I didn't know why. Had he had enough of General Starrett's ill-treatment? Was he annoyed by Sir Arthur's inexplicable, ill-timed departure? Or was it something else? I didn't want to consider the "something else" and was grateful when Officer Corbett didn't make eye contact. Instead, Walter took my hand. "You found the body?"

"Yes, as I said before, I came across him during a hike in the park." Officer Corbett had me describe Henry Starrett when I'd found him, how I knew he was dead, if I'd seen or heard anyone or anything unusual.

"May I ask why you were in the park at that early hour?"

"Are you insinuating Miss Davish had an assignation with my son, only to find him dead?" said General Starrett, who had been listening quietly smoking his pipe.

"No, of course not," the policeman said, shaking his head vehemently.

Why would Starrett think that? I was mortified. I had the impression he knew about the friendship between Walter and me. Then why broach a false accusation? Could the general be thinking of someone else? Did he know something we didn't?

"I know Miss Davish is beyond reproach," Officer Corbett said. Walter shot a glance at me, his countenance clouded with questions. I shrugged.

"And my son is not?" the general said.

"Please, General Starrett, I'm not insinuating anything. I'm trying to learn everything I can so we can catch your son's killer. Now, Miss Davish"—the policeman flipped his notebook to a different page—"you were met in the park at that time by Dr. Grice, correct?" He looked up from his notes.

"Yes," I said, feeling my cheeks burning. I had no reason to be embarrassed. Our meeting wasn't indecent, but nonetheless the policeman's eyes were on me, his countenance radiating judgment. Or was that disappointment I saw?

"What does that have to do with Henry Starrett's murder?" Walter said, the menace in his voice startling me. I'd never known Walter to be defensive.

"He's her physician, for goodness' sake," General Starrett interjected. "As you know, the girl was poisoned at our ill-fated affair the other night." Maybe he was unaware of mine and Walter's personal relationship, after all.

"Of c-c-ourse, I—," the policeman said, stammering slightly. He stole a glance at Walter and then at me. "I didn't mean to imply—" Moments ago this man stood up to General Starrett like few could. So why was he suddenly acting like an awkward schoolboy? I shifted my weight in the chair as the tension increased. I wanted this interview to be over.

"To answer your question, I make it a regular habit to hike early, Mr. Corbett," I explained. "It typically helps to clear the brain so I can be effective and efficient for the rest of the day."

"After the incident on the bridge, I was concerned about her safety," Walter added, "so I decided to accompany her."

"Incident on the bridge?" Officer Corbett and General Starrett said simultaneously.

CHAPTER 23

"Where on earth did you find it?" Rachel Baines said, gazing at the brooch in astonishment.

After explaining to Officer Corbett what had happened to me on the bridge, I'd been more than grateful to end the interview and take General Starrett's offer of his driver and sleigh. Walter volunteered to accompany me. I normally would've walked to Sir Arthur's, but I would have had to cross the Spring Street Bridge again or pass the statue in Grant Park with its bloodstained pedestal stairs. I shuddered at the thought and instantly lamented the loss of a once peaceful place. The sooner I got back to work, the better I would be. I parted with Walter, who wished to clean up after the autopsy, at the De-Soto House Hotel, with a promise to meet for lunch. I had found Mrs. Baines reading in the parlor by the Christmas tree. The tree looked pathetic. Harvey had secured it in a wooden box filled with sand, but with all that'd happened it was bare of any ornaments, garland, or candles. I vowed to rectify the situation as soon as possible. I would not let the death of Henry Starrett rob me of my Christmas.

But first I had to face Rachel Baines. No wonder Sir Arthur had charged me with the task of returning the brooch, discreetly, to Mrs. Baines. Either the exchange would uncover a relationship between Henry and Rachel or it would raise speculation about Henry as a thief. I'm not sure which would be more awkward. Better that I face Mrs. Baines. Sir Arthur wasn't going to embarrass himself.

"In Captain Starrett's room," I said. She looked up sharply at me. "I was hoping, Mrs. Baines, that you could—"

"What were you doing in Henry's room?" she demanded.

"Ma'am?" As I was not expecting her reaction, the question took me by surprise.

"Does Sir Arthur know about this? Don't think I won't tell him; I hate snooping servants."

"I was not snooping, Mrs. Baines."

"Then answer me. Why were you in Henry's room?" Before I could answer, John Baines walked into the room.

"I think the question you should be asking, Mrs. Baines," Mr. Baines said, "is what was your brooch doing in his room?"

"John, are you back so soon?"

"I forgot my overcoat. I heard the whole conversation. Answer the question, Rachel."

"Excuse me, John," Rachel said, "but I think it's highly inappropriate for this . . . this secretary to be nosing around Captain Starrett's room. The man is dead, after all."

"It's not supposed to be general knowledge, ma'am, but we believe that Captain Starrett might've stolen your brooch." In the presence of her husband, I'd decided to avoid mentioning the most probable reason and suggested the alternative.

"Really?" Her entire demeanor changed in an instant. She sank back into her chair, smoothing her skirt. She batted her eyelashes and put a hand to her cheek. "How despicable."

"Yes, it is shocking," I said, though the expression on Mrs.

Baines's face belied any dismay. "But since your brooch was in his possession, I can think of no other explanation."

"No, what other explanation could there be?" *Was that a smile that flashed across her face?*

"If that's true, how could he have gotten to your jewelry?" John Baines said. His nervous wink apparent again. "You keep it in the safe in your room."

"Yes, of course," Rachel Baines said, but suddenly seemed distracted, lost in thought.

"But I don't know if Captain Starrett ever came to Sir Arthur's house," John said.

"Maybe Ida or Mrs. Monday saw him," I said. "I can ask."

"Sir Arthur's house? I'm sorry, what did you say?" Rachel Baines said.

"We were speculating as to how Captain Starrett gained access to your room," I said, "without anybody seeing him." Suddenly the woman blushed, her face turning scarlet red.

"What are you implying, you little imp?" the woman said, raising her hand as if to strike me. Her violent reaction took me unawares.

"I didn't mean to imply anything, Mrs. Baines."

"She's trying to determine how the man got to your jewels, dear," John said bitingly. "How did the man get to your jewels?"

"Now what are you trying to say, John?"

"Maybe he didn't come here at all," I said, scrambling to extricate myself from what seemed to be an escalating domestic spat. "Could you have worn it while you were visiting the Reynards' home, Mrs. Baines?"

"Yes, yes," she said. "That's it. I was wearing it at the dinner party. I took it off when I was nursing the ill."

"Is that true?" her husband said.

"You know I helped nurse Henry Starrett," she said, grabbing her husband's hand. "I must've put it down somewhere in his room." Then she actually giggled. "How foolish of me to forget."

"Darling, that must be it," John Baines said, relief in his voice, taking both of his wife's hands in his.

Rachel giggled again, then looked at me. Her face reddened. I wasn't the only one embarrassed by my presence at this private scene.

"Are you still here, girl?" she said, taking a deep breath, composing herself.

"Well, I really must be going," John Baines said, kissing his wife on the cheek. "Thank you for returning the brooch, Miss Davish. And clearing up any . . . misunderstanding."

"Of course," I said.

"Have a lovely afternoon, darling," Rachel said, waving to her departing husband. The moment her husband was gone she turned on me. "What more do you want?"

"I wanted to convey my condolences to you, ma'am."

Mrs. Baines tilted her head back and laughed. Her whole body shook, convulsing uncontrollably. Again her behavior had caught me off guard. Why was the woman acting so strange? I wondered.

"Are you all right, Mrs. Baines?" I said. "I'm so sorry. Henry Starrett was your friend. You've had a great shock." She laughed, shallow and calm for a moment longer, before taking a deep breath and frowning.

"You misunderstand me, girl," she said, suddenly cold and composed. "It's a tragedy, but I'm not shocked he's dead. I was shocked at seeing Henry Starrett alive."

"Why?"

"You see, you're right, we were friends a long time ago. Though how you would know is a matter to be taken up with Sir Arthur. It only proves you are a snoop after all." I started to protest. "Hush," she said, holding up her hand, demanding my silence, "keep it to yourself or . . ." She smiled again, this time sending shivers down my back. "I'll see to it that you never work again." She looked down at the brooch in her hand. "As I was saying, we were friends long ago, but I thought that he'd been dead for years."

"Why did you think he was dead?" I asked, my heart still pounding from her threat.

"He was a steamboat captain, girl. Think of the *Sultana*. It's dangerous to be a steamboat captain, especially during the war."

"Yes, it was," I said. My mother's brother, Uncle Michael, had died on that ship, where roughly fifteen hundred returning Union soldiers, many rescued from prison camps, burned to death or drowned in the worst steamboat disaster ever. Although I was an infant when it happened, it was a story my mother told me on many occasions. I've never been on a boat, let alone a steamboat, as a result.

"You knew Captain Starrett during the war then, Mrs. Baines?" I asked, hoping to change the subject back to Henry Starrett.

"Yes, we were acquainted. We met when I was a nurse and he was the captain of a hospital ship." I wasn't about to reveal that I'd overheard their conversation at the Christmas entertainment, that I knew that they'd been more than acquaintances. "That reminds me. I've forgotten all about telling Sir Arthur how I met Dr. Kittoe once. He'd like to know that."

"Do you know if Captain Starrett piloted a steamboat named SS *Lavinia*?"

"What?" She again seemed distracted. "Yes, yes, he did." She smiled and seemed suddenly lost in a memory. "It was his own boat, named it after his mother." She scowled as she came out of her revelry. "Why?"

I told her of the photograph I'd come across and that I wanted to verify its authenticity.

"Well, if it's for Sir Arthur's work," she said.

"He mentioned at dinner the other night that he was based out of St. Louis." I was thinking about the subtropical foliage in the photograph. "Do you know if he sailed the *Lavinia* anytime to the Deep South?"

"No, I don't think he did. When I knew him, he was sailing back and forth from St. Louis to Cairo, like he said. In fact, he used to complain that he never got to go to New Orleans, even after the North controlled that city. Why? Is this something else for Sir Arthur?"

"No. It's to satisfy my own curiosity."

"Well, it's not your place to be curious." She picked up her book, Wilkie Collins's *Blind Love*, and began reading. When I didn't leave, she looked up at me and said, "Don't you have work to do?"

I don't know what possessed me, but I suddenly blurted out something that had been bothering me since I found Henry Starrett dead. "I smelled lily of the valley on Captain Starrett when I found him at the base of Grant's statue."

"What of it?" Rachel said with disdain. "It was probably from one of those silly corsages Henry's son-in-law insists everyone wear."

"I thought of that," I said, "but Captain Starrett was wearing a single carnation. Is that lily of the valley perfume you're wearing, Mrs. Baines?"

She clenched her teeth and stared back down at her book. "I'm done talking to you. Get out!"

CHAPTER 24

*D*ring, dring. Someone was ringing the front door bell. *Dring, dring, dring, dring.* As I left Mrs. Baines in the parlor, I looked around for William or Ida, but no one seemed around to answer the door. *Dring, dring. Dring, dring.*

"Yes?" I said as I undid the latch and pulled the door open. Officer Corbett was standing posed to ring again. He hadn't taken long to interview General Starrett's household, I thought.

"Miss Davish," he said, his face growing red at the sight of me. I nodded as he looked beyond me into the hallway. "Is Sir Arthur at home?"

"I honestly don't know, Mr. Corbett." I followed his gaze behind me into the hallway. "I've only been back a few minutes and no one is about."

"May I come in?" I hesitated, but I knew that I was only forestalling the inevitable. I stepped back from the door.

"Please," I said, gesturing for him to enter, "if you would kindly wait right here. I'll see if I can find Sir Arthur."

"One moment, Miss Davish," Officer Corbett said, all formality gone from his voice. "I, I'd like to apologize for . . . I never meant to insinuate that—"

"I know, Mr. Corbett. General Starrett brought it up and you were just doing your job."

"Thank you," he said, relaxing his shoulders and smiling. "I would hate for you to think I had anything but the highest regard for you." His eyes searched my face for a reaction.

"Let me get Sir Arthur," I said, keeping calm but wanting to run away.

"Miss Davish," the policeman said, catching my arm as I turned to leave. "Hattie, I . . ." He held me for a moment in his grip and with his gaze, expectantly. What was I to say? Disappointed by my silence, he dropped his hand and pulled out his notebook. "Better go find Sir Arthur." I nodded.

I walked swiftly down the hall to Sir Arthur's library and turned once to see Officer Corbett, slumped down in the foyer chair, dropping his head into his hands.

What am I going to do now? I thought, then knocked once and, without waiting for an answer, slipped into the library. Although the expression on his face was disapproving, I was relieved to find Sir Arthur hovering over a manuscript.

"Hattie, what's the meaning of this?"

"Sir, excuse the intrusion, but the police are here, *already.*" I emphasized the last word. Officer Corbett obviously saw through my explanation for Sir Arthur and was suspicious. Why else would he have skipped interviewing the dead man's household to follow on our heels back to Sir Arthur's house?

"Okay, time's up then, I'm afraid," he said.

"Time, sir?"

"Yes. I have the whole household searching for my missing revolver and I had hoped to uncover it before Corbett caught up with me." So that was where Ida and William were, busy turning over every drawer in the house. "Maybe if I'd had you help instead of returning Rachel's brooch, we would've located it in time." It was a compliment with the overtones of a reprimand. I couldn't win. Mrs. Baines hadn't appreciated my time and now Sir Arthur was second-guessing my use of it.

"Well, bring him in," Sir Arthur said, snipping off the tip of his cigar.

"Sir Arthur," the policeman said when he entered the library, "I appreciate you finally talking with me." Sir Arthur merely nodded without offering the man a chair.

"If you'll excuse us, Miss Davish," Officer Corbett said. He seemed to have recovered his composure but wouldn't look at me. I turned to leave the room.

"I don't see any reason she should have to leave," Sir Arthur said, indicating for me to sit. Having been in this position before, I was uncomfortable staying but recognized a command when I heard one. Why did he want me to stay, as a witness? Did he expect me to record what was said?

"If you say so," the policeman said.

"I'd also like for her to record what we say," Sir Arthur said. "I don't want any misunderstandings later on." I retrieved a notebook, a pen, and ink from Sir Arthur's desk, relieved to know my presence was merely a practical one, and sat down on the far end of the room.

"Although highly irregular," the policeman said, "I'm happy to oblige." Still standing, he flipped open his own notebook and spent several awkward moments staring closely at it. "You didn't like the victim, did you, sir?"

"Hello? Excuse me?" Sir Arthur bellowed. The policeman's abrupt accusation took us both by surprise.

"Sir, I have spoken to several witnesses that confirm that you and the victim had harsh words on multiple occasions. I believe you even called him, and I beg your pardon, Miss Davish, but it's a direct quote, an 'ass' during a tour of Grant's home. Do you deny, sir, that you and the victim, Henry Starrett, were confrontational every time you met?"

"No, I can't and I won't," Sir Arthur said. "The man *was* an ass. He insulted me, Miss Davish, and represented the opposite of everything I believe in. I can't say I'm sorry he's dead."

"Sir, did you kill Henry Starrett?"

Sir Arthur chuckled. It was an odd reaction to having a policeman accuse you of murder. "You aren't what I thought you were, Corbett. You're made of stronger mettle than I would've given you credit for," Sir Arthur said, smiling. Then he stood up and walked to within inches of the policeman, who to his credit didn't step back. "But to answer your question, no, I didn't kill Henry Starrett." He turned his back on the man. "Now get out of my house."

"Sir, as you are fully aware, the victim was killed by a shot to the chest by a .44-caliber revolver."

"Yes, and . . . ?" Sir Arthur said as he took his seat behind his desk again.

"And, sir, it has come to my knowledge that you own a .44-caliber gun."

"A Remington 'Army' Model 1863 to be exact, Officer. Forty-fours aren't unusual in this town, though Colts seem to predominate. In fact, General Starrett's grandson owns one and it's missing."

"If you are referring to the gun belonging to the boy Edward Reynard, it was in General Starrett's backyard. According to the family, he'd been playing with it and had misplaced it."

"Had it been fired?"

"We didn't check, sir."

"Why the bloody hell not?" Corbett didn't flinch at Sir Arthur's profanity but glanced in my direction, watching for a reaction. He didn't see one. I was accustomed to Sir Arthur's colorful language.

"Because, sir," Officer Corbett said, "the boy's gun is a LeMat and doesn't fall under suspicion at all." For the first time in the verbal volley between the two men, Sir Arthur hesitated.

"A grapeshot, huh?" Sir Arthur said under his breath.

"What's a LeMat?" I asked. My knowledge of firearms only extended to Sir Arthur's collection and those he mentioned in his manuscripts. General Starrett had mentioned the gun when the police were investigating the burglary and Lieutenant Colonel Holbrook's death, but I didn't think to ask then. "I don't recognize the make."

"You wouldn't, Hattie," Sir Arthur said. "It's a rare, unusual gun." The faraway look in Sir Arthur's eyes and the fact that he hadn't noted my interruption told me he was not only contemplating how Henry Starrett came to have such a gun but also devising a way to acquire it for his own collection.

"So why isn't it a possible murder weapon?" I asked. Officer Corbett dropped his eyes and bit his lip and seemed hesitant to answer.

"Because it's a .42 or .36 caliber," Sir Arthur said thoughtfully. "That may prove significant. Write that down." The policeman quickly looked up at Sir Arthur and was about to protest when he saw me writing in my notebook. He had thought the command was for him. He took a deep breath before continuing.

"Considering your confrontational past with the victim, Sir Arthur," the policeman said, "I have to ask if you can produce your gun, sir."

"So I am a suspect, am I?"

"Yes, sir, you are."

"What about Oscar Killian, Horace Mott, or Enoch Jamison?" I blurted out. I couldn't stay silent while Sir Arthur was accused of this ghastly crime when I knew of at least three other possible suspects. As soon as I interrupted, however, I regretted it and waited for Sir Arthur's reprimand. It never came.

"Well?" Sir Arthur said to the policeman.

"We've discussed these men before in connection with the poisoning, but we know now that Lieutenant Colonel Holbrook's death was an accident."

"But that doesn't mean it wasn't intentional," I said.

"So you're assuming there's a connection between the two men's deaths?"

"Aren't you?" I asked.

"Okay, assuming that's true, you're right. Killian and Jamison should be questioned in this matter as well."

"And Horace Mott?" Sir Arthur demanded, almost as if he was trying to provoke the policeman.

"I'm afraid I know nothing more of Horace Mott," the policeman said matter-of-factly to Sir Arthur. Corbett turned to me. "The last time his name came up, General Starrett was a bit . . . uncooperative. Would you share what you know of him now, Miss Davish?"

I told him about the several times our paths had crossed, at General Starrett's house, at Turner Hall at the Christmas entertainment, and the first time as Mott exited Enoch Jamison's house. I emphasized the heated argument Mott and Henry Starrett had the day I finished General Starrett's interview. I wanted to tell the policeman of the journal entries we found in Henry Starrett's room, but then he would know that we'd been there before him. I had to be satisfied knowing that he would eventually find the entries himself.

"And you know nothing of the nature of their association or where I can find this Mr. Mott?"

"No, I've told you all I know."

"Thank you, Miss Davish," Officer Corbett said, with an odd smile on his face. Then his countenance became grave. "You can rest assured that we will not take this investigation lightly and will look into all of these matters."

Again I was struck by the difference in investigation styles between Officer Corbett and others I'd encountered. Archibald

Corbett was a professional and didn't let personal biases and emotion interfere with his work. Maybe I had wrongly misjudged police in general by basing my opinion on only one incident. I'd done the same with physicians and been proved terribly wrong. Walter was nothing like the doctors Terry and Hillman who treated my father. I vowed to be careful not to pass judgment so quickly again.

"May I see your Remington revolver, sir?" Officer Corbett asked Sir Arthur, as if he had never been interrupted.

"No, you may not." Sir Arthur said. The policeman obviously didn't expect *no* for an answer and stood silently taken aback by this response.

"Why not? Before you answer, may I remind you this is a murder investigation. Your weapon may have in fact been the murder weapon."

"You may not because I don't have it," Sir Arthur said.

"Are you saying it has been stolen, sir?"

"That or merely misplaced as Master Edward's had been. Either way, I've had my entire household staff looking for it and it hasn't resurfaced." The two men stood staring at one another for a moment.

"Can you tell me where you were between six and seven this morning, Sir Arthur?"

"I was asleep in my room." The policeman wrote something in his notebook.

"Can anyone corroborate that?"

"No, most certainly not," Sir Arthur said, his eyebrows raised. "My wife is in Virginia."

"Did a maid start a fire? Did your butler bring you breakfast?"

"Is that what you meant? Well, no, I ask that the staff not disturb me before nine," Sir Arthur said.

"Does that include you, Miss Davish?" I looked up, startled

that the question was directed at me. The policeman was looking at his notebook and wouldn't look me in the eye.

"Yes, of course," I said.

"Though this morning was an exception, wasn't it? You
contacted Sir Arthur when you found Henry Starrett's body?"

"Yes, this morning was an exception. And may I say that
Sir Arthur was here, available to take my call. William Finch
can attest to that if you'd like." It was the closest thing to an
alibi Sir Arthur would probably get.

"Thank you, sir," Officer Corbett said abruptly. "I will let
you know if I have any more questions."

"Of course," Sir Arthur said dismissively. The policeman
turned to me.

"And thank you, Miss Davish, you've done some of my
work for me. I promise I will follow up on the other possible
suspects you mentioned."

"You're welcome, Mr. Corbett," I said, sincerely grateful
that I'd been able to help and that the interview was over.

"I'd like to speak to Lieutenant and Mrs. Triggs and Mr.
and Mrs. Baines, if I may."

Sir Arthur looked like he was about to object but instead
reached for the velvet bellpull. William appeared a few moments later. "Would you mind letting our guests know that
Officer Corbett would like to have a word with them in the
parlor in five minutes?"

"Yes, of course, sir," William said, bowing and then backing out of the room.

"Thank you, Sir Arthur," Officer Corbett said, "for your
cooperation. Miss Davish." He tipped his hat at me and left the
room.

"That man is dangerous, Hattie," Sir Arthur said, to my
surprise. I'd been thinking quite the opposite. "Almost as much
as the man who killed Henry Starrett."

★ ★ ★

"Do you mind?" I said, holding up my notebook and sitting unobtrusively in the corner.

"Yes, I mind," Rachel Baines said. I had addressed my question to Officer Corbett, as Sir Arthur had insisted I take detailed notes at this "interrogation," as he called it.

"I don't see why I have to answer any questions from you," she said, indicating the policeman with her chin, "or be recorded in that notebook by that girl," Rachel Baines added, indicating me with a wave of her hand.

"Rachel, a man is dead," her husband said. "The police are merely trying to find out who did it."

"But why question me? I didn't kill him!" she said.

"But you were acquainted with the deceased," the policeman said.

"What do you mean by that?" Rachel Baines demanded.

"Simply that you knew Henry Starrett, ma'am," Officer Corbett said.

"Well, yes," she conceded. "I met Captain Starrett the other night at Mrs. Reynard's dinner party."

She lied again, I thought. *And Mr. Corbett ought to know. But should I tell him?*

Officer Corbett took out his notebook. "And you, Mr. Baines, did you know Henry Starrett?"

"Like my wife, I met the man for the first time the other day," John Baines said. "Of course, we interacted several times over the past few days, but that's all."

"And Lieutenant and Mrs. Triggs? Did either of you know the deceased previously to arriving in Galena?"

"No," Morgan Triggs said for both of them. I hadn't seen much of Mrs. Triggs lately and she was as cheerless as ever. She held her hands in her lap and stared down at them, never once lifting her face to meet anyone's eyes. Not even mine when I greeted her. To me, she had always shown at least a modicum of pleasure. I'd witnessed her recovery from her melancholy and after the joy I'd seen radiate from her at the Christmas entertainment I'd thought her gloom behind her. I was wrong.

What had happened to distress her so? I wondered. *Surely not Captain Starrett's death?*

"Thank you. Now I have a few routine questions for all of you," Officer Corbett said. "Could you each tell me where you were between six and seven this morning?"

"No, I will not," Rachel Baines said. "That implies that I'm a suspect and I will not abide such a baseless accusation."

"I'd have to agree with my wife, Officer," John Baines said. "If we are not suspects, why do you have to know our whereabouts?"

"It's routine, Mr. Baines," Officer Corbett said. "But you are not obligated to tell me, of course."

"Then I'm not telling you anything," Rachel Baines said. "But you tell me this, have you discovered who poisoned us?"

"We are looking into the matter, ma'am," Officer Corbett said.

"My husband and I were in our rooms here, Mr. Corbett," Priscilla Triggs said, the first words she had uttered all morning.

"Yes, yes, that's right," Lieutenant Triggs said, looking at his wife in surprise. I couldn't tell if it was because she had actually spoken or because of what she'd said.

"Thank you for your cooperation," Officer Corbett said. "I have only one more question. Did any of you see Sir Arthur's Remington 'Army' Model revolver, either in the display case with the other weapons or anywhere else?"

"Sir Arthur's revolver?" Rachel Baines cried. "Are you saying Sir Arthur did this? If so, you're completely off track."

"I'd have to agree, Officer," Morgan Triggs said. "Sir

Arthur didn't dislike the fellow enough to want Henry Starrett dead, but I'm sure others did. That 'copperhead' fellow for one. Seems their hatred for each other goes back to the war."

"Enoch Jamison," Officer Corbett said, glancing at me. "Yes, we will be talking with Mr. Jamison too. No, I'm afraid we believe that Sir Arthur's gun, which he claims has gone missing, may be the murder weapon."

"Well, if he claims it's missing, it's missing," John Baines said.

"Then I will ask again," Officer Corbett said, "have any of you seen it?"

"I don't think I like what you're implying," John said. "Are you saying that one of us took the gun? Are we suspects again?" Rachel Baines stood up abruptly.

"I won't stay here another minute being interrogated like this," she said. "Come on, John." Her husband stood, and without another word the couple left the room.

The policeman seemed unperturbed by the Baineses' abrupt departure. He turned to the only other couple in the room. "Lieutenant Triggs, Mrs. Triggs, have either of you any knowledge of this gun?"

"I can honestly say I have no idea where Sir Arthur's revolver is, Officer," Lieutenant Triggs said. Priscilla wrung her hands in her lap and stared out the window.

"This is all so dreadful," she said with a hollowness in her voice that sent shivers up my back. Her husband took her hands in his. "So, so dreadful." And then she would say no more.

CHAPTER 25

"Hattie!" Ida cried as the door flew open.

I had returned from luncheon with Walter a few hours ago and was finishing typing the few manuscript pages Sir Arthur had dictated to me last night. She startled me so that I typed an x for a c.

"Oh, Ida, now I'll have to start over with this page," I said, pulling it out of the typewriter and crumbling it up in frustration.

"But *die Polizei,* they are taking *him* away, *ja?*" I could barely understand the maid, who, from her lack of breath, must have run up both flights of stairs. "And it's all my fault!"

"The police are taking who away, Ida?" I asked. "What are you talking about?"

"Him! *Komm mit!* Come, come, you must come," she said, grabbing my arm and attempting to physically pull me from my chair. I stood of my own accord, straightened the pages I'd been working on, and followed Ida downstairs. We were in time to see Officer Corbett and two other policeman escorting Sir Arthur out the front door.

"Oh, *Gott,* oh, *Gott,* oh, *Gott,*" Ida said hysterically from behind me.

"Sir?" I said, noticing out of the corner of my eye that Ida ran crying back to the kitchen.

"Oh, Hattie, good," Sir Arthur said as if I'd brought him his morning papers. "I'm going to need your help, I'm afraid."

"Of course," I said, looking at Officer Corbett for an explanation that was not forthcoming. The man wouldn't even look at me. "Anything to be of service, sir." I regretted the words before I finished saying them. I knew what Sir Arthur wanted me to do. I wanted to turn around and run back upstairs. Instead, I stood there stoically waiting for my fate to be decided.

I'm a secretary, I thought. *I don't want to play detective again.*

"I'm going to need you to put your detective skills to work." There it was, the request I couldn't but desperately wanted to refuse. "They're arresting me for Henry Starrett's murder. My revolver's turned up, in the river near a break in the ice where the murderer threw it from the bridge. You're the only one I can trust to do this thoroughly. You've caught a killer before after all, haven't you?" He chuckled, not noticing as the blood drained from my face. The police had arrested him for murder. How could he be so calm?

"Did you identify the gun or could it be another like it?" I asked.

"No, it's mine," Sir Arthur said. "Call Hedgeman, my solicitor in Chicago, but under no circumstances are you or anyone to notify Lady Philippa, at least not until after Christmas."

Christmas? I thought. Did he expect to spend Christmas in jail? I couldn't let that happen.

"And, of course, explain the situation to my guests."

"Yes, sir, of course," I said. "And the manuscript?" A feeble question, I knew, but it was all I could think of to say to avoid the question I desperately wanted to ask: *Did you kill Henry Starrett?*

"Set that aside for now, though bring me what you've finished," Sir Arthur said. "I'll expect a visit and an update from you first thing in the morning."

"Are you ready, sir?" Officer Corbett said. Sir Arthur merely nodded and followed the other two policemen to the patrol wagon. "I'm sorry, Miss Davish," Officer Corbett said as if he could read my mind. "I don't like this any more than you do."

"Does this mean you've completed your investigation and have ruled out other suspects?" I asked.

The policeman shrugged his shoulders. "He's the best suspect we've got. It was his gun after all."

"Which could've been used by a number of people," I said. "Sir Arthur said it'd been stolen. Did you have an opportunity to talk to Mr. Jamison or Mr. Killian? Did you find Mr. Mott?"

"No. I haven't been able to locate Mr. Mott, and of the other two, neither was available. As you know, Oscar Killian closed his store and supposedly left to visit relatives. I spoke with Mrs. Jamison, Enoch's mother, briefly. Mr. Jamison wasn't there. She wouldn't tell us if he'd left town or not." Officer Corbett looked down at his hands, strangely empty of his ubiquitous notebook. "But tell me, if not Sir Arthur, who of those others had access to Sir Arthur's gun?"

"Any one of them. Two of them weren't at the entertainment. They could've come into the house and stolen the gun while everyone was out."

"But would they've even known about Sir Arthur's gun?"

"Sir Arthur is an avid gun collector, Mr. Corbett. It's general knowledge that he's acquired guns for his collection since arriving in Galena."

"I'm sorry. We have our suspect."

"What if I do as Sir Arthur asks and investigate this myself? What would you say?"

"I'd say good luck to you, Miss Davish." I looked at him, trying to determine if he was mocking me or was genuinely wishing me well, but he wouldn't meet my eyes. Instead he nodded and put his policeman's cap on his head. "Good day, Miss Davish."

Officer Corbett walked out to the street, pausing to pat the horse between the ears before climbing into the patrol wagon next to the driver. Corbett said something I couldn't hear, and then the wagon slowly drove away. I couldn't see Sir Arthur in the back of the wagon or the other two policemen. Before the wagon was out of sight, I'd begun formulating a plan. I'd find and confront Enoch Jamison first.

"For goodness' sake, girl, close the door. It's cold outside." I turned to see Rachel Baines coming down the stairs. "What's wrong with you?" I had no idea how long I'd been standing in the open doorway. I quickly shut the door.

"Good afternoon, Mrs. Baines," I said, trying to get by her and back to my room with minimal conversation. I needed to type up the list of suspects I had forming in my head.

"Why did you have the door open?" she said, peering into the front parlor. "And where is everyone?"

"You are the first to come down for tea, ma'am, except for Sir Arthur," I said. As I started to run up the stairs, I added, "And Sir Arthur's been arrested and is on his way to jail." I traded seeing the look on Mrs. Baines's face for the few minutes it bought me and ran back to my room.

1. Enoch Jamison
2. Oscar Killian
3. Horace Mott
4. John Baines
5. Frederick Reynard

6. Rachel Baines
7. Sir Arthur Windom-Greene

The list of all possible suspects I developed was impressively long. Henry Starrett, despite his outward popularity, was not a man without enemies. To shorten the list or at least help the investigation become manageable, I included motives, alibis, whether he or she had access to Sir Arthur's gun, and then attempted to reorder my list from the most likely suspect to the least likely. Along with Enoch Jamison's, Sir Arthur's name rose to the top. I decided I needed a more objective point of view. I pulled the list from the typewriter, tucking it into my coat pocket. I pinned on my straw hat with the ostrich feathers, retrieved my gloves from the satin-lined celluloid box Mrs. Madeleine Kennedy gave me for Christmas last year, and bounded down the back stairs to the kitchen. Mrs. Monday was tying ribbons around the roll sandwiches as I came in.

"Terrible thing, that," she said. "You've heard, of course."

"Yes," I said. She had no idea how terrible. Not only had Sir Arthur been arrested for Henry Starrett's murder, but he now relied upon me to prove his innocence. And determined to have him free by Christmas, I had two days to do it. "Unfortunately we've been saying that a great deal lately," I said. It's the same thing Mrs. Monday had said when she heard about Henry Starrett's murder.

"And poor Ida thinks it's all her fault." Ida had said something to that effect when she came to my room this morning.

"Why would that be?" I asked.

"Because Ida dusts inside all the cabinets every other Wednesday. She was so excited about the entertainment that she thinks she forgot to lock the gun cabinet after she dusted. She didn't have the nerve to tell anyone but me."

"So all it would've taken is for someone to break in to the house and walk away with a loaded gun." Sir Arthur kept a bare minimum supply of accompanying bullets for his gun collection. He prized the guns. The ammunition was a side thought, in the rare case he wanted to fire one. With the guns locked up, Sir Arthur never thought to restrict access to the bullets. It wasn't much, but it was a start.

"They wouldn't have had to break in either."

"What do you mean?"

"Hattie, Ida wasn't the only one distracted last night. I feel awful about it. I didn't think any harm would come of it."

"What are you saying, Mrs. Monday?"

She hung her head. "I left the kitchen door unlocked too." Mrs. Monday started to cry. "Ida and I have done a terrible thing. In a way, we killed Henry Starrett." I wrapped my arms around her as she sobbed into my shoulder.

"You are not to blame for Henry Starrett's murder, Mrs. Monday, either of you," I said. "And I see a positive side to what you did."

"What could that possibly be?" Mrs. Monday stepped back and wiped her eyes with the edge of her apron.

"Because it shows that anyone could've come in the door and taken the gun. Not solely Sir Arthur, as the police suppose, but anyone." It was a frightening thought, but I focused on what it meant for Sir Arthur. "The police will have to consider other suspects."

And it was up to me to give them viable alternative suspects. I knew exactly where to start.

"I thought it might be you," Walter said as he crossed the lobby of the DeSoto House Hotel. I'd requested the registration clerk to call up to Walter's room. "They simply said a young lady wanted to see me." He took my gloved hand and raised it to his lips. "Don't mistake me, but didn't we agree you needed a restful afternoon and evening at home?" He took one look at my face. "What's wrong?"

"Walter, I need your help," I said. He frowned and indicated a settee set against the wall. We walked over to it in silence and sat down.

"What is it, Hattie?"

"Sir Arthur has been arrested for Captain Starrett's murder." Walter whistled and for a moment leaned his head back against the wall. Then he perked his head back up and took my hand.

"How can I help, Hattie?"

"Sir Arthur has had me put aside our work together and investigate the murder myself," I said.

"Like you did in Eureka Springs," Walter said. I nodded. "But you don't want to, do you?" I had obviously failed to keep the dismay out of my voice.

"No, I don't."

"But you aren't in a position to deny Sir Arthur this either, are you?"

"No," I said.

"Then what can I do to help?" I was relieved Walter understood how much I relied on Sir Arthur's good graces and couldn't say no regardless of how much I wanted to. I pulled out my list of suspects.

"I've tried to order these in an objective manner, from most likely to least likely, but as you can see . . ." I pointed to Sir Arthur's name at the top. "This won't do."

"No, it won't." He hesitated slightly. "Unless of course he did kill Henry Starrett." We both sat in silence, mulling over the possibility and what it would mean.

"No, Sir Arthur wouldn't do such a thing. He might kill a man, but I think he would do it publicly, in a duel, not at the break of dawn with no witnesses."

"You say that so matter-of-factly," Walter said. I shrugged my shoulders. I'd worked with Sir Arthur on and off for a long time. Until recently, I would've said I knew Sir Arthur well.

But did I?

"We should still consider him, though," I said, "to be thorough."

"Is that why Mrs. Baines is on your list, a love affair gone awry?" I nodded. "Well, I'd put her at the bottom of your list."

"Why?" I asked. "It's unlikely, I know, but not impossible. After all, a woman left her footprints in the snow."

"I know, but she couldn't have inflicted the bruises the captain sustained."

"But she could've shot him," I said haltingly. It was the first time the thought had occurred to me. "Do you realize what we're saying, Walter?" I said.

"That one person could've beaten the man and a different person could've shot him?" Walter said. "Yes, we need to consider the possibility that two people were involved."

I looked at my long list of suspects, mentally rearranging the order of names in two separate categories. *This could change everything,* I thought adding a few more names to the list.

CHAPTER 26

Our first stop was the home of Enoch Jamison. Walter graciously agreed to accompany me. In fact, I recall he insisted. To avoid Grant Park, we took the long way, crossing the wagon bridge at Meeker. I'd hoped that the stroll, arm in arm with Walter, the crisp air, the festive atmosphere on Main Street as bells jingled and Christmas shoppers passed with colorful packages, would embolden me. This time no mob was waving brooms and throwing rotten eggs at the house nor was the strange little Mr. Mott lingering in its doorway. Yet I was more intimidated by approaching the front door than I'd felt before. Walter tapped on the door with the knocker and we waited. Eventually a short, petite maid with a pointed nose opened the door.

"Yes?" she said.

"We would like to speak to Mr. Jamison," I said. The maid looked at Walter and then back at me.

"This would be about?" the maid asked. Walter opened his mouth to speak.

"It's a personal matter between us and Mr. Jamison," I said before Walter could answer.

"You are?"

"Miss Hattie Davish and Dr. Walter Grice," I said. "I am Sir Arthur Windom-Greene's private secretary and Dr. Grice is . . ." I stopped. I had never had to introduce Walter to a stranger or someone who didn't understand our acquaintance. What did I say? How should I introduce him, my physician, my acquaintance, my personal friend, my companion, my beau? Luckily Walter saved me from the awkward situation.

"Miss Davish and I are the ones who found Captain Henry Starrett's body," Walter explained.

"Really?" the maid said with almost a ghoulish glee. "Is it true his face looked like a smashed watermelon, his broken teeth, like so many seeds, on the ground?" I put my hand to my mouth in horror, images of Captain Starrett's mutilated face flashing through my mind. *What kind of person revels in such things?* I wondered, staring at the gaping, eager maid. Walter put his arm around me.

"Mr. Jamison, if you don't mind," he said sternly.

"By all means, please come in, come in." She stepped aside to allow us to enter, though I was beginning to have second thoughts. She ushered us down a long hallway and then indicated a parlor room on the right. "Please sit down."

Cozy, with a blazing fire, overstuffed furniture, and pillows of every size, color, and pattern scattered throughout, the parlor, despite the maid's eerie behavior at the door, instantly put me more at ease. She left us momentarily, but when the maid returned I was surprised not to find Mr. Jamison but a wisp of a woman in her eighties or nineties shuffling along beside her.

"Mrs. Jamison," the maid said, raising her voice, "this is Miss Hattie Davish and Dr. Walter Grice. They found Captain Starrett's body and came to talk to you about it."

Mrs. Jamison, who from her reaction probably hadn't heard

a word that was said, nodded and sat down in the large armchair nearest the fireplace. The maid tucked a white wool blanket with thin indigo stripes around her lap, then swooped up a cat that I hadn't noticed and placed it too on Mrs. Jamison's lap. The maid turned to leave.

"Can we expect Mr. Jamison?" I asked, not knowing whether to address the maid or the elderly woman by the fire.

"Sorry, forgot to tell you," the maid said. "Mr. Jamison isn't here."

"Thank you, Enid," Mrs. Jamison said to the maid. I wasn't sure if she'd heard what the girl had said or not. "That'll be all for now." The maid pouted, then closed the door behind her. I listened for her receding footsteps and didn't hear them.

She's eavesdropping at the door, I thought.

Mrs. Jamison turned from me to Walter as if not knowing who she should address first. It was my turn to save us from the awkward situation.

"Thank you for seeing us, Mrs. Jamison," I said. "I suppose you are wondering—"

"Speak up; my hearing isn't what it used to be." The woman put her hand to the back of her ear. I raised my voice, repeating myself.

"I suppose you are wondering why Dr. Grice and I are here?"

The old woman nodded, indicating she'd heard me. She leaned forward, giving me all her attention, almost too much. Her eyes were a piercing blue that seemed to stare straight into you while giving the impression that she couldn't see you at all.

"Besides being the unfortunate person to have discovered Captain Starrett—," I said.

"I thought you both found Henry Starrett's body?" Mrs. Jamison said, looking at Walter as if for the first time.

"Miss Davish was there first, ma'am. I came along a minute or two after."

"Ah, I see," Mrs. Jamison said. "Go on."

"As I was saying," I said, "besides finding the dead man's body, I am also the private secretary of Sir Arthur Windom-Greene—"

"Yes, Enid told me," the woman said. I took a deep breath. *Un, deux, trois* . . . I had never been interrupted so much in my life, at least not by someone who wasn't paying me to oblige. I looked the woman in the eye. I would not be intimidated by this peculiar woman. Her son may have murdered Henry Starrett.

"Yes, my point is that Sir Arthur has been arrested for the murder of Captain Starrett."

"Hee-hee!" The woman slapped her knee and grinned. "And you think you have a scapegoat in my son?" She turned to me. "Am I right, Miss Davish?"

"My employer is innocent," I said, amazed at how easily I spoke with conviction about something I was not sure of myself. When had I become skillful at deception?

"And you want to prove it?" Mrs. Jamison said.

"Yes," I said. "When will your son be home, Mrs. Jamison?"

"So you can hear him confess to a crime he didn't commit?"

"Oh, no, Mrs. Jamison," I said, distressed that she could see through me so clearly. "I was hoping he could help us, tell us something, anything that might help prove Sir Arthur is innocent."

"If not a confession, then what can he offer?" she said.

"He could explain why Henry Starrett attacked your home, why the captain seemed to hate your son so much?" I said. *Why he tried to run me off the bridge?*

"I can tell you that, my girl. It was mutual; Henry hated Enoch and Enoch hated him, like the Hatfields and the Mc-

Coys. I'll admit that none of us are sad that he's dead. Henry made my son's life . . ."—she hesitated, searching for the proper word—"unpleasant. But Enoch didn't kill him." She sat back in her chair and unexpectedly smiled. She had no teeth. "Now there, it's out in the open. Don't we all feel better?"

"But why did Henry and your son hate each other so much?" Walter asked, his curiosity piqued.

"Because Enoch is a man of conviction and . . . ," Mrs. Jamison said, looking down at the cat on her lap and beginning to stroke its fur with the back of her hand. Her fingers were gnarled and twisted with age. The cat purred loudly. "And Henry was not."

"I've heard that your son was once part of the organization called the Peace Democrats?" I said.

"Enoch prefers copperheads," Mrs. Jamison said, suddenly sticking her tongue out like a snake. I sat back in my chair abruptly to put as much distance as possible between me and this strange woman. I shared a glance with Walter, who merely raised an eyebrow. "I was a copperhead too, you know. Gave much of what Enoch's father left us to undermine that evil war." She smiled again.

"I didn't know. Was Oscar Killian a member of your group as well?"

"Yes, Oscar's a good boy. Married my niece, Elizabeth, you know. He's like a brother to Enoch. They're very close." *Close enough for Oscar to poison Henry Starrett in retaliation for his treatment of Enoch?* I wondered. I'd wait for the right moment to ask.

"Is it true you believed that the Union could never be restored by war, that peace with the rebels was the only way?" I said.

"Yes, that's right, among other things."

"So you were opposed to a cause that many in this town, including Henry Starrett, were fighting and dying for?"

"That was our point, dear girl," Mrs. Jamison. "With peace, no one dies."

"But some called 'copperheads' like yourself and your son traitors, did they not, Mrs. Jamison?" I said. Suddenly Mrs. Jamison jolted forward. The cat on her lap screeched and flew with all fours toward Walter. He put his arms up defensively, but the cat hit the floor before reaching him.

"My son is not a traitor!" Mrs. Jamison shouted, shaking her gnarled fist before her. Then she reached down and struggled to pick up the misplaced blanket the cat had sent sprawling to the floor. She muttered angrily under her breath. I began to rise to assist her, but she managed to grab the blanket between two knuckles and pull it onto her lap. When she looked up, she smiled again. I was astonished by her erratic behavior. "No need to fret, my girl," she said to me. "We know the truth. We loved our country then and we do now. That is why we copperheads fought for its salvation."

"But you were in the minority during the war. You were going against what most people believed," I said.

"You might've heard that Enoch and a few others were wrongly imprisoned for treason at Fort Lafayette. When they were exonerated, they returned to Galena with what you might call a heroes' welcome. This town was deeply divided when the war broke out. I assure you, many believed as we believed. And some of the real traitors were never exposed."

"Ma'am," I said, latching on to what she said, "did you believe Henry Starrett was one of those traitors?" Walter looked at me in surprise. I'd heeded Sir Arthur's request to keep the letter we'd found in Henry's fireplace a secret. But now it seemed relevant to proving Sir Arthur's innocence. I needed all the help I could get. "Someone accused Henry Starrett of that in a letter days before his death."

"My, my, this is news," Mrs. Jamison said. "The police never mentioned such a thing."

"The police don't know," I said, more to answer Walter's questioning stare than responding to Mrs. Jamison's comment. "Did you or your son write that letter, Mrs. Jamison?"

She held up her hands. I felt ridiculous. "I don't do much with these anymore, let alone write. I can barely pet Mouser. As for Enoch, I doubt it. My son has never been much of a writer. With him away now, I'll be lucky if I get a Christmas card."

"If your son didn't write the letter then why would Henry Starrett, after all these years, gather a mob and attack your home all in the name of justice?" The woman leaned forward in her chair and indicated that Walter and I should do so as well.

"Simple. Henry Starrett was an ass." She leaned back again and smiled. Walter and I shared a glance again. This was the strangest old woman I'd ever met. "He was a weak man who was threatened by those he didn't understand. My family has convictions and he didn't know what a conviction was."

"May I ask if you know where your son was early this morning, Mrs. Jamison?" I said.

"No, you may not, but since I've already told the police everything, I'll tell you anyway," she said. "Enoch's in Chicago. He left yesterday."

"Chicago?" I said, stunned that my prime suspect wasn't even in Galena at the time of the murder. Could I trust this woman to tell the truth? Could Enoch Jamison have told his mother that he was going yesterday only to leave after killing Henry Starrett? The image of Enoch Jamison's sleigh racing up the hill away from the bridge yesterday came to me. Was he leaving town then? But why was he in such a hurry? "I encountered your son yesterday on the Spring Street Bridge. Is that when he said he left?"

"Yes, he met Oscar. They decided to spend the holidays with Oscar's sister in Chicago. Though I don't know why.

Oddly, they met in Millbrig and didn't leave from Galena." If it was true, I knew why. They were guilty of trying to poison Henry Starrett, inadvertently causing Lieutenant Colonel Holbrook's death. They had to get out of Galena as fast as possible without leaving a trace for the police to follow. But obviously they didn't count on Mrs. Jamison revealing their plan. If Oscar Killian and Enoch Jamison were both out of town this morning, who killed Henry Starrett? I had missed some of what the old woman said. "Of course, Elizabeth went with them, so I'm all alone for Christmas."

"Maybe you should join them in Chicago?" I suggested, knowing what it's like to be alone at Christmas.

"Now what an idea!" The old woman's face lit up. "I think I may do that."

"Ma'am, do you or your son own a .44-caliber revolver?" Walter asked.

"Is that what killed Henry?" Mrs. Jamison said, raising one of her hairless eyebrows. I shared her surprise but for another reason. It was obvious that the police hadn't mentioned the revolver to her. That was the whole reason they were holding Sir Arthur. Why wouldn't they have asked her?

"I would've thought stoning or tar and feathering more appropriate for that self-righteous hypocrite." My sympathy for Mrs. Jamison's loneliness dissipated as she began to cackle. I wasn't fond of Henry Starrett, but the callous way this woman wished a more torturous death on her son's adversary was inexcusable.

"Or poisoned to death by tainted oysters?" I said. "Would you or your son have had a hand in that?"

"If it made him suffer, absolutely," the old woman said, a glint in her eye. "But he didn't die slowly, though, did he?"

"No," Walter said. "His death would've been almost instantaneous."

"Too bad." Mrs. Jamison stroked her cat, who in turn purred in response.

"If it makes you feel better, Mrs. Jamison," I said sarcastically, "Captain Starrett was first savagely beaten."

"Ah, that does make me feel better, my girl," she said with all sincerity, leaning back in her chair. I was starting to get sickened by this woman's behavior and couldn't stand being in her presence any more than I had to. Only for Sir Arthur's sake did I stay in my seat.

But it was Mrs. Jamison who suddenly stood up.

"I think it's time for you two to go." Her abruptness was on par with all her other bizarre behavior but didn't interrupt my thoughts. I had one more question.

"Ma'am, before we go," I said, standing, Walter at my side, "could you tell me who Horace Mott is?"

"Mott?" The woman seemed genuinely surprised. "Horace Mott?" She indicated for us to follow her into the hallway. "Enid!" she shouted for the maid. As her mistress opened the door the maid scurried away from it, furiously dusting a side table nearby. "Enid, the door." The maid grinned at me and then ran to open the front door.

"Ah, yes, Mr. Mott," Mrs. Jamison said. "He's the little rat of a man who offered to buy my house. Well below what it's worth too, I might add."

"Did he say why? Was he looking to buy it for himself or someone else?" I asked.

"I have no idea," the old woman said as Walter and I stepped down from the threshold and turned to face her. "And I couldn't care less. Good-bye." With that she unceremoniously shut the door in our faces.

"Well, that was strange," Walter said. "Do you think we can believe anything that woman said?"

"I don't know. But for Sir Arthur's sake, I'll have to find out."

"Ah, Miss Davish and her doctor," General Starrett said, making me blush. "I'm sorry, young man, I've already forgotten your name."

"Walter Grice, sir," Walter said.

"Of course, please sit down," the general said, indicating the only two empty chairs in the room.

Henry Starrett's body had been brought home. Having seen the black crape on the door when we entered, I was surprised to see so many callers, and at this evening hour. When my father died only our closest friends called before the funeral. Yet besides Walter and me, Adella, Lieutenant and Priscilla Triggs, Mrs. Kaplan, Mrs. Holbrook, and several men I recognized from the G.A.R. meeting last week were all crowded into the front parlor. Candlelight had replaced the gas lamps and the room was silent but for the occasional sniffle from Adella. I hadn't seen Adella since bringing the news of her father's death, and by the puffiness and redness of her eyes she'd been crying all day. Dressed completely in black paramatta silk and crape, she sat near the head of Henry Starrett's coffin, her hands folded in her lap. The coffin was closed.

"I'm so sorry for your loss, Mrs. Reynard," I said quietly, with Walter echoing my sentiments with a nod.

Adella glanced toward her father's coffin. "I've been thinking over and over what I could've done to save him. If I hadn't been nursing the children that morning—"

"Are your children ill?" Mrs. Triggs interrupted.

"Nothing too serious, Mrs. Triggs, but they both woke up with fevers and I had to stay with them much of the day. They are better now." Mrs. Triggs sighed and leaned back in her chair.

"There's nothing you could've done, Mrs. Reynard," I said.

"Thank you, Miss Davish," she said. "I truly mean that. You continue to serve this family in ways we will never be able to repay." Beyond the reference to Gertrude's accident in the river, I had no idea was she was talking about.

"You have my deepest sympathy," I said, at a loss for anything else to say.

"And you have mine," Adella said, lifting a handkerchief in her fist to her mouth, trying to hold back the tears. "I'm ashamed to say I thank God every hour that it was you and not I who found my poor father like that. Have you—" She stopped mid-sentence no longer able to hold back the tears. When I heard someone else sniffle, I didn't have to turn my head to know it was Mrs. Triggs responding to Mrs. Reynard's tears in kind. "You must excuse me," Adella said, bolting from the room.

The woman's departure must have been the cue for the gentlemen in the room, because suddenly Major McDonnell from the G.A.R. stood and, reiterating his offer to be a pall-bearer, was the first of a mass exodus out of the room. Within minutes, only the general, Mrs. Kaplan, who had volunteered to sit vigil with the body, Lieutenant Triggs, his wife, Walter, and I remained. By the way Morgan Triggs fiddled in his chair, he too wanted to be far away, but with her downcast eyes and dabbing handkerchief he couldn't tactfully get his wife's attention.

"General, sir, you are an exceptional storyteller. I wondered if you would tell us about Henry's adventures in the Deep South during the war?" I asked as a way to not only lighten the mood but glean some valuable information at the same time. "I know Sir Arthur would be most interested."

"Yes, Cornelius," Mrs. Kaplan said. "Tell us a nice story about your boy."

"I would love to oblige you, ladies, but I can't," the general said.

"Sir?" I said.

"I can't because I have no idea what you're talking about, Miss Davish. What gave you the idea that Henry served in the Deep South? He carted cargo and troops up and down the Mississippi River, mostly from St. Louis to Cairo. As far as I know he never got farther south than Cairo."

"While doing research for Sir Arthur's book, I came across a photograph of Henry's steamboat, the *Lavinia*." The general smiled at the mention of his wife's name.

His gaze drifted toward the coffin. "That's one thing I can say about Henry. He loved his mother. That boat was named after her, you know."

"Yes, I know. . . ." I hesitated, not knowing whether these questions were too much of an intrusion on the general's grief.

"So what about this picture?" he asked.

I gratefully continued. "It was obviously taken during the war. The foliage in the picture was subtropical, so of course I assumed Henry had had missions to the southernmost reaches of the country."

"You mean like New Orleans or . . . Vicksburg?" Mrs. Triggs said, sniffling but oddly interested.

"Yes. Louisiana, Mississippi, Florida, Arkansas," I said, remembering the range of switch cane I'd looked up in the latest edition of Chapman's *Flora of the Southern United States,* not being able to identify the species of palmetto from the photograph.

"Why, Mrs. Triggs, have you been to the Deep South?" I asked, curious why this of all topics would interest her.

"No, but—" She stopped mid-sentence, her eyes and mouth frozen wide open. She dropped her gaze to her lap and mumbled, "It doesn't matter."

"Well, I can't help you," the general said, shaking his head. He'd been watching Mrs. Triggs and seemed as confounded by her behavior as I was. "This idea of Henry taking the *Lavinia* down south is news to me. Do you have the photograph? I'd love to see Henry's boat again. A boiler explosion sank it sometime around the time of the siege on Vicksburg, though, as I said, not there, of course. Luckily the boat was docked and no one got killed."

"I have the photograph back in my room at Sir Arthur's house," I said. "I'd be glad to bring it to you."

"Yes, that would be nice. If nothing else, I was proud of Henry in those years. Not everyone can perform the mundane tasks of war and still find glory in it. Henry did. And I'll never forget it."

"I'm sorry to interrupt," Lieutenant Triggs said, standing, "but I think my wife and I will take our leave now. She's not feeling well." He took his wife's hand and helped her to rise. I stood up too. Something in her posture propelled me to touch her shoulder.

"Is there anything I can do, Mrs. Triggs?" I said. She threw her arms around me, her sudden movement taking me aback. I stood with my arms at my sides not knowing what to do.

"Oh, Hattie, your whole life's ahead of you," she said in my ear. "You have no idea what it's like—"

"Priscilla, darling, please," Morgan Triggs said, peeling his wife's arms away from me. "Forgive my wife, gentlemen. As you can see, she's a little hysterical right now."

"Is there anything I can do?" Walter said.

"That's good of you to offer, Dr. Grice," Lieutenant Triggs said. "Priscilla, would you like to take something to help you sleep?"

She slowly nodded her head. "Yes, I apologize for my be-havior. I haven't been myself since . . ." Her voice trailed off and she looked longingly at me. *Since when?* I wondered. Henry Starrett's death? Since she arrived in Galena? Since she finally acknowledged that she'd never have children? "Would

it be all right, Hattie, to steal your friend for a few minutes?"
Again, I blushed from ear to ear. Did everyone think that Walter was my beau? Was he?

"Of course, Mrs. Triggs. Dr. Grice will do everything in his
power to help you feel better," I said. "I do hope you feel better soon." She managed a weak smile.

"Thank you. And it's Priscilla, remember?"

As Lieutenant Triggs gave his apologies and farewells to
General Starrett, Walter escorted the frail Mrs. Triggs into the
hallway.

"I need a glass of water before I go," Priscilla said.

"Of course, Mrs. Triggs," Walter said, and then looked
back once, meeting my gaze. I shrugged. He hoped for answers
I didn't have.

"Okay, Miss Davish," the general said when everyone else
had gone. "We both know you aren't here simply to express
your condolences or hear tales of Henry's nonexistent trips to
Mississippi." This was a shrewd man, despite his frail outward
appearance.

"You're right, General," I said. "I did come by today with
more than condolences to impart, although I truly am sorry
for your family. . . ." I hesitated. "I'm not sure how to tell you
this and I'm equally distressed that it falls to me to have to be
the one to—"

"You've never been one to prevaricate, girl. That's what I
like about you. Out with it." He was right. Why was I hesitating now?

"Sir Arthur has been arrested by the police for the murder
of your son," I said.

The old man whistled. "I don't believe it."

"Neither do I, sir," I said. "That's why I'm doing everything in my power to find the truth behind your son's death."

"So you're not the man's secretary anymore but his Pinkerton detective?"

"If it will exonerate Sir Arthur, yes."

"That may mean making some difficult decisions. You do realize that, don't you? Everyone is suspect. Nothing is sacred. No secret is safe." How much did the general know about Henry's death or the events that might've triggered it? Did he suspect that he and his household might be subject to such scrutiny as well?

"You're right, sir," I said, remembering having to do this same ghastly process before. "I will do anything in my power to find the truth and not everyone will appreciate my dedication."

"You would be right to do so, my girl," the general said. "No one can blame you for uncovering the truth." He nodded, seemingly pleased with himself, and took a long draw on his pipe.

I suddenly thought of the secret letter calling his son a traitor. How would the general react to it coming to light?

"I hope you're right, General," I said. "I hope you're right."

CHAPTER 27

"Ah, miss," the grocer said, "what can I do for you this fine day?'

It *was* a fine day. Crystal blue skies above me, sparkling snow below my feet, I'd hiked into the hills and returned invigorated. I was picking up a few last-minute items for Christmas, including a new felt hat for myself from Mrs. Edwards' Millinery, when I passed Killian's grocery. It was open, so I went in. I was amazed to find Oscar Killian behind the counter.

"I thought you were in Chicago, Mr. Killian?" I asked. His smile disappeared.

"Yeah, I was in Chicago, but I came back. I have a business to run after all."

"Have the police spoken to you yet?" I said quietly. The man's head darted back and forth, making sure I hadn't been overheard. Two young girls, wearing matching trimmed sailor hats with navy ribbon bands, giggled between themselves while admiring Christmas tins filled with bonbons on the other side of the store. Absorbed in adding to their Christmas wish lists, they probably wouldn't have heard me unless I'd shouted.

Oscar Killian pushed aside glass jars of rainbow-colored gumdrops, rock candy, and licorice and leaned forward, resting his elbows on the counter. He motioned for me to come closer.

"Why do you say such a thing?" he whispered.

"Have you heard about Captain Henry Starrett's death?" I said. Killian shook his head slowly, making a clucking noise with his tongue.

"Yes, what a shame."

"It was murder, Mr. Killian." He stood back from the counter and picked up a feather duster. He turned his back and, with a flick of his wrist, began swishing the duster back and forth across the rows of canned vegetables.

"But why would the police come here? What do I have to do with Henry Starrett's murder?"

"Because someone tried to kill him several days earlier by poisoning him," I said. I knew that this might not be altogether true, but I'd already been frustrated by not learning anything that could help Sir Arthur. I'd decided to see if my stretching the truth would glean something out of Oscar Killian.

"My God," he said as he dropped the duster, his hands flying to cover his face. He began muttering a string of words, a jumbled mixture of English and a language I didn't recognize. I couldn't understand a thing he said.

"Are you all right, Mr. Killian?" I said. "You seem terribly disturbed."

Ding-a-ling. The shopkeeper's bell over the door rang. Oscar Killian and I both looked toward the door as Officer Corbett entered the grocery. The policeman grinned slightly when our eyes met. Suddenly the grocer grabbed my arm. I turned to see why.

"I'm innocent," Killian said, tightening the grip on my arm. Tears began to well up in his eyes. "I've never hurt anyone. You've got to believe me."

"Please, Mr. Killian, you're hurting me right now," I said. He released my arm.

"Is everything all right, Miss Davish?" Officer Corbett said, frowning as he approached us. It was obvious he had seen the exchange.

"Yes, thank you," I said, trying hard not to rub the sore spot on my arm. "Mr. Killian and I were talking about the late Henry Starrett."

"Yes, I'm sure you were," the officer said, not quite chuckling. "Sir Arthur warned me you'd be thorough."

"Is that all right with you, Mr. Corbett?" I said, expecting to hear him tell me that I was overstepping my bounds and that I was interfering with his investigation.

"Of course, Miss Davish," he said, "as long as you share with me any evidence or insights you may find."

"Thank you, Officer Corbett," I said, trying to keep the surprise out of my voice. "I have learned that the gun cabinet and kitchen door had both been left unlocked during last night's entertainment. Anyone could've taken Sir Arthur's gun."

"Okay, I'll take that into consideration," the policeman said. "Anything else?"

"Yes, I'm able to tell you now that Mr. Killian denies any involvement in Henry Starrett's murder." I turned to Oscar Killian. "Isn't that right, Mr. Killian?"

"Yes, yes, of course. I had no reason to kill him."

"No, not unless you are a man who holds a grudge," I said. The grocer's head swung around and he stared at me in horror. He started to shake his head violently.

"No, no, I don't know what she's talking about." His hands

flew toward the policeman in supplication. "I didn't kill him. I didn't. I have an alibi."

The two girls, at the bonbon display, did look up at that.

"First things first, Mr. Killian," Corbett said, holding his palm up toward the grocer and trying to sound calm. He walked over to the girls, placed a hand under the elbow of each, and escorted them, astonished and frightened, out the door. He flipped the sign on the door from OPEN to CLOSED as he shut it behind them. The two girls clasped hands and ran as fast as they could down the street out of view. "Now what are you referring to, Miss Davish?"

I'd been waiting to ask Mr. Killian about his involvement in the Copperhead Movement and his friendship with Enoch Jamison and this seemed as good a time as any. But I was beginning to regret my actions, having no idea they would solicit such a strong reaction from the grocer. He wouldn't turn violent with a policeman here, would he?

"I learned yesterday that Mr. Killian and Enoch Jamison, the man whose house Henry attacked, are as close as brothers and have been since before the war. They were even both part of the political movement known as the Peace Democrats, or copperheads."

"Is that true?" Corbett asked the grocer. "I thought you fought in the war?"

"Yes, it's all true," Killian said. "I joined the movement at Enoch's urging after I was discharged." He pointed to the letters tattooed on his hand. "My initials in case I was killed in battle," he said. Without warning, he untied his apron, unbuttoned his vest, and draped them over the counter. Then he yanked his shirttails free and lifted them up to expose his naked stomach. A jagged scar of purplish puckered skin ran from his navel several inches toward his left hip. I immediately averted my eyes. He tucked his shirt back in. "I was sick of war. I wanted peace. We both wanted peace. So why would I kill anyone, even for a friend?"

"But you would poison him, intending to make him sick," I said, remembering Mrs. Monday's story of the cook who inadvertently killed her master with a poisoned cake. Oscar Killian dropped his head in his hands and sobbed.

"How did you know?" Corbett asked.

"I didn't," I said. "It was a reasonable guess."

"Yes, well," Corbett said, "we know for sure that it was the oysters that were tainted. We've discovered several other people throughout town that had fallen ill around the same time as your dinner party. And they all confirm they bought them from Killian's grocery." He turned to the distraught grocer. "You said you had an alibi, Mr. Killian, for early yesterday morning?"

"Yeah, I was in Chicago visiting my sister and her family. You can check. I have my ticket receipts and you can ask my sister." If he was telling the truth I had to check another suspect off my list.

"I'll do that," the policeman said. "Did you deliberately sell bad oysters to the Reynards' cook, knowing Henry Starrett would be poisoned?" The grocer nodded.

"I heard from several families that they had gotten sick from the oysters. It was bad for business, especially this time of year, so I pulled them from my shelves and refunded everyone's money. I was going to dispose of them but—"

"But then Mrs. Cassidy came here looking specifically for the oysters, saying they were the captain's favorite," I said.

"I had a whole case in the back and had already taken a loss. This would be a good payback for Enoch, I thought."

"But what about the other innocent people who were poisoned?" I asked. "Did you think about them? Lieutenant Colonel Holbrook likely died because of you."

The grocer looked at me and his shoulders drooped. All color left his face. I pitied the man. "I'm so sorry," he said. "I didn't know it was for a dinner party. You must believe I thought it was only to be Henry who would eat them."

"Basically, you weren't thinking at all, Oscar," the policeman said. "Now you're facing hefty fines and criminal charges. You will make amends one way or another. You can start by giving Miss Davish here an apology."

"You were at that dinner party, miss?" he said, barely above a whisper. I nodded. "I'm truly sorry for the suffering I've caused you."

"Apology accepted, Mr. Killian," I said sincerely. It was true I'd spent a night miserable on account of him, but the happy consequence was that Walter had rushed to my aid. I personally couldn't begrudge Killian much. But an apology wasn't going to bring Lieutenant Colonel Holbrook back.

"So that is why you are so adamant to find the truth?" he said.

"No, it's because my employer and mentor has been accused of the heinous crime of killing Henry Starrett," I said, simultaneously being overwhelmed by a competing sense of loyalty, gratitude, and potential loss. I wouldn't be who I was or have gotten as far in life without Sir Arthur's support and belief in me. How could I have ever doubted him? "And because I know he's innocent."

Officer Corbett grinned at me again. Was that a look of condescension or was he truly glad I believed in Sir Arthur's innocence? I couldn't tell.

"By the way, Mr. Killian, do you know where Enoch Jamison is?" I asked.

"In Chicago."

"Do you know when he left Galena?" I said.

"Wednesday morning. Why? He had nothing to do with this. He didn't know anything."

"No, that isn't why I asked," I said. The grocer looked from me to the policeman and back again.

"Then why?"

"He's a suspect in Henry Starrett's murder," I said.

"No!" Oscar Killian exclaimed. "Enoch would never do such a thing, no matter how much he hated a man, even Henry Starrett. I told you, we wanted to stop the killing."

"Would he purposely run me off a bridge?" I asked.

"What? No. What are you talking about?" the grocer said.

Could it have been an accident? I wondered. In his haste to leave town and any hint of his involvement in Holbrook's death, could Jamison have simply lost control of his horses on the icy bridge? Maybe. I'd certainly like to think so.

"Well, if he can confirm he wasn't anywhere near Galena at the time of the murder, I'll believe you. Okay, Oscar," the policeman said, waving his hand. "Out from around that counter. You need to come with me."

"Can't you wait until closing time? It's Christmas. I have no one to work the store for me. That's why I had to come back."

"No, you have to close up now," the officer said as he held the door open for me. He tipped his hat. "Good-bye, Miss Davish, for now." I nodded.

"But I can't lose my business," Killian said, waving his arms around indicating all the goods on the shelf. "It's my life."

"Be grateful you'll get to keep it," I heard the policeman say as I stepped into the street and was hit by cool, refreshing brisk air. I started shivering despite my wool coat. I was glad to leave the grocer in the hands of the police. Would I ever understand the drastic measures people took to get revenge? I hoped not. Although he seemed like a decent man, Oscar Killian had endangered an entire dinner party of people, some of

them quite old and frail, all for the sake of getting revenge for the act of one man toward another. And it had turned deadly. But neither Killian nor Jamison could've killed Henry Starrett.
Then who did?

I walked almost a block in my reverie. When I stopped to look about me, I recognized the figure I'd been walking only a few steps behind, Frederick Reynard. If I'd been walking at my usual pace, I probably would have bumped right into the back of him. I stepped into the shadow of a store front entrance and, leaning around, watched from relative safety as Mr. Reynard crossed the street. A woman in a wide-brimmed hat with silk purple violets and matching velvet bow exiting the store eyed me warily and pulled her young son close as they passed. I stepped back onto the sidewalk, smiled as I slipped by the boy and his mother, and from a distance followed Frederick down Main Street. I kept close to the buildings, prepared to step out of sight at the slightest indication that he might see me. But it was for naught. Frederick stared straight ahead and never once looked behind him. He seemed comfortable with the route, never hesitating and barely even turning his head to watch for wagons and sleighs when he crossed the street. I followed at a safe distance for several blocks and was almost surprised when he turned and disappeared from sight. He must have entered a building, so I picked up my skirt and ran after him. I stopped in front of the squat three-story nondescript redbrick building I thought he disappeared into.

Do I go in? I wondered, staring up at the sign etched into the building, STAR CIGAR FACTORY. Frederick Reynard worked here. Although I didn't know his motive yet, I considered him an excellent alternative to Sir Arthur as Henry Starrett's murderer. Frederick had acted so strangely: demanding I not tell anyone that I'd seen him in the street, swearing me to secrecy for a secret I didn't know, and lying to General Starrett about his whereabouts at the time of the murder. And I couldn't overlook the fact that the olive tree leaves discovered near the dead man almost certainly came from Frederick's greenhouse. But what if he was a murderer? Should I be confronting him alone? I knew what Walter would say, but Walter wasn't here and this was an opportunity I'd been waiting for. Before I lost my courage, I opened the door, the pungent smell of drying tobacco hitting me the moment I went in. How did Frederick stand smelling this all day? Maybe that was why he relished his greenhouse and flowers, I thought.

"May I help you?"

I'd walked down a corridor toward the familiar rhythmic tapping of typewriter keys striking paper. The trepidation I'd felt upon entering this strange place dissipated with every keystroke. I heard the voice as I approached a glass-front office. A middle-aged woman sat at a desk, her hands poised above a Hammond.

"Is there something I can help you with?" the woman repeated, looking up at me above her spectacles. I stepped into the office.

"Yes, I would like to speak to Mr. Frederick Reynard."

"And you are?"

"Miss Hattie Davish, secretary to Sir Arthur Windom-Greene."

"Is Mr. Reynard expecting you?" she said, her hands still hovering above the keys.

"No, but if you would announce me," I said, handing the woman my card, "I believe he will see me." The woman took my card and scrutinized every letter. She looked at me again and handed back my card.

"I'm afraid Mr. Reynard does not wish to be interrupted at the moment. If you would care to make an appointment, I'm sure you can be accommodated at a more convenient time." I refused to take my card back and we stood for an awkward moment while her hand extended my card toward me above the desk. Finally she dropped it.

"If you would be so kind to announce me now, Miss . . . ?" I said. Instead of a camaraderie that should exist between fellow workingwomen, a sense of competition often arose. I hadn't had to spar with a fellow professional for a long time, but I was oddly enjoying the challenge.

"Miss Haversham," the woman offered.

"Miss Haversham, what I need to discuss with Mr. Reynard requires discretion and delicacy. Thus if he knew, he would not deny me a few minutes out of his busy schedule. In fact, he would be displeased if I were not to speak to him immediately. Hence we are wasting both my time and yours, which I believe is as invaluable as Mr. Reynard's, if not more. I understand that you may lack the time to announce me, so I will find my own way to Mr. Reynard's office." Success! The woman pushed back from her desk, scraping her chair along the wooden floor, and stood up.

"If you will follow me," she said gruffly.

"Thank you," I said. My satisfaction at besting the factory secretary at the stubborn game was short-lived. The moment I saw Frederick Reynard, grim and bent over a table full of cigar boxes in conference with another man, I realized I'd made a serious mistake in not bringing Walter with me.

"Miss Davish?" Mr. Reynard said, standing up quickly, a look of panic on his face. "What on earth are you doing here?" The whirling, scraping sound of a band saw nearby made me jump.

"I . . . ah . . . I . . ." He took a step toward me and I almost bolted for the door.

"Has something else happened? Are Adella and the children all right?"

"Oh, no," I said, relieved. I thought he was going to accost me for revealing the secret that I didn't even know. Instead he imagined I was again playing the bearer of bad tidings. "No, your family is fine, sir."

"Then why are you here?"

"May we speak privately, sir?" I said. Frederick looked at the man next to him.

"Oh, of course. You're excused, Haversham," he said to the secretary. "If you would excuse us for a moment, Verner." The man and the secretary retreated in opposite directions. "Now, what is this all about?" Frederick said, slightly impatient.

"Sir Arthur has been arrested for your father-in-law's murder, Mr. Reynard," I said. "And he has charged me with the task of finding the real killer." Frederick stared at me for a moment without blinking. Then he shook his head as if to clear his vision.

"What are you talking about?"

"The police arrested Sir Arthur yesterday afternoon. They believe that it was his gun that killed Captain Starrett. But I believe he's innocent and I'm determined to prove it."

"So what does that have to do with me?" His voice rose in pitch with each word. "I didn't kill anybody!"

"Didn't you?" I demanded, setting all caution aside. "Then why have you been entreating me for days not to reveal that I saw you that day in front of the photography studio? Why have you been acting so strangely if you have nothing to hide?" He knotted his brow and stared at me in confusion. "If you didn't kill Henry Starrett, what is your secret, Mr. Reynard? I've been keeping a secret I don't even know."

Suddenly the man laughed. I took a step back. Did he genuinely find what I said funny or was he unstable and dangerous? I wondered.

"Oh, Miss Davish, I have taken unfair advantage of you, haven't I?"

"Sir?"

"You've done nothing but show kindness, bravery, and discretion toward me and my family and how do we repay you? With behavior that I believe tests even *your* patience, I'm ashamed to say." I still had no idea what he was talking about. If he only knew how patience was not one of my virtues and I've only developed a professional veneer of it.

"I'm sorry to say, I don't know what you're talking about, Mr. Reynard." He pointed to the table with the cigar boxes on them.

"Come over here, Miss Davish. I'd like to show you something." I took a few tentative steps toward the table and saw that every one of the boxes was open, revealing the underside of the lid. Each bore a different variation of a portrait of General Cornelius Starrett. "This, my fair secretary, is my secret."

"Cigar boxes?"

"Not boxes, Miss Davish, but what's in them, cigars, a new commemorative cigar," he said. "It's for Christmas. With everything that's happened, I've had to work almost every waking hour for the past few days to be able to present them to General Starrett on Sunday."

"So all this secrecy and furtiveness was to be able to surprise the general with a cigar made in his honor?" Frederick nodded.

"Pathetic, I know, but you have no idea how difficult secrets are to keep." Ah, how wrong he was, I thought. "I've had to lie to my wife, the general, everyone. I've been working on this for months. I was almost done, the charade was almost over, when you saw me on Main Street that day. I panicked. I hope you'll forgive me."

"Yes, of course," I said, mentally crossing another viable suspect off my list. Although I was genuinely relieved that this man was as I had originally thought him, kind and sincere, it was difficult not to feel the weight of another defeat. Sir Arthur wasn't any closer to getting out of jail than when I started.

"But General Starrett said you retrieved something from the library yesterday morning, around six thirty?"

"I woke him up? Too bad. But no, Miss Davish, it wasn't six thirty, it was five thirty. The general's eyesight isn't strong."

"You have workers here who saw you yesterday morning?"

"I can see why you'd be suspicious of me, Miss Davish," he said sadly, "but I assure you several people will be able to verify that I was here at the time of Henry's death. Miss Haversham for one." He pointed in the direction that his colleague Verner had left. "Verner for another. Everyone's been commendable, working early and late to make this happen."

"But then where did the olive tree leaves come from?"

Frederick shook his head. "Probably from one of my boutonnieres or corsages. It's Christmastime. I've tucked the leaves into almost every one I've made."

"Olive branch means peace," I said, remembering the language of flowers.

"Yes, appropriate, don't you think?" I had to agree, though I wasn't blind to the irony that some of the leaves had lain next to a murdered man.

"Could you make a list of everyone you gave flowers to?" I asked.

"I think so, if it will help. I'll do it when I take a break from this." Frederick indicated the cigar boxes on the table with a sweep of his hand.

"So all of this was for a surprise Christmas present?" I said, thinking about what lengths people will go to keep a secret. If Frederick did this for a Christmas present, what would a murderer do?

"Yup," Frederick said. "But what horrible timing! I wonder if I should even give them to him now."

"I think the timing couldn't be better," I said. Frederick tilted his head and looked at me askew.

"Are you mad, Miss Davish?"

"No, General Starrett needs this present now more than ever."

"Indeed? Why is that?"

"Because at least Adella won't be able to refuse him his cigars anymore. Of course, his pipe is another matter."

"You don't know my wife," he said.

"But how can anyone, even Mrs. Reynard, deny General Starrett a smoke of his own cigar?"

Frederick laughed heartily out loud, slapping the table with his hand. "How clever you are, Miss Davish," he said.

With Sir Arthur still in jail and not being any closer to finding Captain Starrett's killer, I didn't feel especially clever.

CHAPTER 28

Someone had been in my room. It wouldn't be difficult. As with all the third-floor rooms, the door was never locked. And the intruder had gone to great lengths to cover up their presence, but I could tell. At first I thought I'd forgotten, in all the confusion of the morning, to straighten up my desk. With all that had happened, I had felt slightly muddled at times. But although I might've left a hat on the chair or forgotten to align my brush with my mirror, I never would've left my pearl-handled letter opener lying haphazardly on top of a stack of manuscript notes, not even if the house was on fire. I always put it in the drawer, especially after it had once been proposed as a weapon. No, someone had definitely been in my room.

Was this going to become common practice? I wondered, this being the second time this had happened to me. I felt violated and annoyed. I took a deep breath and counted.

"Un, deux, trois . . ."

After leaving Frederick Reynard busy at work at the Star Cigar Factory, I'd returned to Sir Arthur's to a message from

Walter inviting me to luncheon at the DeSoto House Hotel. I had thought I'd have enough time to type up my notes and recollections of the day and change for luncheon. Instead I spent precious time making a swift catalog of my notes, my lists, Sir Arthur's manuscript, and my few belongings. Everything on my desk seemed to have been touched and misaligned, but nothing obvious was missing. What could I have that someone would want? What were they looking for?

I realigned the stack of photographs I'd picked up at the photographer's for Sir Arthur. The tintype of Captain Henry Starrett's steamboat, the *Lavinia,* was no longer among them. The intruder must've taken it. But why? It wasn't a great loss to me, for I remembered it well, or to Sir Arthur, who hadn't wanted it for his book in the first place, but I'd promised to show it to General Starrett. Could I have missed something in the photograph, something important? I didn't have time to wonder. I sat down and quickly typed up my notes as Sir Arthur had requested. When I finished, I put a partially typed list back into the typewriter and added more questions than I could answer.

5. Was Enoch Jamison in Chicago at the time of the murder as Oscar Killian claimed?
6. Where was Rachel Baines the morning of the murder? Why wouldn't she want anyone to know?
7. If Frederick Reynard couldn't have killed Henry, where did the olive leaves come from?
8. Who entered my room? Why did they take the steamboat photograph?
9. Could there be a connection between the burnt letter and the photograph?
10. How am I going to free Sir Arthur from jail?

I was staring at the last question when my door began to slowly creak open. Without thinking I grabbed my letter opener and held it behind my back, poised to strike.

"Hattie," Ida said as she peeped around the door. "Are you in there?"

I breathed a sigh of relief and in the next moment was dismayed at how unnerved I'd truly become. Did I actually think the intruder would come back? And if so, with the intention of harming me? I had to admit that it wasn't such a far-fetched idea. Someone stole from my room and someone killed Henry Starrett. Who's to say they weren't one and the same? The thought sent a shiver down my back. I'd been perturbed by the violation and disarray of my belongings, but could I've been in danger?

"Ida," I said, pulling the desk drawer open and dropping the letter opener inside. "You startled me."

"Oh, *verzeihen Sie mir*, but your doctor is here, *ja?*"

Walter! I had completely forgotten about luncheon and here I was still in my street dress. I slammed the drawer closed.

"Please tell him I'll be right down." Ida looked at my dress and shook her head.

"I will first help you dress and then I will tell him you will be right down, *ja?*"

Her small kindness touched me and brushed away the fear and dread I was beginning to feel.

"Thank you, Ida, but I can manage. Too bad it's too soon to wear the bodice to my new dress!" I pulled it out of the wardrobe to show her.

"But Hattie, you don't have a maid," she said, feeling the silk fabric. "Why did you buy it? *Es ist verrückt*, it's crazy, *ja?*"

"It is a little crazy, but it's lovely, don't you think?" I said. "I bought it to wear for Christmas dinner."

"*Ja*, it is lovely." She nodded cautiously and then we both laughed at the absurdity of my owning anything with twenty buttons down the back.

"Ready for lunch?"

Walter stood up abruptly as I entered the parlor. The Christmas tree was still standing bare in the middle of the room. It made me melancholy again to see it, remembering the excitement I'd felt cutting it down, buying and making ornaments for it, only a few days ago. A few days ago Lieutenant Colonel Holbrook and Henry Starrett were still alive, Sir Arthur was happily working on his manuscript, and I still envisioned a festive and happy Christmas. The events over the past few days had changed all that.

"Yes, though I need to see Sir Arthur first, if that's all right," I said.

"Of course, but something else is wrong," Walter said. He must've seen the sadness in my face. "Something else has happened to upset you. Are your ribs still bothering you?"

"No, it's not that. Someone stole the photograph of Henry Starrett's steamboat from my room."

"Why would anyone want it? Let alone bad enough to steal it from you?"

"I have no idea. In fact, Walter, I'm baffled and frustrated by most of this." I told him about Frederick Reynard and what I'd learned from the police at Killian's grocery. I handed him my report for Sir Arthur.

He scanned my notes. "As usual, you are thorough and precise, Hattie. No one could've done better. Not even the police."

"But I've spent part of yesterday and all of this morning searching for anything that'll help Sir Arthur and I'm no closer than when I started." He handed back my notes. "In fact, all

I've done is confirm that Sir Arthur is still the best suspect the police have."

"Let Sir Arthur be the judge of that," he said, putting on his top hat. I nodded and preceded him out the door. Remembering Walter's aggressive driving style, I opted to walk to the jailhouse. The fresh air, I knew, would do me good.

"How is Mrs. Triggs?" I asked as we walked down Bench Street, my hand on Walter's arm.

"She was extremely upset. I had to give her chloral hydrate. I checked on her this morning and she was still sleeping. I don't know the woman. Do you think it characteristic that she'd be this distraught over the captain's murder?"

"She does seem fragile in constitution as well as in mind," I said. "And I think in general she is an unhappy woman," I said. "But I was surprised how she reacted to the murder too. She barely knew Henry Starrett."

"That confirms something I've been thinking. I can't put my finger on it, but I think she knows something."

"Really? Like what?" This was hope from an unseen quarter. Maybe she knew something that could help Sir Arthur.

"I don't know," Walter said, "but after I administered the chloral hydrate, I stayed for a while to observe. I couldn't help hear her mumbling 'murderer, murderer,' over and over."

Why would Priscilla Triggs say "murderer" in her delirium? I never once considered her involvement in any of yesterday's sordid events. But why else would she say it if she didn't know something we didn't? Could she have been a witness? Could she have seen or overheard something that made her suspect someone? Could that be the cause of her intense reaction to Henry's death? A thrill of hope enlivened me.

"When will she be well enough to talk to?" I asked.

"I gave her a strong dose, but she should be up and about this afternoon."

Only moments ago I was dreading more "detective" work and now I couldn't wait.

"You've done an excellent job so far, Hattie, but you must delve deeper," Sir Arthur said after reading the report for the second time. Walter and I sat opposite Sir Arthur, iron bars between us, in a large room in the county jail, an impressive red and limestone brick building on Meeker Street, where only the bars on the third-story windows gave any indication that this wasn't a wealthy gentleman's home.

"Yes, sir. Thank you, sir," I said.

"It can't be a coincidence that someone stole that photograph, Hattie. And where does the letter come in? Who wrote it and is there any truth to it?"

"I've been thinking about that, sir," I said, "and I wonder if a connection exists between the two, the letter and the photograph, I mean."

"In what way?" Sir Arthur said.

"The letter accused Henry Starrett of being a Southern sympathizer and the one photograph that shows evidence that Henry did at least spend time in the Deep South has been stolen."

"Of course, he could've been a Southern sympathizer without leaving Galena," Sir Arthur said, "but I get your point. Especially since no one you've talked to admits knowing anything about it."

"Do you think the person who stole the photograph is the same one who wrote the letter?" Walter asked.

"That's what you need to find out, Hattie," Sir Arthur said. It was a formidable task and my earlier enthusiasm for this type of "research" was gone. "I'd start with looking into Captain Starrett's war record. At least you should be able to confirm or deny whether he had official duty in the Deep South. I have a few friends in the War Department you can telegraph. The scrapbooks in General Starrett's library may also hold some clues."

"Yes, sir," I said. The door opened and Officer Corbett leaned into the room.

"Time's up, Mr. Windom-Greene." He looked at me and smiled, and then took off his hat. "Oh, I didn't know it was you visiting the prisoner, Miss Davish." He hadn't been the officer who let Walter and me in. "You can have a few more minutes."

"Thank you, Officer Corbett," I said. I turned to say something to Walter and stopped short. He was glaring at the policeman as he closed the door.

"What is it, Walter?" I said under my breath, hoping to keep a semblance of privacy between us with Sir Arthur only a few feet away.

"I don't like him," Walter mumbled. Walter shook his head in short, clipped movements before waving his hands in agitation. I looked back at the jail room door as if the answer to Walter's sudden perplexing behavior would be there.

"I don't understand," I said. Walter turned to look me straight in the eyes and gave me a sideways grin.

"Never mind, Hattie," he said, taking my hand and squeezing it lightly before letting go again. "I'm a foolish, jealous man."

My heart thumped hard in my chest. Walter was jealous! Before Walter, I'd never had a serious suitor before, dare I even call him that. What was the likelihood that less than two months after meeting Walter I'd have another man stammering like a schoolboy in my presence? The idea was both absurd and thrilling. Yet Walter had a right to be suspicious. What should I do? I hoped to avoid any misunderstanding between us. Archibald Corbett was a good-natured, professional policeman and, to me, nothing more. Should I tell Walter? Or would not mentioning it at all be best? Either way, the matter could wait. I had a task to do for Sir Arthur and couldn't let any man's fancy get in my way.

"If that's all," Sir Arthur said, looking at me with an amused look on his face, "I think you'd better get to work."

"Yes, sir," I said, embarrassed by the exchange and relieved to be talking about work again. "Though I'd like to mention one more thing. Dr. Grice has something he'd like to add that isn't in the report." Walter told him what he'd told me about Priscilla Triggs.

"Sounds like a promising lead," Sir Arthur said, walking away from the bars, "though I wouldn't get your hopes up." He sat down on the only piece of furniture in the cell, an iron double-decked cot, having to stoop to do so. It was the first time I'd seen Sir Arthur look tired. It frightened me. "Mrs. Triggs is a delicate soul who may simply be emotionally disturbed by the murder and may know nothing at all," Sir Arthur said.

She knows something, I thought. *She has to or else . . .*

I had no illusions about how much my fate was tied up with this man. I had to do everything I could to free him. I had to find the real killer; my livelihood depended on it.

"Walter," I said, trying to keep my voice down. I was ecstatic and wanted to shout. "It's Horace Mott!"

The man, who remained a mystery to both me and the police, had disappeared after the Christmas entertainment at Turner Hall. Now he was being seated at a table a few feet away. He still wore the outdated black suit. Walter and I had proceeded with our plans to dine together at the DeSoto House Hotel. Over a wonderful light luncheon of sliced cold corned beef, fried potatoes, bread, butter, and pickled peaches, we rehashed all that had happened since Henry Starrett arrived unannounced at his father's home seven days ago. Whenever

Officer Corbett was mentioned I sensed a tension that I'd never felt in Walter's presence before. I couldn't let this go on. I'd gathered the courage to speak to Walter about the policeman when Horace Mott walked into the dining room.

"Where?" Walter said, scanning the room. I pointed in the general direction. Mott was seated with three middle-aged men of varying gentility. "I wonder where he's been the past few days?"

"I don't know." I pushed my chair back and stood up. "But I'm going to find out." The courage I'd gathered to talk to Walter propelled me across the dining room. Without looking back, I knew Walter had followed me.

"Excuse the interruption, gentlemen," I said, standing before the table, "but would it be possible to have a private word with you, Mr. Mott?" The strange little man looked down his nose at me and blinked twice.

"Miss . . . Miss . . . I'm sorry I don't recall your name," he said.

"Miss Davish," I said. I turned slightly toward Walter. "And this is Dr. Walter Grice." Horace Mott didn't stand and offer Walter his hand but continued to look over his spectacles at us.

"What can I do for you?" he asked without introducing his dining companions. I knew the man was uncouth.

"May we speak in private, sir?" I said. Mr. Mott looked around the table at his companions and then produced a high-pitched giggle of a laugh. I took a small step back.

"I have no secrets from my good friends here, Miss Davish," Mott said. "Now what could you tell me that warrants interrupting our luncheon?" My apprehension from a moment ago was gone; now I was angry. How dare he call me rude.

"You've been absent from town of late, Mr. Mott," I said.

"Yes, so? You disturbed us to tell me that?" he said, interrupting me and laughing his strange giggle again. "Besides, how do you know I've been out of town?"

"The police have been trying to locate you, sir," I said. A small sense of triumph surged through me when his smug expression suddenly changed. His companions began mumbling to each other.

"The police? Why are the police looking for me?"

"In regards to Captain Henry Starrett's death," Walter said. Mott cast a quick look at Walter and then purposely twisted his shoulders to more directly face me.

"But as you say, Miss Davish, I was out of town when Henry was murdered," he said, some of his overconfidence emerging again. "So obviously I've nothing to tell the police."

"You could tell them exactly where you were when Henry was killed," I said.

"When was that?" the man to Horace Mott's left said. Droplets of consommé, trapped by the man's heavy gray mustache, sparkled above his lip. It was the first time any of them had spoken directly to me.

"Between six and seven yesterday morning," Walter said. Mott and his companions all began to speak at once until the man with the gray mustache put his hand up.

"If that's when Starrett was killed, then Mott is innocent. He was at the mine, signing the final paperwork. We here can all attest to that." The men all nodded in agreement as a sly smile grew on Horace Mott's face.

"What mine?" I said, again seeing another likely suspect slip through my fingers.

"The Starrett-McKinney Lead Mine," the man, whose name I still didn't know, said.

Starrett-McKinney Lead Mine, I repeated to myself, *the SMLM on Henry Starrett's papers.*

"I thought all of the lead mines were exhausted years ago,"

I said, remembering the old newspaper articles I'd read in General Starrett's library while researching for Sir Arthur. For good reason the town was named Galena; *galena* meant "lead" and lead, as early as the 1820s, propelled the town's growth and prosperity. But only fifty years later, the production of lead had dropped drastically and the mines in this region were no longer of national interest.

"Yeah, for the most part, you're right. Lead's heyday in Galena is long past. But Starrett wasn't shy about putting his money on a long shot, was he, Mott?" the man said, jabbing Horace Mott in the ribs with his elbow. Mott flinched. "So me and my crew, we dug and we found it—a small but substantial vein of untapped lead. It's going to make us all extremely wealthy men."

"Hear, hear," one of the company, a man in his mid-thirties, said, raising his glass.

"Too bad Starrett won't be able to benefit from it," the third man said. The comment instantly made me reconsider why Henry was murdered. Could it have been not for his supposed treasonous past or his assault on Enoch Jamison but for money, pure and simple?

"Who inherits Starrett's share of the mine's earnings?" I asked.

"His daughter, of course," Mott said.

Adella! Could her affection for her father all be an act? Did she know she was to inherit a great deal of money? Were there olive leaves in her corsage? Were those her footprints in the snow? Did she kill Henry Starrett? She didn't seem capable of killing a mouse, let alone her own father.

"Did Adella know of the mine?" I asked.

"No one knew of the mine except us and Henry," Mott said.

"Unless Henry told someone else," I said. Mott shrugged.

"It's possible," he said. "Though when I told the general

and Mr. and Mrs. Reynard, they seemed genuinely surprised." I was startled by the news.

"Excuse me? The Reynards and General Starrett know? Wh-h-hen?" I asked, stammering in my surprise.

When had Mott been at General Starrett's house? Why didn't the police or I know that he was in town again? What else didn't I know?

Mott smirked but didn't answer my question. I changed tactics. "So what is your role in all of this, Mr. Mott?"

Before Mott could answer, the man with the heavy gray mustache, who seemed to be their leader, answered for him. "Mott is Starrett's land agent and acts as the go-between for us and Starrett."

"So you were also working on the captain's behalf when you made an offer on Enoch Jamison's house?" I said. Mott nodded.

"Like the man said, Henry liked putting his money on long shots." Mott explained that Henry was interested in buying Enoch Jamison's home and hoped the man, after being harassed, would be willing to sell cheap.

"So he formed a mob and terrorized the man and his mother merely to frighten him into selling his house?" I said. Mott shrugged again. I wondered if Enoch Jamison knew what Henry was trying to do. If so, was it a reason to kill him? But if so, how could Jamison do it when he was supposedly in Chicago at the time? It was a question I couldn't get around.

"Is the mine what you were discussing the day we met, Mr. Mott?" I asked.

"Of course," he said.

"And when you called him away from the dinner party?"

"Then, too. I was there to collect the final payment."

A sudden thought occurred to me. "And where did you meet?"

"Why does that even matter?" he said, reaching for his wine. "I think I'm done being interrogated, Miss Davish."

"Please answer the lady's question, Mr. Mott," Walter said. "Or you'll be answering to the police." Walter probably had no idea what I was getting at but trusted that I was on to something. Mott's eye darted to Walter's stern face; then he dabbed his lips with his napkin. He sighed expansively.

"We met in the general's library," he said. "Are you satisfied?"

"And Captain Starrett got the money from the safe?" I said.

"Are you dense? Of course," Mott said snidely. "Where else would you keep that amount of money, under your mattress?" I ignored Mott's sarcasm, for I was right. Henry had been the one to steal from his father's safe, after he'd left the dinner party but before he was feeling the effects of the food poisoning.

"That money was stolen, Mr. Mott," I said. "The general suspects one of the house staff, but your name was also mentioned." I didn't illuminate for him the fact that it was me who cast suspicion his way.

"I didn't steal anything!" Mott said, squealing in desperation. He looked to his companions, who were staring at him again. "Henry gave me the money, Carter. You remember, we didn't even need it in the end. We uncovered the lead and I gave it all back to him."

"Too bad Starrett's not around to verify that, Mott," Mr. Carter, the man with the heavy mustache, said, eyeing Mott suspiciously. "I'm starting to wonder about our arrangement, Mott. If I didn't know exactly where you were yesterday morning, I'd be suspicious of you too." Mott's eyes widened, his spectacles falling to the tip of his nose.

"I didn't do anything," he whined. He grabbed Mr. Carter by the arm. "I swear I gave it all back."

"Did you give it back to him at Turner Hall?" I asked. I'd been enjoying seeing the man's distress, but I couldn't let it go on.

"Yes, yes," Mott said, nodding his head furiously. He turned to me with hope in his eyes. "Yes, at the Christmas thing. That's when I gave it all back."

"Hattie?" Walter whispered.

"Mr. Mott is telling the truth, gentlemen," I said. "After Henry Starrett's death, General Starrett discovered that all of the stolen money had been returned."

"Good to hear we can trust you after all, Mott." Mr. Carter tipped his head. "My apologies." Instead of appreciating my aid, Mott glared at me, pushing his spectacles slightly higher on his nose.

"You've taken up enough of our time, Miss Davish, Dr. Grice," Mott said. "Please leave now and let us enjoy our meal."

"With pleasure, Mr. Mott," I said. "Mr. Carter, gentlemen, good day, sirs." Walter and I returned to our table.

"Hattie, are you ill?" Walter said, leaning over trying to take my hand. We'd sat in silence and I'd eaten little of our cheese and dessert course since confronting Mott. I knew Walter would be taking my pulse next.

"No, why do you ask?"

"You haven't touched your sponge cake." I laughed despite myself. Walter knew that I never let a cake go uneaten. I took a bite. It was delicious. "That's more like it. I hope you didn't let that little man distress you."

"No," I said, not wanting to admit to Walter how much Mott's demeanor had angered me. "No, I was thinking about what I know and don't know about Henry Starrett's murder. If Enoch Jamison didn't do it, could John Baines have beaten Henry? If Frederick Reynard wasn't there, could his wife have pulled the trigger? What is the likelihood that two unrelated people committed this crime? And if one person beat and shot Henry, who was it? Not Mott, not the general, not Oscar Killian." I didn't want to believe what I was starting to conclude. Walter looked at me with concern on his face.

"Sir Arthur didn't do it, Hattie," he said, reading my mind. "We'll simply have to do what Sir Arthur said, 'delve deeper.' " I nodded and trusted Walter was right. I pushed the dessert plate away, several bites of cake left uneaten, and fought the tears I could feel welling up in my eyes. But what if he was wrong?

CHAPTER 29

"Any luck finding what you were looking for?" General Starrett took another puff from his pipe. I'd spent the afternoon combing through every possible source in the general's extensive library: war history books, newspapers, G.A.R. meeting records, biographies, and autobiographies, trying to piece together his son's war record. I'd noticed that the general was still favoring his pipe and wondered how he would like Frederick's commemorative cigars.

"No, not yet," I said, skimming through one of the scrapbooks Lavinia Starrett had compiled. The general had preferred staying in the library with me over sitting in the parlor with his dead son. Occasionally he would interrupt me with a comment on a particular article that caught his interest, often one that had no bearing on my search. But for the majority of the time we sat reading in companionable silence. At one point he'd been quiet for so long that I looked up to find him fast asleep in his chair.

"Your son had an unusual experience during the war, didn't he, sir?"

"Unusual? What do you mean?"

"Well, I've noticed in doing research that once you can figure out what regiment a soldier belongs to, you can trace what
the soldier did more easily by what the regiment did. But as a
ship's captain, Henry didn't belong to a single regiment. He
had numerous missions involving many regiments, both army
and navy."

"Ah, I see. Yes, I think *tedious* and *boring* are more appropriate words than *unusual*."

"Because he wasn't on the ground fighting battles?"

"Because his main task was to transport goods and people.
No glory in it. Don't get me wrong, what he did was vital, but
you don't win medals for picking up guns and soldiers in one
port and dropping them off at another."

"Papa, are you smoking again?" Adella said, entering the
room. I glanced up from my work and tried not to stare at her.
Could she be capable of killing her own father? "Hello, Miss
Davish," she said sadly.

"Hello, Mrs. Reynard."

"My only child has been murdered," the general said with
more vehemence than I'd expect from him. "Have a heart, girl,
and leave me alone with my pipe." Adella burst into tears and
collapsed into the nearest chair. "Oh, now, I didn't mean to
make you cry."

"He was *my* only father," Adella sobbed. "And now he's
gone."

I was ill at ease being witness to this intimate scene. I set
the scrapbook I was looking at down and stood. "If you will
excuse me, I'll leave you to your privacy." I walked toward the
door, but as I passed, Adella unexpectedly grabbed my hand.

"Please, Miss Davish," she said, "don't go." I looked to the
general for direction. He merely shook his head slowly back
and forth.

"Can I do something for you, Mrs. Reynard?" I asked.

"Yes, tell me about my father."

"Ma'am?" I said, confused. "I'm sorry, but I didn't know your father. I'd only met him last week."

"I know," she said, letting my hand go with a sigh. "I also know that they've arrested Sir Arthur for his murder and that you're trying to prove his innocence." She looked up into my eyes. "Frederick told me about your conversation this morning."

"But I'm not clear how that relates to your request," I said, still confused.

"I want you to tell me why someone would kill him," she said. I was afraid she'd say that. She wanted to know about Henry's secrets, his weaknesses, his unsavory behavior. And she wanted me to be the one to tell her. "Please sit down." Instead of sitting at the table as I had been, I sat in a chair across from her.

"I'm afraid I haven't learned much, Mrs. Reynard," I said.

"Is that the truth, Miss Davish, or do you think I can't cope with the truth?" she said.

"Well, my girl," the general said, "the truth can be hurtful and ugly. What if it mars the memories of your father? Would you still want to know? I'm not even sure if *I* want to know." Adella began to cry again.

"Tell me this, Miss Davish," the general said, "and swear on your integrity that you will tell me the honest truth."

"Yes?" I said.

"Do you think Sir Arthur did it?"

I hesitated, knowing everything, my career, my status, my honor, depended on my answer.

"No, I cannot believe that Sir Arthur is a murderer, sir," I said honestly. "But I'm beginning to doubt my ability to find a more plausible suspect." The general nodded and took a long puff from his pipe.

"I don't think he did it either," he said finally. I was relieved to hear that. "That's why I gave you permission to look through my library. Too bad you aren't having any luck."

"You truly think the murderer is still at large, Papa?" Adella said, dabbing her eyes with a handkerchief.

"Yes, I do. Furthermore, I think we must do all we can to help Miss Davish here find the real culprit."

Adella looked over at the table piled with books and papers as if noticing them for the first time. "What are you looking for, Miss Davish?"

"I think the reason for your father's death may lie in the past, possibly from his time during the war." The general squinted at me. I hadn't explained the exact details of my research, hoping to avoid having to tell him about the accusations against his son. "Specifically I'm trying to determine if he ever had an official duty in the Deep South."

"You mentioned that before," the general said. "I told you I didn't know of any such duty."

"Yes, sir," I said. "But remember the tintype of Captain Starrett's steamboat that was taken in the Deep South? I promised to show it to you?"

"Yes, that's right. You had a picture of his boat, the *Lavinia*. And I remember you said it had something to do with plants." I explained about the palmetto's limited range again.

"So you see, that plant only grows in a few places."

"Yes, yes, that's right. Did you bring the photograph with you?" the general asked.

"I'm sorry, sir," I said. "But I couldn't."

"What does any of this have to do with his murder?" Adella asked.

"I would've thought nothing except that photograph was recently stolen from me."

"Oh," Adella gasped.

"Stolen? What the Sam Hill is going on here!" the general exclaimed.

"I don't know. That's why I thought that if I could trace Captain Starrett's movements throughout the war, I might be able to find an overlap with something we already know."

"Like his wartime relationship with Rachel Baines," Adella said quietly. She obviously hadn't forgotten the conversation we'd both overheard between Henry and Rachel at the Christmas entertainment.

"Yes, like that," I said.

"What relationship?" General Starrett asked. Adella ignored him.

"Would his letters help?" she said. I almost fell out of my chair.

"His letters?" I said, trying to stay composed. When Sir Arthur and I searched the dead man's room, we found business memoranda, the burnt letter, and Rachel Baines's brooch but no wartime correspondence. Who knew what it might reveal? I might prove Sir Arthur innocent, after all.

"My father wrote my mother every day of the war. Sometimes twice a day."

"We all did, write every day, that is. It helped with the tedium of waiting for the next battle to begin. Well, go get them, girl," General Starrett said with almost as much enthusiasm as I felt. "I had no idea such letters still existed," he said after Adella left the room. "It will be almost like having him back again."

Adella wasn't long. When she returned, she hugged a black wooden box against her chest. "I used to read them when Father was away and imagine what he was doing at that exact moment. That's how I started reading travel journey books." She hesitated a moment before handing the box over to me. The initials *AKS* were engraved with ivory inlay on top. "They're all I have left of him," she said.

I took the box with all the reverence it deserved. I sat down, opened the box, and pulled out the first stack of letters, tied with a navy blue ribbon. I began reading their contents as quickly as I could, one letter after another, partly out of my eagerness to find something of value, partly out of fear that Mrs. Reynard would change her mind and take the letters back.

Adella hovered over me and then leaned in. "They aren't comprehensive," she whispered. I snapped my head up to look at her. "Mrs. Baines isn't mentioned." I nodded my understanding and went back to my reading.

"You can whisper all you want, Adella," the general said. "But my hearing is excellent. Now what is this about Mrs. Baines?"

I could vaguely hear Mrs. Reynard explain what she knew to her grandfather while I read Henry's letters. Details about his time acting as a captain of a hospital ship confirmed Rachel Baines's story without mentioning her. Other letters described how he'd spent most of the war doing as the general said, conveying troops and goods from one part of the Union to another. With a letter still in hand, I dragged my notebook across the table, flipped to a blank page, and began a catalog of Henry's missions: St. Louis to Cairo, Cairo to Cincinnati, Mound City to Fort Anderson, et cetera.

When I had finished skimming all the letters, I'd confirmed that Henry had only one official mission to the regions where the switch cane and palmetto both grew. Henry had been to Vicksburg. But if the mission was official, what was it about the photograph of Henry's boat that made someone want to steal it? I read the full letter addressed to his wife, Sarah, dated Christmas Eve, 1862.

Merry Christmas, my love! Arrived at Milliken's Bend, just upstream from Vicksburg, today. It's stormy and cold here but doesn't feel much like Christmas. How I have a hankering for your mince cake with Spanish cream. I can taste it in my dreams. We picked up more infantry troops, (the 12th

and 29th MO if Mother is still keeping track) in Helena
along with supplies and will be heading up the Yazoo soon.
But don't worry, once Sherman's men disembark, I'm head-
ing straight back to Cairo. Give my love to little Adella and
tell her Daddy is bringing home presents.

Something struck me as vaguely familiar. I read it a second
and then a third time. The Twenty-Ninth Missouri Infantry
regiment! I'd almost missed it. Could that be what Priscilla
Triggs knew that she wasn't telling anyone? I had to speak
with Sir Arthur immediately.

"Miss Davish, you're as pale as yesterday's gardenias,"
Adella said. "Are you all right?"

After writing down the name of the regiment that Henry
had transported to Vicksburg, I handed Adella back the letter
box. My hand was shaking.

"Thank you, Mrs. Reynard. Thank you, General Starrett,
sir," I said. "You've both been extremely helpful." I said, gathering up my notes. I threw my coat on, not bothering with my
gloves.

"You've found something, haven't you?" General Starrett
said.

"I believe so, sir. Yes." Before either could ask me another
question, I stuffed my hat on my head and ran out the door.

"He's your guest, sir," I said. "What would you have me do?"

After leaving General Starrett and Adella Reynard gaping
at my abrupt departure, I'd headed straight for the nearest telegraph office. I wired a request to Sir Arthur's friend in the War
Department. When I marked it "Urgent," I laughed out loud,
to the befuddlement of the telegraph operator. Hank, the
operator in the Arcadia Hotel in Eureka Springs, would've
understood. Then I ran, literally, to the jailhouse. I was overwhelmed with what I'd learned and the only way that I could

release the pent-up energy and calm my nerves was to run. Once or twice I slipped on an icy patch on the sidewalk, but I'd kept my balance on both occasions and, despite the ache in my ribs, kept going. I told Sir Arthur everything I'd learned from Henry's letters.

"I'm sorry I haven't had time to type it up properly, sir," I said, "but I thought it more important that I speak to you immediately, to see how you would have me proceed." Sir Arthur stroked his chin.

"You wired Rogers at the War Department?"

I nodded. "Before I came here," I said. "I'm hoping for a prompt response."

"Then we should wait for the response." I wasn't sure I'd be able to wait. It would mean Sir Arthur would languish that much longer in this cell. It would mean I'd have to keep this secret for hours, maybe days. I was already feeling anxious. What if I saw the object of my inquiry at Sir Arthur's house? How was I going to pretend that everything was as it was before?

"Should I continue asking questions?" I asked.

"No, suspend everything you're doing on my behalf until you get the telegram. We'll know where to go from there."

"Sir, what if I only spoke to Mrs. Triggs?" I said.

I'd been eager to speak to Priscilla after lunch and the confrontation with Mott. But when Walter accompanied me back to Sir Arthur's house to check on her, he discovered she'd taken another, unprescribed dose of the chloral hydrate. Walter had been both furious and deeply concerned. Some people have died from overdoses of this medicine. Despite Lieutenant Triggs's assurances he would make sure she didn't take any more, Walter insisted on staying by her bedside until she woke. Knowing she was in good hands, I'd left Walter and the Triggses and gone to General Starrett's house.

"Dr. Grice implied that she might know something of importance." I was convinced more than ever that she knew something. Something she didn't want to face. Why else would she prefer to spend the day in a drug-induced stupor? "And we're on friendly terms. If she'll talk to anyone, she'll talk to me."

"No, Hattie," Sir Arthur said, "leave Priscilla out of this."

I wanted to shout, "Even if she knows something or saw something that could exonerate you?" But I knew better than to question Sir Arthur. Instead, I sighed and said, "Yes, sir."

I had barely slept at all. I was unaccustomed to going to bed with little or nothing to show for a day's efforts. My sole task had been to find something, anything, that would ease Sir Arthur's predicament and yet I'd failed. I'd successfully eliminated several people as possible suspects, but the only evidence I'd uncovered in Sir Arthur's favor had yet to prove significant. Now all I could do was wait. I didn't even have any manuscript pages to type to keep me occupied. Restless, I'd left the house hours before sunrise and hiked several miles beside the railroad tracks that paralleled the Galena River toward the Mississippi River. The rigor of the hike and the burn in my lungs as I breathed in the cold air effectively cleared my head. I returned energized and able to concentrate on the tasks of the day: to wait patiently for a reply to my inquiry and to prepare for Christmas. It was Christmas Eve. Despite Sir Arthur's arrest, he had compelled his staff to act as if he were to arrive home at any minute. That meant the daily newspapers on his desk, a decorated Christmas tree, and a timely Christmas Eve tea.

"A message arrived for you," William Finch, the butler, said as I hung up my coat. He was sitting in the kitchen having breakfast with Mrs. Monday, Ida, and Harvey. My heart skipped a beat. Could it be a telegram from Washington already? "I left it on the table."

"Can I fix you a plate?" Mrs. Monday said, pushing her

chair back and standing up. I picked up the envelope that was addressed to me and carefully peeled it open. I didn't have my letter opener. I scanned the contents and my hopes were dashed. It was from Walter.

"No, thank you, Mrs. Monday," I said, having lost my appetite. Then I noticed the raspberry jelly cakes. "Well, maybe I'll have a jelly cake." She smiled as she set the plate before me.

"Who's it from?" she asked.

"Dr. Grice. He's invited me to luncheon again."

"Then why do you sound so disappointed?" Mrs. Monday said. "My lamb on toast isn't that good." I smiled at her jest.

"No, it's not that," I said, walking over to the stove and pouring myself a cup of coffee. "I was expecting a telegram." I sat down next to Ida at the table and sipped my coffee and nibbled on the jelly cake. The front door bell rang. I experienced a moment of exhilaration, expectation. Could that be my telegram? Then I came to my senses and realized the telegram I was anxious for, especially at Christmastime, might take days to arrive. William took one more gulp of his coffee and then jumped up to answer the door. William returned a minute later. He carried an envelope in his hand. My heart raced again.

"Who was that?" Mrs. Monday asked.

"The mail," he said. "Looks like a Christmas card for you, Mrs. Monday." My hopes dashed a second time, my stomach was tied in knots. *This won't do,* I thought. I had to distract myself or I was liable to become ill with anxiety. I gulped down the remainder of my coffee, grabbed a second jelly cake off the tray, and pushed myself back from the table. Making up my mind had brought back some of the original excitement I'd felt before the two men died.

"Anyone else ready to decorate the Christmas tree?" I asked.

CHAPTER 30

E ven without the candles lit, the Christmas tree was stunning. William Finch had donated the hundreds of tiny
candles and he and Harvey helped secure them while I draped
the garlands and ribbon. We took turns climbing up and down
the ten-foot ladder. Then Ida, Mrs. Monday, and I took turns
trimming the tree. We hung sugarplums, handmade paper cornucopias filled with Brazil nuts and preserved coriander seeds,
gold-painted pinecones, glass ornaments in a myriad of colors,
shapes, and sizes, icicles made of silver foil, and strings of whole
cranberries and unwrapped hard candy in rainbow hues. All
that was missing was the wrapped presents and the angel that
I'd purchased out of my own wages. It waited for Sir Arthur to
do us the honor.

It was the most spectacular Christmas tree I'd ever seen.
Everyone who walked by exclaimed how lovely it was. Sir
Arthur would be proud.

"It's great, Hattie," Lieutenant Triggs said, who with his
wife had spent part of the morning watching us trim the tree.

"Doesn't it look like it should be on the cover of *Harper's*, Priscilla?"

"I've never seen a tree so beautiful," Mrs. Triggs said, caressing the baby Jesus from the nativity scene beneath the tree. Even Mrs. Baines, who had checked on our progress several times, had to admit that it was a "festive, colorful thing."

It almost made everything seem to be all right—almost.

I was standing on the ladder, straightening a few wayward candles, when Ida pushed the door open. She was carrying a bucket of coal and had dark smears on her face and apron. She set the bucket down next to the fireplace.

"Mrs. Monday says tea will be ready soon, *ja?*" she said. Even though Sir Arthur was in jail, the staff had continued as if he was still demanding prompt and proper service.

"Thank you, Ida," I said. I sighed and climbed off the ladder. It was teatime and Sir Arthur was no closer to being home for Christmas than he was yesterday.

After decorating the tree and having a pleasant, diverting luncheon with Walter, I again waited. The afternoon dragged on as I tried to occupy myself. With no manuscript to work on, I wrote a letter to Miss Lizzie in Eureka Springs, read some chapters of William Trelease's *Species of* Rumex *Occurring North of Mexico,* which I'd borrowed from General Starrett's library, retyped some labels in my botanical collections according to the taxonomic changes I'd learned from Mr. Trelease's book, and then set to wrapping Christmas presents. I had set the presents beneath the tree and had just noticed the tilting candles when Ida arrived.

The front door bell rang.

I knew not to get excited anymore. The bell had rung several times this morning while we trimmed the tree. Twice it had been well-wishers who hadn't heard the news of Sir Arthur's arrest; once it was someone delivering an exquisite bouquet of flowers from Frederick Reynard. The former had been a harsh reminder that Sir Arthur was still in jail. The latter, with its sprigs of olive branch, was a grim reminder that Henry Starrett's killer was still free. The last time the bell rang it was Walter arriving to escort me to lunch.

William appeared in the doorway.

"This came for you," he said, handing me an envelope.

I held my breath. This time it was the telegram. I looked around for something to open the envelope with and, seeing nothing, ungracefully ripped it open with my fingers.

THE WESTERN UNION TELEGRAPH COMPANY

NUMBER *17* SENT BY *RM* REC'D BY *JG* CHECK *24 paid*

RECEIVED at *No. 1 Galena, IL*   *Dec 24* **1892**

Dated: *Washington, DC*   *3:47pm*

To: *H Davish*   *112 S. Prospect, Galena, IL*

Received your request, Confirmed 29th MO Infantry transport 12-24-62, soldier listed as POW Vicksburg jail 12-25-62 to 5-20-63, Cahaba Prison, AL dates unkn. Regards to Sir Arthur.
Adm J. Rogers

I was right, I thought. *It's true!*

With my hands trembling, I read the message again. It was not only true but astounding! I'd been right about the transport on Captain Starrett's steamboat but was shocked to discover that this particular soldier had become a prisoner of the Confederates at Vicksburg, the very next day. And Christmas Day of all days! Was his entire regiment captured? If so, how did Henry Starrett and his crew not suffer the same fate? Could that have something to do with Henry's death, almost to the day thirty years later? How does the saying go? "Revenge is a dish best served cold"? I shivered at the thought.

Now I must confront him. But when and how? Should I

tell Sir Arthur what I'd learned first? Should I ask Walter to be at my side? I folded the telegram, put it back in the envelope, and brought it up to my room. I hid it under a stack of manuscript pages. *What if he's the killer?* I thought as I went down to Christmas Eve tea. I took a deep breath.

Everyone was there, except of course for Sir Arthur. I hesitated before entering the parlor.

"Why are you hovering in the doorway staring at me?" Rachel Baines said. It wasn't Rachel Baines I'd been staring at. "Don't you have something better to do?"

"You're making my wife uncomfortable, Miss Davish," John Baines said with a hint of sarcasm. He winked at me. Or was that his nervous twitch? "Please stop hesitating and join us for tea." Rachel sneered at her husband.

"I didn't want you to invite the girl in," she said, under her breath but loud enough for me to hear her from the hallway. I took a few steps forward.

"Yes, join us," Lieutenant Triggs said while his wife patted a chair next to her.

"Yes, please, Hattie," Priscilla said. "Sit with me." William Finch entered carrying the tea tray with Ida behind him, a clean apron around her waist but the coal smudges still on her cheek and brow. She carried a three-tiered cake dish brimming with egg sandwiches, salmon sandwiches, apple bread, scones served with jam, butter, and clotted cream, slices of golden cake and silver cake, cranberry tarts, jumbles, peppermint drops, and chocolate caramels.

"Well, since Sir Arthur's not here and I'm tired," Mrs. Baines said, "we won't stand on ceremony. You may serve the tea, Hattie." Mrs. Triggs frowned. "Unless you want to do it, Mrs. Triggs?"

"No, Hattie may do it," Mrs. Triggs said.

"Very well. I prefer mine weak with two sugars," Rachel Baines said.

"*Bitte,* please," Ida said, bending in a clumsy curtsy, "but I can do that, Frau Baines." Before I could say anything Ida took the teacup I'd prepared for Mrs. Baines.

"For goodness' sake, when was the last time you had a proper washing?" Rachel said, noticing the smudges on Ida's face. Ida offered Mrs. Baines the teacup. "You expect me to drink from that? Being poisoned once this week was enough, thank you."

She pushed the teacup away, almost spilling the tea. Ida glanced at me in a panic. I picked up a clean teacup and poured the tea. Using the tongs, I dropped two cubes of sugar into the cup, and handed it to Mrs. Baines.

"It's okay, Ida," I said. Ida, not understanding the etiquette of tea, thought I was being imposed upon. "I'll serve the tea." With a quick nod toward the door, I encouraged Ida to leave as quickly as she could. Mrs. Baines, like some women of her class, often forgot to treat those who served them like people. I'd worked for many an employer who treated me this way. I was used to the verbal abuse, but Ida was not. But as Ida retreated after William and I poured Mrs. Triggs a cup of tea, I was baffled. Rachel Baines had never passed on an opportunity to make herself the center of attention. And she'd never shown anything but condescension toward me since the moment she arrived. So why had she not poured the tea instead of giving that honor to me? Was it simply because she was tired, as she said? Or was there some other reason?

I handed Priscilla her tea. She smiled weakly at me.

And what do you know? I thought as I returned her smile. As dictated, I'd refrained from asking Priscilla about Henry Starrett's murder. But it hadn't stopped me from wondering.

When I approached Lieutenant Triggs with his tea, he and John Baines were in a conversation about past Christmastide hunts. Again my thoughts turned to Sir Arthur, who loved to hunt. Tomorrow was Christmas. How could I allow Sir Arthur to spend Christmas in jail? I'd dutifully waited for the telegram as I'd been told. And I knew he expected me to consult him before I did anything further. But Sir Arthur hadn't forbid me from continuing my questions after the telegram's arrival. If my questions led to his release, he'd forgive my breach of duty. Hopefully.

I handed Lieutenant Triggs his tea and took a deep breath. I couldn't look the man in the eye. He'd almost always been friendly to me and appreciative of my work. But he was a liar and I had to know why.

"Why did you lie to the police about knowing Henry Starrett?" I said. Lieutenant Triggs spit his tea out and started coughing. His wife leaned over and pounded him on the back.

"Hattie, what kind of question is that?" she said.

"A crucial one," I said.

"I don't know, Miss Davish," John Baines said. "It almost sounded like an accusation." All eyes were on me and I couldn't back down now.

"Sir Arthur is in jail for a crime he didn't commit. I've been charged to discover the true culprit, if possible. My questions and research have led me to a few unexpected discoveries, such as a connection with the murder victim and you, Lieutenant Triggs." Lieutenant Triggs had his wife's handkerchief over his mouth, still trying to compose himself. He merely shook his head.

"What sort of connection?" Rachel Baines asked.

"Like you, ma'am," I said as her cheeks burned red. "They crossed paths during the war. The unit that Lieutenant Triggs belonged to was once on Captain Starrett's steamboat. His regiment was transported to Chickasaw Bayou around Christmas, 1862."

"You knew Henry Starrett during the war?" John Baines asked his wife. His nervous twitch was apparent in both eyes now. She ignored him.

"But I thought Henry never went to Vicksburg or any-where near there?" she said. "How do you know this?"

"I read it first in one of Henry Starrett's letters and then had it confirmed by a friend of Sir Arthur's in the War Department."

"Henry's letters?" Lieutenant Triggs and Rachel Baines exclaimed at the same time.

"Yes," I said. "The captain was a prolific writer during the war. His wife kept every one and left the letters to her daughter, Adella Reynard."

"Did Henry mention me in any of these letters?" Rachel Baines said.

"Why would he?" John Baines demanded.

"Oh, John," Rachel said, dismissing her husband with a wave of her hand. "Well?"

"Not that I read," I said, noticing Rachel frown. John Baines noticed his wife's reaction as well. "No, they're more like a ship's log than anything. He described his cargo, his missions, the tedium. Rarely did he write of anything personal." She blushed again.

"Again, I have to ask, why didn't you tell the police or Sir Arthur that you had met Henry Starrett before?" I asked Lieutenant Triggs.

"I didn't think it was important," he said.

"My wife didn't tell anyone either and that may turn out to be of the greatest import," John Baines said snidely.

"Jack, this has nothing to do with me," Rachel said.

"Did you also think it wasn't important to tell anyone that only days after being on Henry Starrett's boat you were a prisoner at Vicksburg?"

"How did you know that?" Lieutenant Triggs blustered. He stood up abruptly, but his wife, taking his hand, nudged him back into his chair.

"It's true?" Rachel Baines said. "You were in a prison camp?"

"Yes, it's true, if you must know," Priscilla said. "First Vicksburg, than Cahaba in Alabama." I suddenly remembered Lieutenant Triggs mentioning Cahaba after we'd been food poisoned. I hadn't understood the reference at the time and hadn't taken note of it. "My husband suffered terribly, Mrs. Baines, so we don't like to talk about it." She stared at me and frowned.

"Is it a coincidence then that your path crossed with Henry Starrett and a day later you were a prisoner?" I asked. Lieutenant Triggs looked down at his lap. "Or that your paths crossed again and now Henry Starrett is dead?" The room erupted. Everyone, except Lieutenant Triggs, began shouting all at once.

"What are you saying?" John Baines said. "That Triggs here killed Starrett?"

"My husband would never do such a thing," Priscilla protested.

"Oh my God, I'm having tea with a murderer," Rachel Baines said, cowering in her chair.

The shouting had brought Mrs. Monday and Ida from the kitchen. They hovered in the doorway, each looking to me with a questioning gaze before staring at the guests having tea. Mrs. Monday passed the back of her hand against her chin, leaving a smudge of chocolate frosting. It looked like dried blood. Lieutenant Triggs held his hand up and everyone fell silent.

"Some of what you say is true," he said. Rachel moaned in distress but quieted down immediately when her husband flashed her a glance of annoyance and anger. "I actually feel relieved that someone found me out." He chuckled slightly. "Should've known it'd be you."

Priscilla put her hand on his arm. "Don't," she said. He patted her arm.

"It's okay, darling," he said. "I'm glad the truth's out. I don't know why I hid it so long."

"Are you admitting to Henry Starrett's murder, Lieutenant Triggs?" I asked. Rachel Baines and Ida, who was hiding behind Mrs. Monday, gasped. Rachel Baines stared at the women in the doorway until they retreated out of sight. Lieutenant Triggs shook his head.

"No, I didn't kill him, though I had every intention to." Rachel Baines gasped again as I continued staring at him, expecting him to say more. He didn't.

"What do you mean you intended to kill him?" I said. "Did you take Sir Arthur's gun?" He nodded.

"I'm ashamed to say I did. But I didn't use it, I swear." He looked pleadingly to everyone in the room. "The miscreant got what he deserved," he shouted, "but I didn't shoot him!"

"But you did beat him," I said.

"No," Priscilla declared with a surprisingly spirited voice. "He couldn't have. He was with me all that morning, weren't you, Morgan?" She was still clutching his arm.

"No, my love. You have no reason to lie for me. I was there and I did it. I pounded on that pompous, reprobate scoundrel until I couldn't anymore." He rubbed his knuckles, which didn't show any signs of bruising. It was cold that morning. He'd probably been wearing gloves.

"Why?" John Baines asked.

"Because he was a hypocrite, a liar, and a traitor," Lieutenant Triggs said. The letter Sir Arthur and I'd found in Henry's fireplace came to mind.

"You sent him that letter," I said.

"You know about that too?" Lieutenant Triggs said. "What else do you know?"

"Tell us why you did it, Triggs," John Baines insisted.

"Miss Davish was right. Starrett was the captain of the ship that was transporting my regiment to Chickasaw Bayou. I had the misfortune of stumbling on hidden crates of quinine that Starrett was obviously smuggling to the rebs. While 'serving his country' he was making a profit for himself."

How despicable, I thought. And ironic! Henry Starrett attacked and harassed a copperhead at every opportunity for more than twenty-five years all the while hiding his own treasonous past. If Enoch Jamison had known, he might've killed Henry years ago.

"I don't believe it!" Rachel cried. "If it's true, you would've turned him in. Even I would've stopped him from smuggling stolen medicine to the rebels." Tears welled in the woman's eyes.

"Why didn't you turn him in?" John Baines asked.

"Because it's not true," Rachel said.

"Because he stopped me before I had a chance," Lieutenant Triggs said. "One minute I was lifting canvas off crates, the next minute I was gagged and tied next to them."

"And when he handed over the quinine, he handed over you as well," I said.

"So it was 'Merry Christmas, Graybacks!' " John Baines sneered, his lips curled.

"Yeah, you could say that," Lieutenant Triggs said. "And after the battle, I was just one more soldier lost or missing. I spent the next eighteen months in prison."

"He contracted the mumps there," Priscilla said, her voice cracking in despair. "We never could have children after that." She started to sob quietly. Her husband put his arm around her and pulled her close.

"You can see why I didn't want an open confrontation with the man," he said, glancing at his wife. "I tried to just get through the holidays, but I couldn't do it. I admired General

Starrett and was appalled that he, like many others, was unwittingly welcoming a traitor back into this glory-filled community. And Henry had the gall to boast about terrorizing that copperhead and his elderly mother in their own home. At least that Jamison man was honorable in his own way, serving time for his beliefs. No, it was too much. I wrote Henry Starrett that letter and suggested we meet. I knew the cocky, arrogant devil would come. Like I said, I went intending to kill him. But I swear he was alive when I left."

"So why didn't you?" Rachel Baines asked. "Kill him, I mean." She was sitting on the edge of her seat, balancing her teacup on her knee.

"He was unarmed. If I'd killed an unarmed man, I'd be worse than he was. Besides, he had the smell of perfume about him and I thought, if he'd fooled a poor woman into loving him I didn't want her to suffer like my wife had. That poor woman was already suffering enough."

"He smelled of lily of the valley didn't he?" I asked.

"I don't know. I wouldn't know one perfume from the other," he said. John and Rachel Baines exchanged glances and John Baines abruptly left the room.

"I wonder what's gotten into him?" Rachel said, shrugging her shoulders. "So what did you do then?"

"Like I said, I beat him with my fists until I was exhausted. I might've kicked him a few times too. If he'd died from that, I wouldn't have been surprised. But he didn't, did he?"

"No, the coroner confirmed that it was the gunshot that killed Captain Starrett," I said.

"And Sir Arthur's gun?" Rachel said. "The police found it in the river."

"I don't know how it got there," he said. "I threw it down at Starrett's feet, cocked and loaded. I hoped he'd use it on himself." He shook his head. "But he was a bad egg. I should've known he wouldn't do it."

"But someone did," I said, my mind racing. *If not Lieutenant Triggs,* I thought, *then who?* "You'll have to tell this to the police." Lieutenant Triggs nodded. I tugged on the bellpull. "Did you steal the photograph from my room?"

"I'm ashamed to say I did. I beg your forgiveness for invading your privacy."

"But why?"

"When you asked General Starrett about it, I was surprised to learn that no one knew about Henry's visit to Vicksburg. Even Henry denied remembering when or where it was taken. So with him dead, I seemed to be the only one who knew. If the photograph disappeared, no one would be the wiser, would they? Henry's treachery would be my secret alone and the general spared the shame. So I burned it. I didn't know about the letters."

"And you weren't wearing a boutonniere that morning, were you?" I asked. I thought I knew the answer, but I wanted to be certain.

"What does that have to do with anything?" Rachel Baines asked. Lieutenant Triggs, frowning and furrowing his brow, seemed as skeptical as Mrs. Baines.

"It's important. Were you?" I asked again.

The lieutenant shook his head. "No. No, I wasn't. I'm allergic to flowers."

I was right.

William arrived in answer to the bell. "Someone rang?" he said.

"I did," I said. William frowned. "Would you send for the police, please?" William's eyebrows shot up. His eyes took in the scene: Rachel Baines rearranging herself in her chair, fluffing the folds of her dress, Priscilla Triggs softly crying as her husband comforted her.

"Don't worry, PrissyCat," Morgan Triggs said to his wife. "I didn't kill him. Everything will be okay."

CHAPTER 31

Icouldn't stay in that room. While we waited for the police, we sat in awkward silence for several minutes. The Triggses seemed in their own private world while Mrs. Baines, with no reason to stay other than her own sense of drama, pulled a *Harper's Bazar* from the table and began idly leafing through it. I was amazed at her composure. I finally stood up and crossed the hall to Sir Arthur's library. I entered with the intention of tidying up, having the expectation that he would be released soon. It was immaculate. I was disappointed but should've known. Other than his atrocious handwriting, Sir Arthur held order in high regard. So instead, I grabbed a blank piece of paper, dipped my pen, and wrote down the questions that were still unanswered:

1. Is Lieutenant Triggs telling the truth, the whole truth?
2. If so, who shot Henry Starrett?
3. Was it Mrs. Baines's perfume Lieutenant Triggs and I smelled on Henry Starrett?

    4. If so, why was she there?

    5. Where did the olive leaves come from? Mrs. Baines's corsage?

    6. Did she shoot Henry Starrett?

If he was telling the truth, Lieutenant Triggs wasn't the killer after all. *And I'm not any closer than I was before,* I thought.

If Lieutenant Triggs took Sir Arthur's gun as he claimed and left it at Henry Starrett's feet, anyone could've come along and shot him, taking advantage of his incapacitation. Anyone. The idea was overwhelming. Henry Starrett was an obnoxious man who had many enemies. Oscar Killian had thrown away his livelihood getting revenge for Enoch Jamison. What if others knew of Starrett's treachery? Or objected to his treatment of Enoch Jamison and happened to stumble upon him, see the gun, and . . . ? My reflection was interrupted by the front door bell. I left the library, carrying my list. Walter and Officer Corbett were in the hallway. Walter was handing William his coat. Officer Corbett took off his hat and nodded.

"Good afternoon, Miss Davish," he said, smiling. "It's nice to see you again, though once it would be nice to meet under more pleasant circumstances." Walter frowned.

"How is Sir Arthur?" I asked.

"He's fine, Miss Davish," Corbett said, "and if the reason I'm here is because you're a better policeman than I am, then he'll be home for his Christmas Eve supper."

"I hope so," I said, indicating for Corbett to lead us into the parlor.

"By the way," the policeman said, "we have confirmation that Enoch Jamison was in Chicago the day before the murder. His mother followed him there and had him telephone. His story checks out. He may still face charges for Lieutenant Colonel Holbrook's death, but he didn't kill Henry Starrett." Another suspect I'd have to cross off my list. Hopefully Lieutenant Triggs's confession, even to just the beating of Henry Starrett, was enough to clear Sir Arthur.

"I thought I heard someone come in," John Baines said, coming down the stairs. He nodded to Walter and then noticed Officer Corbett. "Ah, the police. Are you here to arrest Triggs then?" Walter looked at me with wide eyes.

"I was on the steps about to ring the bell when he drove up," Walter said, speaking low into my ear. "What's going on?"

"A breakthrough," I said, grasping his hand. I looked into his eyes and smiled. He squeezed my hand and his brilliant smile lit the room. I felt giddy, only the seriousness of the moment kept me from laughing. Walter had always had my heart and he knew it. We let go of each other's hands. Corbett, who had seen our exchange, wore an embarrassed expression. He caught my eye briefly and hesitated, as if to say something, before turning abruptly on his heel.

That's that then, I thought, distressed that I was the cause of a good man's disappointment.

Walter gestured to me with an outstretched arm toward the retreating policeman's back and we followed Corbett and John Baines into the parlor. All three occupants of the room looked up.

"He took Sir Arthur's gun and assaulted Henry within inches of his life," Rachel Baines announced, pointing to Lieutenant Triggs. Walter looked at me for confirmation. I nodded.

"Is this true, sir?" Corbett asked Lieutenant Triggs as John Baines joined his wife, sitting on the arm of her chair.

"Yes."

"But he didn't kill him," Priscilla said pleadingly. "He didn't kill him." She looked at me. "You believe him, don't you, Hattie?" Officer Corbett turned to me, expecting a reply. What was I supposed to say? That my impression of Lieutenant Triggs was that he was incapable of cold-blooded murder? I'd learned the hard way that anyone could murder, if they thought it was for the right reason. Luckily I didn't have to give a reply. As often before, Walter came to my rescue.

"According to the autopsy and the medical examiner's report, the bruises were consistent with what we know about Lieutenant Triggs in terms of strength, height, and the fact that he's right-handed," Walter said.

"But that could describe Sir Arthur as well," Officer Corbett said. Walter conceded that that was true.

"But the lieutenant is admitting to it," Rachel Baines said. "Sir Arthur always claimed he didn't do it."

"You have a point, Mrs. Baines," Corbett said. "But that still leaves the identity of the shooter unknown."

"Well, he probably shot him too," she said.

"No!" Priscilla exclaimed with force. "My husband is not a liar, let alone a killer."

"Once a liar, always a liar, dear," Mrs. Baines said, smirking and shaking her head.

"Truly, Rachel?" John Baines said, his eyes unusually steady. His wife looked up at him in surprise. "You lied about your relationship with Henry, didn't you? Maybe you're lying about shooting him too." Rachel's hands flew to her face, covering her expression of horror. But only for a moment.

"How dare you!" she screamed. Then she slapped her husband across the face. John Baines didn't flinch.

"Tell them or I will," he said.

"Mrs. Baines?" Officer Corbett said. Rachel looked as if she was going to ignore him, but her husband grabbed the brooch she was wearing and ripped it off her dress. The collar tore, exposing her bare neck. Rachel quickly covered the tear with her hand.

"You animal," she declared. John Baines held the brooch before her eyes.

"Tell them or I will." Rachel looked around the room until her eyes lingered on me.

"Not with her here," she said. "I've been humiliated enough already." Everyone turned to look at me. Officer Corbett's face was flush with anger as he turned away from me to face Mrs. Baines.

"You will explain yourself, right here, right now, Mrs. Baines," he said. "Now!"

"All right," she said, waving her hand as if to dismiss the seriousness of her situation. "I was with Henry the morning he died. But he was alive, quite full of life, if you get my meaning, when I left him," she hastened to add. "In fact, he was in high spirits."

"Where did you leave him?" Officer Corbett said.

"On the bridge, the one that goes to the park," she said. "We'd taken a walk along the river and parted on the bridge. He went toward the park; I came back here."

"Do you wear lily of the valley–scented perfume?" I asked. Rachel Baines glared at me and folded her arms across her chest.

"Yes, she does," her husband replied instead. "I'd always been fond of that fragrance. But now . . ." Rachel Baines glanced at her lap unable to meet her husband's gaze.

That answered whose perfume lingered on Henry Starrett that day, I thought. But not whose footprints were in the snow. I mentally checked yet another suspect off my list.

"Did you see Lieutenant Triggs?" Corbett asked.

"No," she said. She looked at Lieutenant Triggs and his wife. "If I had, I'd have stopped him from killing Henry."

"He didn't kill anyone," Priscilla insisted in a whimper.

"But he does admit to stealing Sir Arthur's gun and assaulting the victim," Officer Corbett said. "I'm sorry, but Lieutenant Morgan Triggs, you are under arrest. Please stand and come with me." Priscilla burst into tears and wouldn't let go of her husband's hand.

"Don't worry," Lieutenant Triggs said. "Everything will be all right. They'll find the real killer and then everything will be all right." He turned to me. "You found me out. I have no doubt you'll find the real killer." What could I say to that? I had thought he was the real killer.

"Does this mean you'll release Sir Arthur?" I asked. Before the policeman could answer, William entered carrying another exquisite bouquet of flowers and a box.

"These arrived for Sir Arthur," the butler said to no one in particular. "They're from the Reynards." The policeman took the card that accompanied the gifts.

"I believe they're getting ahead of themselves," he said. He handed the card to me. Instead Rachel stood and snatched it from his grasp.

"I don't think the girl should be reading Sir Arthur's private mail," she said. "You had no right doing it either," she said to the policeman.

"On the contrary, in a murder investigation everything concerns me. As to Miss Davish, she alone in this household has the authority to read Sir Arthur's correspondences. She's his secretary, as you so like to point out, after all." Rachel Baines blushed as the policeman took the card from her and handed it back to me. It was from General Starrett and Frederick and Adella Reynard.

With our sincerest wishes. May you be home for Christmas and the rightful culprit in jail, the card read.

"That reminds me," I said. The flowers reminded me again of the olive leaves.

"Reminds you of what, Miss Davish?" Corbett said.

I hadn't realized that I'd said it out loud. "We still don't know where the olive leaves came from," I said.

"What olive leaves?" It was my turn to blush. I'd inadvertently forgotten to tell Officer Corbett about the leaves. I corrected my mistake, handing him my list of questions, and told him everything I knew: where I'd found the leaves, how I'd verified the species in Frederick Reynard's greenhouse, and how none of the men, with the exception of Frederick Reynard, had been wearing olive leaves in their boutonnieres. A chill went up my spine. I suddenly knew who killed Henry Starrett.

"Were you wearing or carrying flowers with you when you met Captain Starrett that morning, Mrs. Baines?" I said, already knowing the answer.

"I'm not answering to this girl," Rachel said, dismissing me with a wave of her hand.

"But you will answer to me," Officer Corbett said. "Were you or were you not wearing flowers that morning?"

"No," she declared. "Why would I? We weren't meeting to go dancing!"

"And the corsage that Mr. Reynard sent to us the day of the Christmas entertainment? What did you do with that?" I asked.

Rachel scrunched up her nose in a look of disgust.

"I threw it away," she said snidely.

"Why should I believe you, Mrs. Baines?" the policeman said.

"I can confirm it," William said. Everyone, including myself, turned to look at him. I'd forgotten he was still in the room. "With the guests and extra Christmas tasks, I've had to do some of Ida's work. I cleaned the waste baskets and can confirm that Mrs. Baines's corsage had been discarded."

"But she could've thrown it away after she met with Henry," Walter said. The policeman nodded.

"No, sir, she couldn't have because I emptied the baskets before I went to bed that night." My heart sank. I didn't want to be, but I was right.

"Then where did the leaves come from?" Lieutenant Triggs said, innocently curious.

I turned to look at his wife beside him. "A sprig of olive leaves was in each of the ladies' corsages that Frederick Reynard sent," I said. "Some dropped from your corsage when you covered the bullet wound with the dead man's coat. You shot Henry Starrett, didn't you, Mrs. Triggs?"

"What?" Lieutenant Triggs was on his feet and launched himself at me. Mrs. Baines screamed as I scrambled to avoid his grasp and knocked over a chair. Walter and Officer Corbett caught him by the arms and wrestled him to the floor.

"How dare you! Of all people, Miss Davish!" he cried, kicking and wrestling with his restrainers. "I've never hit a woman, but by God—"

"Do something!" Rachel Baines shrieked to no one in particular. Priscilla put her hand on her husband's arm.

"It's true, Morgan," she said, barely audible. He shook off Walter and the policeman and knelt before his wife.

"Why, Priscilla, why are you doing this? I told you I didn't kill him. You don't have to lie for me." She shook her head slowly and put a hand to his cheek.

"I saw you retrieve Sir Arthur's gun from where you'd hidden it in our room and followed you to the park," she said.

"I didn't see you there," Rachel Baines said.

"But I saw you." Priscilla looked Mrs. Baines in the eyes for the first time since they'd met. "I saw what you and Henry were doing." Rachel's jaw dropped and she was stunned speechless. John Baines glared at her, his hands curled into tight fists at his sides.

"Rachel, I should . . ." John Baines seethed. I was concerned for Mrs. Baines's safety until John abruptly stood and walked to the fireplace. He picked up the poker and smashed it against the wall. Tiny fragments of plaster burst from the dent the impact made. The poker clattered to the floor. We all gaped in silence at the man's back as he refused to face the room.

"Please continue, Mrs. Triggs," the policeman said, disregarding John Baines's outburst. Priscilla looked back down into her husband's tormented face.

"I overheard everything you said, Morgan," she said. He dropped his head against her knees. "I never knew how you ended up a prisoner. You never wanted to talk about it."

"I'm so sorry," Lieutenant Triggs said, his voice muffled by his wife's dress.

"I watched you beat that man and I silently cheered on every blow. It was his fault you were sent to that prison. It was his fault you contracted the mumps. I never wanted to be anything but a mother to your children, Morgan. It's why I was put on this earth; you know that. Not a day has gone by that I haven't questioned God for refusing my only prayer. And every day I'd feel guilty for my doubts and conclude somehow I was to blame. But that morning I discovered my suffering: the guilt, the self-recrimination, the faithlessness, had been pointless. We hadn't been denied the blessing of children by God but by a man, a self-serving traitor of a man."

Priscilla paused. Every eye was on her, including John Baines, who'd turned around to listen to her story. Silence filled the room, broken only by the creak of Rachel Baines's chair as she adjusted herself, and the ticking of the mantel clock. I'd been holding my breath. Priscilla shrugged, slightly shaking her head.

"And then there he was, like a Christmas present sent from above."

"So after your husband left, you shot him?" the policeman said.

"I couldn't resist approaching him. He lay there groggy and bloody from his injuries. He probably could barely even see who I was. So I told him."

" 'You have such lovely grandchildren, and I'll never have any,' I told him," she said. Suddenly Priscilla looked around the room and stopped with her eyes on me. "And you know what that man had the nerve to say to me, Hattie?"

"No, Priscilla," I said, slowly shaking my head. "What did he say to you?"

"He said, 'Well, then I deserve a medal. I prevented a Triggs brat from being born into this world.' And then he laughed, a gurgling sound with his lips split and his nose bleeding."

"Then what happened, Priscilla?" I asked.

"I did what any woman in my position would," she said. "I picked up the gun laying at his feet and shot him."

CHAPTER 32

Christmas dinner had been everything I'd imagined it would be. The table, which I had had a hand in decorating yesterday, was warm and welcoming. Red velvet ribbon draped down from the chandelier, red and green festive Christmas crackers marked each place, and single candlesticks glowed in the windows. A fire crackled, its light sparkling off the silverware, the crystal glasses, and the etched vase holding Frederick Reynard's bouquet as centerpiece. As expected, Mrs. Monday outdid herself with the food: tomato aspic, cranberry relish, roast goose, chestnut stuffing, sweet potato croquettes, peas served in turnip cups, dressed lettuce with cheese straws, and ginger sherbet, which, with my stomach fully recovered, I could properly enjoy.

And the company was amiable and merry. Beside Sir Arthur, who had been released after Lieutenant Triggs and his wife had been taken into custody, the guests included the Baineses; Mrs. Kaplan, the feisty widow we'd met at Adella Reynard's dinner party; Walter; and me. I'd thought I would've been satisfied with sharing a simple and relaxing Christmas dinner with William, Mrs. Monday, and Ida in the kitchen. But watching Walter, his face lit by candlelight, tell a scandalous story about a sixty-year-old female patient who insisted on being examined in the nude, I couldn't have imagined a more pleasant way to end the day. Sir Arthur chuckled and John Baines roared with laughter while Mrs. Kaplan grinned, nodding her head.

"I can see the lady's point. But if you examined me, I'd rather you were in the buff, Doctor," she'd said, to the shock and delight of us all.

Even Mrs. Baines, who was uncharacteristically melancholy at the start of the meal, was giggling before long. In fact, she cheered the loudest when Mrs. Monday, given the honors, presented the traditional plum pudding, flames and all.

"I propose a toast—," Sir Arthur said, standing and raising his glass. And then William arrived bearing a letter. With that the gaiety ended.

"I'm sorry to interrupt, sir," the butler said, leaning forward to place the salver within Sir Arthur's reach. "But this was just hand-delivered by messenger." The table conversation stopped. Forks that a moment ago had dipped into the pudding were left suspended in mid-air. I instantly recalled the dinner party and Ambrose's announcement that a man was wanting to speak with Captain Starrett. I wasn't the only one. Mrs. Kaplan licked her lips and inched to the edge of her chair. Rachel Baines looked anxiously toward her husband, who wouldn't make eye contact with her as he pushed his plate away. Sir Arthur set his glass down and reached for the envelope. He took out the card. It was silver with a wide black border. One exactly like it had arrived last night, the invitation to Henry Starrett's funeral.

"It's from General Starrett," Sir Arthur said as he looked up into five expectant faces. We had, until now, been able to avoid the topic of Henry Starrett's murder and the arrest of Morgan and Priscilla Triggs. Everyone had celebrated the day as usual, with church services or Mass followed by presents under the glow of the Christmas tree candles, carols, and games of snapdragon and charades in the parlor. Walter and I had taken a leisurely sleigh ride in the afternoon, his driving tempered by the snow. We had stood arm in arm, looking out over the Mississippi River as it flowed by. Not a word had passed between us of the tragic events of the past few days. But it was inevitable. I took a deep breath and glanced at Walter. He was looking at me and smiling.

It doesn't matter what that card says, I thought. *I've had the best Christmas since my mother died.* I smiled back.

Sir Arthur put on his spectacles and said, "It reads: 'As it is Christmastide, I've been granted three wishes. One to thank you for your kindness and condolences at this sad time, two to thank Miss Davish for her commendable 'Pinkerton' work, and three to wish everyone a Merry Christmas.' "

As the weight of the past few days settled on everyone's shoulders, only the crackling of the fire could be heard.

"What do you think they'll do to Mrs. Triggs?" Mrs. Kaplan said abruptly, her voice booming in comparison to the previous moment's hush. She voiced what we all must've been wondering. "I can only imagine the desperation and emptiness Priscilla Triggs must've felt being denied motherhood. I had nine children, myself. Of course, Henry, no matter what he did, wasn't to blame, but I do hope they are lenient on her, and her husband."

"I don't think she will hang," Sir Arthur said, "if that's what you mean. As to her husband, he won't serve any time, not if I have anything to do with it."

"Why not?" Rachel asked. "He beat Henry almost to death."

"Henry deserved what he got, though, didn't he?"

"But Sir Arthur!" Rachel protested.

"He was a traitor, Rachel, and there's no getting around that," John Baines said. He shook his head. "He betrayed his country and his family. If I were General Starrett, I'd never be able to forgive him for that." He deliberately looked at his wife.

"If only he had never had to learn why his son was murdered," I said.

"Yes," Mrs. Kaplan said, "but you'd be surprised. General Starrett's a good man and more forgiving than most. He'll find it in his heart someday to forgive both Henry and his killer."

"Then he's a better man than me," John Baines said, deliberately looking at his wife again before taking a healthy gulp of port. His eyes were still and piercing, his nervous twitch gone. Rachel Baines looked away, smoothing her hair with her hand. I had to wonder what Rachel Baines's infidelity would cost her. I shuddered to think of what the future held for her if her husband abandoned her and branded her an adulteress. A woman's reputation, as I knew so well, was all she had.

"I have to agree," Sir Arthur said while Walter nodded his approval. "It was vigilante justice, I grant you, but Morgan Triggs had a right to restitution. He won't be convicted by a jury of his peers."

"You never did explain how you knew Mrs. Triggs was the killer, Miss Davish," Mrs. Kaplan said.

"The police and I had eliminated almost all of the obvious suspects. So then it became simply a matter of determining where the leaves I found next to Captain Starrett's body came from," I said. "While preparing for the Christmas holiday, I'd been to every shop that carried fresh hothouse flowers, holly, evergreen garland, and other exotic greenery. No one sold olive branches. The likelihood then that the leaves came from Mr. Reynard's greenhouse was great. Since Captain Starrett was only wearing a single carnation, they had to have dropped from someone else's spray of flowers. I assumed the killer's."

"But the leaves could've been dropped before Henry even entered the park," Rachel Baines said.

"No, it snowed that morning. So they had to have dropped after it had snowed."

"But why Mrs. Triggs and not her husband? He could've easily lost a few flowers while he beat the man senseless," John Baines said.

"Because Lieutenant Triggs wasn't wearing a boutonniere. He's allergic to flowers. And I still hadn't determined which woman's footprints we'd seen. So that made me consider the corsages Mr. Reynard had sent out, including those to us for the Christmas entertainment, one to me, one to Mrs. Baines, and one to Mrs. Triggs. And we all know that William confirmed that Mrs. Baines had disposed of hers the day before."

"But you seemed to know even before William confirmed it," Walter said.

"Because I'd told her I hadn't even gone into the park," Mrs. Baines said. "Henry and I were simply out on a friendly walk together and had parted on the bridge."

"That and the fact you are meticulous about your appearance, Mrs. Baines," I said. "You would never wear a day-old corsage."

"Absolutely not," Mrs. Baines said.

"But Mrs. Triggs, on the other hand, who wore a lace bonnet and brought but two dresses with her, wouldn't notice a small detail like the corsage still pinned to the waist of her dress." Mrs. Baines smiled and nodded her head in vindication.

"But the leaves were next to the body," John Baines said. "Mrs. Triggs shot Henry from a distance."

"Yes, but someone closed his coat over the bullet wound, probably to hide the evidence for as long as possible. Mrs. Triggs must've dropped the leaves then."

"But why Priscilla?" Mrs. Kaplan asked. "Why not Adella or even me? Frederick gave me a hibiscus corsage with a sprig of olive leaves too. Or Sir Arthur? Didn't Frederick send you flowers too, Sir Arthur?" Sir Arthur nodded.

"I admit I never considered you, Mrs. Kaplan. Did you have a motive to kill Henry Starrett?" I asked.

"No, of course not, but simply because I'm old doesn't mean I don't like to be considered dangerous," she said, pouting and crossing her arms across her chest. I had to smile at the old lady's spirit. "So what about Adella then? I've heard she's in line to inherit money from her father's lead mine." *News travels fast,* I thought.

"That's true, and I had considered Adella Reynard as suspect at one point, but she had an alibi, attending to her sick children all morning. Mrs. Triggs did not. Mrs. Triggs had originally given her husband an alibi, but Lieutenant Triggs voided that by confessing to confronting Captain Starrett. As to Sir Arthur, he tossed his away at the Christmas entertainment."

"Who would've known that tree leaves would be so important," John Baines said, slurring his words slightly.

"That's why Hattie is good at what she does," Sir Arthur said, his compliment making me blush. "She can be depended upon to pay attention to the smallest detail!"

"I'm sure she can," Rachel Baines said dismissively. "By the way, have you been holding out on me?" Everyone looked at Sir Arthur, whose countenance revealed he was as confused as we were, then back to Mrs. Baines. It was as she wanted it, all eyes on her. "Whatever was in the box that came for you yesterday, Sir Arthur?" If Mrs. Baines thought it was something he would share with her, she was about to be vastly disappointed. "Bonbons, perhaps?"

"Oh," Sir Arthur said, relieved to finally know what she was talking about. "No, it was a box of Frederick Reynard's new 'General Cornelius Starrett' brand cigars and a rare copy of First Lieutenant B. S. De Forest's *Random Sketches and Wan-*

dering Thoughts or What I Saw While with the Army during the Late Rebellion." Mrs. Baines frowned. "I believe Frederick promised to send a box of cigars for you, John, and you too, Dr. Grice. I'm looking forward to a good smoke after the ladies leave us."

"Well, I'll drink to that," John Baines said, raising his glass in a toast. "To Sir Arthur, a truly generous man and gracious host," John Baines added, raising his glass again. We toasted Sir Arthur, who in turn toasted his guests.

"To Philippa, my wife, who I wish could be here," Sir Arthur said.

"To Lady Philippa," everyone responded.

"To the beautiful women who have graced us with their presence today," Walter said. He toasted in the direction of Rachel Baines, which pleased that woman immensely, but then winked at me when he caught my eye.

"Hear, hear," John Baines said boisterously, and then drained his glass.

"We'll be waiting beneath the mistletoe after dinner, ladies," Walter said, grinning.

"Oh, Dr. Grice," Mrs. Baines said, playfully waving her hand.

"Oh, Dr. Grice, nothing," Mrs. Kaplan said. "I'll be there, first in line and with bells on! And if Sir Arthur's game, watch out, ladies, he's all mine!" For the first time since I'd known him, Sir Arthur blushed. Mrs. Kaplan slapped the table and cackled. Her gaiety was infectious. The table erupted in giggles and laughter.

"What about you, Miss Davish?" Walter said, an impish smirk on his face. "Are you game?" I grinned at his banter but left him guessing for an answer.

"To the best bloody secretary a man could ever ask for," Sir Arthur said, unexpectedly bubbly. "Another job well done!" I blushed at Sir Arthur's public display of appreciation. I wasn't used to it, but I reveled in knowing I'd exceeded his expectations. Sir Arthur was happy and so was I. "To Hattie Davish!" he said, raising his glass.

"To Hattie Davish," Walter said, beaming at me. I beamed back. Everyone was drinking and laughing. The joy was infectious.

This is what Christmas should be, I thought as I raised my glass in one final toast.

"To a Merry Christmas for all and a Happy New Year!"